N
the
Un
mo
for
Boo
anot

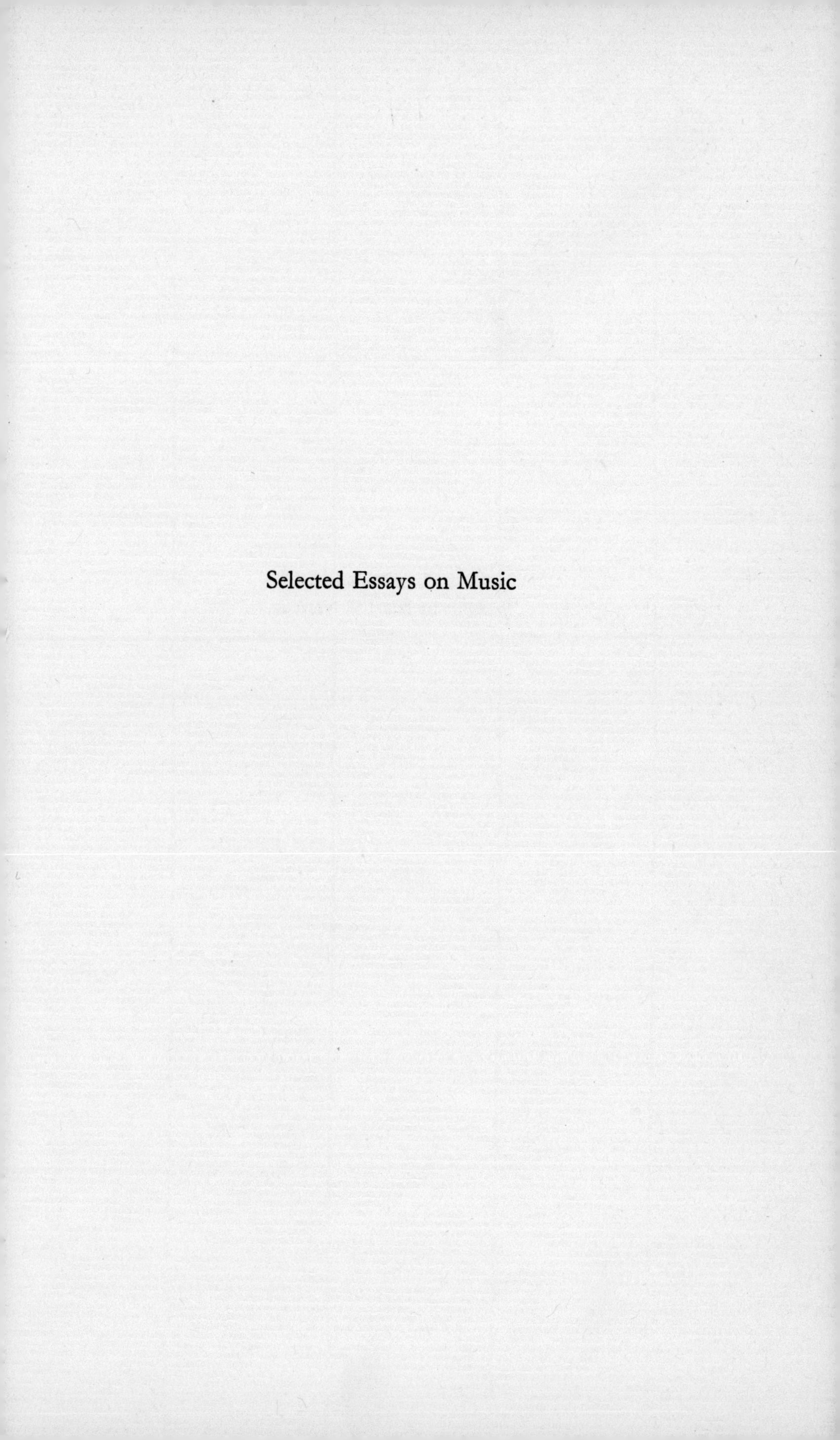

Selected Essays on Music

Florence Jonas also translated
Prokofiev by Israel V. Nestyev

Vladimir Vasilevich Stasov, by Ilya Repin

Vladimir Vasilevich
Stasov

SELECTED ESSAYS ON MUSIC

Translated by Florence Jonas
Introduced by Gerald Abraham

Barrie & Rockliff
The Cresset Press
London

First published by
Barrie & Rockliff, The Cresset Press
2 Clement's Inn, London, WC2
1968
SBN 214.16039.4

Printed in Great Britain
by Spottiswoode, Ballantyne & Co. Ltd.
London and Colchester

Contents

Introduction

V. V. Stasov: Man and Critic

by Gerald Abraham

A recent English book on music refers in passing to "a Russian music critic called Stassov". This is rather like speaking of "an Irish music critic called Shaw". It is true that Stasov was not himself a creative artist, though he stimulated a vast amount of creativity in others, but his intellectual energy and the breadth of his interests, his love of controversy, sometimes even his wit and sarcasm, remind one of Shaw. Actually he was even less a "music critic" than Shaw, for although he wrote occasional concert notices he was never engaged in regular concert criticism as Shaw was for years on *The Star* and *The World*. When the first collected edition of his writings—other than books—appeared in three large volumes in 1894,[1] the first two volumes consisted of art history and criticism, and biographical studies of architects, painters and sculptors, while hardly more than half the third volume is devoted to "Music and the Theatre". And when a small fourth, supplementary volume came out in 1906, the year of his death, the most important study—a survey of "Art in the Nineteenth Century"—gives 178 pages to painting as against 101 to music. Merely to glance at the titles of a few of the articles gives some idea of Stasov's wide-ranging interests: "Notes on two ancient Asiatic bronze statuettes found near Lake Van", "A new Raphael [the 'Madonna del libro'] in Petersburg", "Ornamentation in Russian folk art", "A catacomb with frescoes found in 1872 near Kerch", "The Representation of the Hebrew race in European art", "European capitals and their architecture", "An exhibition of V. V. Vereshchagin's pictures". His book reviews, always substantial, sometimes Macaulayan in proportions, range from Alfred Butler's *The Ancient Coptic Churches of Egypt* to Zola's *L'Oeuvre*. In 1847, at the age of twenty-three, he reviewed Grote's *History of Greece*, Harris Nicolas's *Memoirs of the Life and Times of Sir Christopher Hatton*, Bulwer Lytton's *Lucrezia*, Fenimore Cooper's *Ravensnest*,

[1] *Sobranie sochineniy V. V. Stasova: 1847–1886* (St. Petersburg, 1894).

Disraeli's *Contarini Fleming* and *Tancred*, Dickens's *Pictures from Italy*, Lord Lindsay's *Sketches of the History of Christian Art*, E. F. Apelt's *Die Epochen der Geschichte der Menschheit*, Heinrich Alt's *Theater und Kirche in ihrem gegenseitigen Verhältniss*, Niebuhr's *Vorträge über alte Geschichte*, W. A. Schmidt's *Geschichte der Denk- und Glaubensfreiheit im I-sten Jahrhundert der Kaiserschaft und des Christenthums*, and the first volume of Schiller's correspondence with Körner. Archaeology, history—not only art history but political history and the history of ideas—biography, contemporary writing: here already Stasov's main interests are revealed. And music as well: in 1847, besides the "Review of the Year", reprinted here, he also published a seven-column review of Henselt's piano transcription of the *Freischütz* Overture, making detailed technical criticisms and particularly attacking Henselt for ignoring the contemporary methods of transcription as developed by Liszt. (This is also reprinted here.)

It is only because the Western world is more interested in Russian music than in Russian painting, architecture or archaeology that we read the lives of Russian musicians but not those of Russian painters, and so we know Stasov as the friend and propagandist of the Russian nationalist composers, the first biographer of Mussorgsky and Borodin, the instigator and provider of programmes or scenarios for *Khovanshchina* and *Prince Igor* and Tchaikovsky's *Tempest*, but not as the friend and propagandist of Repin and Vereshchagin, Antokolsky and Kramskoy. He was not a propagandist of Tolstoy or Turgenev, but he was a valued friend. Aylmer Maude tells us in his *Life of Tolstoy* that "his immense knowledge of books, as well as the great library at his command, enabled him to be of much use to Tolstoy when the latter wanted to read up any subject he was dealing with", and also that he was (typically) one of the first volunteers of information when Maude began to contemplate his biography.[1] Incidentally, Stasov makes one anonymous appearance in that *Life*:

> When he [Tolstoy] was over seventy I remember taking a walk with him and a friend of his—a well-known literary man who was still older. The latter was saying that Tolstoy's assertions did not accord with his (the speaker's) own experience of life. He had a mistress and did not consider that it spoilt his life.[2]

The "well-known literary man" was, as Maude himself told me, Stasov.

As a boy, Stasov had wanted to be an architect—which was very natural, since his father, Vasily Petrovich Stasov (1769–1848), was one of the greatest Russian architects of his day, held in high favour by Alexander I and Nicholas I, and designer of the Trinity (Izmaylovsky) and

[1] "World's Classics" edition, II, pp. 428 and 436.
[2] Ibid., II, p. 281.

Transfiguration (Preobrazhensky) Cathedrals, the Imperial Barracks and the Moscow Arch at St. Petersburg, as well as an early masterpiece—the beautiful bell-tower on Arakcheev's estate at Gruzino, near Novgorod.[1] The architect's fifth child, Vladimir Vasilevich, was born on 2nd/14th January, 1824, just too late to be conscious of the Emperor Alexander who "loved to meet and converse with" his beautiful mother when the family were living at Tsarskoe Selo. The mother died in 1831 and it was the father who fashioned the boy in his own image, for he was interested in very much more than his profession, "highly cultivated, reading much, and (above all) of an enquiring mind"; at 79, during the last months of his life, he made Vladimir read to him *Faust*, Hegel's *Aesthetics*, and various travel-books. His favourite saying, "A man is worthy of the name only when he is of use to himself and to others", became his son's lifelong motto.

The Stasov children, five brothers and two sisters, were at an early age taught foreign languages, drawing and music. Their earliest music teachers were of little account but toward the end of the 1830s they had Anton Gerke, the best piano teacher in Petersburg—ten years later he taught Mussorgsky—a Pole who introduced them to the music of Chopin and Schumann. Before this, in 1836, Vladimir had entered the new, so-called Law School (really a school for future civil servants founded by the Tsar's nephew, Prince Peter of Oldenburg) which was housed in one of his father's buildings. Thanks to its founder's passion for music, the School was a hot-bed of musical activity; the pupils were expected to study either a string or a wind instrument and become a member of its school orchestra, and from 1838 the principal piano teacher was Adolf Henselt. The fourteen-year-old Stasov actually studied with the classically inclined Henselt at the School on week-days and with the "romantic" Gerke at home on Sundays; in 1840 he appeared at a School concert as pianist in Hummel's Septet and later as soloist in concertos with the School orchestra. His intimate friend was A. N. Serov, just four years older than himself, later to be famous as musical critic and composer, already a good amateur pianist and like himself an enthusiast for art and literature, though Serov was more interested in painting and German literature, while Stasov preferred architecture and the French classics. Both tried their hands at musical composition. They heard every great performer who visited Petersburg: Thalberg, Pasta, Lipinsky, Ole Bull and, most impressive of all, Liszt. As we learn from Stasov's famous account of "Liszt, Schumann and Berlioz in Russia" (translated in the present volume), it was during Liszt's visit that he got to know the Russian musician who was his lifelong hero, Glinka.

In the field of painting Stasov then greatly admired K. P. Bryullov, the

[1] The Gruzino tower and Moscow Arch are illustrated in G. H. Hamilton, *The Art and Architecture of Russia* (London, 1954), plate 137.

most famous Russian painter of the day,[1] and would visit the Kazan Cathedral in the early morning, waiting for the sun to light up Bryullov's "Assumption", before which he would then sit for hours in adoration. Through another Bryullov picture, the "Crucifixion" in the Lutheran Church of Peter and Paul, he made the acquaintance of the organ—unknown in Orthodox churches—and, more important, of the fugues of Bach which made not only a deeper but a much more lasting impression than the works of Bryullov.[2] Throughout his life he would visit the Lutheran Church to hear an oratorio or the *Matthew Passion.* (But the "Herr von Stassoff" who appears among the early subscribers to the Bach-Gesellschaft edition was his brother Dmitry.) The contemporary Russian writers who influenced him most in adolescence were Belinsky, Gogol and Lermontov; he read the complete works of Winckelmann in German and soon came across Heine, whose work he loved "passionately, though well aware of his unevenness and his shortcomings". All this meant much more to him than what he was actually taught at the Imperial Law School, where the—mostly German—teachers were sound but pedantic. Already at the School, too, he distinguished himself by his gift for sarcasm; on two occasions his victims retaliated with penknife attacks. For his part, during his very first days at the School, when another boy jeered at him he seized him by the ears and threw him to the ground.

Leaving the School at nineteen, Stasov entered the Survey Department of the Ruling Senate. But one reason after another would prophetically direct his steps in his spare time to the Imperial Public Library, first to study in the collection of prints in the art department, then to help a friend in the department of foreign books; and in 1847 another friend, who had been reviewing foreign books for the *Otechestvennïe Zapiski* and was now moving to Moscow, recommended him as his successor to the editor Kraevsky. Hence the astounding crop of reviews described above and hence, also, Stasov's first essay in musical criticism—translated in the present volume. Professionally, he moved from one government department to another until in 1851 he was offered, and joyfully accepted, a chance to escape. He took the post of Russian secretary to the immensely wealthy Prince A. N. Demidov, who had an estate at San Donato near Florence.

In May he resigned from the government service and next month travelled by way of Berlin and Cologne to London, where he stayed at Long's Hotel, New Bond Street, from 30th June (new style) till the end of

[1] In the long letter to his father (1st January, 1844) quoted from below, he brackets Bryullov with Mozart, Shakespeare, Homer and Beethoven. His admiration for Bryullov did not last, however.

[2] Glinka was so amused by Stasov's passion for Bach that he nicknamed him "Bach", and the name was used for many years by his intimate friends. Balakirev usually converts it into an affectionate diminutive: "Bakhinka".

July. He saw all the usual sights, including the Great Exhibition, and visited Windsor Castle and the House of Commons, where he saw Lord John Russell in action. Demidov's influence opened all doors to him. He heard *Elijah* at Exeter Hall and *Figaro* at the Queen's Theatre. But what impressed him most of all was the acting of Rachel in Schiller's *Maria Stuart*. She gave him some of the deepest artistic impressions of his highly impressionable life; he saw her afterwards in Paris and Italy in most of her great rôles and wrote later: "How many lands and cities I have traversed since those times, how much I have seen, how much I have changed! But one thing has not changed—my passion for Rachel". From London he went to Paris and then by way of Basle to Florence, where he had a flat in the Palazzo Ricci Altoviti. Characteristically, he immediately hired a piano on which the first things he played were Beethoven's Sixth and Ninth Symphonies, in four-hand arrangements, with another of Demidov's young secretaries, brother of the then well-known pianist and composer Theodor Döhler. He played Bach's *Forty-eight*, as well as the Viennese classics, and before long he was writing to his favourite brother Dmitry:

> What should I have done here without all my music? Sometimes I should have been completely lost. For me music is not simply a pleasure, like others, but the *sole medicine* for my spleen and my black days. Just like David's music for Saul. Only just as our music towers millions of versts above the poor and meagre music of David's harp, so much deeper and sharper is my pain compared with Saul's . . .

Stasov stayed in Italy until early in 1854, mostly in Florence but also visiting Rome, Naples, Venice, as well as making an expedition to Vienna. The impression made on him by Italy, her people, her cities and above all her incomparable art-treasures—many of which he had copied for Demidov—may be imagined. But he was by no means bowled over by every masterpiece; in the Sistine Chapel he found fault with Michelangelo's "Last Judgement" though the "Creation" was another matter—"that is where he is the *whole* Michelangelo"; as for the Colosseum, he regarded this as an "architecturally clumsy elephant". And while Italy opened his ears to older music, this did not happen at once; hewas bored by Allegri's famous *Miserere* in the Sistine Chapel and a Gloria by Marcello he found "good, but not particularly":

> How far, for example, from the Haydn choruses in the *Schöpfung*, not to speak of the Choral Fantasia [of Beethoven], the final chorus of *Fidelio*, the Sanctus of the *Requiem* [Mozart's] and all our own things (Letter to his family, 29th March/10th April, 1852).

But a couple of months later he had had copies made of Arcadelt's "marvellous" (but, alas, spurious) "Ave Maria" and a number of

Palestrina motets, and his conversion was completed by his meeting with the Abbé Santini, the famous Roman collector of old music. His first thought on seeing Santini's wonderful library, he told his brothers (letter of 29th May/10th June), was to ask the old man to have copied for him "*all* Palestrina, who has now become absolutely my *passion*":

But then I judged it better to begin with those famous names which so far I don't know at all, and so I ordered from him the best things of *Durante*, *Leo*, *Scarlatti, Anerio, Benevoli, Bernabei, Pitoni*; then will come *Jomelli*, *Clari*, various printed things by *Marcello*, *Carissimi*, etc. But I'm awfully afraid this will make away with much of my travel money. What's to be done? I shall arrange things as best I can so as not to lose my present chance, which won't come again.... Santini lets me borrow and take home whatever I like.... Since I've been here I scarcely ever play either Mozart or Beethov[en] any more—always *Palestrina*, *Marcello*, and goodness knows whom else.

He was already thinking of having as much as possible performed in Petersburg by Lomakin, the director of Count Sheremetyev's then famous choir. (This was actually done after Stasov's return home.) It would help if Lomakin would send lists of what he has already and what he would like to have:

church things or secular, long or short, i.e. *motets* or madrigals; *Masses*, requiems, *lamentations* (there are hundreds of them), *cantatas*, with accompaniment or without, etc.

Later he became interested in still older music; before Lent 1853 Santini had had copied for him two Masses by Arcadelt, and *Lamentationes* and Magnificats by Carpentras, Goudimel, Févin, Festa, Lejeune, Cadéac, Certon, Claudin de Sermisy, as well as Handel chamber duets, Alessandro Scarlatti's *Missa in canone* and "a fat book of Palestrina motets chosen by me". And there was much more to come: duets by Steffani and Agostini, works by Lassus and Marenzio, Benevoli's 16-part Mass.... No wonder he could write to Glinka that he had had tons of music copied for him "so that when I return to Russia a long caravan will have to accompany me". Long before this he had been sending home smaller consignments of more ordinary musical purchases: Handel, Gluck, Mozart, Beethoven—and a vocal score of Purcell's *King Arthur*,[1] in which he was impressed above all by "Come, if you dare", to which he refers again and again in his letters. (I will say nothing of his non-musical purchases, which range from treatises on Egyptian obelisks and the manufacture of boric acid to architectural books and a volume of "petits poèmes grecs".) But it was the Santini collection which widened his musical horizon so vastly. He paid tribute to it in an article in the Petersburg *Biblioteka dlya chteniya*

[1] Some passage in one of Walter Scott's novels led him to believe that Purcell was an Elizabethan.

(April and July, 1853),[1] a much extended French version of which, *L'Abbé Santini et sa collection musicale à Rome*, was published in a limited edition of 250 copies at Stasov's own expense in Florence in 1854 on the eve of his departure; he sent copies to Liszt, Berlioz, Fétis and Ulybyshev among others; and more than half a century was to pass before a Western scholar—a German, Joseph Killing—was to write anything of comparable value on the contents of Santini's library. As for the manuscript copies, in 1870 Stasov presented the lot—some four hundred works from the fifteenth to the nineteenth centuries—to the St. Petersburg Public Library.

Stasov began to work in the Library soon after his return to Russia in the spring of 1854. Demidov no longer needed him and he was at a loose end. He found that under a new director, Baron Korff, the Library had become a much more lively and attractive institution; he spent most of his time there, and before long V. I. Sobolshchikov, head of the departments of art and *Rossica*, suggested that he should compile a systematic catalogue of the latter section. "Systematization, arranging in categories, had always been my passion in everything", he wrote later, "and here was my chance to set in order some tens of thousands of books concerned with practically every sphere of human knowledge, in this astonishing, unique section *Rossica*". He did not catalogue without reading and it seemed to him that "in a few months he had learned more new things than previously in many years". He published articles—on a medieval Greek treatise on church song by a pseudonymous "Hagiopolites" which he had found in Paris in the Bibliothèque Nationale, of which he presented a copy to the Petersburg Library, on the autograph manuscripts of musicians in the Petersburg Library, on the sumptuous 1855 French edition of the *Imitatio Christi*—and when in 1856 his catalogue of *Rossica* had been approved by the Academy of Sciences he compiled for Sobolshchikov lists of art books which should be acquired. Before the end of the year he was appointed personal assistant to Korff with the special task of collecting material for a history of the reign of Nicholas I (which had ended the year before); beside this anonymous work, Stasov's labours in the Imperial archives produced a number of monographs, some published, others preserved in the Imperial Chancery and printed for official circulation only. He also arranged a series of exhibitions in the Library, beginning with one of all the engraved portraits of Peter the Great which occupied him for several months. His activity was already indefatigable and many-sided: through a sea-captain he got hold of an eleventh-century Georgian version of the Gospels, an emissary was despatched to Athens to photograph Slavonic and Greek manuscripts, Prince M. A. Volkonsky was induced to collect for presentation to the Library "Athenian popular woodcut pictures of sacred subjects". When

[1] Reprinted in the *Sobranie sochineniy*, III, col. 1.

Glinka died in 1857, Stasov secured for the Library his musical autographs, his autobiography, and some two hundred letters.

In 1856 Stasov had made the acquaintance of the twenty-year-old Balakirev, and soon began to play that inspirational rôle in Russian music with which Western readers are familiar. And not only in Russian music but in Russian art generally. Repin and Antokolsky regarded him as their teacher, and he was closely associated with Kramskoy's Free Artists' Co-operative of 1863 and the Society of Travelling Exhibitions—the so-called *Peredvizhniki*, or *Ambulants* as French critics call them—which developed from the Co-operative in 1870. The period 1856–72 was that of Stasov's chief activity as a historian and of his greatest influence on the minds of his creative contemporaries. At the latter date he became head of the department of art in the Library and was more absorbed by official responsibilities. But he resisted. Twice there was question of his appointment as director of the Library, but he flatly refused. "Neither by nature, by character nor by inclination am I capable of being an administrator or the *head* of anything", he wrote to the Minister. Besides, as he confided to his brother, "there would be the impossibility of writing freely, *democratically*, controversially. . . . Once I had taken on the directorship it would be goodbye to my bold, lighthearted, jolly polemics". And this was in 1899, when he was 75.

Polemics were the breath of life to him. As a young man, he ruefully admitted his "unfortunate habit" of quarrelling about matters of art, "of which, it seems, I shall never cure myself and which has spoiled for me many a pleasant acquaintanceship". He always wanted, indeed needed, to share his enthusiasms—"It is always absolutely essential to me that many others, that *everyone*, should be pleased by what pleases me", he wrote in 1852—and a failure to share his enthusiasms was unforgivable. Serov's lack of sympathy for Balakirev and his circle[1] and for Glinka's *Ruslan* led Stasov to break with his oldest and closest musical friend, and with such bitterness that when in 1865 they met by the grave of Serov's mother, to whom Stasov had been devoted, he refused to take the offered hand of his former friend. But it was this passionate need to share his enthusiasms that made him such a wonderful source of inspiration to others. His ardent love of Russian legend, Russian literature and Russian history made him send Rimsky-Korsakov—he had already tried to send

[1] For whom Stasov inadvertently in 1867 coined the nickname by which they have since been known: "the mighty handful". His article in the *St. Peterburgskie Vedomosti* on "Mr. Balakirev's Slav Concert" (reprinted in the *Sobranie sochineniy*, III, col. 217) ended with the wish, "God grant that our Slav guests may never forget today's concert, God grant that they may forever preserve the memory of how much poetry, feeling, talent and intelligence are possessed by the small but already mighty handful of Russian musicians (*u malenkoy, no uzhe moguchey kuchki russkikh muzikantov*)!" But the Russian musicians actually represented in this programme were not the so-called "five" but Glinka, Dargomïzhsky, Balakirev and Rimsky-Korsakov.

Balakirev—to *Sadko*,[1] Borodin to *Prince Igor*, Mussorgsky to *Khovanshchina*. He sent Tchaikovsky to Shakespeare's *Tempest* and provided him with the outline programme which he actually used, just as he had earlier sent Berlioz the programme for a symphony on Byron's *Manfred*—the very same programme that Tchaikovsky acquired from Balakirev many years later. (In 1852, in Italy, he had wanted to find a comic-opera libretto to wake the sleeping genius of Rossini.) These enthusiasms were twofold: for the subject and for the artist. And when he found an artist whose ideals were nearly, as with Balakirev between 1857 and 1864, or totally—as with Mussorgsky and with Repin until the later years—identical with his own, he boiled over.

Gusto, in both senses, was the real keynote of his criticism: idiosyncratic *gusto* supported by vast learning and spiced with sarcasm. One must not expect from him cool, objective criticism, deep and subtle penetration, or even striking originality of thought. He loved *life* above all and was impatient with Tolstoy's insistence that he ought to be thinking about death, though he did think much of death in his last years, especially after a serious fall in the summer of 1904. "He always thought only of life, activity and creativity", wrote one of his nieces with pardonable overstatement, and much of the value of his criticism lay in his infectious vitality; he is the archetype of the propagandist-critic.

He stated the basis of his critical beliefs very early, in a long letter to his father written on New Year's Day, 1844, the eve of his twentieth birthday:[2]

Hitherto all criticism of the arts has consisted of saying: this is good, this is bad, this is not seemly, here are such-and-such errors in costume, here in proportion, etc. No talent is needed for such criticism as this, only a certain degree of *study* and *learning*, consequently *anybody* (for any untalented fellow can learn and know the technical parts with which such criticism deals—hands, feet, capitals) can *enounce* such criticism . . . and consequently all the criticism written up to this time can be quietly destroyed since it is helpful neither to the works themselves nor to those who look at them.

[1] He exercised strong influence on both *Sadkos*. The original "programme" of the early orchestral piece was his and when, more than a quarter of a century later, Rimsky-Korsakov first thought of using the subject for an opera, Stasov pounced on the first, very limited scenario by N. M. Shtrupp, which the composer had sent him, and enthusiastically urged all sorts of additions—notably the crowd scenes in Novgorod, which are the making of the opera—and the introduction of Sadko's wife. (See the Stasov-Rimsky-Korsakov correspondence printed in *Russkaya Mïsl*, 1910, nos. VI–IX, particularly Stasov's letter of 7th July, 1894; Rimsky-Korsakov's account in his autobiography, which most biographers and critics—including myself—have followed, is very inaccurate.) When the libretto was completed, he vigorously criticised verbal ineptitudes: one phrase sounded like "Tatar or Mongolian or Kirgiz" and one mustn't speak of "pothouse beggars" because there were no "pothouses" (*kabaki*) in Russia before the sixteenth century: to use the word "in Russian antiquity" was "the same as introducing *cannon*, *rifles*, *carriages*, *French quadrilles* and *polkas*", so he offers twenty-two alternatives "and 100 others" if necessary. But Korsakov kept to "pothouse".

[2] Printed in *Pisma k rodnïm*, I (Moscow, 1953), pp. 33–45.

All "so-called aesthetic criticism" falls under this condemnation, although "Plato, Kant, Hegel and some others have said good things about the arts *in general*"; these critics look at works of art as at mirrors, finding only reflections of their own tastes and emotions.

But what should we demand from works of art, what are the arts for? They don't exist for their details but to state *a whole*, concentrated in one point, the product of all its parts, all its elements. . . . This whole . . . is closely connected with the most important questions of mankind, inseparable from universal history; for it doesn't exist for the satisfaction of refined feeling, it exists together with life, with which it decides questions whose origins cannot be separated from conscious life. . . .

Every real work of art . . . bears within itself its *meaning* and its *allotted task*; to reveal both of these for the human race is the task of criticism, and such criticism has not existed for the arts (however, it has begun for *the art of poetry*). So it is not for criticism to invent something new or to invent factual adornment of the existent; its duty is to extract from the work of art itself its vital idea, *by which* and *for which* the whole work exists with all its beauty and greatness; in short, criticism of the arts must show what works have been created in the world up to now . . . by what means they utter their inner thought, and the *meaning* of this thought for the world, i.e. criticism must show the indispensability of these productions to the world. . . .

This thought is so simple and clear that, once it has occurred to you, it seems impossible to take in works of art in any other way; but this has not been the case. . . . A difficult question awaits me on this point: for what have the arts existed for some thousands of years if their real significance was not known? This is one of the first questions of the philosophy of history . . . the inseparable connection between the history of the human race and the arts in this human race, and the examination of it, and likewise the attitude of the whole mass of people existing up to the present time with regard to the arts, all this must be decided by the history of the arts, if only these problems are soluble.

Thus workers in the arts are of two kinds: the *artist* and the *critic of art*. Feeling the inevitability of having to work to the best of my powers as the latter, I first of all had to find the limits of some extensive field lying before me for future cultivation, i.e. I had to *fix on certain products* (and consequently that which had produced them), throwing all else into the river of eternal oblivion; little remained, by way of reward, but that little comprises everything that *to this day* the world needs (it will go further, and therefore the art corresponding to it will be in equilibrium with it); between them exists the law of *inevitable consequence* or *succession*, and this again is a problem of art criticism.

I cannot accept existing appraisals and traditions; from the very start (because on different bases) I was obliged to begin my own appraisals, the result of different *demands*, and thus many former idols were burned. . . .

From what I have said about criticism it becomes clear that such criticism must embrace *all* the arts, absolutely without exception, since they are essentially different sides and means of one and the same general whole. . . . Where one leaves off, there another begins. . . .

Another significant remark occurs near the end of the letter:

The greater the artist, the more he is a man, the more he feels himself connected with the world and his fellow-men. . . .

No doubt much of this, particularly the emphasis on the inseparability of art from humanity, was influenced by Belinsky, who had recently begun to write in this sense. These were the views later adopted more and more widely by Russian intellectuals, especially after the appearance of Chernïshevsky's *Aesthetic Relationships of Art to Reality* (1855) and the writings of Dobrolyubov, which absolutely dominated Russian thought during the 1860s, which Tolstoy developed to absurdity in *What is Art?* in 1898 (by which time they had become "old stuff", as Chekhov said), and which are the foundation of the Soviet doctrine of "socialist realism". But Stasov must have been one of Belinsky's earliest disciples. The remarkable thing is that he never modified his creed. Balakirev and Repin fell victims to mysticism, as Gogol and Perov (the first notable realist-nationalist Russian painter) had done before them; in fact, mysticism in one form or another, with artistic cosmopolitanism, "decadence", aestheticism, impressionism, mysticism, had supplanted the ideals of the 1860s in the Russia of Stasov's later years. But he went on till his death in 1906, fighting faithfully for his old beliefs in the Russia of Chekhov, Skryabin, Merezhkovsky and Dyaghilev's *World of Art*. In 1903 he astonished Rimsky-Korsakov by pronouncing his "realistic" *Mozart and Salieri* to be a masterpiece "side by side with *Snowmaiden*". And his last published article, "A Friendly Commemoration", translated here on p. 195, shows him once more in his early rôle of Schumann's champion.

Next to realism, Stasov placed nationalism; it was the combination of both in Mussorgsky and Repin that specially endeared their work to him. His English disciple, Mrs. Newmarch, has put on record his remark that "if you strip a Russian of his nationality, you leave a man several degrees inferior to other Europeans"[1] and in some cases—for instance, that of the architect Viktor Hartmann, who would hardly be remembered if Mussorgsky had not immortalised the posthumous exhibition of his sketches—he over-valued inferior artists on account of the Russianness of their work. He interested himself in the collection of Russian lace-work and old Russian textiles, and in the totally unrealistic field of ornamentation—provided it was Russian or had Russian connections. Indeed, he was an authority on it and his *Slavonic and Oriental Ornament according to Manuscripts of Ancient and Modern Times* (1884) is a landmark.

"Romanticism" mattered to Stasov mainly in a negative sense, as opposed to classic beauty, beauty for its own sake, and art smelling of the conservatoire. He preferred the irregular townscape of Florence to the classical monuments of Rome, the medieval to the Renaissance, and the Renaissance to the Baroque—for which he had no sympathy at all: "How can one compare the soulless, cold and stupidly correct buildings and churches of the 17th or (still worse) 18th century with the bold, always original, always different, always unexpected, always irregular

[1] Rosa Newmarch, *The Russian Arts* (London, 1916), p. 261.

and hence always beautiful forms of medieval architecture?" Even the Russian neo-classical architecture of the late eighteenth and early nineteenth centuries ceased to please him. He equated originality and irregularity with life, and not only in art; wherever he went, he was more attracted by the lower classes who behaved freely and naturally than by polite and conventional society. He was acutely conscious of the frequent failure of art to match itself against life and, faced as a young man with the experience of Rome and the efforts of the minor artists who sketched and painted it, could exclaim, "How happy I am that I *don't know how to draw*!" His scorn for Goethe in Italy, more interested in pseudo-Greek statues than in the marvellous Italian peasant women, was profound.

Yet other indications that in the end life mattered even more to him than art were his relationships with Balakirev, Repin and Antokolsky. All three drew away from him in their artistic ideals and there were consequent strains in their personal relationships; but there was no bitter break as there had been with Serov. In his last letter to Antokolsky,[1] written in 1902 not long before the sculptor's death, he says, "Maybe we differ in our opinions about art. So be it! There's no harm nor sin in that. There's not the slightest need for everyone in the world to hold one and the same opinion about art . . ." This is very different from the intolerant Stasov of forty years earlier. Not that he had moved an inch from his old positions, but an old friendship was now too valuable to lose for an old opinion. He was delighted when Balakirev in 1900 sent him his First Symphony, begun many years before, but he did not spare him some adverse criticism, and when the still earlier *King Lear* music was printed at last in 1904 he rather touchingly hoped "you didn't destroy and won't destroy the dedication of *Lear* to me. Repin, once being angry with me, destroyed on his marvellous picture 'Liszt' (a full-length) the dedication of this picture to me". But "dear, dear, dear, a hundred times dear Mily" had let the *Lear* dedication stand, and when the score arrived as an eighty-first-birthday present, Stasov sent him in return his latest book, *Shakespeare's "Merchant of Venice"* (St. Petersburg, 1904) and wrote:

> How happy I am that you still remember me and those happy days when I lived in the whole orchestra of life, and when you began and composed *Lear*. So that time and our then still young relationships and transports remain engraved even in music, its sounds and poetry!! How grateful I am![2]

Some years before, he had written to Rimsky-Korsakov's wife that he was "like a bulldog, in that I hold on hard with my teeth to anything I've once got hold of firmly and affectionately": herself, her husband, Pargolovo where he had spent his summers for nearly fifty years. And his mind kept going back to "poor, unhappy" Gussakovsky, one of the minor members of the *kuchka* who, like Lodïzhensky, never fulfilled the high

[1] *Pisma k deyatelyam russkoy kulturï*, I (Moscow, 1962), p. 96.
[2] Ibid. p. 149.

hopes aroused in his youth. He wanted to arrange for the publication of Gussakovsky's works—they are still in manuscript—and his very last letter to Balakirev (25th January, 1906) ended with a request to be told

What can you remember of our poor talented Ukrainian, untimely dead *Gussakovsky*? How I should like to preserve his image! To this day I can't forget, it's as if it were yesterday, how he burst into tears when I read you both one evening the sixth book of the *Iliad* (Hector's farewell to Andromache). Ah, how marvellous was that time!!!

Translator's Note

Although Stasov's writings on music constitute a major primary source for the study of the rise and development of the Russian national school, they have thus far remained little known in the West. Only those with a knowledge of Russian have had access to them. It is my hope that this selection, which includes works covering the entire span of Stasov's activity, will acquaint the reader not only with his views and the broad range of his musical interests but also with the man himself.

An inveterate foe of the cultural establishment at home and abroad, Stasov spent his entire life championing what seemed to him the best of the "new" in art. As spokesman for the idea of a Russian national music, he fought with a passion and zeal which bordered on the fanatical. Many of the arguments and even the words he used sound remarkably contemporary. They might easily serve the cause of avant-garde composers of today.

With his first published essay on music, "Review of Musical Events of 1847", written in his early 20s, Stasov embarked upon a campaign which was to end only with the caustic piece "A Friendly Commemoration", his very last writing on any subject, completed shortly before his death in 1906. It is interesting, in the light of the subsequent direction of Russian music, that at the very beginning Stasov turned toward Berlioz and Liszt.

The long article "Liszt, Schumann and Berlioz in Russia" (1889) holds particular interest for us because of its first-hand reportage of these three Westerners' visits to that country, the reviews of their concerts and the account of their relations with the emerging Russian school of composers. Here, as in the earlier, shorter essays, "Letters from Abroad" (1869), "The Letters of Berlioz" (1879) and "A Letter from Liszt" (1879), the vehemence of Stasov's attacks on the detractors of his idols is tempered only by the ardour with which he himself embraces them.

Of course, no collection of Stasov's writings could be truly representative without one devoted to the Russian composers. For this reason I have included the section "Our Music" from the extended article "Twenty-Five Years of Russian Art" (published in 1882–83). In this, one of his major works, Stasov traces the growth of the national school from its inception with Glinka and Dargomïzhsky through the "Five" right down to the most recent composers of his time.

To lend added weight to his arguments, Stasov quotes voluminously from non-Russian sources. Wherever possible, these have been checked and the Russian translation verified. While occasionally Stasov somewhat compresses the writer's style, his versions are, for the most part, faithful to the original. In the few cases where they vary significantly, the original text is given in a translator's footnote. In certain instances, however, I have found it impossible to consult the source. For example, four of the thirty-five Liszt letters cited in "Liszt, Schumann and Berlioz in Russia" have proven unavailable. These are: the one to Bessel on p. 181; to Balakirev, Borodin, Cui and others on p. 181; to Jurgenson on p. 185; to the Countess Mercy-Argenteau on pp. 190–1. Three of the twenty-two Berlioz letters quoted in this same essay have also not been located. They are: the one to Bernard, p. 147; to Odoyevsky, p. 150; to Vielgorsky, pp. 155 and 156. In view of the accuracy of most of Stasov's translations, there is little reason to believe that these missing sources have been seriously distorted.

In preparing this work it has been an honour to be associated with Dr. Gerald Abraham whose studies have so enriched our knowledge of Russian music. It is fitting that he should introduce the writings of Stasov, and for this and his many helpful suggestions I am deeply grateful. I wish also to express my thanks to Dr. Jacques Barzun for his aid in securing some of Berlioz' letters and for permission to use his translation of the one to Stasov dated 10th September, 1862. I should like, too, to thank John M. Thomson and David Sharp for their invaluable assistance in the preparation of the manuscript.

F.J.

I. Review of the Musical Events of the Year 1847

Stasov's first essay in music criticism, published in the Petersburg *Otechestvennïe Zapiski* in 1847, at once shows the forthright, highly individual nature of his judgements. No "accepted opinions" are accepted; no "established reputation" cannot be disestablished. And nothing is wrapped up in diplomatic phrases, though some things are disguised in sarcastic ones. Everything is intense; the praise is as exaggerated as the blame. The sharp juxtaposition of black and white (e.g. "While neither Liszt nor Berlioz has composed anything that could be considered music, they are both most brilliant heralds of the future") is of course much more vivid than carefully graded shades of grey, and one can often detect in it Stasov's painful striving to convey the precise nature of his own reaction to a composer or a work.

G.A.

AMONG THE very first concerts of the Lenten season were those directed by our two theatre conductors, Messrs. Maurer and Każyński.[1] Every year Mr. Maurer's concerts prove notable only in the fact that at them an attempt is made to perform some great, famous work by a famous composer. This time the work selected was Beethoven's *Pastoral* Symphony, which was, in fact, played. The most noteworthy feature of Mr. Każyński's concert on the other hand, was Schubert's song, the "Erlkönig", as orchestrated by the conductor himself. In saying this we do not mean to imply that the "Erlkönig" was the best piece on the programme—no, for the programme also included the overtures to *William Tell* and *Egmont*. We single out the "Erlkönig" only in order to draw attention to Mr. Każyński himself.

One of the Petersburg periodicals has asserted that Mr. Każyński made a wood spirit out of Schubert's "erlking", and that "an erlking is not a wood spirit but a mystical being that expresses itself in soft, profoundly meaningful sounds, at once enchanting and frightening". We can only

[1] Ludwig Maurer (1789–1878), German violinist, composer and conductor, and Wiktor Każyński (1812–1867), Polish composer and conductor. In 1847 Maurer directed the symphony concerts of the Concert Society and Każyński was musical director of the Imperial Theatre, St. Petersburg.—G.A.

suppose that all this is merely an exercise in rhetoric, since we see no other reason for such a statement. First of all, "erlking" is nothing more than a polite way of saying "forest spirit", and we simply cannot see what kind of "profoundly meaningful" sounds could possibly issue from the mouth of one of the wild creatures of the world of childish imagination, a creature who whispers to a child "Come, come to me into my forests", and, when the child does not go to him into the forests because his father will not let him, strangles him! As for the "mystical" quality, even if there actually were a difference between an erlking and a wood spirit, they might both be permitted to enjoy equally the title of mystical beings, on a par with mermaids, naiads, and even the devil himself. Secondly, Mr. Każyński has an extraordinary knowledge of the orchestra and orchestration—extraordinary even for this day and age when "everyone orchestrates well and can easily make orchestral arrangements".

This same periodical also speaks scornfully about Mr. Każyński's polkas, attacking, in particular, the title of one of them, the *Arab Polka* (the Arabs, you see, have never had polkas). Now, while we ourselves see no great merit in the composition of polkas or any other kind of dance music, we by no means look down on this kind of music, not because of its intrinsic value but because we consider it an expression of the taste of broad masses of the people. Dance music is developing on such a vast scale nowadays that even a person with good taste and a good understanding of serious music cannot but give it serious attention. He must wait and see what the outcome of all this will be, for nothing that has engaged the interest of masses of people has ever failed to yield great results. That is why something of this sort cannot simply be tossed aside and ignored. Like certain kinds of popular fiction, dance music has opened the public's mind to a great deal in serious music that had hitherto seemed obscure. Through its simple popular forms it has begun to educate the ears of a majority of the public musically. It has already made accessible to a great many ears what would have been totally inaccessible to them some ten years ago. It has schooled them in the subtleties and refinements of orchestration. On the other hand, it is gratifying to note how excellently, indeed how magnificently, the composers of dance music have mastered the art of instrumentation. It is no longer a matter of a few fiddles with French horns or a puny little flute. Nowadays the scores of dance music contain all the most intricate effects of large orchestral scores, and a composer of serious music might find it very worthwhile to examine with care some of the little pages of these waltzes, polkas and quadrilles in their orchestral form. In this respect, the progress made by dance music in the space of only a few years is truly amazing. If you compare the present century with the century gone by, you will find a difference that staggers the imagination. We firmly believe that this subject calls for very serious and thorough consideration. There is nothing to be gained from talking lightly about things which seem trivial to us only because we have failed to grasp their significance. I am speaking of those who attach a great deal of importance to the "Erlkönig", but when it comes to something that is really important, have nothing to say. The *Arab Polka*, which provoked this periodical's attack, is remarkable for its orchestration; in this respect it is the equal to Mr. Każyński's *Alexandra Polka*. In both of these words there are colouristic effects which do honour, in the full sense of the word, to the composer. The transcription of the "Erlkönig" is also very deserving of attention—it is virtually flawless.

This transcription has, however, made one thing clear: the piece itself is absolutely devoid of good melody. What sounds rather smooth and flowing when performed by voice and piano alone proves to be quite different when the individual instruments unravel the threads of the musical fabric. The orchestra is the perfect touchstone of the "strength" of a melody. The monochrome of the piano tone blends many things, it deceives with respect to everything having to do with melody; it makes a rather decent melody out of what is in essence a poor one. This difference cannot be stressed too strongly to those who are thinking of orchestrating pieces which were not originally intended for orchestra. Sometimes the transcriber can make very strange mistakes and do the composer the worst possible service: he can expose the composer's weaknesses in all their nakedness. Mr. Każyński's transcription, although splendid in itself, has revealed the hidden poverty of Schubert's "Erlkönig"—a piece which has been enjoying a fame it does not fully deserve. The poverty and inadequacy of this piece have always been masked by a certain kind of beauty in the piano part, a beauty which aids the voice. Indeed, it must be remarked that in general the "Erlkönig" sounds best not as a song, but as Liszt transcribed it for the piano. When performed by voice and piano, it loses a great deal; and, finally, a performance by the orchestra reveals all the secrets which previously had been concealed. The best thing in it is the depiction of the horse's galloping. The short, abrupt phrases uttered by the father, the son, and the spirit have no musical value whatsoever; in and of themselves they express nothing. Whatever they or the piano seek to express separately fails to come through. It is only when the brief sustained phrases of the voice part and the rapidly moving piano part are combined that the song takes on a certain meaning.

In addition to being an excellent transcriber, Mr. Każyński is also a conductor of great ability. Although he has headed the orchestra of the Alexandrinsky Theatre for a very short time, he has already effected a marked change there. The musicians are the same, but they play entirely differently from the way they used to. In this unified group it is impossible to recognize the jarring, ragged playing of former times. Of course, the orchestra does not perform everything equally well; after all, its primary role is to accompany *vaudevilles*. But one can always point with special pleasure to its performances of overtures (a good number of which had not been played in Petersburg for a long time in spite of their fame) and, above all, to its performances of the dances composed by Mr. Każyński.

The Philharmonic Society presented two concerts. The first consisted of a performance of Haydn's oratorio, *The Creation*, and the second included, along with some lesser works, Mendelssohn's First Symphony, a new concerto by Henselt, and Weber's *Invitation to the Dance*, orchestrated and conducted by Berlioz. The second concert in no way equalled the first—not one of the three works mentioned produced anything but the slightest impression. It was quite different, however, with the first concert. Haydn's oratorio produced the liveliest of impressions. Even the Italians were touched to the quick—and, what is still more surprising, so were the people who usually cannot comprehend anything beyond Italian music. Yet this is not really so surprising, for *The Creation* is suffused with an extraordinary beauty which no one can resist. To be sure, there are defects in the very conception of the work, which reeks with the idyllicism and sentimentality of the last century and an inappropriate naïveté. No less an intellect than Berlioz has chuckled over the watery little snows and mist-like rains which are supposed to have enveloped the entire earth, the pitiful lightning bolts, diminutive thunderclaps and sweet north winds. Nowadays all this would be done very differently; it would be fuller, better, closer to the actual natural phenomena. On the other hand, the composers of today could not muster the talent to create the charming beauty which pervades the whole work and imbues every listener with a very special feeling: he hears a new language being spoken; he has a sense of a new striving, a longing of something to take wing. One cannot demand sense and accuracy of the libretto of this oratorio. If in our own day no one has succeeded in producing opera and oratorio librettos which conform to the demands of art or even to those of common sense, what can be expected of a bygone day when no one even bothered about such questions?

The Creation is pervaded with joyousness. The very same song continues throughout, only in different keys. Something is created and at once the chorus sings: "Let us praise, let us glorify"; something else is created—again the chorus: "Let us praise, let us glorify"; finally Adam and Eve make their appearance, and with their first step they begin the very same thing. Thus, the Oratorio consists of restricted, compact little pictures and hymns of praise. With few exceptions, the pictures (i.e. the arias) are very old-fashioned. Most boring of all are the recitatives that precede them, although they do have some good points which might be brought out if they were taken apart and orchestrated. In their present form they are very far from the generally accepted music of today. There is really nothing in these recitatives that could possibly interest anyone; why, then, do they "burden the earth in vain"? There is no music in them; there is nothing of Haydn's genius in them; they do nothing but try one's patience. All the choruses and *morceaux d'ensemble* (trios and duets), on the other hand, are flawless. Here are to be found the power, the beauty, the mastery of detail which only a consummate artist possesses. Here you will no longer find anything old-fashioned; you will not stop to think about the music or anything else. Along with the composer, along with his work, you will be transported into a state of solemn rejoicing, of infinite joy.

In these choruses Haydn's orchestra really comes into its own. It does not yet possess those attributes which the modern orchestra has developed; it cannot yet function in terms of individual sections. It is still on a homogeneous plane, but one of a most perfect and most resplendent kind. As is well known, Haydn is considered the father of our instrumental music; but it was in *The Creation*, written towards the end of his life, that he revealed himself in the fullness of his powers. What he did here was not equalled even in his *Seasons*. This final oratorio, composed on the eve of his death, sums up, as it were, everything that had been begun in *The Creation*. It proves conclusively that the only elements of which Haydn was master were the elements of solemnity and classic beauty. He had not a grain of what we call a dramatic sense or sense of objective truth. Thus, for example, there is no difference between the choruses of the angels and those of the peasants. It was all the same to Haydn. He required only that the words of the libretto give him the opportunity to express all the solemn, triumphant beauty that stirred within him and that received such full expression in his works. Many people believe that the essential quality of Haydn's music is childlike simplicity and naïveté. We cannot share this view, however; it is too one-sided. It applies primarily to his early symphonies and certain sections of his quartets, but not to his major works.

In this concert of the Philharmonic Society not all the tempi were as they should be. For example, the charming C major aria from the creation of Man was taken too fast, and the E flat trio of the second finale too slow. Indeed, this whole trio was performed in a most inartistic manner. The effect of astonishment when the Creator withdraws his hand from the created world, an effect expressed by Haydn with true profundity, was completely lost; it was reduced to something trivial and totally insignificant. Furthermore, the orchestra is very short of stringed instruments. The strings were drowned by even the most ordinary entrances of the brasses, and consequently many passages which depend for their effectiveness on the strings were rendered ineffective. But despite all this, the Oratorio was performed satisfactorily by both the orchestra and the chorus—something which can by no means be said of the soloists. The marvellous voices of the Imperial Chapel choir, with their amazing accuracy of pitch and purity of tone, contributed greatly to the wonderful effect of the whole performance.

During the present Lenten season Petersburg was visited by an old acquaintance, the cellist Borer, and his reception clearly demonstrated, as though on a barometer, the change that has taken place here in the course of a few years. Many performers who pleased us only a short while ago will no longer find favour here! Even though Petersburg's taste is far from impeccable, it has greatly improved. This is due to the fact that during the past five or six years almost all of Europe's celebrities have been heard here. If nothing else, force of habit alone could have brought about an improvement in the level of musical understanding.

Before Mr. Borer made his appearance this season, Petersburg firmly believed that he combined in his playing tenderness, taste, feeling, warmth, a singing quality, the marvellous voice of a Catalani and the bow of a Romberg, in short, that he was a veritable Paganini. Were this true, Mr. Borer would be the foremost musician in the world today, the kind of musician that appears only once in a hundred years, if that. But alas! The only feelings aroused by Mr. Borer's one concert here were numerous and varied feelings of pity. Before us was a wreck, a wreck, moreover, who has been loudly proclaiming his total lack of talent since his earliest years, one who has never been able to produce anything artistic and beautiful. We will not even speak about Mr. Borer's outmoded style of playing. That would not have mattered had there been something to compensate for it. But the only compensation the audience received throughout the entire concert was annoying Germanic gestures and unpleasant glances.

Far above Mr. Borer on the ladder of the arts stands Mme. Cristiani, cellist to the King of Denmark, who was paying her first visit to Petersburg. Before her concert, of course, the question in everyone's mind was: how can a woman play such a bulky instrument without looking awkward? Mme. Cristiani answered this question splendidly. There is nothing the least bit graceless or displeasing when she plays. On the contrary, she proved that a woman looks no less graceful when playing the cello than she does when she plays the harp. As the hands move, now away from now towards each other in the various motions required in playing this instrument, they trace very elegant lines against the background of the dress, especially when the woman's hands are as lovely as Mme. Cristiani's. As for her playing, it was evident from the very first note that she possesses a beautiful, rich tone which, of course, is the first prerequisite of all instrumental playing. Mme. Cristiani cannot, however, be considered a complete master of her art. She plays well and competently, but like a diligent student who has only recently left her teacher. Listening to her, one feels as though he were attending the final examination of a proficient pupil—and, as we know, there is a world of difference between the answers of such a pupil and the statements of a mature professor. Nevertheless, Mme. Cristiani possesses a great many good qualities. First of all, her wonderful tone, which we have already mentioned; secondly, warmth of feeling; and, finally, considerable tonal clarity and accuracy of intonation. In conformity with the current mode, her programme consisted primarily of well-known excerpts from the favourite Italian operas. These she played simply, effortlessly, without intricate embellishments—all in all, quite decently. At one of her concerts, however, she decided to play a cello transcription of the *Élégie* which Ernst had played only a few days before, and this was an entirely different matter. If Ernst had not been here, everyone would have been satisfied with Mme. Cristiani's performance of the *Élégie*. But this elegy is Ernst's favourite piece. He is said to have composed it on the death of a woman he had loved. Can you imagine how he must have performed it, this man who is one of the greatest violinists of our time?

In this case, the enormous difference between a student and a mature master immediately became evident. When Ernst came to Petersburg the public was assured that he was a second Paganini, that—Paganini excepted—the world had never known such a violinist. We cannot agree with this, however, for Ernst has always scored his greatest success with *The Carnival of Venice*, a musical farce consisting entirely of tricks. In this piece, the violin is made to produce all sorts of squeaks and screeches, to imitate the chirping of sparrows and the sounds of other animals—to the delight of the audience. There is no denying that in order to accomplish such tricks, a violinist must have a good command of his instrument or must be able "to do whatever he wants to with the violin", as they say. But we are firmly convinced that what is most important about an artist's technique is that it be used for legitimate artistic purposes. It ought not to be used for the sake of wildness or oddity, much less for banality. For this reason we think that Ernst did his best playing in his *Élégie*. This piece does not call for tricks, but it does demand a complete mastery of the instrument. Indeed, only complete mastery could draw from it such passionate, such profoundly stirring tones and infuse them with the simplest kind of truth! For his performance of this *Élégie*, Ernst can rightfully take his place among the greatest musicians of our day. However, in other pieces (at least in those he played at his three Lenten concerts here), we very rarely found his tone completely flawless. Invariably it had a certain rather unpleasant sound, and after a few measures, the tricks—all sorts of leaps and skips—began. The distinctive qualities of Ernst's playing are facility and straightforwardness. He tosses off a two-octave scale as if it were a joke; all the notes pour forth one after the other with amazing speed—even, smooth, the last just like the first, without any roughness, without a single interruption. Or he begins one of those increasingly widening trills in which the notes of the theme are heard, and he does this so beautifully, so perfectly, that it seems as though two violinists were playing—both of them the greatest masters! One naturally might have expected Ernst to play Desdemona's "Willow Song" in much the same way as he did the *Élégie*, but he did not. In this piece there was neither intense passion nor pensive sadness. There were some correct notes, but that was all; it did not differ much from the performance of the march from *Othello*. This latter piece posed a strange problem; that of playing a grandiose march, originally composed for a huge orchestra, by means of some double-stops on an insignificant little violin! No wonder the result was so strange.

Before leaving Petersburg to go abroad, those long-time favourites, Vieuxtemps and Blaz[1] gave farewell concerts which, of course, were extremely well attended. These two musicians are so well known to our audiences, and the virtues of each are so fully appreciated that we shall not speak at length about them. In reference to Vieuxtemps we will permit ourselves only to point out something which has hitherto not been remarked upon: in his own compositions he displayed an excellent knowledge of the orchestra, which, as everyone knows, is very rare among solo performers. The last time he appeared at one of the concerts with *tableaux vivants* given by the directorate, he played the adagio and finale from his large-scale Concerto in A. This adagio contains instrumental effects that are truly striking in their originality.

In addition to the musical events already mentioned, a number of less imposing concerts have been given in various nooks and corners of Petersburg, and each of them without exception made use of the services of Mr. Versing and Mme. Walker (the soloists of *The Creation*)—sometimes separately, sometimes jointly. But whether they appeared individually or together, with all their tireless activity and their various well-known arias (from *Figaro, Don Giovanni, Fidelio, Titus, Der Freischütz*, etc.) never once did they create a sensation in the concert hall—quite the contrary.

To our great astonishment, we must add, of the several dozen overtures played during the *tableaux vivants* and at concerts held in various quarters of Petersburg, not one was performed entirely satisfactorily except Berlioz' *Roman Carnival* overture, which the composer himself conducted at his first concert. Since overtures are played more often than any other kind of music, it would seem that every musician ought to know most of them almost by heart. Of the many performances of overtures during this Lenten season, however, some have been merely passable, others downright bad. The most famous ones, such as *The Magic*

[1] A well-known clarinettist of the day.—G.A.

Flute, *The Marriage of Figaro*, *Don Giovanni*, *Oberon*, *Fidelio* and *The Hebrides*, have fared the worst. Of the rest, the best performed was the overture to Méhul's *Joseph*, which Mme. Cristiani played at her first concert.

But all these concerts, large and small, good and bad, were overshadowed by the two given by Berlioz in the Assembly Hall of the Nobility. These were the most magnificent, most crowded, most brilliant (in terms of both orchestra and applause) most deafening concerts that were presented this year. Everyone flocked to them; how could they do otherwise, when Berlioz has such a colossal reputation throughout all of Europe? The truth must be told, however: probably nowhere else has Berlioz' arrival been preceded by such widespread prejudice as it was in our country. No sooner did it become known that he was coming than the public began to receive reports through letters from abroad and in other ways that Berlioz is utterly worthless, that he composes in the manner of a washerwoman wringing out her laundry, that he is a noisemaker, a *tapoteur*, etc. Even after attending his concerts, some people continued to say such things. Others added that Berlioz belongs to that young generation which "has sown its wild oats, spent itself, and become staid and respectable"; that, of course, Berlioz has very lofty ideas, but none of them has been embodied in melody. "Melody is the soul of everything," say these people. "Take any melody you like, sing it to a Hottentot and he will say, 'You have sung my joy, my sorrow, my anguish, my happiness'. Just as poetry without an idea is not poetry, so music without melody is not music. If you take the song 'Po Ulitse Mostovoi' and transcribe it for a large orchestra, it will sound no worse than any of the large works that Berlioz has composed for enormous instrumental forces. When it comes to such things as the marches from *La Vestale* or *A Life for the Tsar*, there is no point in even trying to make a comparison—there just isn't any." Besides all this, these people exclaim: "No, no! Say what you like, we simply do not understand Berlioz' music!" A third part of the public, unable to bring itself to the point of speaking candidly, has decided that there are some good things in Berlioz' music after all, such things as the "combination of instrumental sonorities", "tonal colours", "their sudden rise and fall"; that in his music the erudite is combined with the accessible but not as clearly as in the works of Mozart, Weber and others. Nowhere else has Berlioz been received with such hostility, for the very simple reason that many people here do not follow the dictum not to pass judgement on something that they have never seen or heard, in short, that they know nothing about.

Leaving aside these regrettable human failings, let us try to say something about Berlioz himself. First of all, it seems to be quite impossible to regard Berlioz as a man of no significance and of no talent. The reputation he enjoys and the extraordinary impression he makes on everyone cannot possibly be ascribed to fashion alone, as is sometimes the case with men who, though not entirely without talent, are far from great. Since Berlioz does produce such an effect everywhere, we ought to try to find out what this effect consists of and by what means it is produced, for although most people are not aware of it, behind every effect there lies a cause.

We cannot and must not say that Berlioz' music is good or bad, that it contains melodies or does not. Before anything else, we must state that Berlioz' works are utterly devoid of music; he has no gift for musical composition whatsoever. On the other hand, he is enormously gifted as a performer; his talent in this regard is fully on a level with the amazing talent of Liszt. Indeed, these two men are strikingly alike in every respect—in taste, ways of thinking, and in their entire manner of performance, down to the smallest details. Liszt is generally regarded as a performer at the piano, and nothing more. How many times have we heard or read comparisons between Liszt's playing and compositions and the playing and compositions of Thalberg, Field, Hummel, and any number of other pianists? How many times have we listened to the same sort of discussions about Liszt's melody or lack of melody that we have become accustomed to in reference to Berlioz? But the whole tenor of Liszt's life has been entirely contrary to that of any other pianist. One of our "respected" critics quite recently asserted, in *Biblioteka dlya Chteniya*, that "up to this time there have been four periods of piano composition: the first began with the classical sonatas of Mozart; the second comprised the epoch of Hummel and others, during which the form of the Mozartian compositions was slightly altered; the third, initiated by Herz and Czerny, consisted entirely of variations; and finally, the present period, which began with Chopin."

Without going into the question of the earlier periods, which is irrelevant to this discussion, let us only point out that the whole trend of present-day piano playing and the manner of composing for the piano was started by Liszt. But in this case it is different, for while everyone has trailed along after him, has imitated him in one way or another, they have done so without taking note of anything and sometimes without grasping the essence of his thought. As Liszt himself said in 1839 in the preface to his transcription of Beethoven's Fifth Symphony, "By virtue of the extraordinary advance in piano performance, the piano has in recent years acquired the importance of the orchestra." It follows that a transcription bears the same relation to an original piece of music that an engraving does to a painting, and that the performer of a transcription takes on the rôle of an orchestral conductor. Viewed thus, piano music as it used to be composed has been killed at the root; the piano music of today has assumed the importance of that written for the orchestra. This is the reason for the countless transcriptions and arrangements which are flooding the musical world these days. But of all the musicians who have thrown themselves into this new music and this new way of playing, Liszt is utterly unique. He is the only one for whom the piano has not been an end in itself, but only a means by which he might perform as a conductor. He alone has fathomed the mystery of the piano.

What the piano is to Liszt, the orchestra is to Berlioz. Just as Liszt knows all the innermost secrets of the piano, so Berlioz knows the orchestra. He compels it to venture upon new paths, to produce sounds such as have never been heard before. He forces it to bow before his baton and to play in such a way as no one has ever been able to play before. While neither Liszt nor Berlioz has composed anything that could be considered music, they are both the most brilliant heralds of the future. It is truly incredible to think what plans Berlioz has still to carry out, what hints he has given us of as yet unheard-of resources, what mysteries of rhythm and instrumental sounds he has still to unveil. It would be absurd to compare the music of Berlioz with that of Beethoven—a single bar of Beethoven's best music (I say "best" because Beethoven wrote many weak things) reduces to naught Berlioz' entire *oeuvre*. It must be admitted, however, that Beethoven did not know a tenth of what Berlioz has discovered in the orchestra. Probably no one else has ever delved so deeply into the art of musical performance as he has; no one else has ever experienced the joy he does when "playing the orchestra" (as he himself puts it). His amazing ear catches every nuance, even the most elusive. He never permits a single one to slip by; he brings each one out through the thunder of the entire orchestra. Under Berlioz' direction the orchestra is like a steed that feels the full power of its rider. Leading it, Berlioz is a veritable general, adored by all his forces, inspiring them by some kind of extraordinary power to accomplish unprecedented feats. Under him, they do things it would have seemed no one on earth could have made them do. It is as though the musicians seated before him were not men but a row of keys; he plays on them with his ten fingers, and each one produces just the sound, just the degree of tone that is needed. Berlioz arrives in a city. He gathers together musicians of all kinds and calibres. He seldom has more than two or three rehearsals—sometimes, very rarely, four (here, I am proud to say, there were only two rehearsals for each concert). Then suddenly this group is transformed into an orchestra; it becomes one man, one instrument, and plays as though all of its members were finished artists. Berlioz' concerts end. He leaves. And everything is as it was before—each man for himself. The mighty spirit that had inspired everyone for a moment is gone.

One might think that it would be best if Berlioz performed only the works of the great masters, especially Beethoven, whom he finds so congenial and of whose spirit he has such a profound understanding. But if he did, he could not make known his own rhythmical and instrumental discoveries—the very discoveries which make him so powerfully effective. At his concerts at the Paris Conservatory, however, he quite frequently conducts his favourite works of Gluck and Beethoven.

In order for Berlioz' exceptional gifts to be realized to the fullest, it seems that he would have had to be, as he is, a thoroughgoing romantic. For him the only possible subjects for a work of art are the most powerfully objective phenomena in man and nature, and the most bizarre nightmares: executions and witches' sabbaths, the reveries of a Harold and the orgies of brigands, storms, flights of gnomes and fairies, choruses of drunkards in Auerbach's cellar, etc. If he is portraying a man in love, he tries, above all, to depict in the music, the sighs, the transports of the lover's heart. In a pastoral scene, what is most important to him is an echo and the sound of birds. In Shakespeare's play, *Romeo and Juliet*, one of the characters for some reason casually mentions the fairy queen, Mab. Even though this has nothing whatever to do with the plot of the play, Berlioz devotes a whole movement of his symphony to depicting the scarcely audible flight of the swarm of tiny insects which carry the court of the microscopic Queen Mab through the air. Completely non-musical subjects such as these are more conducive than any others to the development of instrumental music; they compel the composer to find ways of exploiting the hitherto untapped resources of the instruments. And this Berlioz succeeds in doing most wonderfully.

Berlioz' scores are strewn with indications to the musicians on how they are to play their instruments: how to produce the right tone, how to draw the bow with a certain kind of pressure against the strings, how the timpanist should play his kettledrums. I say "play the kettledrums" because in Berlioz' music the kettledrum is not an instrument designed for making noise, but is just as much a musical instrument as the others are. There may be two, three or four timpanists, each of them playing a separate instrument tuned to its own special note, so that the four instruments together constitute a complete chord; in combination with the basses and other timbres they produce an unusual sound. Recall, for example, the beginning of the triumphal march from the *Symphonie Funèbre et Triomphale* (composed in 1842[1] on the occasion of the erection of the Bastille column). All the double-basses begin to play one of their deepest notes; to this sustained note is added the quivering roll of the snare drums and kettledrums, at first scarcely audible and then continually increasing in volume; all of this forms an entirely new, rich sound upon which, as though upon the undercoat of a painting, the resplendent fanfares of the other instruments sparkle as they enter, one after the other. Then the whole orchestra enters. Finally the two orchestras join together . . . This accumulation of sound produces an effect of unbearable power and then, at the point when the ear is strained to the utmost, this

[1] *Grove's Dictionary of Music and Musicians* and Jacques Barzun in *Berlioz and his Century* both give 1840 as the date of composition. [Trans.]

whole huge mass of sound suddenly subsides into the ponderous tread of a triumphal march. It is in his marches that Berlioz comes closest to creating real music—in this one, for example, in the Hungarian march from *Faust* and in the march of the pilgrims from the symphony *Harold in Italy*. But, of course, one does not need any special talent to write marches! Surely, no one who knows anything at all about orchestration would ever make the strange statement that if "Po Ulitse Mostovoi" were played by such a huge orchestra, it would sound just as good as this march by Berlioz. The unusual instrumental effects are so closely bound up with this piece's rhythm—its syncopation, its antiphonal phrases which constantly divide the orchestra—that only a hopeless ignoramus would make such a statement as that quoted above. Instead of declaring that if you sang any old melody to a Hottentot, he would say, "You have sung my joy, my sorrow," etc., etc.—(a Hottentot, by the way, would never say this no matter what melody you sang to him; it is more likely that he would fall asleep or start making extremely pitiful grimaces. Besides, it would be rather interesting to find out from those gentlemen who, on so many occasions, repeat what they have heard about the melodies of Mozart, Haydn and Beethoven how many of these composers' works they actually know. It might very well turn out that they have never heard a single one of them or that when they did, they could not wait to get back to the comfortable arms of the Italians.)—instead of exclaiming, "No, no! We don't understand Berlioz' music" (as if anyone cares whether they do or not!), instead of all this talk, it would be a great deal more useful to try to understand the rare gifts of a man like Berlioz, to grasp what it is that makes for the special character of his genius, that enables him to take so enormous a step forward in music.

Although we fail to see a Byron in Berlioz, as some of his well-wishers have called him ("Oh, these friends of mine, these friends!" Pushkin used to say), we leave each of his concerts in a most extraordinary mood, a mood entirely different from that produced by the usual concerts. We feel shaken, uplifted, as if we had been in the presence of something great, yet we cannot account for this greatness. We recall that for a moment we caught a glimpse of beauty in all its splendour, something wonderful indeed—and then everything dissolved in a mist of vague yet lofty aspiration. This vagueness endows each work with a sense of incompleteness, of uneasiness, a sense of reaching out for something, of futile seeking after form. It is as though you saw before you shades wandering disconsolately along the banks of the Lethe, finding no repose. Who can deny Berlioz' poetic feeling, his poetic nature? Yet all musical forms elude him; he always remains himself, leaving others with an unquenched thirst, an unfilled desire. Even so, everyone is awakened to a sense of music's enormous and inexhaustible resources. It is this that intoxicates the wonderstruck listener. Rare are the evenings when he finds himself so profoundly moved. Because of this we cannot be content with only two or three concerts. We long to know everything that this extraordinary man has done, this man who offers new wonders, new discoveries in each new work. Thus, for example, although Berlioz has on several occasions taken as his subject the portrayal of fantastic spirits, never before has his orchestral treatment of such scenes been so charming and delightful as it is in the *Ballet of the Sylphs* from his latest work, *Faust*. No sooner do the last sustained notes of the chorus of the sylphs die away than the whole orchestra becomes scarcely audible, answering melodically the slowly articulated thread of the bass. It is impossible to distinguish the individual instruments; all merge into a series of wonderful harmonies, rapidly following one after the other, the like of which have never been heard before. The music flows smoothly along in $\frac{6}{8}$ time, punctuated only occasionally by a short outburst from the whole orchestra, and then returns once again to its measured harmonies. Suddenly an unusual sound is heard—it is two harps playing one note—and then the orchestra returns without them. Again the very same note is heard in syncopation against the entire orchestra, like the peal of a bell resounding through the air. These amazing notes are repeated several times and then everything —this whole transparent microscopic Paradise—vanishes. The effect of this little picture is most extraordinary; everyone is struck by it.

In his symphony *The Damnation of Faust*,[1] Berlioz' manner of composition shows a marked change. In this work he finally decided to adhere strictly (at least in most of the movements) to contrapuntal devices, a practice he had previously scorned. One finds here instrumental fugues and canonic devices of all kinds for chorus as well as for orchestra. Even though the use of these devices does not improve his compositions— where there is no content but only the poetic transports of the composer, no compositional technique will be of any avail—it can and should be expected to prove very beneficial to those aspects of Berlioz' talent which we have already mentioned so many times. As we know, orchestral writing gains immeasurably from the use of strict contrapuntal devices. They give rise to innovation; they heighten rhythmic effects to the utmost. That is why this latest symphony gives fuller expression to Berlioz' talent, incomparably more than any of his earlier works. One has the

[1] Many people here and abroad believe that Berlioz is the creator of a new form which has been called the "dramatic symphony". But this is not true. First of all, Berlioz' symphonies stem directly from the oratorio, differing from it only in that the instrumental part is given a larger rôle. Secondly, these works of Berlioz owe even more to Beethoven and to his little-known Ninth Symphony (the symphony with the chorus on Schiller's *Ode to Joy*). Beginning with the Third Symphony (the *Eroica*), one constantly hears in Beethoven's orchestra both the solo voices and the entries of a whole chorus. All of his symphonies, from the Third to the Ninth, are developed strictly according to a dramatic programme. Berlioz himself has never denied that his symphonic form was derived from Beethoven's Ninth. See his *Italian Journey* and numerous articles in the *Débats*.

feeling that this man will go on developing forever; there is no way of knowing what new wonders can be expected of him. And it is even more heartening to think of those musicians who will come after Berlioz, musicians whose talent for music will equal his enormous talent in all the techniques of musical composition. They will assimilate everything that Berlioz has done and in the end a new genius, a new Berlioz will stand on the conductor's podium and perform unheard of marvels in an unheard of manner. All future music will be linked in the closest and most indissoluble way to the Columbus-like discoveries and undertakings of Liszt and Berlioz.

For the most part Berlioz has composed music in honour of great national events. Thus, the *Requiem* was written for the memorial service in honour of those who perished during the July revolution; the *Symphonie Funèbre* for the dedication of the Bastille column; the cantata *Le Cinq Mai* on the occasion of the transfer of Napoleon's remains to Paris, etc. Consequently he is constantly dealing with huge masses of instruments and military bands. He has worked with almost every orchestra and military band in Europe, and after all of these he speaks with the highest praise of our orchestral and band performers. Indeed, one cannot but wonder how some peasant who, after having spent half of his life in bast shoes behind a wooden plough, then entered a regiment, upon appearing on the stage at a Berlioz concert suddenly becomes transformed into a performer capable of satisfying all the demands of someone like Berlioz, a performer who seemingly senses all of the composer's most subtle intentions, enters into the spirit of the music and plays with the restraint and assuredness of a master. This is truly one of the marvels of our national character and it indicates something great. . . .

At the beginning of this year, a book was published in Paris under the title *Introduction au code d'Harmonie*; the author was the Petersburg voice teacher Giuliani. This work, the preface to a larger study, sets out to demonstrate the inadequacy of all previous books on harmony. The chief targets of its attack are Reicha's famous work on this subject, which is used as a manual at the Paris Conservatory, the writings on harmony by Professor Fétis, Director of the Brussels Conservatory, and Berlioz' articles on the same subject published in the *Revue et Gazette musicale de Paris*. As a corrective to errors in musical harmony, this book is of out standing importance. But whereas a grammar generally confines itself to the forms of a language and the rules that govern them, Mr. Giuliani's book also undertakes to deal with the very essence of musical composition. The author continually interjects irrelevant and erroneous observations on the present-day method of composition and present-day orchestration, alleging that they overstep their bounds, and he attempts to lead harmony back to all the rules formulated by the Frenchman Rameau and developed by Rousseau and d'Alembert. But Rameau's system was so unnatural, so artificial that when its narrow limits were exceeded and new harmonic combinations were introduced, they clashed violently with what that system permitted. Among his examples Mr. Giuliani includes a number of excerpts from the latest music which seem to him entirely impermissible. However, far from offending the ear, they even afford it the pleasant sound of dissonances being resolved. No composer is ever bound by what he is permitted and what he is forbidden to do. On the subject of harmony, Mozart used to say: "It would be a fine thing for us if we did what they order us to". Books on harmony should not presume to indicate the limits to which harmony can go. Harmony stems from man's inner self, not from observations and mathematical computations. Books on this subject should undertake only to give instruction on how to *write correctly*—it is not their business to go any further than that. To be sure, the writings of Fétis and Berlioz contain some paradoxes, but these could easily be omitted and this would not invalidate the splendid purpose of their works: to break down unnecessary restraints which only clutter up the minds of students. No one who has given any thought to the matter can question that harmony must be treated as a science; but certainly it need not be bound by the limits which obtain today—as Mr. Giuliani would wish, by the way. In the prospectus of his contemplated large work, appended to the present introductory volume, we noticed, among others, a chapter devoted to the question: "Is harmony conditioned by melody, or melody by harmony?" It seems to us that in view of the prevailing concept of the art of music and of the arts in general, this question is too naïve; it might, perhaps, be permissible in a chatty *feuilleton*, but it certainly is not in a serious book. However, we have no way of knowing what Mr. Giuliani will actually say in his book. When it is published, we will try to give the readers of *Otechestvennïe Zapiski* a detailed report of it. Until then, let us repeat that as a "grammar" on the method of writing music, the recently published *Introduction* is of great importance.[1]

* * * *

During the month of May there appeared, in the Odeon music store, a transcription by Henselt of Weber's *Freischütz* overture. The edition is fairly inexpensive (1 rouble, 50 kopecks), neat, and without errors; the transcription itself does not present any special difficulties, it is very easy to play; and the overture is one of the long-time favourites of audiences everywhere. Consequently, it is to be expected that this transcription will not remain long on the shelves, but will find a ready market. Henselt is so famous that, of course, anything bearing his name is certain to be considered a real contribution to the literature of the piano. However, since

[1] *Otechestvennïe Zapiski* (1847), V. 51, "Miscellany", p. 216.

in this case he is appearing in a field entirely new to him, that is, presenting not an original composition but his first transcription of a major work (we do not attach any special significance, positive or negative, to his earlier arrangements of little songs), he must be judged from an entirely different standpoint.

If there is a great difference between a writer and a translator, there is an even greater difference between a composer and the person who transcribes an orchestral work for the piano. The translator works within the dimensions of his original, not reducing it by a single word, a single dash. Perhaps the highest praise that can be given him is that he has not only caught the whole spirit of the original and conveyed it perfectly in his translation, but that, in spite of the differences between the two languages, he has succeeded in preserving the author's style, has retained all the original words in their original order and, at the same time, has rendered them into language that is fluent, not strained but so natural that he seems not to have been translating but speaking in his own right, expressing not someone else's thoughts but his own. The work of the transcriber is entirely different. He must not follow the original blindly but must compress it considerably, must cut and, above all, transform it—not for the purpose of sparing the performer difficulties and awkwardnesses (this is irrelevant and unworthy of serious consideration) but because this is the very essence of his work. This is the one and only rule of transcription. But it is precisely this that you seldom find in any of the countless transcriptions. At the very first glance you can see that all the changes from the original have been made for only one purpose—ease and comfort of execution. But how can a transcriber concern himself with something that is so non-essential and moreover so purely relative? What is difficult for one performer may not be at all difficult for another and may even be too easy for a third. If you take something like this as your criterion, God only knows where it will stop and what strange results it may lead to. Actually, nothing could be more pitiful than the present run of transcriptions of operas, oratorios, etc. No one has ever considered this kind of work as of the slightest importance; not a single composer for piano of any note has ever thought of doing it, because everyone has regarded it as meaningless hack work, not worth wasting time on. Besides, all first-rate musicians have always looked down on transcriptions of famous compositions. "Bah! How can anyone play such things on the piano!" they would say. "It is a sacrilege, a desecration. No, I cannot listen to this on the piano—I have heard it played by an orchestra."

But it is an old story, known to everyone, that when someone who is really born for his work appears on the scene, he immediately changes everything. Usually work that had previously been considered unimportant and trivial suddenly turns out to be of the utmost importance—

the prime, the only necessity—and almost everything that had been regarded as important and great somehow becomes unimportant, and, sometimes even worthless. Undoubtedly one of the most outstanding reformers of this kind is Liszt. When he started out on his true mission, he immediately brought about a decisive revolution, and what had previously been considered of little consequence and not at all worthy of notice immediately assumed the highest importance. Liszt began composing fantasias on all sorts of operas. Of course, other composers had written variations, that is, free fantasias on various themes from operas before this. But these earlier compositions bear no resemblance whatever to those which originated with Liszt. The latter, being a novelty, at once became the rage. Everyone started to write in the manner of Liszt; they began to regard him as an outstanding composer for the piano. The only virtue we can see in Liszt's compositions, however, is a desire to present, in a small piano piece, a kind of dramatic replica of a famous opera—a desire which the composer carries out by selecting a few characteristic passages from the opera and interspersing the various themes with lyrical effusions of his own. But since Liszt has no talent whatever for composition, his intentions have remained only intentions. He has not been able to realize them, and consequently the most noteworthy feature of his pieces is the way in which he has arranged the various themes for performance on the piano. This kind of arrangement was so new, so original, and so suited to the resources of the piano (which he exploited to the utmost) that it became apparent at once that, compared with Liszt, the greatest of the earlier composers for the piano had not really known the instrument at all.

It was to be expected that entire pieces would be arranged for the piano just as separate themes had been, and in fact Liszt began to turn out numerous transcriptions of whole orchestral works. From then on he found his true métier and the character of the revolution he had brought about fully revealed itself. Now it was no longer a matter of simply composing pieces but of the meaning of the piano as an instrument. Before this composers had written sonatas, concertos and many other kinds of music for the piano as they had for the other instruments. It had been the same kind of solo instrument as the violin, flute, and so on. Now it no longer requires this kind of music; it is a miniature orchestra, a veritable replica of it. And just as the music written for orchestra must have definite content, that is, it must aim to express one idea or another (as sculpture and paintings do, although the subjects treated by each of these arts differ, one from the other), so must the music written for the piano.

When Liszt turned to transcription, he went full sail, so to speak. Here all the knowledge he had gained through the deepest study of his instrument revealed itself. Here all the techniques of his magical playing, playing the like of which had never been heard before, were presented in a form accessible to the public. It might be said that there is a kind of acoustical deception in the way Liszt's arrangements are made. What is written in the arrangement differs from what is to be found in the orchestral score, and yet the effect produced is exactly the one that is desired and required. Sometimes you can scarcely believe your own fingers: you cannot understand why it is that some figure with a certain disposition of notes sounds altogether different from the way it apparently should sound. The reason for this is that not all the sounds on the piano are of equal quality; each tone has its own properties. Some tones are stronger than others and sound very different from those of the next octave. Musicians whose concern is with the orchestra are well acquainted with similar differences peculiar to the various timbres of the instruments. Just as no one knows all the hidden properties of the different orchestral instruments in their various combinations as well as Berlioz does, so no one can be compared with Liszt in his knowledge of such properties of the piano. Furthermore, after the endless study required for the greater and greater development of his brilliant piano technique, Liszt arrived at a new formulation for piano music (perhaps the same one Berlioz introduced into instrumental music), according to which entire complicated figures which seem to be used for melodic purposes can exist solely for the sake of the general harmonic impression. It would be a terrible mistake for an orchestra or pianist to perform melodically those parts of the music which are supposed to produce a general impression on the listener. When an orchestra is playing contrapuntal music there are a great many themes which (just as in a fugue) exist independently of one another and must not be permitted to get lost or to be drowned by the other themes. In the music of Liszt and Berlioz the melodic figures are not meant to be heard independently but only to contribute to the overall effect.

The vogue of Liszt's compositions has gradually passed away. Now they lie untouched in the music stores. But before? It was really a great occasion every time something new appeared under his name. Lately he has leaned more and more toward transcription, and it seems doubtful whether we can expect anything else from him. This is just as well, for his own compositions are as worthless as his transcriptions are great. These transcriptions point directly towards future musical composition for the piano, the limits of which have now been expanded beyond belief. Nothing seems impossible any longer; there seems to be nothing that could not be performed on the piano. There are not many orchestras in the world, but by means of the piano they can be increased almost infinitely, just as a writer's manuscript can be reproduced endlessly through the process of printing. Clearly, all that is lacking now is a composer who would not have to confine himself to arranging the works of others but would be capable of composing in his own right.

One of our Russian magazines recently advanced the curious idea that men ought not to play the piano; that this is too trifling a rôle for them, a rôle which should be left to women because men have to devote themselves to more serious pursuits. We do not know whether many readers were taken in by these views (which were set forth at great length), but we are quite sure that they date back to the time when the human race was divided into the serious and the non-serious, i.e. men and women, and when only a superficial rôle was allotted to the women. Nowadays women are expected to concern themselves with serious matters just as men are; and along with this rectification of ideas, ideas about the arts have also been rectified. An attempt is now being made to eliminate from the arts everything that is unimportant, trivial, and to retain only that which actually has meaning. This is why Liszt's ideas of what constitutes piano music have caught on so strongly.

Consequently any arrangement which does not adhere to the ideas conceived by Liszt immediately strikes one as old-fashioned, lifeless, unsuitable for the present day.

It must be confessed that Henselt's arrangement of the *Freischütz* overture is one of those works which have not kept pace with contemporary developments. Indeed, it is so far behind the times that someone who did not know when it was made might think that it had been written and published fifteen years ago. This cannot be said of any of Henselt's own compositions. Such is the difference between using the piano for trivial pianistic purposes and using it for its true purpose and exploiting its resources to the full. The orchestra cannot be fitted *completely* into the space of the two piano staves. Consequently, omissions and alterations are necessary. This is the crux of the matter: to understand instinctively what must be left out and what must, without fail, be retained so that the effect of the original may be reproduced. In short, one must have the ability of a portrait painter to capture, above all, the essential features of the face, those which define the whole physiognomy. Henselt lacks this gift of seeing keenly and accurately. Everything in his arrangement seems fortuitous. God alone knows why one thing is left out, why something else is added and, it goes without saying, that additions which cannot be explained are unforgivable.

Liszt has made an extraordinary number of transcriptions: many of Schubert's songs; Beethoven's songs on the sacred poems of Gellert; Beethoven's "Adelaide"; two compositions of Berlioz (*Les Francs-Juges* overture and the *Symphonie Fantastique*); the whole of Pacini's famous aria "I tuoi frequenti palpiti", with the full introduction and recitatives; the *William Tell* overture and the *Freischütz* overture; and the Fifth and Sixth Symphonies of Beethoven. He had, therefore, to struggle with all kinds of difficulties. Even so, the most striking quality in all these transcriptions is their astonishing fidelity to the original, the way Liszt strives to express all the nuances of the composer's thought. What could be more difficult than transcribing for two hands such complex orchestral compositions as Beethoven's Fifth and Sixth Symphonies? Yet these transcriptions turned out to be Liszt's finest works, the crowning achievement, thus far, of his activities as a transcriber. They are on a par with his two fantasies on operatic themes: the marvellous, passionate duet with chorus, punctuated by the beats of the timpani, from Bellini's *Norma* and Don Giovanni's drinking song, *Finchè dal vino*, from Mozart's opera. Of all of Liszt's superb transcriptions these four may be considered the best.

In the case of such difficult transcriptions you never cease to wonder how Liszt managed to fit almost the entire orchestra into ten fingers and do it so easily. In Henselt's case, on the other hand, you ask yourself with astonishment why he made such unpardonable omissions in the overture to *Der Freischütz*—omissions not of the sort that are scarcely noticeable, but in the most important, most famous sections and, moreover, in sections with no special difficulties which might serve as an excuse. Thus, the widely known main theme (taken from Agatha's aria), which appears first in E flat major and then in C major, has a syncopated accompaniment throughout. Henselt omits this syncopation altogether, and in so doing completely changes the character of this section, to which the syncopation gives a joyous forward thrust. Later on, at the overture's climax, the minor key suddenly resolves into the brightest of major keys and two brilliant fanfares proclaim the triumph of good over evil. Between these two fanfares, there is a long pause, and before the second one begins, the first and second violins rush swiftly upward; then, after the last note of the violins, the entire orchestra enters triumphantly. This whole violin figure, of course, follows the triadic intervals of the tonic, the third and the fifth, except for one extraneous note (the augmented second, D sharp) which occurs near the beginning, in the lower part of the figure. Henselt constructs this figure of completely different intervals, piles up several sharps and non-chord tones, and destroys the pure brightness which is necessary at this point, replacing it with noise. Immediately following this figure, Agatha's flowing melody returns for the last two times, played by the loud, joyous chorus of the full orchestra. It is at this point that power is called for—the accompanying syncopation is even more necessary here than when this melody first appeared in a not so triumphant form—and what do we find in the transcription? The only difference between the way Agatha's melody appears in the first part of the overture and the way it appears here is that at first it is played by a single voice, a single note, and here it is in octaves. How could Henselt do such a thing? What is there in his transcription to express the powerful, augmented sound of the whole orchestra? Can octaves possibly make all that difference? What could have been easier than to make every quarter note a full chord in both the right and left hand? This would have presented no particular difficulty. In any case it is not a question of difficulties; it is sufficient to know that the composer wanted the full force of the orchestra. This means that the piano must do everything it possibly can with ten fingers to capture the sound of the orchestra—and that is a great deal. Because of this omission, the entire close of the overture turns out, in Henselt's transcription, to be extremely weak in comparison with the first half, where octaves are used a great deal, and as a result it is impossible to notice any difference in the relative power of the orchestra at the beginning and end; there is no gradual development, no crescendo whatsoever.

The overture opens with part of the orchestra in unison, to which the violins respond in unison with a half-phrase. For this response Henselt introduces octaves. Further on, at the first *tremolando*, accompanied by dull claps of thunder, the timid and trembling voice of Max is heard, played by the cellos alone. Again Henselt uses octaves. Why? In the very middle of the piano keyboard the alto-range notes for this recitative (E flat, D, C) are so full and resonant that there is no reason to reinforce them with octaves. It is because of things like this that the relation between the volume of sound in this section and the volume of sound in the concluding section of the overture is so disproportionate. In addition to the two just cited, there are a number of other instances of error and carelessness. Thus, in the opening bars of the Vivace a strong syncopation occurs, growing in volume. For this crescendo and for the volume of the syncopation wide chords were needed and Weber supplied them. But in Henselt's arrangement the whole support of the basses is chopped off and the chords that remain are compressed together near the middle of the keyboard and lose all trace of importance and power. What was the point of leaving out the octaves in the basses? A contrary example: a few bars before the second appearance of Agatha's theme, instead of E flat major leading to G major, there is a rapid bass melody in the key of B flat minor. Just before this melody the whole string section of the orchestra descends in a two-measure scale passage from D flat to D flat. In Henselt's transcription this scale is played in octaves in the very lowest region of the piano, with the result that when the B flat minor theme begins, one is conscious of a jolt—all this for no good reason and directly contrary to the composer's intention. Nor is this all. The *tremolando* which accompanies the bass melody is divided into two parts—the second violins with the violas, and the first violins—which answer one another in such a way that the first violins intercept and introduce the change in tonality. This nuance is completely left out in Henselt's transcription. But Henselt's most unforgivable error occurs when he permits himself (aside from a number of other modifications of the chords) to make an arbitrary and extremely unpleasant resolution of a chord in Agatha's main melody, one which does not appear in Weber's score at all. In the sixth bar of this E-flat major melody Weber had two E-flat major chords; in the following measure there is a seventh chord on the dominant F, for the modulation to B flat major in the eighth measure. Probably because he considered this modulation to be insufficiently prepared, Henselt changes it: in the sixth bar he replaces the E-flat major chord with an E-flat minor chord, which completely alters and distorts the flow of Weber's musical idea. This arbitrary change in chords is all the more strange in that when the same melody returns later on in G and in C, Henselt not longer considers it necessary to use a similar resolution. Or should this be considered a misprint? In fairness to Henselt, bearing in mind that he always wanted to preserve the intentions of the composer, let us assume that this change of chord is nothing but a typographical error (albeit a very strange one).

The conclusion to be drawn from all that has been said on this subject is that, although Henselt's transcription is comfortable to play and presents no difficulties, it lacks those attributes Liszt has accustomed us to regard as indispensable. It lacks fullness; it lacks complete fidelity to the original; the liberties taken are not justified by necessity or by the intention to produce certain nuances; many voice parts are omitted which could very easily have been included. In a word, this transcription is no better than many of the two-hand and four-hand transcriptions made in previous years by Czerny and many others. Finally, it gives no evidence of a knowledge of the piano and of the special hidden resources existent in the very nature of the instrument—the kind of knowledge which would have been required in order to reproduce the full orchestral effect of the original. Nowadays we can no longer be satisfied with transcriptions like the earlier ones, which were made when the piano was thought of as an inadequate and weak instrument. Nowadays everything is possible on the piano. They say that Liszt is presently transcribing all of Weber's overtures. We can be certain that they will be magnificent. But if Liszt has decided to devote himself to this kind of work, which is his true calling and forms an inseparable whole with his astonishing playing, who would not hope that after completing the Weber overtures, he will transcribe for the piano—for all the "conductors" to play—many, many other great works of music, as brilliantly as he transcribed the extraordinary Fifth and Sixth Symphonies of Beethoven?[1]

[1] *Otechestvennïe Zapiski* (1847).

II. Letters From Abroad

This is Stasov's reaction to two musicians in Munich in 1869: Wagner, whom he did not meet, and Liszt, whom he did. His extremely malicious account of the preliminaries to the performance of *Das Rheingold* at Munich in 1869 should be compared with the facts as narrated by Ernest Newman, *The Life of Richard Wagner*, IV (London, 1947), pp. 210 ff.

The change of attitude to Liszt as a composer is not at all remarkable; most of the works which built Liszt's reputation as a composer had been written in the two decades since 1847.

G.A.

ON MY very first free day, I am sitting down to write the letter I promised you. I am not going to begin, however, with the main purpose of my journey—the International Art Exhibition in Munich—nor with the Berlin aquarium, the synagogue or other interesting and curious things that have caught my eye. All this will appear in my future letters. First I want to talk about something quite different, though certainly no less interesting than exhibitions, aquariums and synagogues: I want to talk about two great men who have been in Munich during my stay.

God knows there are not too many great men in the world today, and the number of great works being produced in our time is also rather small. This being so, we ought to cherish more than we ever did before those great men and great works we do have. One thing is certain: there is always some pleasure or benefit to be derived from observing great people or associating with them.

Before saying a single word about the two great men I am about to discuss in my letter today, I must confess that one of them I really consider "great", indeed, I venerate him; the other—not quite. But I am getting ahead of myself. What I mean will become clear in the course of this letter.

One of these men is Liszt; the other—Wagner.

Both of them came to Munich in connection with Wagner's new opera, which is called *The Rhinegold*. Because of this opera, crowds of people flocked here from everywhere—from all over Europe, even from America. Everyone who heard or read about *The Rhinegold* wanted to attend the first performance (and of course, the newspapers wrote so much about it that everyone's curiosity was aroused). Liszt also came, even though he is an abbé and lives under the very wing of the Pope. But what happened was this: the opera was prepared, rehearsed, mounted—in short, everything that had to be done was done for the scheduled première "the day after tomorrow"—and then? "The day after tomorrow" never arrived. In spite of the fact that the opera had been prepared, rehearsed, and mounted, it was not performed. Wagner himself had come here to see to it that the opera be staged, but even that did not help. So, Wagner and Liszt simply left, without seeing or hearing anything. This is the story—*en gros*. But *en détail*, many other things occurred which deserve more extended discussion.

All this happened very recently, as a matter of fact only a few weeks ago. I gather from the Russian newspapers that something of this strange story is known in Petersburg. But the information that was given the Russian public is rather inaccurate. It was taken from the *Neue Freie Presse*, which is Wagner's arch-enemy and so hostile toward him, his operas and the whole tendency of his art, that it devoted columns to gloating over his present setback, and with loud huzzas declared that perhaps now at last we might be spared both Wagner's operas and the composer himself. "Now", exclaimed the correspondent of the *Neue Freie Presse*, "it is as if an evil spirit has vanished from our beautiful theatre, and we are free once and for all of Wagner's baneful influence." What can one say about such senseless talk? Isn't this rejoicing really unseemly? Isn't this fear of an "evil spirit" really ludicrous? What could be more ludicrous than the notion that the whole situation is going to change immediately simply because one Wagnerian opera happened to suffer a temporary setback in Munich? The fact is that Wagner's operas will continue to be performed here. They will not be dropped from the repertoire for a long time to come. After all, the German people have not stopped liking them!

Therefore, let us ignore all these infantile notions, fears and joys; animosity and hostility are poor advisers and reporters. We can do without them. Here is what actually happened.

Everyone knows that Wagner has often taken the plots of his operas from ancient German poetry. *The Flying Dutchman, Tannhäuser, Tristan and Isolde* are all based on old legends, tales and songs. But this was not enough for Wagner. One day he took it into his head that all that was needed was to choose the right subject, set it to his Wagnerian music, and the result would inevitably be a great national monument of German dramatic art. Accordingly, he chose the poem which many naïve Germans even now regard as a kind of home-grown *Iliad* and *Odyssey*, that is, the *Nibelungenlied*. The assumption was that the minute Wagner's *Nibelung's Ring* appeared, the German art world would have still another great creation, a creation which would be the musical equivalent to Homer's two epics. Unusual ends required unusual means. Wagner deemed it necessary to turn out of his workshop not one drama but three at one stroke, as if to say, "I have so much material, it is impossible to cram it all into one opera. Ladies and gentlemen, wouldn't you like to listen to my triune opera three days in a row? This sort of thing, a tragedy in three parts, has been done before, by the Greeks, by Shakespeare and by Schiller; am I not as good as they are?"

All this was told and retold a hundred times and in a hundred different ways to the German public by all the newspapers dedicated to spreading Wagner's fame, and of course, it attracted the widest possible attention.

However, as the time to present his opera in the great Munich theatre drew nearer, Wagner began to do everything he could to prevent its being put on. There's a wonder for you—a composer who does not want his own works performed! What could have happened? There were explanations galore. Some said that Wagner, who has been thoroughly spoiled by highborn patrons (with whom he has always loved to hob-nob, despite his everlasting talk about democracy), has a great contempt for the public and the critics and does not want to grant them the honour of hearing his opera. Others said that when he saw even his most ardent admirers doubtfully shaking their heads upon hearing his great musical poem, he suddenly became apprehensive about its merits. "What kind of opera is this?" many people asked. "What kind of subject is this—the amorous adventures of the gods, and German gods to boot! There's a timely topic for you! How very interesting, indeed, to watch crowds of gods engaging in love affairs on the stage! Is *this* the revolution in opera? Is *this* 'das Kunstwerk der Zukunft', is *this* the destruction of the old hackneyed stuff and nonsense? We thought that the only thing these German Olympians were fit for was an Offenbach satire, and here we are, expected to take this old nonsense seriously, to actually enjoy it!" Whether it was this sort of talk or something else that swayed Wagner, no one knows, but the fact is that he insisted that his *Rhinegold* not be performed publicly, but privately, for a select few. One can easily understand how the theatre directorate reacted to his preposterous demand.

"But, dear friend, is there any sense at all in what you're saying?" they argued. "If you didn't want your opera performed publicly, then why in the world did you sell it to us for such a fantastic sum? It's all very well for you to say, 'Don't put on *Rhinegold*, don't put on *Rhinegold*! I don't want you to. You mustn't do it!' But what about us? How can we possibly give in to such whims? First we were asked to pay money for the opera—we paid for it, and paid a great deal, too. Then, we were asked to alter the stage, to reconstruct it for this *Rhinegold*—we altered it. Then, we were asked to stage the opera magnificently, sumptuously enough to suit the Herr Composer—we staged it exactly as the Herr Composer wanted it, at a cost of some 60,000 thalers. And then, we were asked to invite the baritone Betz to come from Berlin to sing the rôle of the 'God

Wotan'. 'But that will cost a fortune', we said. 'What do I care? Get me Betz. I want him. I need him!' So we did this, too. We asked Betz to come from Berlin and began paying him at the rate of 3,000 thalers a month. And now, suddenly, after all this, we mustn't perform the opera for the public, but privately, just for your friends! Really, what kind of madness is this, and how is it going to end?"

But Wagner refused to listen. He just kept saying, "Don't put on my opera. Don't put on my opera. I don't want it put on."

"Very well, we don't want it either," said the directorate. "After all, there's a limit to everything. We've had enough of your carrying on and your silly nonsense, Herr Genius, Herr Wagner!"

And thereupon, the Intendant of the Royal Theatres, Baron von Perfall, declared categorically that if he could not do what had to be done, if the genius Wagner did not stop making a nuisance of himself with his absurd notions, did not stop interfering in the direction of an opera that he had sold and no longer had any rights to, he, the Intendant, would resign. The King supported the Intendant. For, in spite of his deep admiration for Wagner, he finally realized that his protégé, the great man, had carried his disgraceful behaviour too far! Baron von Perfall did not resign, and the opera went into the final stages of production.

At last the day of the dress rehearsal arrived. Crowds of people, especially visitors from out-of-town, managed to get into the theatre; it was filled. And then what! Suddenly, in the midst of the rehearsal, the conductor Richter declared—some suspect on Wagner's instructions, for he is one of the composer's most ardent admirers—that the opera had not been *staged* as it ought to be, that the *production* did not do justice to Wagner and his superb creation, that things could not go on this way, and that he no longer wanted to conduct the opera. They tried to reason with him; they reminded him that the première of the opera was only two days away, that everything was ready—posters had been printed, tickets had been distributed, the public was waiting. The furious Richter refused to listen.

"What's the matter with you?" they urged. "After all, you're supposed to take care of the music. You're satisfied with the orchestra, the singers. What else do you want? It should be pretty obvious that we, too, want the production to be good—we've already spent 60,000 thalers on it. Anyhow, all the things you're complaining about are mere trifles, petty details, not worth discussing. They can easily be corrected, changed. Everything that can possibly be done will be done by the day after tomorrow."

But Richter just kept saying, "No, I don't want to. No, I can't. How can the great Wagner's great operas possibly be presented *like this*? No, I don't want to, I can't." Finally the Intendant lost patience, even though he was a German.

"Now, you listen here, Mr. Richter," said Baron von Perfall. "What are you trying to do? You seem to have forgotten that you're a paid employee and that you're here not to satisfy your own whims and fancies, but to do what your superiors think should be done."

"Superiors!" shouted Richter. "The only superior I ever had or ever will have is Wagner." And with that he declared that he was resigning and that he would not listen to another word.

What to do? It is not so easy to find a conductor, especially for something as difficult as a Wagnerian opera. Richter really thought that he had the Intendant on the spot and that after sulking a bit, the latter would refuse to accept his resignation and everything would work out just as he and Wagner had planned. But it did not work out that way. The Intendant stuck to his guns, accepted Richter's resignation and decided to present the opera as soon as possible, come what may. After all the money that had been spent to buy and stage it, a protracted delay was out of the question. They approached one conductor, then another, and finally chose Wüllner—first, because he is very able and secondly, because he knows Wagner's music very well. He soon got his bearings with the orchestra and the singers and was ready to conduct the new opera. It was performed just a few days ago.[1]

Meanwhile, what about Wagner? From the very beginning, he had been kept informed by telegraph, in Lucerne, of everything that was going on, and as soon as he learned of this sudden turn of events, he rushed back to Munich and started all over again, arrogantly insisting that all his demands be complied with: first, that *Rhinegold* be staged exactly as he, Wagner, wanted it and secondly, that Richter be reinstated.

"But what do you want now!" the directorate objected. "Aren't you the one who kept saying that you didn't want *Rhinegold* put on at all? Now all of a sudden, you want it. And not only are you once again burning with a desire to see your opera staged—you're still making the same old fuss about trivial details in the production. What do you expect us to do? What are we supposed to think? How long is this nonsense going to go on? As for Richter, he was the one who flew into a rage, who insulted everybody, who left. Do you really expect us to take him back after he's caused so much trouble and made us lose so much money?"

"Yes, take him back and produce the opera exactly as I say. And spend all the money that's required. What do I care about your 60,000 thalers?"

"And suppose we don't do as you say?"

"I'll complain to the King."

"Go ahead and complain."

So Wagner did. But by that time the King was as angry with him as

[1] Actually on 22nd September, a fortnight before the publication of Stasov's article.—G.A.

the directorate and public were—not simply because of the *Rhinegold* affair but because of another affair even less tolerable than that. So, in order to avoid seeing his erstwhile favourite and adviser, the King left Munich just as Wagner was arriving. What could Wagner do? He looked about here and there, got into some arguments, and went back to Lucerne. But the matter did not end there. The Munich press and public (if not all, at least most of them) were simply enraged at the way Richter and Wagner had behaved. Day after day, the newspapers were filled with reports and stories about this scandalous business, and just at this point, popular indignation at Wagner was further inflamed by the other affair. This had to do with Liszt's daughter Cosima, the wife of the famous conductor and pianist Bülow. For years, Wagner, Liszt and Bülow (a former pupil of Liszt's) had enjoyed an intimate friendship. For years, Bülow and Liszt had thought only of how they might further Wagner's success and fame, and had done everything they could to promote the performance of his operas. But Wagner, who thought nothing of ties of friendship, placed Liszt and Bülow in a position where they had no choice but to break with him. I do not know exactly how he managed it—whether through his good looks or something else—but somehow he turned Mme. Bülow's head so completely that she left her husband and went to live with him.

Now the entire press launched an attack on Wagner. "Well, what's the meaning of this?" they asked. "What kind of poetic licence is this? Did you really have to put your poetic morality into practice, Herr Wagner, and play the role of Tristan to Cosima's Isolde and Bülow's Marke?[1] One would imagine that the time has passed when the only way a genius could achieve fame was by enacting the rôle of a charming rogue!"

At the same time, the press rejoiced in the hope that perhaps now Wagner's insufferable despotism would end.

"Is it really possible" some asked, "that we are living under the rule of a tyrant who is going to hurl his thunderbolts at us from Lucerne and prescribe not only aesthetic but moral laws as well?"

How do you imagine Wagner answered all these attacks by the press? He published a lengthy article[2] in which he said that he did not intend to present any proof in confirmation or denial of anything, since all the attacks on him were anonymous and since it would be futile to entrust the real facts to a press that published so much falsehood. In addition to generalities of this kind, which, of course, neither said nor proved anything, Wagner's article contained one very extraordinary passage:

"Since you reproach me for first wanting my new opera performed

[1] In Wagner's *Tristan and Isolde*, the hero Tristan seduces Isolde, the betrothed of his friend and benefactor King Marke.

[2] In the *Berner Bund* (16th September, 1869); reprinted in Richard Wagner's *Gesammelte Schriften*, ed. Julius Kapp (Leipzig, 1914), II, p. 179.—G.A.

and then changing my mind, I think you should know that I have always done everything I have been able to do—not only now but in the past as well—to prevent my operas from being produced in German theatres. If you want the truth, so far as authentic performances are concerned, the theatre in Germany is so inferior to theatres in other countries that, at the present time, it is useless even to think of successfully solving the lofty tasks posed by German genius. And so it will continue until the Germans have developed a style of their own. This is why I am firmly convinced that it is still much too early to have my works performed publicly. I have always opposed the performance of my works in Munich, and if, in spite of everything, I have sometimes consented to have them given, I have done so only to afford singers an opportunity to perform dramatic works in every possible style—this in the hope that they might become accustomed to performing them correctly and that thus a company might develop in Munich which would make it unnecessary for us to import foreign artists."

Do you realize what Wagner is saying here? Is it not curious to find such a view expressed by the very man who, a thousand times before, had said and written exactly the opposite? Wagner does not want and never has wanted his operas performed! But isn't he the one who droned on and on to everyone in Europe that he had composed such-and-such operas at such-and-such times but that malicious enemies had prevented them from being performed? Can a single book, article, or (I suspect) even one personal letter be cited in which he does not make such complaints, and does not picture himself as the most miserable, persecuted creature on earth, a victim of general ignorance, stupidity and enmity? Only a few months ago he pulled the most absurd trick of all! He published a pamphlet entitled "The Jew in Music" (*Das Judenthum in der Musik*), in which he once again expatiated on this point, in the most appalling detail, hoping to convince the world that if, for more than twenty years, he had had to suffer and struggle against countless enemies who were trying to keep his works off the stage, it was because of the Jews, all of whom despise him, persecute him and continually seek ways to hinder him.

In this pamphlet he also complained about a universal obtuseness, stupidity, and lack of understanding with respect to art. Well, if things are really in such a state, what is he making such a fuss about? It would be sheer madness suddenly to read Shakespeare's plays to Tahitians or New Zealanders! Better by far to lay them aside, sit by the sea and wait for better weather. But, as we know, Wagner has never done this; he has spent his entire life trying to find ways to get his operas put on here, there and everywhere. One need only recall how many times he has tried unsuccessfully to take Paris by storm; he has told the whole story himself, in his books. And now, suddenly, we are supposed to believe that he never tried to do any of this, and that if he did, it was only because of a burning desire to produce better performers for Germany! The only reason he had his operas performed was to afford a *means* for the development of German singers and a German style! Does this sound a likely motive for a person like Wagner? Just see how his deeds correspond to his words—how well the Cosima-Isolde episode coincides with the endless talk, in his operas, about pure, noble, innocent, virtuous love. Why, all his heroes and heroines are forever indulging in the most romantic daydreams about chastity and purity; some of them even die at the awful thought that on one occasion or another they failed to preserve their dove-like chastity. Furthermore, the poets and musicians in his operas are forever extolling pure love and innocence. And—what does Wagner himself do at the first opportunity?

It is clear that all his preachments, musical and moral, are only words, words, words—they have nothing at all to do with his own ideas and actions. This is all Wagner is—nothing but phrases and rhetoric from head to toe. His entire behaviour belies everything he preaches.

Who bemoaned more loudly than Wagner the absurdity of earlier operatic subjects: their "puppet-ness", their emptiness, and their conventionality? Yet who ever composed operas with plots more absurd, more inane, more lifeless; with plots more improbable and ludicrous, more conventional and formal?

What are all his phantom ships, condemned to sail the seas forever; swans that turn into murdered youths;[1] heroes, who, like the legendary Wandering Jew, have a mystical "curse" hanging over their heads that can be removed only by the love of a pure, innocent woman; knights who appear out of the blue and return again simply because here on earth they are asked to reveal their identity; poets and musicians who oscillate endlessly between Venus and the Pope, and finally die from ultra-virtuous pangs of conscience; and what are all these amorous adventures of the gods on the German Mt. Olympus? What has any of this to do with our times? Isn't it only the same old romantic nonsense, without rhyme or reason? Do the audiences of today really need all these everlasting marches, processions, interminable ceremonies—all this gaudy trash that fills Wagnerian operas and doesn't differ by a hair from the trash that filled earlier operas? What a strange, strange great man!

In music, Richard Wagner is the German equivalent of a Slavophile, and it is this, more than anything else, that accounts for his success among many sections of the German public. To these people the music is not as important as the chauvinistic, myopically nationalistic spirit of his operas. What is dear to them are the stories drawn from old German fairy tales and legends, however nonsensical and meaningless these stories may be.

[1] Elsa's brother had not been murdered; Ortrud had only changed him into a swan.—G.A.

And the Germans firmly believe that Wagner's music is as good, as national, and as much to be treasured as his librettos are. We cannot resist saying, however, that we find Wagner's concern over the requirements of contemporary art strange, indeed, and stranger still his desire to compose operas only so that he may complain that they are being performed now instead of a hundred years from now!

II

At the very time when the senseless, farcical Wagner episode I described in my first letter was taking place in Munich, Liszt was also here. I wanted to see him if only to reassure myself that not all the "great men" of our day are cut from the same cloth as Wagner, that there are also some among them who deserve to be considered great not only because of their superior air and cavalier treatment of the masses (who are still prone to enjoy such treatment) but because of their intrinsic worth, the actual contribution they have made to the common good. I recalled that Liszt's extraordinary talent had made him famous when he was still a boy; and that he could easily have rested on his laurels and spent the rest of his life garnering wealth and adulation! But this is not what he wanted; he could not bear the thought of following the path of his predecessors and contemporaries, most of whom did nothing but entertain Europe with meaningless virtuosity.

As he crossed the length and breadth of Europe he always seemed to be saying, through his playing: "Here is something you have never heard before, or if you have, you have heard it played poorly or incorrectly. Just listen, I am going to play for you with my ten fingers, that is, my orchestra, and you will learn something you have never known and never even dreamed of." With this as his avowed task, Liszt devoted his whole life and his genius to disseminating the greatest music that had ever been written, music which most people had not known before. He rescued a great many important composers from obscurity. During a very important period in European art, he was her mentor in matters of music; he forced her to a sudden awareness of her own riches, riches of which she had previously been ignorant. With his mighty effort he advanced Europe's musical culture; without him, it probably would have taken her much longer to achieve the high level of understanding and development she has now attained. And when, at last, the time came for his own creative work, he followed only the dictates of his own feelings and thoughts. True, these feelings and thoughts have been dimmed by that unfortunate veil of Catholicism in which he has so unexpectedly and inexplicably wrapped himself during recent years; but in pursuing this course, he is not lying, he is not pretending: this is the very essence of his soul. He does not seek to deceive or beguile anyone. All his creations, even the most recent, bear the stamp of an extraordinary sincerity, of deep conviction, and this is why they have such a powerful effect upon the listener, why, in spite of their religiosity and medieval piety, they mean so much to the men of today. What could possibly be more precious in any work of art than deep, sincere conviction and a true spiritual union between the creator and his work?

In all this Liszt differs from Wagner precisely as the spiritual, the inner life and everything that truly expresses it differs from the merely decorative, the external, the outer trappings that can be put on and taken off at will. Is it not strange that of these two men, Wagner—the free-thinker, the democrat, the republican, the man who has cast off all prejudices (if one judges only from what he says and writes) and Liszt—the Catholic, the obscurant, the man who has devoted himself now of all times to all the prejudices of a dead past, seemingly has nothing whatsoever in common with the temper and needs of our day, it turns out that of these two men, the pious obscurant and Catholic is more valuable, more needed, a million times more closely linked with our time than the progressive and democrat, the free-thinker? What has this free-thinker expressed in all his operas but a veneration for the Middle Ages, before which he genuflects and whose nonsense and ugliness he lovingly recreates in every scene? What is new in all this, how does it serve contemporary needs? Yet, it is precisely on the meeting of these needs that Wagner places even greater stress than he does on his music. He insists that his operas be regarded not simply as operas, but as revelations in which we must give our primary attention not to the music, the voices and orchestra, but to the underlying idea. It is the idea that we are expected to discover the great path along which Wagner is guiding contemporary humanity. After all, aren't his operas "the art works of the future", creations the like of which never existed before, and therefore models which all the art of the present and future should eagerly seize upon and imitate? But in the final analysis, what do we find in these new creations save a pitiful, old-fashioned puppet show, gaudily painted sets, and purely external effects that are just as painful to the eye as those in any Meyerbeer melodrama? How can this possibly be compared with what Liszt set out to do in his music and is doing, even today, in the pious period of his life, when he has locked up half of his house, as it were, and is living only in the other half?

I wanted to see once again this extraordinary man who, even though he has embarked upon a strange, incomprehensible life (he is now an abbé), is still one of the most influential teachers and leaders of contemporary art. It seemed to me that a visit to Liszt might dispel the feeling of disgust with which Wagner's latest Munich episode had left me. I wanted to convince myself that in Germany, where (save for our own small musical world) all the most promising musical activity is concentrated, there are other forces besides Wagner, forces whose influence is greater than his and will be more beneficial in the days to come.

I wondered: could Liszt have turned completely to sacred music, does nothing else interest him? After all, until just recently, he was the most enthusiastic apostle and champion of Wagnerism. He was the first to want the Germans to hear Wagner's music; to insist that they listen to it, then that they respect it and finally that they love it. He was the first to get the German theatres to accept Wagner's operas; had it not been for him, God knows how long it would have taken for Wagner to become known. Considering the relationship between these two people, if what has just happened to Wagner in Munich had happened a few years ago, that is, if unexpected obstacles to the performance of a new "great" opera had been put in his way—oh, how Liszt would have set to work! How he would have hurled his thunder and lightning, how he would have written in all the journals, how he would have attacked right and left, how he would have begged and argued with some, cajoled others until he finally gained his objective and handed Wagner another triumph. But now all this has changed. Now Wagner has to fight alone. Liszt is here in Munich, but he will not lift a finger to help his former friend and idol. Could it be that he has changed so greatly that nothing concerns him now except the church and sacred music? Could it be that all that was best in him has been completely destroyed; that he has lost his former ardour and, like most people after they have lost their youth, grown indifferent to all his former interests?

Besides all this, I wanted to see with my own eyes whether the passage of years, failures and the false path of outmoded Catholic piety could have harmed a man of genius.

When we met, I found a man who, in spite of everything, still burned with the same fervour, the same unquenchable desire to affect his fellow-men through one of the most powerful means known to man—art; the same need to imbue them with the poetic feelings which burned within him. I found him as unswerving in his devotion to his work as he had been when I first knew him twenty-five years ago. As before, I found none of those qualities—self-adulation, morbid self-concern, inordinate arrogance—that usually characterize pseudo-great men like Wagner. I had known Liszt when he was still a young man; I had seen him at the pinnacle of his fame as a virtuoso pianist. He had struck me then as a glorious, powerful eagle, with his head thrown proudly back and with flashing eyes, amidst the adoring crowd and thunderous applause that shook the concert hall. Liszt was now living in small quarters. In one room hung a crucifix that was so large it occupied almost as much space as the bed beneath it. The other room was occupied mainly by a handsome piano surrounded by piles of manuscripts and published music. The Liszt I now saw was an old man of nearly sixty, with the humble air of a monk, attired in the long, sombre cassock of an abbé. But his head was still crowned by a thick mane, and his eyes had lost none of their sparkle, strength and keenness. When he begins to talk with you his hands are folded tightly on his chest as if he were about to rub them together—a gesture of humility often observed among Catholic priests. But once he becomes caught up in conversation, his clerical posture vanishes. His movements lose their restraint and pious humility; he raises his head and shedding, as it were, his monkish pose, once again becomes forceful, dynamic. You see before you the old Liszt, the genius, the eagle.

He has lost none of his old interest in art, and his present trip to Munich is the clearest proof of this. He is old now, he is an abbé. He spends all his time fussing over Palestrina masses and the papal choir. He has broken completely with Wagner—through no fault of his own—yet, the moment news of the new Wagnerian opera reached Rome, news that an important musical event was to take place (so, at least, the pro-Wagner newspapers promised), Liszt immediately forgot his sixty years, Palestrina, the papal choristers and Rome, and rushed off, hundreds of miles, to hear the new opera. Next year will be the hundredth anniversary of Beethoven's birth, and Liszt is devoting the entire winter to composing a large work for orchestra and choruses in honour of this occasion. He himself will travel to Weimar to conduct one of Beethoven's most colossal creations—his Second Mass. His head is filled with plans for large compositions; he is continually creating new, important works. He does not forget his art, his work for a moment. He knows no rest, no leisure. Yet he does not concern himself only with his own compositions. He is keenly interested in everything new and follows avidly all that is being done in the world of music, even outside Germany.

How mean, how contemptible that person must have been who thought he could win Liszt's favour by bringing him articles in which he had attacked and crudely caricatured Berlioz. The author of these articles knew that in recent years Berlioz and Liszt, who had long been friends, had broken with each other because their artistic outlooks were diametrically opposed. Presumably Liszt should have been "delighted" to see these vulgar attacks on his present "enemy". What a revolting assumption! How mean and vile it must have seemed to the noble, generous, forthright Liszt! Still, this actually happened this very summer while Liszt was in Munich. No, miserable tricks of this kind, which might perhaps please Wagner, would certainly not win Liszt's approval. His mind, his feelings are taken up with much purer and nobler considerations and motives than this. For this reason, it seems almost certain that it could not have been personal relations alone that so completely altered his attitude toward Wagner. When people who have been very close, almost passionately enamoured of each other, suddenly turn away and break forever, external circumstances alone cannot possibly be the sole cause of the break. In such cases many other factors must have gone awry. Is it possible for a man to be base and vile in his everyday life and at the same time be a wonderful, a superb, a great artist? Every work such a man creates must inevitably bear traces of his baseness and vileness, the imprint of something revolting, foul or false that can never be erased. No doubt Liszt's eyes have been opened to many things in Wagner's operas since that moment when the two men broke with one another; many things must now seem not quite the works of genius he thought they were, not nearly so profound and sincere. Despite this, he rushed from Rome to Munich to hear *Rhinegold*, to immerse himself in the amorous adventures of the ancient German gods and watch the curious procession of dwarfs, giants, mermaids, etc. set to music. He still expects a Wagner work to be a step forward in music; he still has faith in his former idol.

While the life of an abbé and Palestrina masses did not keep Liszt from travelling to Munich to contemplate ancient German mythology on the stage, so far as his own music is concerned, there seems to be a kind of interdict on his best works, a barrier that separates the earlier from the present ones. In vain I begged him to play at least a few excerpts from the compositions of his middle period, which must be considered the most brilliant of his creations. In vain I implored him to play something from his *Totentanz*, from *Faust in the Tavern, Nächtlicher Zug*, *Hunnenschlacht* or *Dante*. But he was adamant and replied to all my pleas: "All these are works of *that* period! No, I don't play them any more." To no avail I told him that it is the works of "that" period which are loved by everyone in our country who understands music; to no avail I asked him to explain the principal variations in *Totentanz*, for which no programme is given (contrary to the practice Liszt has followed in all his symphonic works). He flatly refused to play this piece, and as for its programme, he said only that he felt it was one of those works whose content must not be made public. A strange secret, a strange exception, the strange effect of his life as an abbé and his stay in Rome! On the other hand, I did hear at least the beginning of *Ce qu'on entend sur la montagne*, those wonderful poetic pictures which no one before Liszt had ever thought of portraying in musical colours. Need I say how it was performed?

I was very happy to hear Liszt play again after twenty-five years—and how he played! The same marvellous orchestra beneath his fingers, but now an orchestra performing not a piano fantasy on some fashionable opera of earlier days but the magnificent *Ce qu'on entend sur la montagne*. He played only a bit of it, however. Then, as if he had suddenly remembered something, he stopped. He said that it recalled too vividly an earlier period, an earlier state of mind, and he began to play his new Mass for me and for his other guest, a chaplain from Regensburg who conducts a church choir. I listened to this mass with deep interest; after all, it was Liszt playing and a Liszt mass. But I thought sadly to myself: Why did Liszt have to change so terribly, why did he have to become an abbé?

Liszt will not come to Russia again. He was invited there last year and again this year. But he feels too old and too tired, and in spite of the wonderful memories he retains from his two trips to Petersburg and Moscow, he does not want to undertake such a long journey.

What a loss this is for us! In recent years the best, most gifted European conductors have visited our country, but Liszt has not been among them, and this will always remain an enormous void. This great, poetic, profound artistic nature—in spite of its many failings—how magnificently it must express itself in an orchestral performance, in the conducting of the greatest new works! After all, in the exemplary performances of present-day conductors, we have heard only earlier works or, of the latest ones, only those of Wagner and his school. We should like to hear many other things—conducted by Liszt.

I left Liszt with a feeling of sadness. The joy, the enthusiasm I had felt during the morning I spent with him was gone.

S.-Peterburgskie Vedomosti. 23rd and 24th September, 1869, Nos. 262 and 263.

III. The Letters of Berlioz[1]

In 1879 Daniel Bernard published a volume of *Correspondence inédite de Berlioz*, the first collection of his letters to be printed but full of inaccuracies. Stasov's review, in *Novoe Vremya* (18th/30th January, 1879), is self-explanatory.

G.A.

THE PUBLICATION of Berlioz' letters is an important and valuable event for all musical Europe, but for France it has a quite special significance. It constitutes additional proof of the change in public attitude towards a great man who all his life was ridiculed, hissed, and spat upon. Berlioz has been dead only ten years, but his country has already granted him the recognition which she denied him for thirty-five long years. This change has taken place rather quickly, almost as quickly as it did here in our country in the case of Glinka and much more quickly than in the case of Dargomïzhsky.

Whether France has actually come to appreciate Berlioz or is only yielding with condescension to the insistence and enthusiasm of her leading arbiters of musical matters, one cannot say, but it is clear that in France today the recognition of Berlioz as a man of genius is encountering no sort of opposition. The conservative French critics, who succeeded in ruining a good many days of poor Berlioz' life, have now stopped their yelping and along with all the others are bending over backward to glorify and interpret this great man.

Daniel Bernard, an elderly reactionary, a bigot, and one of the bigwigs of an important clerical newspaper in Paris, has also seen fit to bring his forget-me-nots to the grave. He has taken it into his head to publish Berlioz' letters. For this purpose he took space in all the major musical publications, asking everyone in Europe who was in possession of such letters to communicate them to him. In view of the importance of this undertaking, I disregarded Bernard's clericalism, immediately gathered together everything in the way of a Berlioz letter that I was able to obtain in Russia and sent them to him. But I was cruelly punished for my trustfulness.

Of the Berlioz' letters I had collected, letters written during the years

[1] Unless otherwise indicated, all footnotes to this essay are the translator's.

1848 to 1868 to various persons in Russia, this old Frenchman Bernard decided to throw out almost half, and he concealed this fact from me until the very last moment. No doubt the same thing happened to other letters as well. Those that Bernard included were published in a very slipshod fashion: almost nowhere is there any indication of where the letters were sent from, who sent them, the circumstances under which they were written, or to whom they were addressed.[1]

These letters are particularly important because they corroborate fully everything that Berlioz recounted in his *Memoirs* concerning himself, his friends, and his enemies. He was often suspected of fabrication, falsehood, exaggeration, and distortion. But the letters triumphantly refute all these stupid fictions. Written at the very moment when the events they relate were taking place, imbued with the fire and inspiration of battle and strife, they depict even more clearly and vividly than do the *Memoirs* all the truth and tragedy of Berlioz' life. The present volume covers a period of fifty years (the first letter dates from the year 1819, the last from 1868), and what do we find? This man remained true all his life to the noble ideals of his ardent youth, and he went to his grave, an old man of sixty-six, an implacable champion of all that was lofty and magnificent in his art, an invincible foe and denouncer of everything that is false, mouldy, and stupid in music. He never yielded a single iota; he never made a single concession to either his enemies or his benefactors. He was as poor in his old age as he had been in his boyhood, and neither the persecution of the mediocre nor the jeers of the ignoramuses who called him a "half-educated auto-didact" and "arrogant upstart" ever caused him to deviate a single inch or for a single second from the work and the path he had charted for himself while still a youth. It was probably because of this that everything Berlioz did turned out to be so vast, so grand, so powerful.

There was only one strange and puzzling quirk in Berlioz' nature: his aversion to a free and independent life for the French people; his distorted understanding of every one of the nation's aspirations, even those which were most legitimate and reasonable; and his unshakable devotion to the two Napoleons. Granted, his devotion to Napoleon I is more or less understandable. All sorts of people were confused and taken in by him, even the most profound, brilliant and independent minds of our century (Byron and Heine, for example). But Napoleon III! How can we explain that? Berlioz believed in him, he preferred him to the French people, he considered him the very ruler France needed.

Consider how unjust, how short-sighted, how blind Berlioz was in his attitude toward the political upheaval of 1848; how completely wrong his interpretation of it was, how exactly his views coincided with those of the most desperate reactionaries, slanderers and liars of that time. In

[1] Stasov returns to this matter in "Liszt, Schumann and Berlioz in Russia" (see pp. 117–8.

December, 1848, he wrote to one of our fellow-countrymen, Lenz, in St. Petersburg:

. . . Our Republican cholera is giving us a slight respite at the moment. There is not much doing in the way of political clubs; the Reds are champing at the bit . . .

. . . How you in your country must be laughing and jeering at us, we who call ourselves "advanced"! Do you know what we call woodcocks when they are overdone, high? We call them, too, "avancées" . . .

And you are still thinking about music! What barbarians you are! What a pity! Instead of working for the great cause, the radical destruction of the family, property, intelligence, civilization, life, humanity, you busy yourselves with the works of Beethoven!! . . . You dream of sonatas! . . . [1]

These little gibes of Berlioz have a special appeal nowadays to certain old people in France. Because of them these old folk can make their peace with Berlioz the reformer, Berlioz the bold titan, who all his life toppled lies and falsehoods from their age-old pedestals. He stumbled—they instantly applauded him and burst into song. The best example of this is my dear Bernard.

Berlioz complained of only one thing with respect to Napoleon III: his lack of understanding of music. In January, 1856, he wrote: ". . . The emperor is unapproachable and detests music like ten Turks."[2] He found the Emperor wonderful in every other respect. He looked forward with joyous anticipation to the moment when he might read his libretto of *Les Troyens* to Napoleon III, and he quite often sought invitations to the Emperor's dinners and audiences. Even the Empress Eugénie was, for him, nothing less than "la charmante impératrice". How different all this would have been with Beethoven!

The anti-musical atmosphere that prevailed in France in those days was a constant source of torment to Berlioz. He chafed and struggled like a caged beast. In his *Memoirs*, we read:

Why did the Lord God take it into his head to have me born in our "beautiful France". Even so, I begin to love it, this amusing land, the moment I manage to forget art and our idiotic political agitations. How gay life can be here sometimes! What a range of thought (at least, of words)! How they tear the whole country and its ruler to shreds with their pretty little white teeth, their pretty little nails of polished steel! How their brains rattle! How they pirouette on a phrase! How they attitudinize!

In March, 1848, Berlioz wrote:

. . . The arts are dead in France now, and music in particular is already beginning to putrefy; let it be buried quickly! Even from here I can smell the noxious fumes it exudes . . .

True, something always makes me turn automatically toward France whenever a happy event occurs in my career; but this is an old habit, an out-and-out prejudice, which I will shake off in time.

[1] Letter to Wilhelm Lenz, Paris, 22nd December, 1848.
[2] Letter to A. Morel, Paris, 9th January, 1856.

France, from a musical point of view, is nothing but a country of fools and rogues; one would have to be infernally chauvinistic not to see that . . .[1]

In January, 1856, he wrote:

. . . As for the Parisians, it is the same old story of indifference and frigidity . . .

. . . I cannot undertake anything of any importance in music in Paris; there are obstacles to everything everywhere. No hall! No performers (none I would want). There is not even a Sunday on which I might give my small concert! . . .

Farewell! Enough of this, too much. What's the use of recrimination? Cholera exists—everyone knows that. Why shouldn't Parisian music exist also?[2]

Even Berlioz' fervent devotion to Napoleon III and his adoration of all that is great and noble in the spirit of the French people could not dispel the dejection caused by the public's antipathy and crass lack of understanding. In August, 1864, he wrote:

. . . There is a house in the Rue de la Victoire, where Napoleon lived, as the young Commander-in-Chief of the Italian army. It was from there that he set off to Saint-Cloud one day to throw the representatives of the people out of the window. In a square, called Place Vendôme, there is a tall column which was made, on his order, out of the bronze from cannons captured from the enemy. On the left of this square you can see an immense palace, called the Palais des Tuileries, where a devil of a lot of things took place . . . As for the houses in certain streets, you cannot imagine what a throng of ideas they awaken in me . . . There are countries like this which exercise a powerful sway over the imagination. But I am terribly bored here all the same . . .[3]

The essence of Berlioz' nature was passion and love. Note the fervour with which he poured forth his feelings, even in his last years, even in a moment of misery, when he was racked with the pain of a thousand wounds. In January, 1858, he wrote to Hans von Bülow:

Thank you for your charming letter, charming in its style, in the warmth which prompted it, in the good news it brings me; charming in every respect. I read it with pleasure, as a cat laps up milk . . .

Your faith, your ardour, even your hatreds delight me. Like you, I still have some terrible hatreds and volcanic ardours; but as regards faith, I firmly believe that there is nothing true, nothing false, nothing beautiful, nothing ugly . . . Do not believe a word of this, I am maligning myself . . . No, no, I adore more than ever what I find beautiful and, in my opinion, the cruellest disadvantage of death is this: that one can no longer love, no longer admire. True, then one does not realize that he no longer loves . . .[4]

All his life Berlioz adored Beethoven and Gluck above all others. His passion for them was unbounded. Page upon page in his articles and books on music and in his *Memoirs* is devoted to the expression of his

[1] Letter to Joseph d'Ortigue, London, 15th March, 1848.
[2] Letter to A. Morel, Paris, 9th January, 1856.
[3] Letter to Mme. Damcke, Paris, 21st August, 1864.
[4] Letter to Hans von Bülow, Paris, 20th January, 1858.

enthusiasm for these two great musicians. In his letters, too, he very often speaks of them. On one occasion, for example, he wrote to a certain Théodore Ritter (whose identity remains unknown to us,[1] thanks to the meticulous care of publisher Bernard):

My dear, very dear Théodore:
Remember the 12th of January, 1856!
This was the day on which, for the first time, you began to study the marvels of great dramatic music, when you caught a glimpse of the sublimities of Gluck!
As for me, I shall never forget that your artistic instinct, without any hesitation, recognized and ecstatically adored this genius who was unknown to you. Yes, yes, you may be certain that whatever people of little feeling and little knowledge, those with only half a heart and one lobe of their brain may say, there are two great Supreme Beings in our art—Beethoven and Gluck. One reigns over the infinite realm of the mind, the other over the infinite realm of the passions; and although the former may far surpass the latter as a musician, there is so much of the one in the other that these two Jupiters form but a single god, who should engulf our admiration and our respect.[2]

In another letter, written in 1862, Berlioz said:

. . . As for symphonies, Mozart wrote seventeen, of which only three are beautiful—and the rest! . . . Haydn, the good soul, composed a great quantity of "pretty" things in this form. Beethoven created seven masterpieces. But then, Beethoven is not a man. And when one is only a man, one should not pretend to be a god.[3]

Berlioz' devotion to Beethoven and Gluck did not prevent him from appreciating other composers, however. Indeed, he understood and loved every musician of talent. Not only his articles, but also his letters bear witness to his fervent love for the music of Liszt, Schumann, Meyerbeer, and others. He was so truthful and free of bias that he genuinely admired the better compositions of Mendelssohn (with whom he had become acquainted in Rome in his youth), even though, save for one or two songs which Mendelssohn praised tepidly, he never understood Berlioz' music at all.

In September, 1831, Berlioz wrote from Italy to Ferdinand Hiller in Paris:

. . . Has Mendelssohn arrived? His talent is enormous, extraordinary, superb, prodigious. In speaking thus, I cannot possibly be suspected of cliquishness, for he told me frankly that he does not understand my music at all. Remember me warmly to him. He has an utterly pure character; he still has beliefs. His manner is somewhat cold, but, though he does not suspect it, I like him very much.[4]

[1] Théodore Ritter (1841–1886) was a French pianist and composer of operas and piano music, a pupil of Liszt.—G.A.
[2] Letter to Théodore Ritter, 12th January, 1856.
[3] Letter to August Morel, Paris, 2nd March, 1862.
[4] Letter to Ferdinand Hiller, Rome, 17th September, 1831.

At the beginning of 1832 Berlioz again wrote to Hiller:

> . . . The first movement [of Mendelssohn's symphony] is superb; the adagio did not make a very clear impression on me; the intermezzo is fresh and piquant; the finale, intermixed with a fugue, I detest. I cannot understand how such a talent can become a weaver of notes, as he has in certain cases. But he himself understands it . . .[1]

Two months later, Berlioz wrote:

> . . . As usual, I knew from a letter received prior to yours that the exquisite overture to *A Midsummer Night's Dream* was played at the Paris Conservatory. It is spoken of with admiration; there is no fugue in it . . .[2]

How could it be otherwise than that Berlioz' ideas should differ from those of Mendelssohn? Berlioz was a reformer, a man of the new age, a musician of penetrating intellect, a creator of new forms and explorer of new paths; while Mendelssohn, for all his natural talent, was a man spoiled and crushed by classical training, that is, one who blindly followed the dictates of his elders. How could Berlioz possibly have sympathized with what Mendelssohn regarded as the holy of holies? In a letter dated 16th December, 1856 to a certain Abbé Girod, author of a book called *On Religious Music and the Practical Knowledge of the Organ* (we are given this information by Bernard, a surprising exception to his usual procedure; but then, how could he possibly omit such information when it has to do with a Catholic priest?), Berlioz said:

> . . . The only points on which I regret to say I disagree with you are those relating to the classical fugue on the word "Amen" and the mixture stop of the organ.
>
> Undoubtedly a beautiful fugue of a religious nature could be written to express the pious wish "Amen"! But it should be slow, very solemn and very short; for, however well one may express the sense of a word, that word becomes ridiculous when it is repeated over and over again. Instead of being restrained and expressive, fugues on the word "Amen" are invariably very fast, violent and turbulent, and sound more like drinking choruses interspersed with peals of laughter, especially since each part vocalizes on the first syllable of the word "a . . . a . . . a . . . men," which produces a most grotesque and irreverent effect. These traditional fugues are nothing but senseless blasphemies . . .
>
> . . . If I were still the militant artist I once was, I would say to you: *Delenda est Carthago*! But I am weary and have to admit that absurdities are indispensable to the human mind and breed there like insects in a swamp. Let us leave them to their buzzing.[3]

We cherish Berlioz not only because he was a composer of genius, the direct successor to Beethoven and the creator of a new type of music, *programme music*; not only because all his life he was a vigorous fighter for

[1] Letter to Ferdinand Hiller, Rome, 1st January, 1832. This was the *Reformation* Symphony; Mendelssohn himself took a not dissimilar view of it and it was withheld from publication during his lifetime.—G.A.

[2] Letter to Ferdinand Hiller, Rome, 16th March, 1832.

[3] Letter to the Abbé Girod, Paris, 16th December, 1856.

a just cause; but also because, together with Liszt, he was the first to recognize the Russian school of music, beginning with its leader and founder, Glinka. As early as 1845, when Glinka, disheartened by the scorn shown in Russia towards his work of genius *Ruslan and Ludmila* (which was regarded as an "unsuccessful opera"), left Russia and with despair in his heart went to Europe in search of more discerning judges, Berlioz was more sympathetic and enthusiastic towards him and his great compositions than perhaps anyone else in Paris. He performed Glinka's *Lezginka*,[1] a work which he particularly liked, at his own concerts. On the other hand, Berlioz made a tremendous impression on Glinka, so much so that, although Glinka disliked writing letters, in fact, writing of any kind, he wrote a beautiful and ardent letter to Kukolnik expressing his feelings in this regard.[2]

The extent of Berlioz' interest in our great composer, who otherwise went almost unnoticed in Paris amid the stupid craze for the Italians, may be judged from the following letter. This letter, long forgotten, I recently found in an issue of *Severnaya Pchela* from the year 1845. It is included in Bernard's collection.

> It is not enough, sir, to perform your music [wrote Berlioz], and to "tell" many people that it is fresh, alive, charming in spirit and originality. I must give myself the pleasure of writing a few columns about it; what is more, this is my duty.
>
> Must I not keep the public informed of all the most noteworthy events of this kind that take place in Paris? Will you therefore be good enough to give me a few notes about yourself, your early studies, the musical institutions in Russia, your works, and after going over your score with you so as to have a less imperfect knowledge of it, I may be able to write something tolerable and to give the readers of the *Débats* some idea of your excellence.
>
> I am dreadfully bothered with these cursed concerts, the pretensions of the artists, etc.; but I will find the time to write an article on a subject of this nature. I do not often have such an interesting one."[3]

Glinka, who was modesty incarnate, did not send Berlioz any information about himself. This was done by a certain Melgunov,[4] who happened to be in Paris at the time and knew Glinka very well. On the basis of this material Berlioz published an enormous article.[5]

In 1847 Berlioz was in Russia, but he carried away with him only memories of the brilliant hospitality extended to him by various notables and of the perfection of the Imperial Chapel. At the homes of his hosts there was no mention of Russian music or musicians. Twenty years later,

[1] The *lezginka* from *Ruslan*, in his concert of 16th March, 1845.—G.A.

[2] 6th/18th April, 1845.

[3] Letter to Glinka, Paris, January, 1845.

[4] N. A. Melgunov (1804–1867), one of the members of Herzen's circle in Moscow. —G.A.

[5] *Journal des débats*, 16th April, 1845; separate reprint, *M. Glinka par Hector Berlioz* (Milan, 1874).

that is, in 1867, when Berlioz again came to Russia, he found something quite different. New talents had emerged in our country—fresh, powerful, original talents, striving to carry even further the cause that had been bequeathed to them by Glinka. But along with these men of talent there had also come into being a whole new tribe of critics, who were wearing themselves out trying to prove that we had no gifted composers, no school, but only some outrageous self-taught upstarts, detrimental to all great, true, "real" music. How well Berlioz understood this, how he sympathized with our new musicians, how he appreciated their talent—and how well he remembered what he had gone through when some miserable Fétises and Scudos (the Rostislavs, Famintsyns, Solovievs and Laroches[1] of his time) crucified him every day in their articles and tried to prove to him and the whole world that he was an ignoramus, who was only wasting good paper and covering music with shame! In the last of the letters published by Bernard, dated 21st August, 1868, Berlioz wrote to me:

> . . . I received letters . . . asking impossible things of me. They want me to speak highly of a German artist of whom I do, indeed, think well,[2] but on condition that I speak ill of a Russian artist,[3] whom they wish to replace by the German and who, on the contrary, deserves the highest praise. This I will not do. What kind of devilish world is this?

Here we see the lengths to which the blockheads of all the Russias went in their animosity: they sought slander from a complete outsider to back up their own lies. But this man was not one of their ilk—he was Berlioz, whose great genius was matched by greatness of heart and soul; and men such as he cannot be made to act basely by any means—by neither persuasion nor force, flattery nor bribery.

By the way, I once related this shameful episode, which became known to us through Berlioz' letter, in a circuit court, during Russia's first lawsuit over music, in which I happened to appear in the rôle of the accused. This letter of Berlioz' constitutes one of the important pages in the history of Russian music. The reactionaries had succeeded in forcing Balakirev, then the representative of the new school of Russian music, to resign his post as conductor of the Russian Musical Society concerts. Nevertheless, his and his comrades' cause was not lost, and were Berlioz to return to us today he would see, once again, for the third time, the old familiar scene: on one side, men of original and independent talent; on the other, a whole pack of stray mongrels yelping at them.

The fact is that, in general, Berlioz was not at all receptive to the advice

[1] Conservative Russian critics.

[2] Kapellmeister Seifriz.—V.S.

This was Max Seifriz, composer and violinist, for many years *Hofkapellmeister* to the Prince of Hohenzollern-Hechingen, later at Stuttgart. As a conductor he was a champion of the "New German school".—G.A.

[3] M. A. Balakirev.—V.S.

of others. He never listened to anyone; he followed only the voice of his own conscience, which was always honourable, upright, and magnanimous. At the end of the year 1867, when he was in Petersburg, the Moscow Musical Society invited him to conduct a number of concerts. He agreed. In a letter dated 10th December he wrote to his friends in Paris:

> . . . These gentlemen of the semi-Asiatic capital have irresistible arguments, whatever Wieniawski may say; he believes that I should not have accepted their offer immediately. But I do not know how to haggle, and I would be ashamed to . . .[1]

What a lesson for the music merchants, who think only in terms of money!

No, Berlioz never could haggle, even though he lived all his life on a mere pittance. Up to the time he was sixty years old he received a salary from the Conservatory amounting to—can you guess how much?—118 francs a month. You can be sure that not one of the haughty lackeys of those lordly gentlemen who never attended Berlioz' brilliant concerts but preferred to listen to their dear Italians would have accepted such a sum. And when, in 1863, only six years before his death, the Minister increased his salary to 236 francs a month (how wonderful!—fifty roubles, in our money), he immediately wrote his son about it, confessing, poor man, that the increase would be "very helpful"!

Whatever profit Berlioz made from time to time out of his huge and matchless concerts went, in the beginning, to pay the debts of his first wife, a former actress and theatrical manager, and later on, to take care of the caprices and debts of his son, a naval officer, who at the age of thirty was a drain on his poor father. But Berlioz adored his son, he treated him with tenderness and gentleness, and sometimes when his son heaped heartless reproaches and demands upon him, this man who was austere and proud as an eagle with everyone else, even lowered himself to the point where he offered excuses and apologies! Some of Berlioz' letters to this son wring the reader's heart! Exactly the same as it was in the case of Beethoven and his repulsive nephew. Two poor, unfortunate King Lears, crushed in everything that was most precious to them, both in their art and in their families!

Thousands of failures in Paris and colossal triumphs outside of his native land—in England, Germany, and Russia; perpetual torment with surcease only during the moments when he was passionately at work on his compositions—creations of genius, such as the *Te Deum*, *Faust*, *Romeo*, and a vast number of others—or during those hours when he was conducting the orchestra in his astounding, magnificent concerts; friendship and a constant exchange of ideas with the best and most profound talents and intellects of his time, people such as Liszt, Schumann, Heine,

[1] Letter to the Massarts, Paris, 10th December, 1867.

Meyerbeer, George Sand, Balzac; hatred of Italian music and of everything in art that is hackneyed or false; persecution and triumphs without measure, never any compromise whatever—this was Berlioz' life, and it is with this that the present volume of his correspondence, however incomplete, is replete. It contains such a wealth of material that no excerpts can possibly suffice. Anyone who is interested in such a genius as Berlioz must read the entire book for himself.

1879

IV. A Letter From Liszt

A typical piece of Stasovian enthusiasm, printed in *Golos*, 7th October, 1879. Stasov quotes the letter from Liszt again, seventeen years later, in "Liszt, Schumann and Berlioz in Russia" (see p. 184) but this time from La Mara's *Franz Liszt's Briefe*, II (Leipzig, 1893), p. 285, where the editor took it upon herself to change the "14 petites pièces" to "16" because two more pieces had been added in the meantime.

G.A.

THIS SUMMER, Liszt sent the following letter to the four Russian composers A. Borodin, C. Cui, A. Lyadov and N. Rimsky-Korsakov:

Dear Sirs:

In the form of a jest you have created a work of serious value. I am delighted with your *Paraphrases*: nothing could be more ingenious than these 24 variations and 14 little pieces on the favourite obbligato theme:

Here, at last, is an admirable compendium of the science of harmony, counterpoint, rhythm, fugal style and what is called in German *Formenlehre*! I shall gladly suggest to the teachers of composition at all the conservatories in Europe and America that they adopt your *Paraphrases* as a practical guide in their teaching. From the very first page, Variations II and III are true gems, as are all the subsequent numbers, including the Fugue Grotesque and the Cortège which gloriously crowns this work. Thank you, Gentlemen, for this feast, and when any of you publishes a new composition, I beg you to bring it to my attention. You have had my warmest, highest esteem and sympathy for many years; please accept also the expression of my sincere devotion.

F. LISZT.

15th June, 1879, Weimar.

How true is the French saying [*sic*]: "Nul n'est prophète en son pays!" The Russian connoisseurs of music long ago proclaimed the leaders of the new school of Russian music utter ignoramuses and boorish know-nothings, but one of the greatest musicians of our century considers one of their compositions so skilful and instructive that he intends to recommend it as a manual to the teachers at conservatories in Europe and America. These oh-so-very-clever experts scornfully reject the best works of the new school, but a musician like Liszt declares that he is delighted with one of their very minor works and calls it a "true gem"!

There is nothing new in this, of course. This unfortunate school has long been denied recognition here in Russia just because it is independent, original and talented, whereas all during this time it has been recognized and genuinely respected by the foremost musicians in Europe from Berlioz and Liszt to Saint-Saëns, von Bülow and others. Liszt, we are told, always keeps Balakirev's marvellous fantasy *Islamey*, which is almost totally unknown here, on his piano; what is more, he continually assigns this piece to his best pupils. He also greatly admires and respects the symphonies of Messrs. Borodin and Rimsky-Korsakov, Cui's *Ratcliff*, etc. He is constantly pointing out to the musicians who come to him that "if there is any school of music today that offers great promise for the future, it is the Russian school." (These are his exact words.)

These views differ so greatly from those generally held in our country that perhaps it is fitting that they be brought to the attention of our compatriots.

The composition, *Paraphrases*, of which Liszt speaks in his letter, was published a few months ago by the music firm of Büttner and Co. It consists of 24 variations and 14 little pieces for the piano on the well-known theme reproduced above. They are dedicated to young pianists capable of playing the theme with one finger of each hand.

Even though no one here is aware of its publication, this work merits everyone's interest for its ingenuity, brilliance and sparkling humour. The variations are extremely interesting. It need only be pointed out that while the theme remains the same throughout, the character and rhythm of the variations change from moment to moment, and there is no end to the composers' inventiveness. Each variation consists of only eight measures, but how much imagination, charm and gracefulness are to be found in each of them!

From an artistic point of view the little pieces are even more remarkable than the variations. They include polkas, galops, waltzes, minuets, gigues, tarantellas, a fugue and a fughetta, as well as a lullaby, funeral march, triumphal procession and a piece called *Bells*—all based on the same theme for two fingers, without a single note changed throughout. Rimsky-Korsakov's *Lullaby* is truly charming. His *Bells*, in which at one point the theme appears simultaneously in four different rhythmic forms —sixteenths, eighths, quarter-notes and half-notes—is astonishingly beautiful and majestic. The longer *Waltz* by C. A. Cui sparkles like champagne and captivates with its *élan*. The other *Waltz* by A. K. Lyadov is completely different: it is the quintessence of grace, beauty and elegance. Borodin's *Funeral March* is unusually comical; his three-part *Requiem*—for solo with chorus and organ—is splendid. This latter piece adheres to the strictest liturgical form (Catholic), yet it, too, is based on the same childish, trivial theme. Finally, the whole composition is "gloriously crowned", as Liszt so appropriately says, with Lyadov's *Procession*, which is charged with vigour, originality and grandeur

To be sure, this naïve theme, repeated without alteration and at times over-insistently, may weary the listener's attention. But after all, no one has to play every one of the 24 variations and 14 pieces at one sitting! Meanwhile, it must be noted that though this theme itself may be poor and comical, it offers the composer a very intriguing challenge: it consists of two scales which begin on the same note and move in contrary motion. It closely resembles the theme which once captivated Bach and led him to write his magnificent organ fugue:

In conclusion, let me point out that, even before our four composers, someone else composed a piece for pianists "who can play with only one finger". This someone was the great Dargomïzhsky, who wrote the wonderful piano duet *Tarantelle Slave* for four hands. But this composition is extremely talented, original and elegant—so, of course, it is virtually unknown in our country!

1879

La Mara, Vol. II, page 285
Liszt to Borodin, Cui, Lyadov, and Rimsky-Korsakov, 15*th June,* 1879
Très honorés Messieurs,

Sous forme plaisante vous avez fait une oeuvre de valeur sérieuse. Vos *Paraphrases* me charment: rien de plus ingénieux que ces 24 Variations et les 16[1] petites pièces sur le theme favori et obligé. . . . Voilà enfin un admirable compendium de la science de l'harmonie, du contre-point, des rhythmes, du style figuré, et de ce qu'en allemand on nomme, *Formenlehre*! Volontiers je proposerai aux professeurs de composition de tous les conservatoires d'Europe et d'Amérique de prendre vos *Paraphrases* pour guide pratique de leur enseignement. Dès la première page, les Variations II et III sont de véritables bijoux; non moins les autres numéros continûment, jusqu'à la Fugue grotesque et le *cortège* qui couronne glorieusement l'ouvrage. Merci de ce régal, Messieurs, et quand l'un de vous publiera quelque nouvelle composition, je le prie de m'en faire part. Ma très vive, haute et sympathique estime vous est assurée depuis des années: veuillez agréer aussi l'expression de mon sincère dévouement.

F. LISZT.

15 Juin 1879, Weimar.

V. Twenty-five Years of Russian Art: Our Music

Printed as "Our Music during the last 25 years" in *Vestnik Evropï* in October, 1883. As always with Stasov, it is a fiercely partisan survey—though many of the things he says were long accepted as dogma. For him Russian music began with Glinka, and it is true that Glinka was the first of a "school" which included Tchaikovsky as well as the composers of the "mighty handful" of Stasov's closer friends and associates, the first Russian composers to attract general European attention. But there had been Russian composers of consciously Russian music nearly half-a-century before Glinka, and Stasov is not even quite fair to Lvov and Verstovsky. (To say that he is unfair to Wagner would be a glorious understatement; but Wagner can look after himself.) He is, of course, very much more than fair to his friends. When we read that Cui, of all people, in his portrayal of "love in all its various manifestations" surpassed "anything ever achieved not only by his colleagues in the Russian school but perhaps by anyone in the whole field of music", we can only smile indulgently. But let there be no mistake: when Stasov writes something like that, he means it. He almost unfailingly reacted to art in superlatives. And if the love-duet in the last Act of Cui's *William Ratcliff* is not "the finest love-duet ever written", as Stasov asserts, it is too good to deserve the total neglect that has overtaken it.

G.A.

HALF A CENTURY ago the Russians firmly believed that they had already achieved their own national, truly Russian music. The reason for this was that they had a "national anthem", which had been written on commission by Lvov[1] and was being assiduously disseminated, and also Verstovsky's opera *Askold's Tomb*, whose quasi-gypsy, quasi-popular melodies (such as *In the Famous City of Slavyansk* and *The Goblets Pass Round the Table*) excited many listeners. But the belief that these constituted a national music was only an illusion. Neither the anthem nor the opera had any national character, and despite the expectations of the authorities and the public, they did not give rise to any national music or school of composition whatsoever. Both authors were too lacking in

[1] In 1833.

national feeling to have initiated such a school; what is more, judging from their compositions, both were completely untalented musicians. The new music and new national school were brought into being not by official prompting or the public's crass taste and enthusiasms; they were born out of the innermost need of the times. Our music followed the same path in the thirties that our literature had during the first quarter of the present century with Krylov, Pushkin and Griboyedov, a path which none of our other arts had as yet embarked upon.

At the beginning of the thirties, Glinka went to Italy as if it were a treasure house of the classics from which he might derive all manner of inspiration, enlightenment and learning. He did not find these things there, however. Something totally unexpected happened to him instead. He brought back from Italy, not what he had gone there for, but something entirely different—the idea of a national art, of a Russian music. As he attended the Italian theatres and concert halls, listened to Italian music and famous Italian singers, he suddenly came to feel that this was not what he or his people wanted. He realized that the Italians are one kind of people and we Russians another; that what suits and satisfies them does not suit us. This sudden questioning, this moment of uncertainty about what he had till then so firmly believed in, was the decisive moment in the history of Russian music. Then, for the first time, our music entered upon a genuine, full life of its own. Glinka thought that he was creating only a Russian opera, but he was mistaken. He was laying the foundations of Russian music, of a whole school of Russian music, of a whole new system. In the fifty years that have elapsed since then, our national school has grown and flourished, and has brought forth works of singular beauty, genius, and power.

For a long time our composers were denied recognition; they were looked upon with scorn and condescension. Even in 1860 Dargomïzhsky wrote: "How many of our leading experts dispute the very existence of a Russian school, not only of singing but even of composition. Nevertheless, it has clearly broken through. It is too late, now, to stifle it. Its existence is already inscribed in the annals of art." Indeed, the Russian school has existed since the time of Glinka, with special features which differentiate it from all other European schools.

What, then, were the forces that produced the special features of our school, the factors that determined its unique development and character?

A primary factor was open-mindedness—the absence of preconceptions and blind faith. Since its very inception, with Glinka, the Russian school has been marked by complete independence in its views and attitudes towards the music of the past. It has never accepted without question the judgements of "recognized authorities", but has insisted upon verifying everything for itself, on determining for itself whether or not a composer is great and his works important. While such independence of thought is found all too rarely among European musicians even today, it was still rarer fifty years ago. Only a handful of them—men like Schumann, for example—dared to apply their own critical judgement to the established idols. Most of the musicians in the West blindly accept all the opinions of the authorities and share all the tastes and prejudices of the crowd. The new Russian musicians, on the other hand, are dreadfully "irreverent". They view traditional attitudes with scepticism and will not value anything they are supposed to until they themselves are persuaded of its worth. Thus, in 1842, despite the widely held view to the contrary, Glinka told Liszt frankly that he found Weber "very unsatisfying (even in *Der Freischütz*) because of his excessive use of the dominant seventh in the root position".[1] In those days no one else would have had the courage to voice such a criticism of the universal idol Weber. For all its renown, Glinka later was just as critical of Mozart's *Don Giovanni*, before which not only the Germans but the entire world genuflects even today. He told everyone he met that this opera was "a masterly (bandmasterly!) but by no means an exemplary work". As far as he was concerned, Don Ottavio's aria "Il mio tesoro", which has always delighted listeners everywhere, was nothing but a "rather sweet cavatina".[2] On the other hand, in spite of the very low esteem in which virtually everyone held Berlioz at that time, Glinka hailed him as "the foremost composer" of our day.[3] Glinka was heard to express many opinions of this kind, opinions which in those days were bold and novel.

It was with respect to Italian music, composers and performers that Glinka differed most sharply with his contemporaries. He went to Italy as a young man, gifted but with little musical training. At first he still shared many of the biases and false notions of the crowd. He even "went into ecstasies" and "shed copious tears of tender emotion" over the operas of Bellini. But it was not long before he realized that everything Italian was utterly alien to him. "We northerners respond to things differently," he wrote, "we are either completely unmoved or moved to the very depths". By the time his talent reached its fullest maturity,

[1] *Memoirs:* see *M. I. Glinka: Literaturnoe Nasledie* I (Leningrad and Moscow, 1952), p. 230.

[2] A typically Stasovian manipulation of evidence. This is all based on a passage in Glinka's memoirs (*op. cit.*, p. 233): "in 1843 Ulybyshev sent me his work on Mozart. I read through part of it and studied afresh all Mozart's operas in the orchestral scores. Count M. Y. Vielgorsky's remarks and criticisms, and these activities, awoke in me a critical vein which later developed further!" [But he means an interest in musical criticism itself, not adverse criticism of Mozart; we know from Lvov that Glinka was enthusiastic about Ulybyshev's panegyric of Mozart.] He then goes on to describe a bad performance of *Don Giovanni* under Ciprian Romberg, with Italian stars, in Petersburg the same year: "Rubini tried to be a *thundering Jove* and sang the rather sweet [*sladenky*] cavatina "Il mio tesoro" like *a pirate*, threatening the public and brandishing his right arm . . . Romberg seemed to be in the conspiracy against Mozart, whose masterly (though not exemplary) work he made the orchestra play affectedly and without energy . . . I wept with vexation . . .".—G.A.

[3] Letter to Kukolnik, 1845.

Glinka "had come to detest fashionable Italian music".[1] On the other hand, the artificial, exaggerated and mannered performances of operatic virtuosi, Italians and non-Italians alike, irritated him from the days of his youth. Even in the early part of his stay in Italy, he found the singing of Rubini, who was then looked upon as a god, pretentious and unnatural. Later, although everyone he knew regarded this singer as the quintessence of talent and taste, and went so far as to call him "Jupiter the Thunderer", Glinka found his singing "ridiculous, affected and exaggerated". Of the noted French tenor Dupré, Glinka said: ". . . he sang in the *French manner*, that is, affectedly, giving special emphasis to each note". Glinka also strongly disapproved of the much-admired singing of the Russian ladies, young and old. According to Mme. Karmalina, in her *Memoirs*, he denounced the vocal style of Mmes. Bilibina, Shilovskaya, Girs and others as a "mixture of church, gypsy and Italian singing". Lastly, he even had some reservations about the then renowned orchestra of the Paris Conservatory. During his stay in Paris in 1845, its playing struck him as "very mannered". "This orchestra plays excellently", he wrote to Kukolnik, "but it overplays. Each detail is performed with such precision, so elegantly, that the overall effect is spoiled". To this very day our new Russian school still cherishes these sound views, sober criteria and convictions as a legacy from Glinka.

As far back as 1844, during his first tour of Europe, Dargomïzhsky wrote to his father:

> Meyerbeer is not strong dramatically. The subject of *Robert* is a legend, a fantastic tale of the Middle Ages, which suits Meyerbeer's way of thinking perfectly. *The Huguenots* deals with religious fanaticism and is intensely dramatic. The violence of the people and the malice of Catholicism are excellently expressed; they have a satanic quality that is congenial to Meyerbeer's pen. But the dramatic scenes are noisy, contrived and very unrealistic! During the performance I followed the libretto. I knew each scene of the drama beforehand. But as I listened to the music, I could not find a single inspired idea. Meyerbeer's skill and intelligence are incredible, but neither skill nor intelligence can simulate the human heart. *The greatest craftsman is still not a poet.*

In other letters Dargomïzhsky said that the music of Meyerbeer and Halévy was "often banal". Regarding Félicien David's symphonic poem *Le Désert*, he wrote in 1845:

> I had difficulty getting a ticket. The French have gone mad over it, but we look at it with different eyes. There is no denying that David has some talent, but he is no more a Beethoven than my thumb is the Colonne de Vendôme.

Dargomïzhsky had as little liking for Italian singers as Glinka. "The naturalness and nobility of the Russian school of singing cannot but gladden the heart after the pretentiousness of the Italians, the shouting of the French and the mannered style of the Germans," he wrote in 1860.

[1] *Memoirs*, p. 144.

We find the same way of thinking and the same quest for truth and sincerity of expression among all the best Russian musicians who came after Dargomïzhsky.

Further, none of our great musicians, from Glinka on, have ever put much faith in academic training. They have never regarded it with the servility and superstitious awe with which it is regarded even nowadays in many parts of Europe. It would be ridiculous to deny the value of learning in any field, including music, but the new Russian musicians, unfettered by Europe's age-old scholastic tradition, look learning boldly in the eye. They respect it, they avail themselves of its blessings, but they do not exaggerate its importance or genuflect before it. They reject the notion that learning must necessarily be dry and pedantic. They refuse to have anything to do with the academic capers to which thousands of people in Europe attach so much importance. They do not believe that it is necessary to vegetate dutifully for years and years over erudition's ritualistic mysteries.

"Generally speaking, I was not fated to study with the strict contrapuntists", Glinka remarks in his *Memoirs* about the noted theorist Raimondi whom he failed to meet in Naples in 1832. In recounting his youth he also says, "Somehow I never managed to meet the famous contrapuntist Miller who was in Petersburg at that time. Who knows? Perhaps it was for the best. Strict German counterpoint does not always go well with a fiery imagination." In Milan, in 1830, Basili, the director of the Conservatory, "tortured" him with the various intricacies of counterpoint, ". . . but my fiery imagination could not submit to such dry and unpoetic labour," he writes, "and I soon gave up my lessons with him".

It was not until Glinka was thirty years old, that is, not until the idea of a Russian music began to stir powerfully within him, that he applied himself seriously to the study of musical composition. Returning to Russia from Italy, he stopped off in Berlin where, in about five months, he went through exercises in musical theory with Professor Dehn. Everything that Dehn taught him filled only five small notebooks. But neither this nor the fact that Glinka spent such a brief time on these studies prevented him from becoming an outstanding master of his craft. Later, Dargomïzhsky also mastered this subject very quickly. "Glinka lent me Professor Dehn's theoretical notes which he had brought from Berlin," he says in his autobiography. "I copied them out and soon assimilated the so-called wisdom of thorough-bass and counterpoint." It was the same, later on, with Dargomïzhsky's colleagues and successors. Unlike the Germans, they did not waste endless years on the grammar of music; they learned it quickly and easily, like any other grammar. But this did not prevent them from learning it solidly and thoroughly. This attitude towards the so-called "wisdom", so revered by other schools of music, saved the Russian composers from writing pedantic, routine works, something they have never done. This is one of the major differences between our school and the European schools that preceded it.

Another important distinguishing feature of our school is its constant search for national character. This began with Glinka and has continued uninterruptedly until the present time. No such striving is to be found in any other European school of composition. The historical and cultural conditions of other peoples have been such that folk song—that expression of the simple, spontaneous musicality of the people—has long since all but disappeared in most civilized countries. In the nineteenth century who knows or ever hears French, German, Italian or English folk songs? There were such songs, of course, and they were once widely sung, but they were mowed down by the levelling scythe of European culture, which is so inimical to all folk art and customs, and nowadays it requires the efforts of musical archaeologists and curious travellers to unearth remnants of them in remote corners of the provinces. In our country it is a completely different matter. Folk songs are heard everywhere even today. Every muzhik, carpenter, bricklayer, doorkeeper, cabman; every peasant woman, laundry-maid and cook, every nurse and wet-nurse—all bring the folk songs of their villages with them to Petersburg, Moscow, to each and every city, and we hear them the whole year round. We are constantly surrounded by them. Every working man and woman in Russia sings endlessly while working, just as their ancestors did a thousand years ago. The Russian soldier goes into battle with a folk song on his lips. These songs are a part of each and every one of us; we need no archaeologists to unearth them so that we may come to know and love them. This being the case, every musically gifted Russian is surrounded, from the day of his birth, by a truly national music. Moreover, it so happens that almost all of the most important Russian composers—Glinka, Dargomïzhsky, Mussorgsky, Balakirev and Rimsky-Korsakov—were born, not in the capitals, but in provincial towns or on their fathers' estates and they spent all their early years there. The others also spent much of their youth in the provinces, in frequent and close contact with folk songs and folk-singing. Their earliest and most deep-seated musical impressions were derived from folk song. The fact that we were so long in producing an art music of our own was due solely to the unfavourable conditions of Russian life in the eighteenth and nineteenth centuries, when everything national was trampled in the mud. Nevertheless, the need for a national music was so basic and widespread that even during the time of Catherine the Great, a time of courtiers and powdered wigs, one of our composers after another tried to incorporate folk melodies into his poor operas which were patterned on the poor European operas of the day. This is precisely what Verstovsky did later on. Of course, in such cases the folk material appeared in the most unfortunate form, but still it was there, and this, in itself, testified to a need which did not exist among other peoples. No sooner did the times begin to change, however, no sooner did the Russian folk become a topic of discussion in life and literature, no sooner was interest in them rekindled, than gifted people appeared who wanted to create music in the national idioms that were dearest and most congenial to them. No doubt European composers (at least the most gifted of them) would have followed the same path as ours did, beginning with Glinka, but such a path was no longer open to them. Proof of this is the eagerness with which they have always seized upon the folk material of other peoples, even in fragmentary form. We have only to recall, for example, Beethoven's attempts to use Russian folk themes, Schubert's to use Slovak, and Liszt's to use Hungarian. Yet they did not create Russian, Slovak, or Hungarian music. For music does not consist of themes alone. To be national, to express the spirit and soul of a people, it must be rooted in the people's life. And neither Beethoven, Schubert nor Liszt immersed himself in the life of the people. They simply took the beautiful gems, the fresh, ever-new and sparkling creations which had been preserved by one or another people, and mounted them in the setting of European art music. They never immersed themselves in the world from which these exquisite fragments came; they only chanced upon them, toyed with them, admired their beauty, and displayed them, brilliantly illumined by their own talent. The situation of the Russian composers was entirely different. They were not guests, they were "at home" in the world in which our folk-melodies, indeed all Slavic melodies, originated, and therefore they were able to use them freely, to present them in their true colouring, flavour and character. Today Glinka's achievement is universally known and recognized. He blazed a new trail; he created a national opera in a manner not to be found anywhere else in Europe. His successors followed in his footsteps, guided by his brilliant example and initiative.

Along with the Russian folk song element there is another which distinguishes the new Russian school of composition. This is the Oriental element. Nowhere in Europe does it play such a prominent rôle as it does in the works of our composers. At one time or another every truly talented European architect, sculptor and painter has tried to reproduce the unique forms of the East. Thus far only the musicians have lagged far behind their fellow artists. Mozart, Beethoven, Weber and certain others, who wrote pieces "alla turca", made a few attempts to incorporate something Eastern,[1] but their efforts only demonstrated their interest in this element. They were never really successful. Félicien David, who lived in the East, introduced several *truly* Eastern melodies

[1] Mozart in his opera *The Abduction from the Seraglio*, Beethoven in his incidental music to *The Ruins of Athens*, Weber in his opera *Oberon*.

into his symphonic ode *Le Désert*, but he had little talent and produced nothing of importance. It was a completely different matter with the new Russian musicians. Some of them visited the East (both Glinka and Balakirev spent some time in the Caucasus), and although the others never actually went there they were exposed to Eastern influences all their lives, and therefore were able to reproduce them vividly and clearly. They shared the interest which Russians in general have in everything Eastern. This is hardly surprising, since so much of the East has always been an integral part of Russian life and has given it such a special, distinctive colouring. Glinka himself was aware of this, and that is why he wrote in his *Memoirs*: "There is no doubt that our Russian song is a child of the North, but it has been affected somewhat by the denizens of the East." As a result, many of Glinka's best works and those of his heirs and successors are replete with orientalisms. To view this merely as some strange whim or caprice on the part of the Russian composers (as our music critics have often done) is ridiculous and short-sighted.

Finally, there is one other feature which strongly characterizes the Russian school of music—that is, its strong predilection for "programme music".

After having lived for several months in Paris, Glinka wrote to his friend Kukolnik in April, 1845:

> The study of Berlioz' music and the taste of the Parisian public has had extremely important consequences for me. I have decided to enrich my repertoire with a few concert pieces for orchestra to be called "Fantaisies pittoresques". It seems to me that it ought to be possible to reconcile the demands of art with those of our time and, by taking advantage of the improvements in instruments and performance, to write pieces equally accessible to connoisseurs and the general public. I will begin working on the proposed "Fantaisies" in Spain—the originality of Spanish melodies will be a great help to me.

This was the origin of the *Jota*, *Night in Madrid* and, somewhat later, *Kamarinskaya*.

These works are important not only because of their great musical merit but also because they were the prototypes of "programme music" in Russia. In writing them, Glinka was following the general trend of the time, a trend that had manifested itself first in Beethoven, then in Weber, Berlioz and Mendelssohn, and later in all the most important new composers, such as Liszt and Wagner. Of course, these composers expressed their programmatic ideas with varying degrees of clarity. Some embodied them in rather nebulous and embryonic form; others in much clearer, more sharply outlined form. But generally speaking, the programmatic element is present in all of them. What are most of Beethoven's overtures (*Leonora, Coriolanus, Egmont*, etc.), certain parts of his last quartets, many of his sonatas, and all save his first two symphonies if not "programme music?" In some cases the subject is more discernible than in others.

Sometimes the composer himself aids our understanding with an inscription: *Eroica* Symphony; "March in Memory of a Hero"; *Pastoral* Symphony; "Peasants' merry-making"; "Storm"; "Canzone in the Lydian Mode in Gratitude to God for My Recovery". In other instances, he mentioned in conversation the programme of works whose content was not indicated elsewhere. For example, concerning the theme of the first movement of his Fifth Symphony, he once remarked, "Thus Fate knocks at the door"; and when asked what his great F-minor sonata was about he replied, "Read Shakespeare's *Tempest*". In still other instances the music itself plainly suggests the subject. Thus, in the Andante[1] of the Seventh Symphony, we easily recognize a procession; in the finales of both this and the Eighth Symphony, we clearly hear the sounds of war. The overtures of Weber, Mendelssohn, and Berlioz are also programmatic. All of this music is far, far removed from the "absolute" music of earlier days. In his orchestral compositions Glinka followed the same path, not only because of his "study of Berlioz' music" (as he wrote to Kukolnik in 1845), nor because this was the prevailing trend at the moment, but primarily because of his own innate need. This he made unmistakably clear when he wrote, in the above-quoted letter to Kukolnik, "My unbridled imagination has need of a text or concrete facts. *Concrete facts* are the basis of musical creativity—they constitute, of course, the basic element of 'programme music'." The content of Glinka's three great orchestral works is clearly "programmatic". It is easy to follow, easy to relate.

Towards the end of his life, however, Glinka developed a dislike for programme music and, in conversation with friends, he often denied that many of his earlier works had a programme. Thus, for example, he even denied that he had intended to depict a "rainbow" in the Bard's opening song, "waves" in one of the variations of the Persian chorus in *Ruslan*, and many other little scenes of this kind, which Serov and I cited in our discussions with him. But the words themselves are proof enough of his earlier tendencies and intentions. I do not think, either, that we should give much credence to his denial, in his *Memoirs*, of a programme in *Kamarinskaya*.[2]

What Glinka began was continued by his successors. Virtually all Russian symphonic music is programmatic, as the following account will show. It is quite clear that the propensity for this kind of music is much stronger in our country than almost anywhere else in Europe.

These, then, are the principal characteristics of the Russian school of music. In noting them, I have not meant to suggest that our school is superior to other European schools—that would be stupid and ridiculous. Each nation has its own great men and its own great achievements.

[1] He means the Allegretto.—G.A.

[2] *Memoirs*, p. 169.

It is only that I felt it necessary to define the special features of our school's character and tendencies which, of course, are very interesting and important.

Now I will discuss the fortunes of our national school of composition during the period after Glinka.

II

Throughout his youth, Dargomïzhsky was a pallid, feeble imitator of either Glinka or the Frenchmen Auber and Halévy. Glinka he imitated in his songs, of which he composed countless numbers, and the Frenchmen especially Halévy, in his youthful opera *Esmeralda*. Only now and then could one catch a glimpse of Dargomïzhsky's individuality; it was almost imperceptible. It was not until he was approaching his forties that he became conscious of his own individuality and gifts.

In the early 1850's, Dargomïzhsky began to work on his opera *Rusalka*. In this opera he set himself new and profound goals. In 1853 he wrote to Prince Odoyevsky:

> I am hard at work on my *Rusalka*. The more I study the elements of our folk music, the more I discover how varied they are. Glinka, who has been the only one thus far to extend the boundaries of Russian music, has, it seems to me, touched only one aspect of it—the lyrical. The dramatic parts of his works are too mournful, the comic lack national character. I am speaking now only of the character of his music; technically it is superb. In *Rusalka* I am making every effort to develop our dramatic elements. I shall be happy if I succeed in this only half as well as Glinka.

Apparently Dargomïzhsky did not fully grasp what Glinka had achieved, for not only the "lyrical" but also the "epic" element finds brilliant expression in his operas. The Bard and the entire introduction to *Ruslan*; the pagan choruses, scenes of sorcery and choruses of the nurses in the same opera; Susanin, the chorus of the people arriving in the boat, the women's choruses, and the "Slavsya" in *A Life for the Tsar*—these are not just lyrical; they are mighty, sweeping, epic. Aside from this error of judgement, however, Dargomïzhsky was quite right in observing that many sides of the Russian character had not been successfully expressed by Glinka. These were the very ones which best suited Dargomïzhsky's temperament and talent. There is no denying that all of Glinka's loftiest creations have a content, structure and character which were utterly beyond Dargomïzhsky's reach, but Dargomïzhsky possessed certain creative gifts which Glinka lacked completely.

The national element plays a large rôle in the works of Dargomïzhsky and he handles it with great mastery. This is true, above all, of *Rusalka*. However, his principal strength lay, not in his ability to write in the national idiom, but in his gift for profound dramatic expression, his ability to reproduce in music all the nuances, colours and inflections of human speech. In *Rusalka* he showed himself to be a great master of this kind of musical expression, that is, declamatory recitative. In his next opera he expanded his ideas even further. In this he has no peer. Even the best recitatives and declamatory scenes in Meyerbeer's *Huguenots* and *Prophet* never attain anything like the realism, power and extraordinary naturalness of similar scenes in Dargomïzhsky's operas. Actually, he had only one rival in this regard—Gluck. But then, Gluck was an idealist, not a realist like Dargomïzhsky. Moreover, it is doubtful that Dargomïzhsky even knew Gluck's music. In declamatory recitative Dargomïzhsky was just as original, fresh and creative as Glinka was in his lyrical writing and epic sweep.

Fully half of *Rusalka* consists of traditional set numbers—arias, duets, trios and ensembles—which are not at all original but simply pale imitations of Glinka or of the French operatic composers of the thirties. (An example of the former is the Prince's rôle; of the latter—most of the Miller's.) But in the remainder of the opera, in all those passages in which he abandons the conventional forms of his predecessors, Dargomïzhsky is a different man, and he moves us deeply with his realism and depth of expression. The scenes between Natasha and the Prince, between Natasha and her father; the portrayal of the crazed Miller, Natasha's plea after her transformation into a water nymph are absolutely unique.

It was many years before our public was able to understand and appreciate Dargomïzhsky's talent and daring innovations. "I am under no delusion", he wrote in 1857.

> My position as an artist in Petersburg is unenviable. Most of our dilettanti and newspaper scribblers consider me uninspired. Being creatures of habit, they are always looking for melodies that please the ear, which is not what I am after. I do not intend to debase music to the level of entertainment. I want the sound to express the word exactly. I want truth. This they cannot understand. I hear plenty of uncomplimentary remarks, but I am used to them and they do not bother me . . .

In his autobiography Dargomïzhsky says further:

> Those in charge of the repertoire, the conductor and the regisseur consider *Rusalka* a poor opera which, as they put it, does not contain a single melody. Consequently, it is seldom performed (only in the summer months, never in the winter) and is produced in a slipshod manner with second-rate artists . . . I believe I am not mistaken in thinking that the Theatre Directorate's unfavourable attitude is due solely to their belief that my talent is inferior to that of other Russian composers.

This was written in 1866, that is, ten years after the first performance of *Rusalka*. Thus, this opera suffered the same fate as *A Life for the Tsar* and *Ruslan and Ludmilla*. For years the Russian public turned its back on all three operas. Dargomïzhsky had to endure in the fifties and sixties what Glinka had in the thirties and forties. He fell heir not only to Glinka's talent but also to his tribulations. At the end of the sixties, however, something of a reaction suddenly set in; the public and the Theatre Directorate began to take a greater interest in these operas and even to treat them with respect. Serious efforts were made to have them produced; the best singers chose them for their benefit performances. Ultimately, all of them won their rightful place on our operatic stage and entered the standard repertory. In his autobiography Dargomïzhsky calls *Rusalka's* success unbelievable, puzzling.

During these ten difficult years Dargomïzhsky did not sit idle, however. He did not lapse into a state of dejection as Glinka had done towards the end of his life. (In 1854, Glinka wrote to Kukolnik: "I very seldom have a feeling of elation," and the following year he again wrote: "I no longer have the urge or desire to compose.") When Dargomïzhsky was fifty, he did not lose his enthusiasm and creative impulse; he did not stop composing. On the contrary, during these ten years he created his most important works. Although he never completed the Russian fairy-tale opera *Rogdana*, two of its choruses—that of the fairy maidens watching over the sleeping Princess Rogdana and that of the Eastern hermits—rank among the most magnificent creations of the new Russian school. A number of the songs written during this period also show a considerable advance in the development in Dargomïzhsky's creative individuality. Some of them—"The Paladin" and "The Old Corporal", for example, are very poignant and intensely dramatic. Others—such as "O Maid my Rose"—are amazing for their Eastern colouring. Passionate and poetic, they differ completely in form and character from anything Glinka wrote in this vein. Lastly, there is a third group of vocal works which gave birth to an entirely new musical genre. These are comic, sometimes satiric scenas which delve as deeply into everyday Russian life and portray it with the same unadorned truthfulness and humour as Gogol did, but in a way never before attempted in music. Such are the scenas "The Worm", "The Titular Counsellor", "As the Peasant Came from Behind the Hill", and "I Hasten to Thy Embraces". Here, too, that "truth", that dramatic realism which Dargomïzhsky had sought in his opera *Rusalka* is paramount, but it is given still fuller and more profound expression.

Even all this activity did not exhaust Dargomïzhsky's creative powers, which were continually developing and maturing in spite of the outward lack of success and recognition. During these ten years between his two operas, he also wrote three very important works for orchestra—the *Ukrainian Kazachok*, *Baba Yaga* and *Finnish Fantasy*. These are thoroughly original Russian 'scherzos', pendants to Glinka's *Kamarinskaya* but marked by an unusual, original and distinctive kind of humour. Dargomïzhsky was never an outstanding orchestrator (least of all when it came to creating the sort of massive or subtly poetic colouristic effects that fill the scores of *Ruslan* and the *Jota*), but in the *Finnish Fantasy* he achieved, even in the scoring, an extraordinary freshness and effectiveness which aptly express the novelty and power of this remarkable orchestral piece.

Important as the music written during this period from 1856 to 1866 may have been however, it was only a prelude to Dargomïzhsky's greatest, his supreme creation, the opera *The Stone Guest*. It was this work which ensured his immortality and established him forever as the equal of the creator of *Ruslan*. In 1866 he wrote to his former beloved pupil Lyubov Karmalina:

> I have not altogether taken leave of my muse. I am trying something that has never been done before. I am writing music for scenes from Pushkin's *Stone Guest* just as they are, without changing a single word. Of course, no one will come to hear it . . .

Two years later, in April, 1868, he again wrote Mme. Karmalina:

> I have begun my swan song. I am writing *The Stone Guest*. It is a strange thing: my nervous condition[1] is generating one idea after another. It costs me practically no effort . . . It is not I who am writing, but some force that is unknown to me. I became interested in *The Stone Guest* five years ago, when I was in perfect health, but at that time I shrank from so enormous an undertaking. Now, ill as I am, I have written almost three-fourths of the opera in two and a half months . . Of course, this work will appeal only to a few . . .

Now we can thank God that in 1863 Dargomïzhsky "shrank from so enormous an undertaking", for at that time he was not yet "ready" for it. His musical nature was still growing, still maturing; he was still ridding himself of the awkwardness and roughness, the formal defects, the Italianisms and Gallicisms which are sometimes found in the works of his early and middle periods. With each new work he took a step forward. By 1866 the preparatory stage was ended. The mighty musician was ready for the mighty task. Freed of all the minor but sometimes ugly flaws, matured in spirit as he was in talent, this man found the will-power and strength of character to complete the opera while lying in bed, suffering the most painful attacks of his final, fatal illness. What is more, he created an opera that is absolutely unique in the history of music. In it was embodied and expressed everything that the great reformer Gluck had striven for a century before—but in a framework even broader and deeper than Gluck's. Here there are no Greek gods and heroes, no classical subject and characters. Gone are all the conventions and formal practices which had grown like an ugly excrescence on European music. There is not a trace of the arias, duets and trios that had been devised for opera just as the conventional *pas* had been for ballet; there are no choruses, no ensembles, no symmetrical, four-square forms. In keeping with the demands of common sense and operatic realism, *The Stone Guest* consists entirely of declamatory recitative, of musical speech which pours

[1] His final illness which ended in an aneurism and death a few months after the writing of this letter.

forth from the lips of the characters in an irregular, unsymmetrical stream just as it does in everyday conversation and in drama. Yet, despite the closeness of this recitative to human speech with all its twists and turns, its form is musical, artistic and poetic. This was an experiment in a new musical genre, the like of which had never been heard or seen before. "When my friends listen to my opera, many of them wonder: is this music or blind stupidity?" Dargomïzhsky wrote Mme. Karmalina two months before his death.

That was fifteen years ago, and most people in our country still regard this opera as nothing more than "blind stupidity". Once again, as in the case of *Ruslan*, the Russian public has failed to understand that here, before their very eyes, is one of the most brilliant works ever written. Even today we can read in the press here and abroad that *The Stone Guest* is a mistake and a blunder, an aberration and a clumsy absurdity. More than a decade has passed for naught as far as the public is concerned; there has been no progress whatsoever. Why, there are even Germans who claim that in this opera Dargomïzhsky was only an "unsuccessful imitator of Richard Wagner, who unfortunately went still further than Wagner did".[1] What utter nonsense! No two people could be more opposite than Wagner and Dargomïzhsky.

It was not only in *Rusalka*, which he wrote in 1855, that Dargomïzhsky rejected traditional form and chose the path of "truth". He had sought long before this, in some of the songs of his youth, to bring music close to life and the spoken word. This was an entirely new system, a system which he adopted consciously and adhered to all his life. In *The Stone Guest* he simply embodied it in all its power and brilliance. At the time that he conceived and began to carry out his reform, he had not heard a single note of Wagner's music; it is doubtful whether he had even heard of Wagner. He was only responding to the deep-seated, instinctive demands of his own nature. Indeed, Wagner was so remote and alien to him that when, in the summer of 1856 (that is, after *Rusalka*), Serov decided to enlighten him about his (Serov's) latest musical idol and gave him *Tannhäuser* to look through (for the first time), Dargomïzhsky immediately wrote to Serov:

> I have looked through half of the opera. You are right; there is a great deal of poetry in the scenario. In the music he shows us a new and sensible path. But in his unnatural melodies and spicy, though at times very interesting harmonies, one senses a kind of strain—*will und kann nicht*! Truth—truth above all—but there must also be good taste as well!

These words epitomize the difference between Wagner and Dargomïzhsky. The former was much less an artist than a pondering, fabricating, consciously inventing mind; the latter was an artist from head to toe,

[1] This view is expressed, for example, in the biography of Dargomïzhsky in the most recent edition of Riemann's *Musiklexikon*.

one who created from inspiration and with every fibre of his being. For all his reforms, Wagner adored "magnificent spectacles", ballets, marches, processions and all the accepted conventions, sham and claptrap of the theatre. Dargomïzhsky despised all this outmoded theatrical falderal; in *The Stone Guest* he had only one purpose in mind—to be true to life and the human spirit. Wagner had little talent, was extremely affected and completely devoid of a gift for realistic recitative. Dargomïzhsky was a fiery, passionate genius, spontaneous, enthralled and enthralling; an artist alive with a sense of drama and pathos, as well as of the humorous and the comic, the true and the natural and, what is more, he possessed a matchless gift for realistic recitative. Lastly, Wagner was a thoroughgoing idealist; Dargomïzhsky—a thorough-going realist. It was in this last respect that these two differed most sharply and definitely. Dargomïzhsky was the father of musical realism. Before him there had been only a few tentative attempts at it.

In Dargomïzhsky's second opera, *The Stone Guest*, poetry, love, passion, gripping tragedy, humour, comedy, subtle characterization and a supernatural phenomenon (the appearance of the Commandant, for which Dargomïzhsky invented a thunderous, terrifying scale[1] never used before) are all fused into a wonderful organic whole. At the same time, realistic expression attained such power, finish, and artisty in this opera that it inaugurated a new era in music and will, without any doubt, serve as the basis for the future development of music, for European *Zukunftsmusik*. The "music of the future" is not to be found in Wagner's operas, but rather in Dargomïzhsky's *The Stone Guest*. Wagner's operas contain few seeds that bear promise for the future; they are too limited and lacking in talent. *The Stone Guest* is the brilliant cornerstone of the new period of music drama. In its formal aspects it has been worked out to perfection. The only element that is missing is the chorus. The matter of the chorus, which must be completely and radically reformed for the purposes of music drama, was the only one Dargomïzhsky failed to deal with.

Thus far Dargomïzhsky's opera has not yet won acceptance in our country. First of all, it was not until three years after the composer's death, that is, in 1872, that the Theatre Directorate deigned to permit it to be performed. Even then a public subscription had to be opened to obtain the modest additional sum needed to acquire the opera from Dargomïzhsky's heirs because the Directorate refused to pay anything above the paltry fee they were authorized to pay at the time. In this case the Directorate was only being true to itself. Fifteen years earlier, when Glinka's sister, Ludmila Shestakova, had brought up the question of her brother's operas with a certain Minister, he had replied: "We don't care who the composer was or what he composed. As far as we are concerned,

[1] The whole-tone scale, which Glinka had already used in *Ruslan*.—G.A.

music is good only when it brings in a profit."[1] Our public remained true to itself, too. Out of a sense of duty, they subscribed the sum necessary to put on *The Stone Guest*,[2] but once it was produced, they did not support it. Those who saw it did not understand it and did not like it, despite the brilliant performance of O. A. Petrov as Leporello and the first-rate performances of Yu. F. Platonova as Donna Anna and F. P. Komissarzhevsky as Don Giovanni. The critics almost to a man let forth shrieks of horror and indignation. They hated *The Stone Guest* with all their hearts. The audience yawned and left. Needless to say, the opera "did not pay" and therefore it was dropped from the repertory. Everything was as it should be. And so it has remained to this very moment. Gounod's *Faust*, Rubinstein's *Demon*, Serov's *Rogneda* and all of Verdi's operas are flourishing. They bring in a profit!

III

Throughout all of Glinka's career and during the first half of Dargomïzhsky's, the musical life of our country revolved around only two poles: one—the composer, the other—the public and critics. At the end of the fifties, a third pole made its appearance—the music school. Before this, our musicians had acquired their musical education fortuitously, independently of each other—some by their own efforts, others under the guidance of a teacher or professor here or abroad. After a while certain people began to talk about the need for a school, a conservatory, and professional rights, titles and privileges for musicians. The advocates of this were those who always regarded everything that was done in Europe as perfect and blindly accepted all of Europe's prejudices. Europe had conservatories, therefore we ought to have them, too. Many people supported the idea; they considered it a truly patriotic and very urgent undertaking, and things went full steam ahead. It was held that the level of music was still too low here and that something had to be done to raise it. In pursuit of this aim and to disseminate a genuine musical education in our country, the Russian Musical Society was founded in 1859 and its chief agency—the Conservatory—in 1862.

Early in 1861, shortly before the Conservatory was opened, *Vek* published an article by Anton Rubinstein entitled "Music in Russia", which was intended to prepare the public for this event by pointing out the sad state of music in our country and setting forth the only measures by which this situation could possibly be remedied.[3] Among other things, the author asserted that "only amateurs are engaged in music in Russia".

[1] *Glinka's Last Years*, p. 13.

[2] The trustee of Dargomïzhsky's heirs regarded as insufficient the maximum honorarium that the Imperial Theatres were entitled to pay for the right of performance. As the result of a public appeal by Cui (see Cui, *Izbrannïe Statii* Leningrad, 1952, p. 176), the balance was quickly subscribed.—G.A.

[3] *Vek*, No. 1 (1861).

The fact is, however, that by the end of the fifties and beginning of the sixties, works by the young Russian musicians, Glinka's progeny, had already begun to appear on concert programmes and in print. Balakirev's Overture on Russian Themes and his Overture to *King Lear* had been composed and performed publicly; most of his songs had been written and published. A scherzo by Mussorgsky and one by Cui had been performed, and several of the latter's songs had been published. Were all these only the works of "amateurs"? The aim to improve and develop Russian music was, of course, a laudable one, but was such improvement and development really needed when an independent and profoundly national school had already come into being in our country? Any discussion of Russian music should have begun with a definition of our new music and new school, its character and special features and what, precisely, needed to be done to further its growth and preserve its individuality. But the would-be benefactors of music in Russia neither understood nor wanted to understand this. Gazing down from the lofty heights of the European conservatory, they viewed our fatherland as a kind of *tabula rasa*, a wild and desolate country whose untilled soil needed the good seeds of Europe. These seeds were enumerated and their wonder-working properties minutely described in Rubinstein's article. No one questioned any of this. It was as though the promises set forth in *Vek* were based on some God-given truth and we had only to await their fulfilment. Furthermore, they were to be fulfilled in the immediate future. Actually, Rubinstein's article read like the manifesto of a group which possessed great authority and power in the realm of music.

Only a few people disagreed with the views expressed in *Vek*; only a few saw the establishment of a routine European conservatory in our country, not as a blessing, but as a mistake. I was one of them, and since this matter seemed very important to me, I published some observations on the *Vek* article in *Severnaya Pchela*, in the hope that the question of setting up a conservatory might be reopened for general discussion and that some people might come forth with clear thinking, new ideas and solid facts.

> Give musicians a title, set up a conservatory (they say), and then suddenly everything will change, everything will be as it ought to be [I wrote]. But we strongly doubt that a title will necessarily further the development of music in our country . . . When a person's well-being can be furthered and his standing as an artist enhanced only by the granting of titles and special privileges, he inevitably succumbs to the promptings of his own selfish desires. Such desires bear no relation to the furtherance of art . . . For years many academies in Europe have been handing out titles to people in the various arts—and they are still doing so. Yet they have produced not artists but only people who crave status, titles, privileges. Multiplying the numbers of musicians by means of such enticements does not advance art . . . Our writers have been given no titles, or special status; nevertheless a truly national literature has emerged and matured in our country. This is the way it should be with music . . . The

establishment of conservatories and progress in art are by no means synonymous. Even if not one, but many conservatories were to be set up here, there is no certainty that this would really benefit art. On the contrary, such a step might even prove harmful.

Nowadays the prevailing opinion in Europe is that academies and conservatories serve only as a breeding ground for mediocrities and help to perpetuate deleterious artistic ideas and tastes. Because of this, in the matter of art education, the best minds are seeking ways of getting along without "higher" educational institutions. "Higher" institutions for the arts are altogether different from higher institutions for the sciences: there is a vast gulf between them. Universities confine themselves to disseminating knowledge. Not content with this, conservatories meddle most harmfully in the student's creative activity. They dictate the style and form of his works; they try to force him into a particular academic mould, to impose their own fixed practices on him and, worst of all, to control his very thinking. They impose upon him opinions about composers and their works which it will be extremely difficult, perhaps even impossible, for him to shake off in later years . . .

The conservatories in Italy and France did not raise the musical level of those countries; they did not further musical education or even produce the valuable school of teachers they were expected to. In Germany the golden age of music *preceded* the establishment of the conservatories; all of her greatest talents were educated *outside* them. All the music teachers in our country are foreigners; they were trained in conservatories and schools. Why then, are people complaining about the poor musical instruction given here? Is it likely that the teachers coming out of our future conservatory will be better than those sent to us from abroad? . . . The time has come to stop transplanting foreign institutions to our country and to give some thought to what would really be beneficial and suitable to *our* soil and *our* national character. The experience of Europe shows that while the lower schools which confine themselves to teaching the rudiments of music are useful, the higher schools, academies and conservatories are harmful. Is this experience to be lost on us? Must we stubbornly ape what is done in other places only in order that later we may have the pleasure of boasting about the vast number of teachers and classes we have, the meaningless distribution of awards and prizes, mounting piles of worthless compositions and crowds of mediocre musicians? . . .

What I had hoped for in writing this article never came to pass. I was preaching in the wilderness. No one responded; no one raised a voice against *Vek*; no one came forth to examine the pros and cons of the matter. Some months later a conservatory was opened in Petersburg, and afterwards a second one in Moscow. Of course, what was to have been expected happened. Viewed as schools for general musical instruction and for the training of performers, our two conservatories have rendered a great service. In the twenty years of their existence, they have turned out hundreds of people who know the rudiments of music and how to play some instrument or to sing more or less satisfactorily. A considerable number of them have joined orchestras or choruses or have become soloists. This is all very well. However, when we consider the level of music in our country, we cannot but see that it has not been raised in the slightest. The conservatories have not furthered our musical culture;

they have merely produced a tremendous number of musical artisans who have little to do with art, are infected with conservatory tastes and have a very poor understanding of music. They are unable to distinguish between the most banal, hackneyed music and the most original; in fact, they invariably prefer the former. And now this musical infection is spreading all over Russia. Has anything really been gained by this, has it really been beneficial? Would it not be better if we had no "musicians", of this kind, if these people engaged in some other pursuit and left art, which is completely alien to them, alone? The false bait has lured them to music to no purpose. But most deplorable of all is the fact that our conservatories have turned out to be purely foreign institutions—German. Within their walls Russian music, the Russian school, the Russian trend are never mentioned, and hundreds of young men and women are being taught to worship only what is worshipped at the conservatories in Leipzig and Berlin. Most of the "musicians"—performers, composers and theorists—who graduate from our conservatories, are even somewhat contemptuous of Russian music. The exceptions are very rare—only the truly gifted people who, after having somehow or other entered into the conservatory, find that they cannot subscribe to its views and, upon graduating, as their talent matures, move further and further away from them. How could the sympathies and attitudes of the conservatories possibly be otherwise when the Russian Musical Society, their head and heart, is basically anti-national and thoroughly permeated with the views of the German conservatories? This Society has either completely ignored the new school of Russian music or treated it with condescension. It has acted exactly as our Academy of Art has towards the new school of Russian painting. The sixties reverberated with clashes between the adherents of the old and new schools of thought, between the representatives of the conservatories and classicism, on the one hand, and those of the movement towards a national Russian art, on the other.

But before giving an account of the events of this period, we must first consider one important man who played a very prominent rôle in our musical life during the sixties, at the same time as did the conservative faction represented by the Russian Musical Society and the conservatories.

IV

This man was Serov.[1] At first glance it may seem strange to bracket him with the conservatories and the Russian Musical Society, for throughout the better part of his life he was very hostile towards them and was engaged in a running battle with them. The truth is, however, that in the final analysis there was no difference between his aims and theirs.

[1] The intimate friend of Stasov's youth, indeed up to his mid-thirties.—G.A.

Western-oriented, both were motivated mainly by their opposition to the new, independent, native Russian school; both wanted to check and destroy this movement which had already begun here, to impose a foreign pattern on us and force us into a foreign mould.

Serov's activity was twofold: he was a composer and also a music critic. In both fields he displayed considerable talent, wide learning, intelligence, vigour and brilliance. In both, however, he lacked the most important, the highest qualities. His gift for composition was second-rate and completely unoriginal; his critical gift lacked depth and solidity. His chief trait was instability and vacillation in his convictions. As a consequence, neither his musical nor his critical works have left any lasting mark, and they cannot possibly affect the future course of Russian music. They did, however, exert a very strong influence in their day.

Serov made his appearance as a composer very late, after he was forty. He was entirely self-taught as a musician: he never studied privately or at any music school, but acquired a solid technical knowledge of music solely through his own initiative and perseverance. Unfavourable circumstances, extreme irresoluteness, a lack of self-confidence amounting to weakness and, above all, the lack of genuine inspiration hampered Serov for a long time and prevented him from composing in his youth. He lost nothing by this, however. Had he composed during his twenties or thirties, he would have gone completely unnoticed and would probably have long remained only another of the belated imitators of Mozartian opera for, in the first period of his life, despite his vast musical knowledge and erudition, he regarded the operas of Mozart as the supreme ideal of operatic music. When he was about forty, however, he came to know *Tannhäuser* and *Lohengrin*, and this gave him the decisive stimulus, the clearly-defined direction he most needed. It seemed to him that Wagnerian opera fulfilled all the requirements of modern opera, that there should be no other kind of opera but this. With that idea in mind he began to compose.

Wagner's system particularly suited Serov not only because in many respects it really met the demands of reason and conformed to the intellectual concept of what opera ought to be, but also because Serov was totally incapable of developing themes, of treating form so as to build entire musical structures on a single melody or motive. He had so little creative ability and inventiveness that after stating a theme, he did not know what to do with it, and he either repeated it again and again or immediately tacked another one on to it. Wagner did the same thing, but for an entirely different reason. He was a born symphonist, a master of form and the techniques of development. If he did not write operas in the "formal" vein, it was only because he saw no good reason to and did not want to, not because he was unable to. But Serov was not a master of form, and just as he could never have written an overture or symphony, he simply could not have written that part of an opera which called for logical musical development. Even such a simple, uncomplicated piece as the "Dance of the Clowns" (in *Rogneda*) was obviously extremely difficult for him. For this reason the Wagnerian system, which gave him a chance to keep stringing together new and different bits of music—motives and melodies—served his purposes perfectly. Of course, this system, applied on a broad scale, characterizes all the latest and most advanced music of our time—Wagner's operas, Liszt's symphonic poems, and many of the songs, operas and instrumental works of the new Russian school. It is a bad thing, however, when this kind of writing stems, not from a system, but from lack of talent and skill.

In opera the first prerequisite is a great gift for setting declamation, the sort of gift that Dargomïzhsky and Mussorgsky had, and this Serov lacked completely. That is why from the strictly musical point of view his operas were unsatisfactory. In all fairness, it might be said that Serov ceased being a crow but never became a peacock. He was in a kind of indeterminate state, forever suspended between heaven and earth. He wanted reforms in Russian opera but all he could do was "want" them; he did not have sufficient artistic ability to effect them. Our opera was reformed, not by Serov, but by other, greater talents. He never acquired a mastery of form nor was he ever truly inspired. What is more, the whole psychological aspect of drama was absolutely alien to him and beyond him. You will not find a single passage in any of his three operas which expresses heartfelt emotion, genuine warmth of feeling, or passion. They fit perfectly his own characterization of himself—a fire that gives out light but no heat. Yet, the subject matter of all his operas called for the expression of feeling. What was Serov to do, when that was precisely what he himself lacked most! He succeeded only when it came to the minor, so-called "decorative" details of opera, its superficial background—a Russian carnival, an ancient sacrificial chant, the shouts and fanfares of the chase, the wild war song of a Holofernes, Eastern choruses and dances. All this came easy to Serov because of his artistic nature, his sense of the picturesque and the elegant. But these are only secondary details, unessential insertions which might easily be omitted from a libretto. On the other hand, when it came to the most important, the essential elements of opera—characterization, the portrayal of emotional states and varied nuances of feeling—Serov always failed miserably. Indeed, his treatment of these elements was dull and unimaginative, especially when it took the form of lifeless, non-musical recitatives, made up of a chance collection of notes, or poor, insipid and sometimes hackneyed arias and ariosos. This is true particularly of *Rogneda*, which became a favourite with the public precisely because of the Verstovsky-like banality of many of its passages. In terms of fame and fortune this was Serov's greatest success, even though compared with *Judith*, his first and best opera, it represents a definite step backward. For while *Judith* is hardly an important opera, it has a serious oratorio-like quality; in it the composer was at least striving to express something profound and meaningful and, occasionally, as in the arias of Akhior and Avra, he achieved a measure of success. But *Rogneda* was written without any serious intent; it was just dashed off, so to speak, and the result was an *Askold's Tomb*, something fit for a side show. Serov's third opera, *Hostile Power*, called for the portrayal of a wide variety of characters—strong, weak, morose, ascetic, wanton, poetic, tender—and an equally wide range of emotions. What was needed in this case was a musician with the gift of an Ostrovsky—and this Serov was not. Instead of creating convincing characters in various emotional states, he succeeded only in drawing a picture of Carnival time. And while the latter is drawn graphically, even realistically, it must be admitted that it is somewhat easier to portray a motley crowd in one of its most superficial manifestations than it is to delineate the human soul.

It is doubtful whether Serov's operas will find any successors. They are too lacking in character and originality. If we try to view Serov as a reformer of opera (which is what he wanted to be), we find that he was not sufficiently independent to play such a rôle; he was merely a disciple of Wagner who contributed nothing new, nothing of his own to European music. When we consider him from the nationalist standpoint, we have to bear in mind that he was born and lived in the capital and had little in common with the life and spirit of the Russian people. His musical nationalism was purely intellectual, contrived. His greatest abilities appeared in his orchestration, where he often achieved astonishingly colourful and, at times, even poetic effects.

As a music critic, Serov was amazingly inconsistent. Lacking principle, he continually wavered right and left. During his twenty years as a critic, his opinions and views on music shifted constantly, now forward, now backward. At one moment he passionately loved Meyerbeer; at another he considered him "harmful to art" and his works "not music at all"; one moment he angrily attacked the Italians, their formalism, banality and affectation; the next he declared *La Sonnambula*, a masterpiece, "the most inspired expression of Bellini's gentle talent" and went into ecstacies over Rubini's singing and "matchless" acting. Towards the end of his life he began to extol Patti and composed songs for her to perform. In the first half of his life his views on music were progressive. This was the best and most important period of his career as a critic. At that time he rendered a great service to our public, championing sound principles and good, honest music. But this did not last long, only from 1851 to 1858. During the second period of his critical activity, that is, from 1858 to 1871, he became an out-and-out conservative and reactionary. Throughout both periods he displayed more wit than wisdom.

He was rather an adroit, sparkling polemicist than a sound critic. He liked to talk about "organic unity" and "relentless logic", qualities he himself was most deficient in. In his criticism as in his music, everything was fortuitous and unrelated.

In 1860 Serov wrote to M. P. Mavromikhala: "I have somehow become accustomed to regard myself as a vessel from which many good artistic ideas are to flow to mankind." This never happened because it never could have. Serov was too shallow for such a purpose. He did not understand this, however, even at the age of forty. Actually, he engaged in rather simple pursuits. For example, he spent several of the best years of his life arguing with such writers on music as Ulybyshev, Rostislav (Theophilus Tolstoy) and Lenz, with whom it was completely meaningless to carry on a prolonged polemic since these writers carried little weight in our country and exerted almost no influence on our public. True, when he started out, in the fifties, he did align himself with the right cause (even though to no avail), defending Beethoven and Mozart against their senseless deprecators and idolaters Ulybyshev and Lenz, and true music against the dilettante tastes of Rostislav.

In 1855 Glinka wrote to Kukolnik: "These presumptuous Ulybyshevs and Rostislavs ought to spend a little more time on the ABC of music and learn something, at least, about the mysteries of art and the geniuses who fathomed them." But Serov did not realize how insignificant his antagonists were, and he willingly wasted his ammunition on them. He delighted in easy victories over weak and juvenile opponents. He strutted about in this empty rôle for a long time. Once he even attempted something of this sort in real life. At a concert in the Assembly Hall of the Nobility, he climbed onto a chair and heatedly exhorted the audience to pelt the conductor, Lazarev, with rotten potatoes because he had mangled Beethoven's works which (according to Serov) he was not fit to touch.[1]

In the sixties, after Serov became acquainted with Wagner and his operas, he took it upon himself to champion Wagner and began to fight with everyone who would not accept him or accord him the recognition Serov thought he deserved. To him Wagner was a musician who had "pondered worlds", and his operas the embodiment of the modern ideal of opera, the ultimate in the art of music drama. Serov was as inflexible about Wagner and opera as he had been, earlier, about Beethoven and the symphony. He had declared that after Beethoven there could be no more symphonies; that Beethoven had exhausted all the possibilities of this form and that nothing written since his time was worthy of being called a symphony. On these grounds, he "detested" the wonderful

[1] This is literally true except that the concert was not in the Assembly Hall. The "chevalier Alexandre de Lazareff", the "Abyssinian maestro, *amico di Rossini*", was a complete charlatan; his concert in aid of the Syrian Christians was given on March 26, 1861. The audience was already in very high spirits before Serov's intervention.—G.A.

symphonies of Schubert and Schumann; he considered Schumann, in general, only half a musician. He rejected completely the idea of instrumental programme music (obviously under the influence of his idol Wagner), and accordingly thought very little of the works of Berlioz and Liszt. He maintained that, for the most part, neither of these composers was "truly inspired", that their music was too often "only a product of the brain".

In view of all this, it is easy to understand Serov's attitude towards the gifted young Russian musicians who appeared on the scene at the end of the fifties and beginning of the sixties. By then his mind was made up and he refused to budge. They, on the other hand, believed in the new life, the new direction in art, and they moved boldly ahead. They deeply loved the work of the very masters—Schumann, Liszt and Berlioz—whom Serov did not understand and did not like. This only served to intensify his dislike for these masters, and in almost every article, he disparaged them. The new Russian composers did not care much for Wagner's operas but they passionately loved Glinka's *Ruslan*. This prompted Serov to write numerous articles in which, while praising Glinka's talents as a musician, he denied his ability to write effectively for the stage. As proof, he cited *Ruslan*. In a series of articles entitled "Ruslan and the Ruslanists", he argued that it was much better to listen to this opera than to see it, since dramatically it was dull, boring and ridiculous; that it was nothing but the "caprice of a great artist", a caprice he might just as well have foregone, since he had already laid the foundations for Russian opera in *A Life for the Tsar*. According to Serov, practically everything about *Ruslan* was poor: the fantastic plot (although Wagner's absurd, mystical moralizing plots did not strike him as poor); the atmosphere (i.e., Glinka's failure to preserve the light and playful mood of Pushkin's poem—as though a composer is duty bound to repeat his original source literally and slavishly); and the libretto (i.e., its disconnectedness). (This last, by the way, was not the fault of Glinka but of his friends and advisers. Proof of this is the initial plan of *Ruslan*, which was excellently drawn up by the composer, a fact others suspected but Serov deliberately chose to ignore.) As far as Serov was concerned, there was so much wrong with *Ruslan* that whenever he praised the music, he found it necessary to object to many other aspects of it, which, of course, robbed his praise of all meaning. He finally prophesied that "in five years" *Ruslan* would no longer be performed.

The main object of Serov's hatred and attacks, however, was the new Russian school. At first, in 1856, he wrote a series of articles about *Rusalka* which were so laudatory that he even justified the imitation or borrowing of something good from another composer. "Music cannot do without this kind of noble imitation and assimilation of forms happily discovered by other artists", he declared in *Muzykalny i Teatralny Vestnik*.

However, ten years later, in the sixties, when he saw that Dargomïzhsky had formed close ties with the new school, Serov suddenly downgraded him and shortly after his death, called him nothing but a "pallid imitator". Serov always represented the works of our young composers as absolutely worthless and unimportant. Towards the end of his life, when he became increasingly the exponent of rigid, stagnant thinking, despite his dislike for the conservatories and their adherents, he suddenly began to agree with them on one point—on attacking the new school for its "innovations" and persecuting it for its "irreverence" towards tradition, towards what had gone before. In this Serov showed himself to be just as conservative as the enemies he aligned himself with.

V

The year 1855 marked the beginning of a new stage in the development of Russian music. An eighteen-year-old youth, destined to play a major rôle in the fortunes of our art, arrived in St. Petersburg from Nizhni-Novgorod. This was Balakirev. Glinka, who met this youth during his (Glinka's) last months in Russia, shortly before his final journey abroad, at once recognized and appreciated his extraordinary musical gifts. He foresaw that Balakirev would have a very important future. By then Glinka himself was no longer composing; he was completely immersed in the classics—Bach, Handel and Gluck. "I no longer have the urge or desire to compose," he wrote to Kukolnik on 19th January, 1855. "If my muse should suddenly awaken, I might write something without a text, for orchestra. I am abandoning Russian music as I am the Russian frost." Nevertheless, he received Balakirev very warmly as a composer, especially as a composer of Russian music. Glinka was not mistaken in seeing in this youth his heir and successor.

While still in his provincial town, Balakirev had come to know and love a great deal of the best European music, such works as Mozart's *Requiem*, Beethoven's symphonies, sonatas and quartets, Weber's *Freischütz*, Mendelssohn's overtures, and much of the music of Chopin. But at the same time he also passionately loved Glinka's operas; he valued them more highly than almost anyone else in our country dared to in those days. He admired not only Glinka's genius but also the fact that his greatest creations incorporated elements of a truly Russian style. The latter circumstance particularly endeared Glinka to this young man, who had been born far from the capital and had spent his childhood and youth in the countryside, in the very heart of Russia. In Glinka he found a kindred spirit, someone he could understand, someone he needed. Balakirev had an innate, spontaneous disposition towards musical nationalism. His first benefactor, Ulybyshev, in whose home he spent his youth, was a lover of the European classics. His adoration of Mozart, whom he considered the greatest composer of all time, was such that in Mozart's honour he even belittled Beethoven. Yet, despite Ulybyshev's influence, Balakirev did not become classically oriented. So strongly was he drawn to national music that virtually his first compositions were the *Fantasy on Russian Themes for Piano and Orchestra* and a fantasy for piano on the trio "Do Not Grieve, My Dearest", from *A Life for the Tsar*.

Balakirev's friendship with Glinka further strengthened his inherent tendencies and firmly fixed his artistic personality. He benefited considerably from Petersburg, where he had an opportunity to hear a great deal of new music, both operatic and orchestral, and also to come into contact with musicians and the musical world. In the final analysis, however, his achievement was due primarily to his own efforts. He acquired his musical education on his own and soon became the leader and centre of a whole new school of music.

Balakirev had all the essential qualities for this: an amazing store of initiative, love and knowledge and, to back it all up, limitless energy. By the end of the fifties the talented young musicians Cui and Mussorgsky had gathered around him; in the sixties they were joined by Rimsky-Korsakov and Borodin. Balakirev taught and guided all of them with his advice and criticism. At the same time that he himself was studying, he instructed his friends in all the fine points of music—theory, form and orchestration. He suggested themes for their compositions, then looked through and carefully analysed what they had done. His friends willingly deferred to his judgement because they sensed the keenness of his perception and soundness of his ideas. He painstakingly went over with them, in four-hand arrangement or full score, all the most important music that had been written from Bach and Handel to the present day in Europe and, beginning later on, also in our country. For his friends these discussions amounted to veritable lectures, to a course in music such as is given at a high-school or university. Probably most important of all were Balakirev's critical observations. No other musician seems to have possessed such a gift for musical analysis. Even if he had not been the great composer we know him to be, he still would have been outstanding for his extraordinary critical ability. Only Schumann might be considered his equal in this respect. Another attribute seldom found in other musicians was Balakirev's unusual and abiding curiosity about new music. Over a period of a quarter of a century, from 1855 to 1883, not a single noteworthy piece of music written here or in Europe escaped his notice. He knew each and every one of them; he studied and analysed them, first for himself and then for his colleagues. Out of this there arose in our country a school of music, a group of fresh young talents thoroughly acquainted with everything that had been created by the art to which they had dedicated themselves. How rare! In most cases artists know far too little; entire areas of art remain unknown to them. In this regard Balakirev gave our young school sound guidance and brought it to a high standard.

Not having been trained at a conservatory, these young people were free from the preconceptions handed down by tradition and were not afraid to regard as old-fashioned or uninspired some of the music that was highly esteemed by academic standards. Moreover, they did not feel bound to regard as perfect everything written even by the great composers they admired most. They carefully distinguished the best and loftiest of these composers' works from the poorer or weaker ones. The members of our school pursued the same independent path in their own work. They refused to adhere to traditional forms and tried to work out forms of their own. They considered Beethoven and Schubert the best representatives of the earlier period; Berlioz, Liszt and Schumann—of the modern. Above all, they felt an indissoluble kinship with the great national trend initiated by Glinka and Dargomïzhsky. Even so, the group did not limit themselves to this sphere alone but strove to create something of their own. It was this that gave rise to the deep dissension and hostility in our music world.

At first the worshippers of the "old" were merely displeased, but their displeasure was fairly mild because they were not unified, they had no rallying point, so to speak. For its part, the Balakirev group issued no public pronouncements; it made its tendencies known only through its works. And although these works (Balakirev's *Lear*, for example) did not suit the taste of its opponents, there were no public objections or denunciations of them. All this changed in the early sixties, however. In 1860 the Russian Muscial Society began to present concerts and two years later, in 1862, the Free Music School, founded by Lomakin and Balakirev, also started to give concerts. At that point the centres became clearly defined, and two musical camps began to emerge in our country—one conservative, the other progressive. Needless to say, they were soon at war with each other. The German faction of the Russian Musical Society was horrified at the thought that, as one of our most gifted musicians jestingly wrote me at the time, "music may pass into the hands of the new Russian musicians and if that happens, a wild, uncontrollable flood of Russian barbarism will sweep away the beneficent seeds of German musical culture which certain virtuous men have succeeded in planting here." The animosity inevitably grew more intense, especially towards the end of the sixties. As the talents of the members of the new school developed and matured, their music became increasingly more novel and daring, and therefore more at variance with the tastes and ideas of the opposing faction and the general public which was closely aligned with them. Even those who at first had acknowledged the talent of Balakirev, Cui, Rimsky-Korsakov, Mussorgsky and Borodin and had received their early compositions warmly (especially the songs), now began to shy away from these composers and to regard their works as musical monstrosities. Attendance at the Free School's concerts steadily declined, despite the excellence of the music performed, Balakirev's profound understanding of it, and the fire and brilliance of his conducting. The public had little liking for the great creations of Schumann, Berlioz and Liszt, whom they accused Balakirev of favouring. At the same time they were quite indifferent to the best, though little known works of Glinka and Dargomïzhsky, whom Balakirev ardently championed. The writers who shared the Conservatory's views complained bitterly because none of Rubinstein's music was ever performed. Meanwhile, the small number of supporters of the new nationalist trend and the Free School grew still smaller after Lomakin left the school and with him went the last remnants of the familiar, "accessible" music which the ordinary concert-goers favoured.

It was precisely at this time, in the mid-sixties, that Serov joined forces with the Rostislavs, Manns and other such banal writers who were voicing their indignation and opposition to Balakirev, his concerts, aims and school. At one time, not long before this, Serov had considered Balakirev a great talent. But now that Balakirev and his group would not acknowledge the enormous importance not only of Wagner but even of Serov's own operas (*Judith* and *Rogneda*), he began to pronounce Balakirev a man devoid of artistic insight and creative gifts, an even worse conductor than Rubinstein (Serov's pet aversion), worse than the "last violinist in a vaudeville orchestra", and to call the group an insignificant "nest of ignorant braggarts", etc. Once, when *Sadko* appeared, Serov praised both the piece and its composer Rimsky-Korsakov to the skies, but this was obviously only a manoeuvre by which he hoped to irritate and humiliate Balakirev. Serov died without ever understanding the importance of the new Russian school. When in 1869, thanks to his efforts and those of his worthy colleagues, Balakirev was forced to resign his post as conductor of the Russian Musical Society's concerts (a post that had been given him in 1867, after his brilliant conducting in Prague, which was acclaimed throughout Europe), Serov declared jubilantly that "this is as it should be". Later on, when Rimsky-Korsakov replaced Balakirev as director of the Free School and conductor of its concerts—offices he administered ably and energetically—he, too, was subjected to the ignorance and hatred of the conservatives.

It was in this kind of disquieting, contentious atmosphere that Balakirev and his colleagues had to carry on their work in Russia. Not many musicians have had to endure such a difficult lot. Glinka and Dargomïzhsky were free to do as they pleased; they had no ties. Had they wished, they could have lived in seclusion. They could have seen no one, heard nothing about what was being said and done in the music world and could have composed peacefully as their inspiration dictated. The situation of Balakirev and his colleagues was quite different. They were not individual artists whose works pleased some and did not please others, were understood by some and not by others—they were a group who professed doctrines which threatened the general musical climate, a group who spurned accepted ideas and sought to change the thinking of others through public concerts and printed propaganda. Their situation somewhat resembled that of Wagner and the Wagnerites in Germany. They, too, were hated and persecuted in their own country, though much less than our school was in Russia because they were much less daring and resolute. Unlike our school, they did not challenge earlier musical precepts nor defy prevailing views. Wagner treated most of the established composers with respect; the only ones he attacked were Rossini and Meyerbeer. He acknowledged as great and important all those who had long been so regarded by the general public, the conservatories and the critics. Furthermore, along with all its innovations and its symphonically conceived recitatives, Wagnerian opera was so filled with banalities of all sorts (marches, arias, processions, "magnificent spectacles", trite melodies like the "Lied an den Morgenstern"), at times it came so close to Verdi and the Italians, that it found its way into the hearts of even its severest opponents, the defenders of the old order. The new Russian school did not concern itself with the public but tirelessly pursued its own exacting ideals. And this is seldom forgiven.

Even though the "Balakirev party" (as Dargomïzhsky called it) was closely knit and in complete accord as to its manner of thinking and artistic direction, its works did not bear the stamp of sameness and uniformity. They were as totally unlike as the natures of the composers themselves. While these young musicians shared a common purpose, each of them retained his own individuality. Taken as a whole, the works of each represents his own world, a world separate and distinct from that of the other members of the school. Each remained true to his own character, his own basic nature; each pursued the path towards perfection, towards the development of his art in his own way.

The first to emerge as a composer was Balakirev. His creative work is characterized by poetic feeling, passion and breadth of conception. His songs (1858–1860), the first important works of his twenties, are charged with poetry and passion. Particularly remarkable are "Come to Me", "Lead Me, O Night", "Rapture", and, perhaps best of all, the "Song of the Goldfish". A charming eastern colouring distinguishes the "Song of Selim" and "Song of Georgia". All these are songs of love and passion. But Balakirev was not content to deal with this theme alone, and sometimes he turned to other, even more profound ones. His "Hebrew Melody" ("My Heart is Heavy"), for example, depicts the strength and nobility of a proud soul steeped in suffering, a heart on the point of breaking, seeking surcease in music.

Most of Balakirev's instrumental works and, after him, most of those of our new school are *programmatic*. In this the school was not only following the example of Glinka; it was responding to the spirit of the times. Our period is growing less and less interested in the "absolute" music of earlier days and insisting more and more upon music with concrete, clearly-defined content.

To be sure, Balakirev wrote some excellent non-programmatic orchestral compositions—the *Overture on Russian Themes* (1858) and *Czech Overture* (1867),[1] for example. Both are very beautiful and highly artistic, especially the earlier one, which is so throughout. In the *Czech Overture* only the introduction and ending are striking in their lyricism and wondrous colouring. For all the excellence of these pieces, however, Balakirev's greatest achievement lay in the realm of programme music.

The overture and incidental music to *King Lear* (1858–1861) are so rich in content that they might be said to amount to a full opera. This work surpasses a similar one by Glinka, the overture and incidental music to *Prince Kholmsky*, in many passages of which one senses the strong influence of Beethoven's *Egmont*. Rachel's beautiful Hebrew song "A Mist Fell from the Mountains" is virtually the only exception. The Overture to *King Lear* is a magnificent tone poem, which depicts the savage epoch and semi-barbaric court of Lear. Against this background is set the majestic figure of the unfortunate old man, generous and loving, but misunderstood and rejected by two of his daughters. Halfway through the Overture the anguished King appears in a field, amidst the thunder and lightning of a raging storm. Beside him is the gentle and devoted Cordelia. The Overture concludes with the sufferer's agonizing death. The incidental music enriches this powerful picture with portrayals of the enmity and bickering of the two sisters, the court jester, a stately court procession in which all the main characters are presented, the battle and finally, Lear's apotheosis.

The overture *A Thousand Years*[2] is also descriptive in content. In this marvellous work Balakirev depicted some of the most important moments in our history which were then powerfully stirring his imagination in colours now bright, now sombre, in moods sometimes austere, sometimes riotous. The emerging new life is expressed in an enchanting, truly inspired melody of wondrous beauty. This overture was written for the approaching commemoration of the thousandth anniversary of the founding of the Russian state. In all these works the orchestration is astonishingly colourful and masterful.

In 1869 Balakirev composed the piano fantasy *Islamey*, based on

[1] Later published as a symphonic poem, *In Bohemia*.—G.A.
[2] Later published as a symphonic poem, *Russia*.—G.A.

Georgian themes. It, too, is a programme work abounding in Eastern scenes which had once captivated the composer in the Caucasus. This is the finest, most finished piano composition to come out of our Russian school and one of the major creations in all piano literature. Liszt, the greatest pianist in the world, thought very highly of it. He always kept it on his piano and had all his pupils play it. But, to our shame, almost no one in our country knows *Islamey*, and none of our pianists ever performs it at a concert.

Balakirev's supreme achievement is *Tamara*, a fantasy for orchestra which was begun in 1867, then laid aside for a long time, and completed only in 1882. It is one of the most perfect musical creations of our century. Gone are the occasional flaws one noticed in some of the composer's youthful compositions—excessive attention to detail, contrivance, toil. *Tamara* is perfect and amazing throughout. Intense poetry, love and tenderness, the wild sounds of a passionate orgy, the disconsolate "farewell" at the end and, framing the whole, a remarkable evocation of the Caucasian landscape with its mountains and the river Terek enveloped in mist—all this forms a work commensurate with Lermontov's great poem upon which it is based.

We cannot conclude a survey of Balakirev's work without mentioning his *Collection of Russian Folk Songs*, which was published in 1866. This collection is exemplary in both the choice and harmonic treatment of the material. It was the first collection of truly scholarly and national significance to be made in our country. The entire school subsequently made wide use of it.

In 1882, after a twelve-year absence from music, the group and the Russian musical movement he had created, Balakirev resumed his activity and once again took his place in the forefront of our country's musical life. An address given in his honour at a concert marking the occasion, on 15th Feburary, 1882, stated:

> The founders of Russian music, Glinka and Dargomïzhsky, recognized you in your early youth as their heir and successor. Through your many years of work you have fulfilled their hopes and expectations. Through your own magnificent creations and your beneficent influence on our present generation of musicians, you, as the leader of a group of gifted colleagues, have ensured the Russian school of music a unique place in our national art, one which has been acclaimed both in our own country and by the foremost representatives of music in the West. Together with our entire new school, you were made to endure a great deal of hostility and even hardship at the hands of obdurate musical conservatism. Your friends and admirers were saddened by your temporary withdrawal from the field of work in which your true service to your country lies and, joyfully greeting you today on your return to your former activity, ardently hope that you will never again abandon the path on which you will unquestionably help Russian music to advance still further.

This address faithfully describes Balakirev's position and significance in our national school of composition.

After Balakirev, the next to emerge as a composer was Cui. He was entirely self-taught as a musician. The initial instruction in the principles of music which he received from Moniuszko in Vilna at the age of fifteen can hardly be taken into account. It was his friendship with Balakirev that exerted the most decisive influence on him in his youth. He was the first of the group with whom Balakirev undertook a critical survey of the music of the great composers. While studying himself, Balakirev taught his friend to examine closely the stylistic characteristics of the various composers; to analyse the meaning of their works thoroughly and completely independently, without regard to their fame or reputation; and, finally, to delve deeply into all the fine points of musical form and orchestration.

Cui, by the way, had little bent for orchestration and he never became a skilled orchestrator. Besides this, he also lacked talent for two other elements of music—the national and the comic. Whenever he attempted to handle them, he invariably failed. There is as little suggestion of humour in the portrayals of Leslie in *William Ratcliff* and of Galeofa and the *sbirri* in *Angelo* as there is of the national element—Scottish or Italian—in these operas. There is not a trace of anything Russian or "Eastern" in any of Cui's works either. Because he himself had little propensity for writing in the national vein, Cui never fully understood or appreciated "nationalism" in the works of others. His gifts were too exclusively lyrical, too exclusively psychological. The character of his talent took shape while he was still in his twenties, and it became discernible in his earliest works, most of which were songs. Like Dargomïzhsky, with whom he formed a friendship early in life, he at first leaned strongly towards the forms and style of French light opera. Traces of Auber appear frequently in his early works. One of them, the comic opera, *The Mandarin's Son*, was written almost entirely in this style. But soon afterward, under the influence of Schumann, whom he adored passionately, and of the best works of Dargomïzhsky's last period, Cui's style and direction changed completely. Then his own creative personality revealed itself in its full strength and beauty.

The principal characteristics of Cui's music are poetry, passion and an extraordinary warmth of feeling and tenderness which move the listener to the very depths of his soul. True, Cui concerned himself almost exclusively with presenting love in all its various manifestations (jealousy, despair, self-sacrifice, etc.) and therefore, his may seem to have been a very one-sided talent, but in depth and intensity, his portrayals of this emotion surpass anything ever achieved not only by his colleagues in the Russian school but perhaps by anyone in the whole field of music.

Although traditional symphonic form was little suited to Cui's creative needs, he sometimes displayed a great deal of talent in this genre.

Thus, for example, his Scherzo in F major (composed in 1857), whose principal themes are based on his wife's name and his own initials; the overture to *The Captive of the Caucasus*; the entr'actes for *William Ratcliff*; and the overture to *Angelo* are replete with skill and beauty. Cui's real forte, however, was vocal composition. Many of his songs, such as "My Soul is Aflame with Love", "Fare Thee Well", "Aeolian Harps", and "In the Quiet of the Night" are deeply moving in their beauty, feeling and ardour. It was in opera, however, that his gift for vocal composition received its fullest expression.

In his first opera *William Ratcliff* (1867), Cui still adhered to the conventional forms—arias, duets and choruses. At the time he was composing it, Dargomïzhsky had not yet undertaken the musical reform he was to carry out in *The Stone Guest*, and Cui was no born reformer. Nevertheless, despite its shortcomings—inadequate dramatic interest, excessive narration, and lack of lifelike characters—*Ratcliff* ranks among the major works of our time. Intense passion, tender love, sombre and terrible tragedy, expressed in the new and captivating manner of the post-Schumann period, endow this opera with a truly unique quality. All its amazing poetry and artistry were wasted on the Russian public, however. Corrupted by the banalities, artificiality and formalism of Italian opera—the effect of its twenty-five years as a guest in our country—they did not understand the importance of *Ratcliff*, found it boring and jeered at it. The critics supported the public in their crass derision and senseless condemnation. Serov, for example, wrote that "the most mediocre bravura arias of a Donizetti or Verdi are worth more than the whole of *Ratcliff*, which is filled with outrageous music and incredible pretentiousness". The rest of the critics distinguished themselves in a similar way. Like Serov, they and the public were especially irritated by the "scene at the Black Rock" which, in its expressive power and masterful evocation of a gloomy landscape, is without doubt one of the wonders of art. No one—neither the public nor the critics—understood that in terms of beauty, passion and extraordinary depth of feeling, the duet in the last act is the finest love duet ever written. *Ratcliff* was given only nine performances and has never been revived in the fourteen years since then. Thus, once again, we see a repetition of the shameful treatment accorded the operas of Glinka and Dargomïzhsky. Even the most worthless Italian, French, German or Russian operas have never suffered such a fate in our country.

Nevertheless, like his great predecessors, Cui did not lose heart. Even though his magnificent creation was ignored he continued to compose. First he wrote several marvellous songs ("I love, though Silently", "Weary with Grief", and "Meniscus") and then, in 1875, his second opera *Angelo*. This opera is his most mature, his best work. The subject, tense, poignant and passionate, is better suited to Cui's temperament than that of *Ratcliff*. In terms of form it far surpasses the earlier opera. Following the example set by Dargomïzhsky in *The Stone Guest*, all the most important scenes contain melodic recitative, rich in dramatic effect, truth, feeling and passion. In the intensity and emotional expressiveness of this opera, Cui attained, it would seem, the very limits of creative inspiration. As in *Ratcliff*, the male characters are much more pallid and ordinary than the female, both of whom are perfectly drawn types—one, gentle, tender, submissive, loving; the other, strong, fiery, consumed with unbridled passion. Compared with these two characters, whose contrasting natures are so convincingly and sharply delineated, most other operatic heroines seem colourless. The only weak parts of the opera are the folk scenes and those which require comedy.

After *Angelo* Cui composed only one work of comparable perfection and maturity—a song to Mickiewicz's poem "Although We Had to Part". It was painted, so to speak, with colours from the palette used for his second opera. None of his most recent works, whether vocal or instrumental, has attained such a high level. However, in his "children's songs" one finds much that is charming. Undoubtedly in his next, his third opera he will reveal himself anew in the full power of his mature talent.

In 1864, Cui began to work as a music critic and here, too, he showed considerable ability. His sparkling, witty articles in the *S.-Peterburgskiye Vedomosti* proved very helpful to the cause of our new music. They denounced reaction and conservatism, assailed the backward taste of the public and narrow views of the critics (including Serov) and pointed out the importance of our new school. These articles reflected the thoughts and ideas of the school, especially of its leader Balakirev. Cui's bold and independent evaluations of many of the earlier, classical musicians, long regarded as great and, as it were, sacrosanct, incensed many people, particularly the reactionary and conservative elements of the public and in the conservatories. These opponents of the new school began to label its exponents "musical nihilists", "musical Slavophiles", "radicals". They accused them of an utter contempt for the rest of musical Europe, which, in reality, was not true. Furthermore, in their writings they tried to convince the public that our young composers were antagonistic towards learning and training, that they shunned everything European and wanted to erect upon the ruins of earlier music only their own works, the fruit of self-taught ignoramuses. These enemies of our school bitterly denounced all its works, its predilection for programme music, its realism, and even its brilliant orchestration, which strove to achieve the breadth and fullness of Berlioz and Liszt. Mr. Famintsyn, for example, wrote:

Side by side with a patriotic fervour which preaches the idea that music has had its day in Europe and can hope to progress only in Russia, there has also been developing of late, among some of our composers and critics, a kind of hatred for the West and an extraordinary liking for everything Eastern. Ever since *Ruslan*, almost every Russian composer has tried to write something "eastern", meaning by this anything that is bizarre, strange—in a word, not European. . . . Many people think that we already have Russian instrumental music and they even call it "national". But is music necessarily national because its themes are derived from trivial dance songs which automatically call to mind disgusting scenes in front of a drinking house? If that is "nationalism", then we can indeed boast of a Russian national music, for we have quite a number of trepaks of various kinds in this style [meaning all the trite dance songs of the common people—V.S.]. We have several Russian trepaks, a Cossack, a Czech and a Serbian trepak, and in time we shall most likely also have a Tatar, a Georgian, perhaps an Ossetian trepak and others as well . . . (*Golos*, 12th December, 1867, No. 343).

These contemptuous remarks were aimed at many of our composers' best instrumental works; Glinka's *Kamarinskaya*; Dargomïzhsky's *Cossack Fantasy* and *Finnish Fantasy*; Balakirev's *Czech Overture* and *A Thousand Years*; Rimsky-Korsakov's *Serbian Fantasy*. Such were the views and taste of the reactionaries. Others (such as Laroche) were forever preaching that it was most important to study zealously fugue and all kinds of archaic, scholastic forms used by the composers of the Middle Ages. In the name of olden times, they demanded servile respect not only for the Josquins des Prés and Goudimels of the fifteenth and sixteenth centuries but also for the Dalayracs of the eighteenth century; they persistently tried to inculcate our country with the narrow views of the most mediocre German writers on music, such as Hanslick and others (*Russkii Vestnik*, July, 1869, etc.). Still others, like Rostislav, headed a "special committee on music" of the Russian Musical Society for the express purpose of "protecting the purity of music", "encouraging eclecticism", and "checking the pernicious influence of those who deny the value of study" (*Golos*, 28th December, 1869, No. 357).

These obsolete ideas, lies, nonsensical and slanderous charges had to be exposed in all their ugliness, and this Cui did with true talent—in a lively, entertaining, spirited and bold fashion. Many people did not like his articles but everybody enjoyed reading them. Most of our enemies dreaded them, and this, of course, was the highest possible compliment that could be given them, for it proved that they were achieving their aim. But around 1874, Cui's writing changed considerably. He became less bold, gave way on many of his views, repudiated some, modified some, withdrew others, and began to find talent in many undeserving musicians and works. In short, from an exponent of progress he became an exponent of moderate, even excessively moderate liberalism. His criteria in matters of musical composition—form, melody, harmony and rhythm—began to approximate to those of the conservatives. On the whole, his standards deteriorated and in many respects sank to the level of the commonplace. Our enemies immediately noted this change and gleefully pointed it out to the public. Since then, unfortunately, Cui's influence has waned and his articles on music are no longer respected as before. Actually, however, the cause of the new school has lost nothing as a result; it has already established itself and stands firmly on its own feet. It no longer needs to propagandize its ideas; they are not only well known, but they constitute the very foundation of the new period of Russian music. The achievements of our national school are increasingly becoming the property not only of all our musicians but of our society as a whole.

The third person to join the Balakirev group was Mussorgsky. Together with Dargomïzhsky, he is the chief exponent of musical realism in our country. In this respect the character of his art is clearly defined and is achieving major importance. Like Dargomïzhsky he was a born dramatist and throughout his career was interested primarily in vocal composition. He wrote little for orchestra, even though he sometimes displayed talent and originality in this medium. At the outset his teacher and counsellor was Balakirev. Under his guidance Mussorgsky became acquainted with musical form and the best musical literature. During this period he composed several instrumental pieces, the most noteworthy of which are the Scherzo in B minor[1] and *The Witches, or Night on the Bare Mountain*, the latter inspired by the fantastic works of Berlioz and Liszt (*La Reine Mab, Totentanz*, etc.). Later he also wrote the *March of the Slav Princes* for the opera-ballet *Mlada* and the Persian dances for *Khovanshchina*. Nevertheless, it is Mussorgsky's works for voice that hold the central place in his art. His gift for this medium of expression was extraordinary. He was not interested, however, in writing in the usual operatic and song style; to him, as to Dargomïzhsky, this kind of writing seemed too artificial and stylized to express life and reality. He felt the need for that realism, that approximation of human speech in music which Dargomïzhsky had striven for and which can be achieved only through declamatory recitative.

"The artistic representation of beauty alone, in its material sense, is crude childishness—art in its infancy", he wrote to me in 1872.

"Life, wherever it manifests itself; truth, however bitter; bold, sincere speech—these are my leaven", he wrote in 1875.

"I am trying to outline as sharply as possible the changes of intonation that occur in the course of the characters' conversation, seemingly for the most trivial reasons, in the most insignificant words. Herein, it seems to me, lies the secret of Gogol's powerful humour," Mussorgsky wrote to Cui in 1868 regarding his opera *The Marriage*, based on Gogol's comedy.

[1] Stasov has here confused two orchestral works: the Scherzo in B flat and the *Intermezzo in modo classico*, which is in B minor.—G.A.

This was the very thing that Dargomïzhsky had wanted and had tried to do. In his approach to vocal composition Mussorgsky owed a great deal to Dargomïzhsky, with whom he formed a close friendship while still a youth. He dedicated "Yeremushka's Lullaby", one of the finest songs he wrote in the sixties, to Dargomïzhsky with the inscription: "To the great teacher of musical truth". But in carrying out his ideas, Mussorgsky went even further in some respects than his predecessor and teacher. This is true, particularly, of his depiction of various types, characters and scenes from Russian life and of the way he extended the boundaries of the little vocal pieces which, in accordance with the earlier custom, are still called "romances". Dargomïzhsky was, clearly, a national composer. He was born in a village; he made a deep study of our folk music, understood and loved it. He portrayed many aspects of the life of the people with great talent and realism (for example, the matchmaker in *Rusalka*; the chorus "Weave the Fence"; the songs "The Titular Counsellor", "The Worm" and "As the Peasant Came from Behind the Hill"). But his greatest masterpiece, *The Stone Guest,* and many of his best works, such as the choruses from *Rogdana* and the songs "The Paladin" and "O Maid my Rose", have nothing whatsoever to do with Russian life, and their wondrous drama, feeling, poetry and beauty are totally unrelated to it.

All of Mussorgsky's greatest works, on the other hand, are Russian to the core; his main strength and inspiration came from Russian life and the Russian folk. He was born on an estate and spent his entire childhood and adolescence far from the capital.[1] The impressions he received during this period left an indelible mark on him and formed his artistic personality. It was the ordinary Russian people who were nearest and dearest to him, and he drew them with matchless truthfulness, simplicity and naturalness. His are not abstract Russians; he was ten times more faithful to "history" than Dargomïzhsky, Glinka or any of our other composers, for that matter. True, he never achieved the sweep and epic grandeur of Glinka, but when it came to "historical realism", he surpassed the best that Glinka ever did in this vein. The scenes and people in *Boris Godunov* are far more "historical" and real than any of those in *A Life for the Tsar*, which are highly idealized and in some cases drawn sketchily. All in all, *Boris Godunov* represents a major advance in opera. Every character in it is more lifelike and more truly Russian than any ever before portrayed in opera. Dargomïzhsky understood this fully and he said many times that Mussorgsky would go further than he had in expressing the true spirit of our people. It was exactly the same with Mussorgsky's "romances". He extended the boundaries of this genre far beyond their earlier limits. His are no longer "romances"; they are veritable scenes from operas or music dramas which might readily be performed in a theatrical setting—with

[1] Actually he went to Petersburg at the age of ten.—G.A.

costumes, scenery and all. Mussorgsky did not even attempt to treat the limited (though often beautiful and touching) subjects to which most Russian composers both before and after him confined themselves. Love themes did not satisfy his artistic needs, and from the moment he began to compose, he broke out of this enchanted circle. He shunned the overworked theme of ideal love and turned to other, new subjects which the life around us offers in incredible abundance.

"One can safely say," I stated in my biography of Mussorgsky, "that his songs will never grow old but will always be treasured by the Russian people. Each of them is a vignette of the people's life, their sufferings and joys, their humdrum, everyday existence."

The grim, terrible tragedy which unfolds in the magnificent palace of the dying Tsar Boris; the agony of the pitiful, drunken muzhik freezing to death in the blizzard-ridden depths of the forest; the wit and humour in dozens of scenes drawn from all levels of life; the exuberant gaiety, revelry, even, occasionally, the broad sweep of a Russian epic—all this makes Mussorgsky's songs and operas the equal of many of Gogol's greatest creations.

The content of Mussorgsky's songs and his operas *Boris Godunov* and *Khovanshchina* is so rich, the characters so varied, that it would be impossible to examine them in detail here. They constitute an entire world, embodied in music with extraordinary genius, power and originality. Both individuals and masses of people pass before us in a multitude of scenes encompassing the widest possible range of human feeling and experience. Tsars and simpletons, muzhiks, boyars and monks, old peasant women and princesses, sextons and police officers, young ladies, functionaries and nurses, *streltsi* and Old Believers, innkeepers, seminarists, and a host of others form a rich national gallery, the like of which is not to be found in any other opera anywhere. Children, drawn with a realism that fully reveals all the subtle nuances of their infinitely rich natures, appear in many tender little scenes which comprise a whole separate work entitled *The Nursery*. No one before Mussorgsky ever treated this appealing and varied little world in music so faithfully and convincingly.

Mussorgsky's first opera *Boris Godunov* received its initial performance early in 1874 in a comparatively favourable climate. By then the public had learned to understand and appreciate Glinka's operas and Dargomïzhsky's *Rusalka*; they had heard *William Ratcliff*, *The Maid of Pskov* and *The Stone Guest*, as well as many of Mussorgsky's songs, which had been sung at concerts. Little by little they had grown accustomed to the new style of music. Consequently, when *Boris Godunov* was performed, the audience was much better educated or, at least, better prepared for it than they had been before. Moreover, the realism (so rare in opera) of Mussorgsky's expressive means made a deep impression on many listeners who had not yet been completely ruined by Italian music. A considerable section of the more cultivated among them not only liked Mussorgsky's opera—they were enthusiastic about it, a phenomenon which is rare, in fact, altogether unheard of in our country. What impressed them most, as might have been expected, were the profoundly original and realistic scenes from Russian history: the scene of the people, under the lash, imploring Boris to assume the throne; the scene of the monk Varlaam and the soldiers in the inn; and that of the people taunting the captured boyar. But the critics and the opera management were dead set against this truly national work and they did everything possible to thwart its success. The critics talked about Mussorgsky's musical ignorance and blunders, his brazen violation of academic rules and practices, his excessive realism, and the "ugliness" of his musical workmanship. In short, they showed themselves totally incapable of understanding Mussorgsky's brilliant innovation, the newness of his aims and the depth of his musical expression. All they cared about were the rules of composition. Those in charge of the production also treated the composer like a stepson. One of them, the conductor,[1] no less, gave the lines of individual characters to the chorus,[2] and cut the best and most characteristic passages of the opera; others omitted altogether some of the most important scenes (as had once been done with *Rusalka*), such as the one in Pimen's cell and the one in which the enraged people jeer at the boyar Kruschov. Finally, *Boris* was withdrawn, even though after the death of the highly gifted singer O. A. Petrov, the original Varlaam, this wonderful role was performed brilliantly by Stravinsky.[3]

Mussorgsky's second opera, *Khovanshchina*, suffered an even worse fate. The theatre committee, which was composed of poorly trained opera singers and an inartistic conductor, rejected it and never permitted it to be staged. Obliged to abide by the decision of a few artisans, the public was deprived of the right to hear the opera and judge for themselves. What an outrageous and arbitrary way to treat the creation of a genius! Nowhere else in Europe would mediocre hacks be allowed to meddle freely in a field that is alien to them, the field of art! Those who condemned *Khovanshchina* on the grounds that there were enough operas with "radical" music did not know what they were doing. They did not understand that realistic opera is the opera of the future and that Dargomïzhsky and Mussorgsky were the immortal creators of this great manner of expression which will someday be adopted by the entire musical world.

Among Mussorgsky's most original compositions are the two satires,

[1] Mr. Napravnik.

[2] In Scene 1 of the Prologue, the scene on the square; in Act IV, the scene of the Duma, etc.

[3] The father of the composer.—G.A.

The Classicist and *The Peep Show*, in which he attempted to draw musical sketches of our reactionaries and the foes of the new school. These essays in a new musical genre proved to be both masterly and successful. The humour, wit, acerbity and novelty of these little portraits astonished our entire musical world, from the public to the very reactionaries they caricatured. Two editions of *The Peep Show* were soon sold out.

Like all other composers of the new school, Mussorgsky wrote a number of splendid works incorporating eastern elements. His "Hebrew Song", two Hebrew choruses ("Destruction of Sennacherib" and "Jesus Navinus"), Jewish types in the piano cycle *Pictures from an Exhibition*, and Persian Dances from *Khovanschchina* are all ingenious and wonderful creations.

Mussorgsky died in 1881 at the very peak of his powers and talent but without ever realizing to the full all the potentialities of his great genius. Illness and a nervous disorder, disappointments and poverty struck him down before his time. Indeed, they curtailed his creative activity during the last two or three years of his life.

The fourth composer to become affiliated with the new school was Rimsky-Korsakov. His artistic development and activity resembled that of Balakirev in many respects. First of all, like Balakirev he was self-taught; even though in his youth he benefited greatly from Balakirev's advice, suggestions and criticism, he learned the rudiments of music on his own and developed and perfected his rich gift for orchestration through his own efforts. Secondly, both he and Balakirev compiled excellent, truly exemplary collections of Russian folk songs which had and are still having an enormous influence on the new Russian school and will certainly exert an even greater influence on future generations of Russian composers. Finally, over a period of many years both of them—first Balakirev and later Rimsky-Korsakov—directed the Free School of Music and conducted its concerts; that is, they were both leaders of the new musical movement. Nevertheless, despite these general similarities in their activities, the talent of Rimsky-Korsakov was quite distinctive and unique.

By temperament and inclination Rimsky-Korsakov was primarily a symphonist and orchestral composer. Even so, his songs and operas rank among the most important works of the new school. By some miracle his earliest compositions—a symphony (the first ever written by a Russian),[1] an overture, and several songs won immediate acceptance. The charming, highly lyrical symphonic poem *Sadko* (1867) also found favour with the public and even certain critics. Even in 1869, Serov was still expatiating in the *Journal de S. Pétersbourg* on its poetic quality and masterful orchestration. This piece led other critics to launch an attack on Rimsky-Korsakov, however. Thus, Mr. Famintsyn, who had just returned to

[1] This is one of the most commonly repeated of Stasov's errors.—G.A.

Russia imbued with the routine ideas he had acquired while studying at the Leipzig Conservatory and with various German professors, filled column upon column in the newspapers with disquisitions on the "triviality" and "banality" of this music, asserting that the disgraceful things found in *Sadko* were impermissible and that if its author persisted in introducing such things into music he "must give up all pretensions to the title of composer" (*Golos*, 12th December, 1867, No. 343). When Rimsky-Korsakov wrote his second symphony *Antar* (1868) and following this, the opera *The Maid of Pskov* (1871), the public and critics alike deserted their former favourite and turned their backs on him. All the beauty, descriptiveness and wondrous poetic quality of the symphony, all the might and power expressed in its scherzo (an amazing portrayal of savage hordes locked in dread conflict) proved utterly beyond their comprehension. It was exactly the same with *The Maid of Pskov*: the charm of its varied scenes produced no effect upon either the audience or critics. They remained deaf and blind to it. They understood none of the beauty and majesty of the choruses (particularly the magnificent one with which the people greet Ivan the Terrible and the one with which the opera concludes); nothing of the splendid scene of the *veche* (popular assembly); nothing of the nurse's fairy tale, that extraordinary epic masterpiece; nothing of the profoundly poetic scene in the forest (introduction to Act V)[1] nor of the character Matuta, which is drawn with such fidelity, wit and humour. All this was either missed or ignored. Even Rimsky-Korsakov's colourful orchestration counted for nothing. The only thing the public and critics were able to observe and understand was that the opera lacked dramatic interest.

The excellent songs which date from this period—"Night", "The Secret", and "Hebrew Song" (1868) "I Believe I Am Loved" and "To My Song" (1870)—are even now virtually unknown here. Each of them possesses that lyrical beauty which characterizes all of Rimsky-Korsakov's songs. "To My Song", we might add in passing, is suffused as well with ardour and passion.

Rimsky-Korsakov's second opera, *May Night*, contains much that is beautiful. Most remarkable of all is the fantastic element which the composer clothes in wondrous colouristic effects—the game of "raven" and the water nymphs' *khorovod* (choral dance) in the last act. All of the choruses are charming and the humour which pervades throughout is delightful. However, in many respects *May Night* is inferior to the *Maid of Pskov,* and for this reason the public preferred it.

Two splendid orchestral pieces, the Overture on Russian Themes and *Legend* (based on Pushkin's prologue to *Ruslan and Ludmila*), went almost completely unnoticed.

[1] A mistake for Act IV, which is equivalent to Act III of the definitive version of the opera.—G.A.

Rimsky-Korsakov's third opera, *The Snow Maiden* (1881), a true masterpiece and his most mature work, has never received the acclaim it deserves. It was so magnificent, so nearly perfect that it met the same fate that all our best musical works had before it: the public was indifferent to it, in some cases even hostile. Nevertheless, some of its passages are worthy of Glinka and *Ruslan*, and others attain the heights of the best music ever written anywhere. Among these are the "seeing out of Butterweek", an astonishingly imaginative and effective depiction of the ancient pagan rite; the scene of the magic metamorphoses in the forest (Act IV); the wonderfully lyrical picture of the coming of Spring; the "melting away" of the Snow Maiden; Kupava's impassioned incantation to the bees and hops; and the comic scenes of Bobyl and Bobylikha. In his scoring Rimsky-Korsakov often achieves even greater beauty and a subtler variety of colours than he had in any of his previous works. All in all, *The Snow Maiden* is one of the major musical creations of our century.

Among Rimsky-Korsakov's other important contributions to music are the wonderful orchestrations he made of *The Stone Guest* and *Khovanshchina* after the death of their composers.[1]

The fifth and last person to join our group of composers was Borodin. He was twenty-eight years old at the time (the eldest of the group) and by no means a novice in music. Until then he had been a "rabid Mendelssohnist" and had been interested mainly in chamber music, in which he had played the cello at the homes of friends. His entry into the Balakirev circle in 1862 brought about a decisive change in him. As in the case of the others, Balakirev strongly influenced his musical education and helped him, within a short time, to develop his talent to the full. During the twenty years that followed Borodin composed works which, though far less in number than those of his colleagues, almost without exception bear the imprint of maturity and perfection. Nothing he wrote is poor; the weakest, perhaps, are his string quartets, but even they contain passages of marked talent.

Borodin's prodigious gift expressed itself equally well in the symphonic, operatic and vocal genres. The principal stylistic features of his music are giant strength and breadth, colossal sweep, drive and dynamism combined with astonishing beauty, tenderness and depth of feeling. His gift for humour and declamatory settings matched that of Dargomizhsky and Mussorgsky. In certain parts of his unfinished opera *Prince Igor* he displayed the same inimitable ability for comedy as these two, his models and teachers in this medium. However, he rejected the progressive forms employed in *The Stone Guest, Boris Godunov* and *Khovanshchina*

[1] Later, Rimsky-Korsakov also orchestrated Mussorgsky's *Night on the Bare Mountain* and some numbers from *Boris Godunov*. [This, of course, was written before he made his complete version of the opera.—G.A.]

and for the most part adhered to the earlier symmetrical forms—arias, duets, etc. It was exactly the same with his symphonies. Even though with his extraordinary talent Borodin could easily have adopted the new, free, completely asymmetrical form first originated by Liszt in his *Symphonische Dichtungen*—the most characteristic feature of modern orchestral music—he did not want to align himself with the radical innovators but preferred to adhere to established tradition. This devotion to the old forms, and a certain, at times excessive thickness in his writing are the chief, indeed, virtually the only defects in his music. Nevertheless, within the limits of traditional forms, Borodin manifested, in opera as well as in his symphonies and songs, a creative power and inspiration seldom matched in all of music.

Like that of Glinka, Borodin's music is epic in the broadest sense of the word, and as "national" as any written by the best composers of the Russian school. The eastern element plays as large and important a rôle in his works as it does in those of Glinka, Dargomïzhsky, Balakirev, Mussorgsky and Rimsky-Korsakov. By temperament Borodin was one of those composers who feel the need for a programmatic basis in their music; like Glinka he might have said: "My unbridled imagination has need of a text or concrete facts." Both of his symphonies are magnificent; both are unusually original, vigorous, passionate and exciting. Yet the second (1872) is even greater than the first, not only because it is more mature but because it is thoroughly Russian and programmatic. In it we sense the flavour of an ancient Russian epic; in mood and character it is akin to the composer's opera *Prince Igor*. We can almost discern, in the adagio, the figure of a bard and, in the finale, the warriors' sumptuous feasting and revelry.[1]

The wealth of characters and personages in *Prince Igor*, the abundance of Russian folk song and eastern (Polovtsian) elements, the alternating tragedy and comedy, passion, love and humour, splendid characterization and depiction of scenes from nature—all these make Borodin's opera (which recreates dramatically the most representative scenes from the *Lay of Igor*) a monumental achievement in the history of Russian music, related, in power and originality, to Glinka's *Ruslan* in some respects, to Mussorgsky's *Boris Godunov* in others, yet fresh, original and striking throughout. Borodin's tone poem *On the Steppes of Central Asia* (1880) is one of the most poetic works ever written. In this, as in everything he composed for orchestra, Borodin's brilliant, colourful scoring matches the brilliance of his creative ideas.

Finally, Borodin's songs, unfortunately few in number, also bear the stamp of a rare talent. "My Song is Fierce and Bitter" (1868) is a wonderful outburst of passion, like a flash of lightning falling from heaven, setting the heart on fire. "The Sleeping Princess" (1867) and "The Queen of

[1] Borodin himself drew my attention to this.

the Sea" (1868) are epic pictures painted in the same charming colours as Glinka's song "She Is My Life" and the fairy tale from Rimsky-Korsakov's *Maid of Pskov*. In its breadth and power "The Song of the Dark Forest" (1868) is a veritable heroic chorus from some opera. "The Sea" (1870) presents another picture drawn with the fervour of a giant's brush. In the opinion of some, this is the most magnificent song in all of European music. "The False Note" (1868), which strikes one at first as a mere trifle, is a witty, caustic, graceful satire quite in the spirit of Heine.

As was to be expected, Borodin's wonderful creations, his symphonies and songs, like all the other wonderful music of our new school, have remained till now virtually unknown here. The Russian public prefers the most ordinary products of the foreign or domestic muse. For their part, the critics have regarded Borodin's works with scepticism or aversion; Serov treated them with scorn and hatred.

It was inevitable that the musical fellowship of such highly gifted men as Balakirev, Cui, Mussorgsky, Rimsky-Korsakov and Borodin—their joint development, growth and creativity, mutual influence and assistance—would yield major results. United by a common outlook and common understanding, by identical likes and dislikes, by commonly shared study of and admiration for the great composers of the West, these five Russian musicians worthily continued and expanded the work begun by Glinka and Dargomïzhsky.

They appeared before the public as a group in a variety of ways. First of all, their views and outlook were set forth in a series of articles which Cui wrote for the *S.-Peterburgskiye Vedomosti* during the years 1864 to 1874. Secondly, in 1872, four of them—Mussorgsky, Rimsky-Korsakov, Cui and Borodin—collaborated on an opera entitled *Mlada*, commissioned by the then Director of the Imperial Theatres, S. A. Gedeonov, who wrote the libretto. This opera was never performed but scenes and parts of it (composed individually but in an identical spirit) were subsequently incorporated into others of the composers' works and rank among their most important creations.[1] In 1878 Borodin, Rimsky-Korsakov, Cui and a gifted young colleague, Lyadov (who will be discussed later) collaborated on the *Paraphrases*, a series of variations and short pieces by turns serious, comic, impassioned, graceful, all based on a set theme. This ingenious musical joke was very well received here (two editions were quickly sold out), especially after the publication of a

[1] For example, Rimsky-Korsakov used his marvellous "kolo" (*khorovod*) for the water nymphs' *khorovod* in *May Night*: Mussorgsky turned the "Procession of the Slav Princes" into an orchestral piece *Marcia alla Turca* and used the fantastic scene of "The Offering to the Black Goat" for the "scene on the bare mountain" in his third opera *The Fair at Sorochintsy*; the entire fourth act of *Mlada*, composed by Borodin, was incorporated in the most important passages of his *Prince Igor*. [The last statement is not quite accurate.—G.A.]

letter from Liszt, expressing his sincere, high regard for the authors' inventiveness and technical skill. Finally, at the initiative of Glinka's sister L. I. Shestakova, Balakirev and Rimsky-Korsakov, again in collaboration with Lyadov, prepared an edition of the enormous scores of *A Life for the Tsar* and *Ruslan and Ludmila*. This was a major contribution. These two operas of genius, which our composers of the new school have always regarded as the sacred testament of Russian national music, will certainly continue to be regarded as such by our future generations of musicians.

At this point mention must also be made of two gifted women who played an important rôle in the fortunes of the new Russian school. These were the Purgold sisters, both of whom were exceptionally talented musicians and quite unique among the multitude of women who pursued this art in the days of Glinka and Dargomïzhsky, or, in fact, who pursue it today. The elder sister, Alexandra Nikolayevna (Alexandra Molas, by marriage) was a singer who was taught first by Dargomïzhsky and later by Mussorgsky. Her singing style, not being of the conventional operatic variety, was excellently suited to the interpretation of honest and unaffected music, whether passionate, tragic, comic or tender—to the recitative style which forms the basis of all the songs and much of the operas written by our new school. Indeed, her singing was so true to the spirit of the music that now and then one of these composers would say that his work had two authors—himself and the performer. The other sister, Nadezhda Nikolayevna (later the wife of Rimsky-Korsakov), was not only more highly educated musically than any of our other women engaged in music; she not only had an instinctive grasp of music and its forms but she was, herself, a gifted composer. Her compositions include an orchestral fantasy *Night*, based on Gogol's story *St. John's Eve*, and a piano fantasy. She transcribed many of her friends' orchestral compositions for piano four-hands and orchestrated several passages of *The Maid of Pskov*. Moreover, even while she was still under Dargomïzhsky's tutelage, she was such an excellent accompanist that Mussorgsky constantly referred to her as "our orchestra". From the end of the sixties and beginning of the seventies, the Purgold sisters took part in preliminary readings of all the songs and operas being composed by the members of the group and afterwards also participated in full rehearsals of their works.

At first the group gathered mostly at the home of Glinka's sister, L. I. Shestakova; later they met at the houses of the Purgold sisters' uncle. These homes were like small academies of music. *The Stone Guest*, *Ratcliff*, *The Maid of Pskov*, *Boris Godunov*, *Angelo*, some of *Khovanshchina* and all the groups' songs and instrumental works were performed at these small gatherings.

VI

In the mid-sixties, another of our extremely gifted musicians—Tchaikovsky—embarked upon his career, quite independently of the new school. Although his was a very great talent, his taste—influenced by his conservatory training—became too eclectic and undiscriminating and this adversely affected his works. At first he was very sympathetic to the composers of the national school and their new artistic trend, so much so that in 1869 he wrote an article expressing bitter indignation over Balakirev's dismissal as conductor of the Russian Musical Society's concerts. Later, however, he moved further and further away from the new school and closer to the leaders of the conservatories and the Russian Musical Society.

By temperament Tchaikovsky was an orchestral composer; his best works are programme works in this medium. His overtures *Romeo and Juliet, The Tempest* and *Francesca da Rimini* rank among the outstanding creations of modern music. The element of love predominates in all three pieces and it is expressed with wondrous poetry. This is not passionate, impetuous love but a love that is tender and deep-felt, sometimes (as in *Francesca da Rimini*) suffused with regret and poignant memories.

Tchaikovsky has not always been successful in handling folk material, but he has created one masterpiece in this idiom—the finale of his Symphony in C minor, based on the Ukrainian folk-song "The Crane". In terms of colour, *facture* and humour this movement (in C major) is one of the most important creations of the entire Russian School. Another of Tchaikovsky's programme works in the national vein is the splendid String Quartet No. 3, written in memory of his friend and fellow-musician, the violinist Laub. Particularly noteworthy is the third movement (*andante funèbre*) which contains an instrumental recitative in the style of Russian chant with a sombre funereal cast. The Scherzo, too, is excellent in its humour and originality.

Tchaikovsky has also composed a large number of non-programmatic instrumental works. Many of them possess superb qualities, especially the Second String Quartet, which is splendid throughout and has an exceptionally fine scherzo.

It is in vocal composition that Tchaikovsky has proved least gifted. He has written a number of operas but hardly anything worthy of note. His works in this form are simply a succession of errors, blunders and misconceptions. He even attempted to set one, *Vakula the Smith* (after Gogol's story *Christmas Eve*), in the style of the new Russian school, that is, in the declamatory style of Dargomïzhsky and Mussorgsky, but he failed completely, largely because of his utter inability to write recitatives. Lack of discrimination in the choice of material, ordinary, at times banal themes, and hurried, slipshod workmanship also contributed to making *Vakula the Smith* as undistinguished as all the rest of Tchaikovsky's operas. This did not, however, prevent the Russian Musical Society from awarding it a prize in a competition for the best setting of Gogol's story. The other operas, written in a variety of styles, old and new, display skill in the handling of form and expert craftsmanship, but they totally lack the quality of genuine creativity and inspiration because of the composer's continuous, endless overwriting and his lack of self-criticism. The same is true of Tchaikovsky's songs. All these are competent works but they are mediocre and, unfortunately, often trite in terms of melodic content and effects.

In this respect Tchaikovsky is a disciple of Anton Rubinstein, his former teacher at the Conservatory. Rubinstein, in his youth and throughout his mature years, was not simply a first-rate pianist—he was an absolutely phenomenal one. Not content with this, for more than a quarter of a century, he sought to win the same laurels for his compositions that he had won so deservedly for his matchless piano playing. But his creative ability and inspiration in no way equalled his performing talent, and few of the many works he has written in all genres (operas, songs, symphonies, trios, duets, quartets, quintets, sextets, etc.) has ever risen above mediocrity. The exceptions have been, first of all, some compositions incorporating Eastern elements (such as the *Persian Songs* and the dances from the operas *The Demon* and *Feramors*: here at times he even achieved something noteworthy, interesting and original); secondly, some works of a humorous cast (such as *Don Quixote*); and thirdly, a few, though very few, scherzos (such as the truly marvellous one in 5/4 time in the F major String Quartet). Rubinstein had no talent whatsoever for writing in the Russian national style. This is clearly evident even in his comparatively more successful musical portrait *Ivan the Terrible*, a piece which is about as "Russian" as something a foreigner might casually dash off on a Russian subject.

Tchaikovsky is an incomparably more gifted composer than Rubinstein, but, as in the case of his teacher, the Conservatory, academic training, eclecticism and overworking of musical materials laid its dread, destructive hand on him. Of his total output, a few works are first-rate and highly original; the remainder are mediocre or weak.

VII

The noble work of the group is still being carried on even though two of them—Mussorgsky and Borodin—have been struck down by premature death. The others, now in their mature years, are continuing along the path charted for them in their youth. But they are not alone. In recent years they have been joined by new colleagues, worthy successors and fellow-champions of their cause.

Our most recent composers, who share the artistic aspirations of the group, have produced excellent works both instrumental and vocal. It might be noted, however, that thus far, with one exception, they have favoured instrumental rather than vocal composition. The single exception is Lodïzhensky. This gifted composer, whose music first attracted attention as early as the end of the sixties and beginning of the seventies, composes only for the voice. His songs are suffused with poetry, beauty and intense passion. Examples of this are "Again I Am With Thee", "Entreaty", "I have Died of Happiness", "Dawn", and "My Tears Are Flowing". Despite the excellence of these songs, however, our public considers them unworthy of attention and ignores them. Of course, they will just as stubbornly ignore Lodïzhensky's most recent set of four charming songs entitled *Requiem for Love*; of course, they will also long ignore his wondrously lyrical *Rusalka* (for voice and orchestra), just as they do all the most exquisite, the finest songs of our new school. At present it is difficult to tell whether Lodïzhensky will ever write any instrumental music.

While Lodïzhensky's colleagues have also produced many noteworthy vocal compositions, it is primarily in the field of instrumental music that they have exhibited their real talent. Thus, although a few of Shcherbachev's many songs, such as "Asra", "Der Schneidergeselle" and, above all, "Vergiftet sind meine Lieder" are truly remarkable, his piano compositions *Valse-caprice, Zigzags* and *Pantomimes et féeries*—a series of vignettes charged with poetic feeling and emotional depth—are much more remarkable, more original and far superior to them.

The same holds true of Lyadov. He, too, has composed some marvellous songs, among them "Someone's Poor Grave", which is outstanding in its beauty and warmth of feeling. But, again, his instrumental works are incomparably better and more original. He began as a devoted follower of Schumann and his earliest piano pieces, the *Biryulki* and *Arabesques*, bear traces of Schumann's influence. Even some of the pieces which constitute the *Biryulki*, however, are fresh and highly original as, for example, No. 6 in 5/4 time, which has Russian overtones. Somewhat later, in the *Paraphrases*, Lyadov displayed greater self-assurance and independence. Here, despite the hazards of working alongside older colleagues, he showed extraordinary originality in his charming, graceful waltz and even more in the majestic *Procession* which brings this unique collaborative work to a glorious conclusion. Lyadov's talent achieves still freer and more mature expression in his *Intermezzi* (the most important of which are those in the keys of B flat, D and C). Here every trace of outside influence has disappeared, and the composer's own musical personality stands forth in its full strength and beauty. In essence, these seeming "little" pieces are symphonic and orchestral in character. There is good reason to expect large-scale symphonic works from one so richly endowed with musical ideas and a sense of form. For that matter, even before the best of the *Intermezzi*, besides his marvellous orchestral *Scherzo*, Lyadov composed something which gave every indication that he was destined to become a major composer. This was a setting of part of Schiller's *Bride of Messina*, written for his final examination at the Conservatory in 1879. Both the recitatives and duet from this work are splendid and reveal a singular creative gift. At the same time, the concluding chorus, "Requiem", evinces a depth of feeling, a breadth and profundity of expression which relate it to the amazing "Requiem" from Schumann's *Manfred*.

The last to join the ranks of our young composers is Glazunov. His truly astonishing, enormous gift for composition revealed itself at once, in his very early years, when he was still little more than a child. He was only a youth of thirteen when he began his theoretical studies with Rimsky-Korsakov, but it became evident within a few months that this youth was progressing at a much faster rate than any of his great predecessors had at that age. Indeed, he assimilated the principles and techniques of music so quickly that by the time he reached eighteen, he was already a true master of his art. Not only was he thoroughly acquainted with all the technical aspects of music and every great and important work that had ever been written but he was, himself, the author of a small library of compositions, so to speak. Unlike his predecessors and contemporaries, however, Glazunov has thus far shown little inclination to compose for the voice. He has done his best work in the sphere of instrumental music.

The first of Glazunov's compositions to be published was a string quartet (1883). Masterly in form and even more remarkable for its inspired musical ideas, it is the finest string quartet produced by the entire Russian school (except for Lyadov's marvellously lyrical quartet which, though begun some five years before, unfortunately, remains uncompleted). The year 1883 also saw the publication of a charming piano suite on the theme S–A–S–C–H–A (the diminutive of the composer's name, Alexander). These were by no means his first compositions, however; he had already written many other instrumental and piano works. A symphony and two overtures based on modern Greek themes (from Bourgault-Ducoudray's collection) have been performed publicly. In addition, Glazunov has also written a tone poem, *The Forest*, filled with magical colour and the supernatural phenomena of ancient Slavic mythology (forest spirits, water nymphs, will-o'-the-wisps); two programmatic orchestral suites, a Spanish serenade and a bolero. He has almost completed two full-blown symphonies, a Spanish overture, two other overtures—*Stenka Razin* and *The Tempest* (on Shakespeare's play),—[1] and several piano pieces. Given Glazunov's extraordinary creative gift, mastery of form, drive and facility of composition, one can be certain that all these works will soon be completed. The principal characteristics of his music thus far are an incredibly vast sweep, power, inspiration, wondrous beauty, rich fantasy, sometimes humour, sadness, passion, and always amazing clarity and freedom of form. The only defect in his writing is occasional repetitiveness and overabundance of detail, clearly the consequence of an excessively inflamed youthful imagination. Glazunov very often uses Russian and Eastern material and does so with great skill and imaginativeness. It seems certain that he will one day be the leader of our nationalist composers.

Our most recent composers have not escaped the fate which befell the founders of the Russian school—they are either disparaged or completely ignored. Our present music critics, worthy successors of the Rostislavs and Lenzes, Serovs and Laroches, Famintsyns and Manns in their hatred for this school and their total lack of understanding of the aims, innovations and gifts of its adherents, are very limited individuals, themselves unfulfilled or frustrated composers. They heap the same contempt and abuse upon our new generation of composers as their predecessors did upon Balakirev, Cui, Mussorgsky, Rimsky-Korsakov and Borodin. How different is the attitude of the leading musicians and critics of the West. Berlioz and Liszt, Saint-Saëns, von Bülow, Bourgault-Ducoudray, Daniel Bernard, Pougin, Riemann and many others have always treated the work of our new composers with genuine respect.

Foremost among the Europeans was Liszt, who continually voiced his belief in the great importance of the Russian school for the music of today as well as that of the future. He never tired of saying that it is only through the efforts of the modern French and Russian schools, especially the latter, that music will advance. Similar views were expressed repeatedly in German music journals after the performances of Rimsky-Korsakov's *Antar* at Magdeburg (1881) and Borodin's First Symphony at Baden-Baden (1880) and Leipzig (1883). German writers found not only "talent" but even "genius" in these works.[2] And only recently, on 1st June, 1883, one of Germany's leading music critics, Langhans, wrote in the journal *Der Klavier-Lehrer* that he has "long been saying in the German press that *young musical Russia* will without doubt soon become a dangerous rival of Germany in the struggle for musical supremacy," and that he is "becoming more and more convinced of this after hearing the most recent Russian works." But our wretched critics do not know and

[1] The Spanish overture and *The Tempest* overture are totally unknown, and not even mentioned in E. E. Yazovitskaya's very complete list of Glazunov's works (including unpublished juvenalia, etc.) in the collective two-volume work on the composer (Leningrad, 1959 and 1960).—G.A.

[2] Article on Borodin's Symphony in the Leipzig *Musikalisches Wochenblatt*, 9th July, 1880.

do not want to know this. Why, not long ago, one of them,[1] after hearing a symphony by Glazunov (a finished and mature master, despite his seventeen or eighteen years) advised him to go and study at some German conservatory or other, thus repeating exactly the advice given the nightingale in Krylov's fable: "Ah, what a pity you don't know our rooster—you'd come on quite a bit if you took a lesson or two from him."

In 1861, four years after Glinka's death, a few of his ardent admirers petitioned the Governor General of Petersburg, Prince Suvorov, for permission to place a bust of the composer on the stage on 27th November, the date of the anniversary performance of *A Life for the Tsar*. This petition was forwarded to the Tsar's Chamberlain who replied officially that "unfortunately this request cannot be granted because according to the records of the Imperial Theatres, no bust has ever been placed on a Russian stage, and also because it would be extremely awkward to set such a precedent, contrary to the regulations established by the Directorate of the Theatres, simply to comply with the wishes of private individuals."

That was twenty years ago and many things have changed since then. The requests and wishes of private individuals have begun to carry some weight. A bust of Glinka has been displayed on many occasions in the theatre and at concerts, and one is now installed permanently in the foyer of the Russian opera. What is more, a statue of Glinka now stands in the square of one Russian city, Smolensk. Who knows, perhaps in a few years the ideas, taste and sympathies of the public and its spokesmen, the music critics, will undergo a complete change and with that will also come a change in their attitude towards our new school of composers, the heirs of Glinka.

1882–83

[1] K. Haller.

VI. Liszt, Schumann and Berlioz in Russia

This is one of Stasov's most valuable writings on music and musicians: a long first-hand record of events and impressions, originally published in the *Severny Vestnik* (July and August, 1889), later separately with some revision in 1896. The numerous excerpts from letters and press-notices are fascinating in themselves. If Schumann's visit to Russia left no impression on his music and had no bearing on the influence his music was later to exercise on certain Russian composers—for instance, on Borodin and Lyadov—both Berlioz and Liszt not only influenced all Stasov's musical friends but were effective propagandists of Russian music in the West.

G.A.

FOR MANY reasons I would like to make public what I know about the visits of Liszt, Schumann and Berlioz to Russia and the relations of Liszt and Berlioz with the Russian musical world. First, of all the great Western musicians of our time, none has exerted such an enormous influence on our music and musicians as these three. Secondly, the present generation knows very little about their visits to Russia. Most of those who were alive at the time and actually saw them are gone and, of course, no one nowadays has the slightest notion of what the newspapers and magazines wrote about this forty years ago. Still less is known about the personal relations and correspondence between our composers and two of these Western musicians, namely Liszt and Berlioz. Thirdly, all three of them were in Russia during my lifetime and, as an eyewitness, I knew a great deal that was not known to others. Fourthly and finally, I have amassed a vast amount of relevant material, both printed and written—articles, letters, memoirs, etc.—most of which has never been published.

It was only a few years ago, after Berlioz' death, that the French musical world began to appreciate this great man. For many years, the French had either laughed at him or completely ignored him. Suddenly, during the seventies, all of musical and shortly afterward non-musical France remembered him. They became very excited about him. Concert programmes were filled with his works, and scores of admirers began busily collecting his letters and material about his life. One publisher issued an appeal in all the European press, asking that all of Berlioz' letters and other material relating to the composer be sent to him. Many people in various countries responded to this appeal, I among them. I gathered together all the letters I could find here in Russia and sent them to this publisher, Daniel Bernard. He included only a fraction of them in his book *Correspondance inédite de Berlioz* (Paris, 1879), however. Out of some strange caprice or simply from a failure to understand what he was about, he omitted a great deal of very important material that I had sent him. I then requested that he return everything to me and I turned it over to the French music critic and writer Octave Fouque, who was very pleased to publish it in his book *Les révolutionnaires de la musique* (Paris, 1882). Subsequently Jullien used some of this material in his extensive and now very famous work *Hector Berlioz, sa vie et ses oeuvres* (Paris, 1888). Unfortunately, it must be admitted that however painstakingly this book was compiled, however famous it may be, it leaves much to be desired, for the author has little understanding of music, he is biased, and therefore he has presented many things in a false light. Moreover, this book is practically unknown in our country.

As for Liszt, shortly after his death I wrote to his friend, the well-known German writer on music Marie Lipsius, who has published a number of musical biographies and collections of letters under the name of La Mara, suggesting that she collect and publish all of Liszt's letters. At the same time, I promised to send her all the letters that I could obtain in Russia. She agreed, and in the fall of 1893 this collection was published in Leipzig by the well-known music firm of Breitkopf and Härtel. The letters I collected far exceeded in number and importance anything that La Mara had dared hope for. Subsequently she several times expressed her surprise and gratitude to me.

Schumann never corresponded with any of the Russian musicians and knew nothing either about them or about Russian music. Nevertheless, there are interesting facts relating to his brief stay in Russia, and I shall present them as they are related in his correspondence with his German friends and relatives.

Having such a wealth of material at my disposal, I have decided to make use of it and, to begin with, to extract from it everything that helps to give a picture of the relationship of these three great composers of our century to the Russian school of music.

* * *

The first to appear in Russia was Liszt. He came to St. Petersburg in 1842, not only because at the time he was making a grand tour of Europe (which he had begun in 1840), but also because he had received several special invitations to come here. During his stay in Paris, he had become acquainted with various Russian families (among them the Obrezkovs), and as he was then a fashionable celebrity, many of them begged him not to forget to include Russia in his future tours.

Among the many concerts Liszt gave in Rome at the beginning of 1839, a particularly important one was that given at the home of Prince Dmitri Vladimirovich Golitsyn, the Governor General of Moscow who had been living there quite a long time. This concert had been arranged for charity by Count Mikhail Yurevich Vielgorsky, a well-known Russian music lover and amateur composer of the time. Included among the distinguished audience were a great many members of the Russian nobility, Roman cardinals and ambassadors from various countries. The most remarkable feature about this aristocratic concert was the fact that Liszt was the only performer; no singer or other instrumentalist appeared during the entire evening. In those days this was something altogether new. No one before Liszt had ever dared to give an entire concert alone, to attempt to hold the attention of a large gathering for a whole evening—and a gathering of capricious, spoiled unmusical aristocrats at that. Despite this, Liszt made a tremendous impression; he simply transported his listeners. It is not unlikely that some of the ecstatic Russians invited him once again to Petersburg.

During the following summer of 1840, Liszt gave a concert in Ems and spent three days there. Every evening he played for Empress Alexandra Fedorovna, who was also in Ems at the time.

The very first time Liszt was presented to the Empress [wrote his biographer Lina Ramann[1]], she asked him sternly, "How is it you have not yet been to Petersburg?" [The wife of Nicholas I, we might note, simply assumed that all European celebrities were eager to go to Petersburg and would consider themselves fortunate to appear there.] Then she pointed toward the piano and Liszt seated himself at it. But the instrument proved to be worse than bad—it was simply worthless—and with Liszt's powerful playing, the strings began to break one after the other. Everyone sat stiff and erect in accordance with the official tone. The first piece made no impression whatever. Even the Empress seemed to be paying little attention to Liszt; she was engaged in lively conversation with Meyerbeer. The only one who was gracious to the great pianist was one of the young grand duchesses. But it was not long before Liszt scored his triumph. After tea he was asked to play again and the ice melted. He played his own transcription of Schubert's "Ave Maria" and in such a way that the Empress was deeply moved. Her eyes filled with tears, and the ladies and gentlemen of the court hastened to change their tone. They all looked entranced, moved, excited and showered Liszt with exuberant praise. The fantasy on *The Huguenots* produced the same effect. From this day forth, the Empress was an ardent admirer of Liszt.

Liszt did not come to Russia until a year and a half later, however. This was in the spring of 1842, following a visit to Berlin, where he gave twenty-one enormously successful concerts. (I do not think that he had ever given that many concerts in any one city before.) The latest newspaper accounts of Liszt's colossal triumphs in Berlin kept arriving in

[1] Lina Ramann, *F. Liszt als Künstler und Mensch* (1880), Vol. II, p. 84. This is as Liszt himself subsequently related it to his biographer.

Petersburg one after the other, and they aroused widespread interest and anticipation. Everyone knew that Liszt would be coming here from Berlin.

He finally arrived on 3rd April. The very next day he was presented to Emperor Nicholas I who, as soon as he entered the audience chamber, ignoring all the generals and dignitaries waiting there, turned first to Liszt with the words: "Monsieur Liszt, I am very glad to see you in Petersburg", and then began conversing with him.

Four days later, on 8th April, Liszt gave his first concert before an overflow audience of more than three thousand in the Assembly Hall of the Nobility. Everything about this concert was unusual. First of all, Liszt appeared alone on the stage throughout the entire concert: there were no other performers—no orchestra, singers or any other instrumental soloists whatsoever. This was something unheard of, utterly novel, even somewhat brazen. What conceit! What vanity! As if to say, "All you need is me. Listen only to me—you don't need anyone else." Then, this idea of having a small stage erected in the very centre of the hall like an islet in the middle of an ocean, a throne high above the heads of the crowd, from which to pour forth his mighty torrents of sound. And then, what music he chose for his programmes: not just piano pieces, his own, his true metier—no, this could not satisfy his boundless conceit—he had to be both an orchestra and human voices. He took Beethoven's "Adelaide", Schubert's songs—and dared to replace male and female voices, to play them on the piano alone! He took large orchestral works, overtures, symphonies—and played them too, all alone, in place of a whole orchestra, without any assistance, without the sound of a single violin, French horn, kettledrum! And in such an immense hall! What a strange fellow!

In my reminiscences of the Imperial School of Jurisprudence (which I attended with Alexander Serov, with whom I was very friendly at the time), I wrote:

As people began streaming into the hall, I saw Glinka for the first time in my life. He was pointed out to me by Serov, who had met him not long before and of course, rushed up to him all smiles, handshakes and questions. But Glinka did not spend much time with Serov. A shrivelled old lady, Mme. Palibina (who, by the way, was an excellent pianist) began calling him. [Here follows Mme. Palibina's conversation with Glinka about the opera *Ruslan and Ludmila*, which he was completing at the time] . . .

Suddenly there was a commotion in the crowded Assembly Hall of the Nobility. We all turned around and saw Liszt, strolling arm in arm through the gallery behind the columns with the potbellied Count Mikhail Vielgorsky. The Count, who moved very slowly, glowering at everyone with his bulging eyes, was wearing a wig curled *à l'Apollo Belvedere* and a large white cravat. Liszt was also wearing a white cravat and over it, the Order of the Golden Spur, which had recently been given him by the Pope. Various other orders dangled from the lapels of his frock coat. He was very thin and stooped, and though I had read a great deal about his famous "Florentine profile", which was supposed to make him resemble Dante, I did not find his face handsome at all. I at once strongly disliked this mania for decorations and later on had as little liking for the saccharine, courtly manner Liszt affected with everyone he met. But most startling of all was his enormous mane of fair hair. In those days no one in Russia would have dared wear his hair that way; it was strictly forbidden.

Immediately the hall began humming with remarks and comments about Liszt. My neighbours, whose conversation had been interrupted for the moment, began talking again. Mme. Palibina asked Glinka whether he had ever heard Liszt before. He replied that he had, the previous evening at Count Vielgorsky's. "Well, then, what did you think of him?" inquired Glinka's importunate friend.

To my astonishment and indignation, Glinka replied, without the slightest hesitation, that sometimes Liszt played magnificently, like no one else in the world, but other times intolerably, in a highly affected manner, dragging tempi and adding to the works of others, even to those of Chopin, Beethoven, Weber, and Bach a lot of embellishments of his own that were often tasteless, worthless and meaningless. I was absolutely scandalized! What! How dare some "mediocre" Russian musician, who had not yet done anything in particular himself, talk like this about Liszt, the great genius over whom all Europe had gone mad! I was incensed. Seemingly, Mme. Palibina did not fully share Glinka's opinion either, for she remarked, laughingly, "Allons donc, allons donc, tout cela ce n'est que rivalité de métier!" Glinka chuckled and shrugging his shoulders, replied, "Perhaps so."

Just at that moment Liszt, noting the time, walked down from the gallery, elbowed his way through the crowd and moved quickly toward the stage. But instead of using the steps, he leaped onto the platform. He tore off his white kid gloves and tossed them on the floor, under the piano. Then, after bowing low in all directions to a tumult of applause such as had probably not been heard in Petersburg since 1703, he seated himself at the piano. Instantly the hall became deadly silent. Without any preliminaries, Liszt began playing the opening cello phrase of the *William Tell* overture. As soon as he finished the overture, and while the hall was still rocking with applause, he moved swiftly to a second piano facing in the opposite direction. Throughout the concert he used these pianos alternately for each piece, facing first one, then the other half of the hall. On this occasion, Liszt also played the Andante from *Lucia*, his fantasy on Mozart's *Don Giovanni*, piano transcriptions of Schubert's "Ständchen" and "Erlkönig", Beethoven's "Adelaide" and in conclusion, his own *Galop chromatique*. This last, though a very poor and inconsequential piece, is fascinating rhythmically and interesting harmonically.

After the concert, Serov and I were like madmen. We exchanged only a few words and then rushed home to write each other as quickly as possible of our impressions, our dreams, our ecstasy . . . [In those days we were continually writing each other, as Serov had already left the School of Jurisprudence and I was still completing my studies there.] Then and there, we took a vow that thenceforth and forever, that day, 8th April, 1842, would be sacred to us, and we would never forget a single second of it till our dying day. We were delirious, like lovers! And no wonder. We had never in our lives heard anything like this; we had never been in the presence of such a brilliant, passionate, demonic temperament, at one moment rushing like a whirlwind, at another pouring forth cascades of tender beauty and grace. Liszt's playing was absolutely overwhelming, even in such poor things as Beethoven's "Adelaide" and the Andante from *Lucia*, a favourite with all European audiences.

At the second concert, on 11th April, the most magnificent playing came in a mazurka by Chopin (in B-flat major) and Schubert's "Erlkönig"—the latter in Liszt's own arrangement but performed, certainly, as no singer in the world has ever performed it. It was truly a picture, charged with poetry, mystery, magic, colour, and the ominous thud of horses' hoofs, alternating with the desperate cries of the dying child. I thought I would never again hear anything like it. I was sorely mistaken, however, for later I heard Rubinstein play both the "Erlkönig" and Chopin's Mazurka many times, and I am delighted to say that in these works, he was in no way inferior to Liszt. However, for all the brilliance of Rubinstein's playing (in the music of Chopin and Schumann), I never heard him play the symphonies of Beethoven as we heard them played at Liszt's concerts. But then, Rubinstein rarely undertook to perform great orchestral works on the piano; his was a more intimate kind of art. Except for the *Egmont* overture, the march from *The Ruins of Athens*, and dances from *The Demon* and *Feramors*, he concerned himself only with piano pieces.

At this second concert, Liszt also played the entire second half of the *Pastoral* Symphony. At that time Serov and I did not know this symphony at all, and therefore we were even more amazed, delighted, enraptured. Only once in my life did I ever again hear the scherzo and storm performed like this. That was when Berlioz conducted them in Petersburg. But then, Liszt and Berlioz were kindred spirits in genius and poetic depth!

At his third concert, on 22nd April in the Engelhardt Hall, Liszt played Weber's *Konzertstück* and Beethoven's *Sonata quasi una fantasia*. [*Here follows a detailed account of Liszt's playing.*] . . . Serov and I attended all of Liszt's concerts after this . . .[1]

On the day of the first concert, Serov (who was only twenty-two at the time) wrote to me:

First of all, permit me to congratulate you on your initiation into the great and sacred mysteries of art, and then—let me collect my thoughts. It is now almost two hours since I left the hall, and I am still not myself. Where am I? Where are we? What is this—is it real or a dream? Did I really hear Liszt? I must confess that I had expected a great deal from the reports; that because of some mysterious conviction I had expected a great deal, but the reality far exceeded all my hopes! How fortunate we are to be living in 1842, when there is such a musician in the world and this musician has visited our capital and given us an opportunity to hear him. I realize that I'm gushing too much, but I can't help it—I can't restrain myself. I must pass through this lyrical crisis before I can express myself sensibly . . . Don't be angry with me . . . Oh, how happy I am! What a festive day this has been! How different all God's world seems! And one man did all this by his playing! Oh, how great is greatness in music! I simply cannot be coherent—my whole being seems in a state of unnatural tension, inexplicable ecstasy, of blissful rapture . . .

The first review of Liszt's concert appeared two days later, on 10th April, not in a Russian newspaper but in a German one, the *S. P. Zeitung*. In this article, as well as in two subsequent ones, the author went into ecstasies over Liszt, declared him "unique, peerless, unapproachable", gave a detailed and rhapsodic account of his impressions but at the same

[1] My article "The School of Jurisprudence Forty Years Ago" (*Russkaya Starina*, June, 1881) contains many other details concerning Liszt's Petersburg concerts and the effects they produced on Serov and myself.

time expressed amazement at the pianist's "unprecedented technique". These were very decent, run-of-the-mill articles written with warmth but very little colour, pendants to the kind of writing that was being done all over Germany at the time, especially in Berlin.

The first Russian publication to comment on Liszt's concert was *Severnaya Pchela*, and now the writing began to take on a special colour and odour. In his column "Journalistic Odds and Ends," Bulgarin, the great writer, critic, journalist and general arbiter of the time wrote, on 11th April:

> What can we say about his playing? Everything has already been said and said again in all the journals of Europe. In our opinion, Liszt's playing bears the stamp of our time, the stamp, that is, of out-and-out romanticism, in which the imagination knows no bounds but those of elegant taste, is subject to no laws but the will of the genius who, overthrowing all theories, makes of art something wondrous, unique, infinite and eternal. Liszt's playing is to music what Victor Hugo's dramas are to French literature, Goethe's *Faust* to German literature, Tegner's rhapsodic hymns to Swedish literature. In it there is terror, charm, thunder, the morning sun, death and roses . . . With his fingers, Liszt *sings* the duet from Mozart's *Don Giovanni* and *with his fingers, he narrates* the German ballad "Erlkönig". Truly a miracle! You have to see Liszt's face, Liszt's eyes when he plays! Passions race, like clouds through a clear sky . . . then suddenly lightinng . . . thunder . . . and once again the sun! If you have never seen a genius in action, even if you do not like music, watch Liszt when he plays!

A week later, this same Bulgarin was still extolling Liszt to the skies in his banal journalistic style (he could not have done otherwise, the prevailing sentiment being what it was) but this time he let his long ear stick out.

On 18th April he wrote in the same "Journalistic Odds and Ends":

> Paganini did not generate half the excitement Liszt does. This is very understandable. The piano is a lady's instrument, almost every woman plays or has played it. All of them understand the mechanics of piano playing, and they divined the genius of Liszt's playing before the men, who simply took their cue from the fair sex and joined them in the general chorus glorifying the brilliant virtuoso. Everyone agrees that Liszt is a marvellous virtuoso, but the general public has not understood him as fully as the Germans have, and our feeling toward him is calm, composed—the usual tribute to talent. We are not so easily moved by music as the day-dreamy Germans are. We have neither books, poems, wreaths, nor an Olympian retinue to offer Liszt, but everyone who knows and loves music admires him and all worthy people esteem him . . .

Bulgarin went on to praise Liszt's generosity and various benefactions, pointing to the many benefit performances he had given for poor musicians, artists, orphans and others in need, for memorials to great men, such as the Beethoven Monument, for the city of Hamburg, which had been almost completely destroyed by fire, and so on. The reader can see that these were nothing but trite, quite perfunctory tributes, a mixture of praise and covert disparagement (what is it but disparagement to say,

"We are not easily moved by music!"). Sometimes the disparagement was not even veiled—it was quite open. Thus, for example, in his last article, written after Liszt had left Petersburg, Bulgarin once again called him "great, peerless" and so on, praised his performance of Hummel's Septet, Weber's Concerto, etc., but then added:

> But Liszt did not play Chopin's Mazurka as it poured from Chopin's soul. It is possible to err and Liszt erred—he did not understand the character of this mazurka. He did not take the trouble to understand this superb work, and instead of playing it softly, sadly, plaintively, he played it loudly, bombastically, like a dance! Sorry, Liszt, but the truth is the truth: even Homer was caught nodding . . .

Such was the state of musical affairs in our country at that time! An utter ignoramus like Bulgarin decided what Liszt played *correctly* and what he played *incorrectly*. He even dared to publicly accuse a musical genius of "not taking the trouble to understand" a certain piece of music. How do you like that! And no one raised a voice against this impudence and ignorance. Well, what could you expect! He was Bulgarin after all! Russia's legislator of all matters public, scientific, artistic and whatever else under the sun! And is it any wonder, considering that his views on everything coincided exactly with those of vast numbers of our public of that day. He was right in step with the whole crowd of military and civil functionaries, business men and so-called connoisseurs, who really cared very little about anything except their government departments and superiors, their businesses and shady dealings, and even less about such things as music or some Liszt. They only went to concerts because they had to to be in style. Actually they cared as much about all this as they did about last year's snow. In a letter to me, on 11th April, Serov drew a very faithful picture of these people, their ideas, tastes, cultural level and attitudes:

> A scene from the life of the social set—verbatim. Dinner in the Assembly Hall of the Nobility; interval between soup and the second course.
>
> Kh: (a Major in the transportation service): By the way, N.N., have you heard Liszt?
> N.N.: Yes, I heard him on Wednesday.
> Kh: Tell me, what does he play—the piano?
> N.N.: Yes, the piano.
> Kh: Is he any good?
> N.N.: Marvellous!
> Kh: You mean nothing's too difficult for him?
> N.N.: Absolutely. He can do anything he wants to with the piano.
> Kh: But really, I have to confess—I don't like the piano at all. What kind of instrument is it, a strumming thing, a gusli!
> N.N.: I agree. I'd much rather listen to a singing instrument, like the violin or cello.
> Kh: And did Liszt play alone, without any other musicians?
> N.N.: Yes, absolutely alone, without any orchestra.
> Kh: Too bad, too bad. Not much pleasure without an orchestra!

N.N.: That's true, but the way he plays, he really doesn't need an orchestra.

Kh: But to pay fifteen roubles just to listen to the piano. It's all the fault of those damned newspapers! If you'd listen to them, you'd go through fire and water to get there, and what would you find—a charlatan!

N.N.: No, Liszt isn't a charlatan, but I suspect he's out for the money.

Kh: And how much did he rake in on this concert?

N.N.: Oh, fifty thousand or so and besides, mark you, he gave the concert in the afternoon so he wouldn't have to pay for the lighting, and he got the Assembly Hall for nothing.

Kh: It's just too bad we couldn't get a few thousand out of him, at least enough to buy some new furniture for our hall.

N.N.: And I think he could at least pay for the hall, to help our impoverished noblemen. But you mustn't say a word about that now! The public is very stupid. When it comes to a fad, there's no use arguing. Besides, nowadays there are so many starry-eyed addlepates wandering around in a daze of poetic ecstasy—they either don't see the truth or don't want to see it. Would you believe it, I myself have heard a lot of people even admire Liszt's looks, whereas he's really a freak, a scarecrow, with his spindly legs, unkempt hair and face that looks like a mummy's!

Kh: He must be some beauty.

N.N.: Charming, indeed. And what grotesque manners! Sometimes he even forgets the ordinary proprieties. Imagine, he didn't even take the trouble to look over the hall or the stage before the concert. Now, in mounting the stage, in order to face the royal family, he was supposed to use the steps opposite the imperial box. But did he? No. When the clock struck two, he elbowed his way through the crowd, pushed his way to the platform, bowed low, then glanced at the stage, shook his thick hair and, as you might have expected, thanks to his long legs, leaped about four feet onto it.

Kh: Ha, ha, ha! How charming, how very respectful! How come his breeches didn't burst?

Z.: (a lieutenant in the Guards) Yes, everybody says his manners are ridiculous. He's like some kind of savage. But all is forgiven when he plays. What playing—it's marvellous!

N.N.: Nobody denies that. He's a past master.

Z.: But you know, even though I'm quite delighted with his technical skill, I must confess that he doesn't move me very much. Somehow he's cold. He doesn't play with enough feeling.

N.N.: But what do you expect from the piano?

Z.: Yes, of course. But all the same, it seems to me that the man has more mechanical skill than musical soul! . . . etc., etc.

After this vivid, lifelike account, Serov concluded his letter:

There you have a sample of the daily conversations between crass ignorance, cold practicality and those insignificant creatures who talk because they think they have to, even though they have neither opinions, ideas nor souls. Despite all this, Liszt's impact on the general public is powerful and unmistakable . . .

I have quoted above from Bulgarin's articles on Liszt. These were the views of a person who was not only completely unmusical but never claimed that he had the slightest understanding of music. Now, in contrast, I shall present the views of a totally different critic, one who considered himself a musical authority and was considered so by everyone else. This was Senkovsky, a friend of Glinka, Bryullov, Kukolnik and practically all the artists and writers of the time, a man who was forever writing articles about everything and everybody in the arts which were widely read and carried great weight with the social set. In the May issue of his magazine *Biblioteka dlya Chteniya*, Senkovsky wrote:

Liszt's presence overshadows all other news of this kind. All conversations and discussions about music revolve around only one subject—Liszt . . . Opinions have already been formed about him, and these opinions, while unanimous as to the amazing technical perfection of his playing, differ widely when it comes to other aspects of his brilliant talent. Many people complain that they are not moved; that this wonderful playing leaves them cold; others complain that they are positively ill from the emotion and excitement engendered by his concerts . . . Many pianists nowadays have achieved the technical perfection which almost everyone regards as the matchless attribute of this extraordinary artist, and if they have not yet achieved it, they will . . . Mr. Liszt's true greatness, that which places him above all other famous pianists, lies in the intellectual aspect of his playing. Of all those who play the piano, only Mr. Liszt has a complete command of this huge, complicated, awkward and soulless instrument, which no one else has ever mastered. He alone understands it, has conquered it, knows what can be said well on it and says it with indescribable intelligence, feeling, dexterity, clarity, power, tenderness and distinctness. His rich and fertile mind is evident in everything he does . . . This is the speech of a wise and skilful orator. These are real tonal pictures, painted with an intelligent, deft, and subtle brush . . .

If there is any flaw in Mr. Liszt's playing [concluded Senkovsky], it is that at times it is too cerebral; some pieces are so weighted with cleverness that there is no room for feeling. One finds the same defect in many writers who are overly clever. But even so, one cannot fail to recognize Mr. Liszt's wonderful acumen. It is always difficult to express emotion on the piano—this can only be suggested. The difference between this instrument and the cello or violin is the same as that between the spoken and the printed word. It always requires more conscious effort to express oneself in print than to do so in speech. Aided by the pleasant inflections of the voice, one can create an effect even when talking sheer nonsense. In order to convey feeling on the piano, one has to help the ineloquent instrument a little with gestures and facial expressions, and this Mr. Liszt does to perfection . . .

Thus, there was little difference between the judgement of Bulgarin and that of Senkovsky, between the perceptiveness of the acknowledged musical ignoramus and that of the acknowledged connoisseur and authority. Both of them praised Liszt and even praised him very highly, but in all this one sensed an element of insincerity and hypocrisy. What these writers really thought was completely different from their pretentious phrases and high-flown words. Liszt is a genius, to be sure—but somehow not quite. This in him is great, that is wonderful, but the most essential element "soul", "expression", "feeling" is missing. Both of our great literati, leaders and arbiters for a considerable part of the Russian public, understood this very well. One went into raptures over Liszt's goodness and nobility; the other over his mind. Both of them said all there was to say about his "mastery of the most unbelievable difficulties", his "unprecedented skill", his "limitless technique". But not one word was said about—a mere trifle, of course—the artistry, the poetry of Liszt's playing and conceptions. His powerful performance of the giant Beethoven; his tender, impassioned, subtle performance of the other masters—this our cognoscenti simply overlooked. They did not notice it at all. What is more, they considered Liszt a fraud, virtually a charlatan, who cleverly affected sad or soulful facial expressions. This was the sum total of the impression Liszt made on the Russian ignoramus and the Russian expert who wrote regularly for the press. There is no doubt that a considerable number of Russians in Petersburg felt and thought exactly as Bulgarin and Senkovsky did.

At the same time there were a great many people in the capital with no pretensions to being experts who admired Liszt deeply and wholeheartedly. The May issue of *Otechestvenniye Zapiski* carried some fairly decent verses by Countess Rostopchin called "After the Concert", in which the author expressed her own sentiments and those that predominated at the time:

> They shower him with laurels and flowers . . .
> They exalt, they glorify him . . .
> Giddy with ecstasy, dazed by beauty
> They fling their hearts at his feet . . .
> He is surrounded by honour, acclaim
> And artful flattery . . .
> I have no words to express
> The depth of my feelings!
> I utter no words, no tribute,
> I only listen, and adore . . .
> . . . .
> A tear quivers in my eyes—
> A tear more precious than momentary roses!
> There is more truth in it than in speeches,
> Or frenzied applause!
> He will leave us—in a day, in two,
> He will forget our noisy city . . .
> But his song is now part of our soul
> So deeply stirred, so deeply inspired!

One of our writers on music, Yuri Arnold, later described to Lina Ramann (who recorded this in her biography of Liszt) how shaken he had felt after Liszt's concerts in those days, especially after hearing the "Erlkönig". "I was completely undone by the sense of the supernatural, the mysterious, the incredible," Arnold said. "As soon as I reached home,

I pulled off my coat, flung myself on the sofa, and wept and wept the bitterest, sweetest tears . . ."

Do you know what? [I wrote Serov at the time] Old Carelli [our music teacher at the School of Jurisprudence, a violinist of the old school] has risen enormously in my estimation since he told me simply and frankly the day after Liszt played at the Prince of Oldenburg's that he places him *über alle Clavier-spieler*. This is a great deal for an old man who heard Field and grew up in the mildew of pseudo-classicism.

Very few Russians of that day had ever heard Liszt before, abroad, and consequently they had no way of knowing that he came to our country at just the right moment, that is, at the very peak of his tremendous development as an artist. One of those who had heard him and could see the difference between the old and new Liszt was the Moscow professor, Shevyrev, a man who wrote a great deal about the arts (and not always too nonsensically). Here is what he had to say in *Moskvityanin*, the magazine published by his friend and associate Pogodin:

I heard Liszt for the first time in 1839 in Rome. That was not so long ago, but if I had not actually seen this artist in person, I never could have believed that this was the same Liszt I had heard four years ago. He had changed so, he had grown so enormously during this time. He himself was aware of this change and admitted it to many of his admirers.

In the days when his creative powers were still in ferment, he indulged in a kind of wild, impetuous playing. His instrument and everything around him often fell prey to his musical paroxysms. In accounts of his concerts in Parisian magazines, one frequently ran across such statements as "four pianos were broken by Liszt's furious playing". Some compared him with Cassandra, possessed by strange apparitions; others with a madman; still others saw him as a demon, venting his rage on the piano and destroying it in the process. From then on, it became commonplace to see something demonic in Liszt's playing which, of course, was not so then and is certainly not so of the Liszt of today, who has come to us a mature genius in his very prime . . . No, there was nothing demonic or forced in the furious outbursts of Liszt's earlier playing, as the future proved: this was simply the young artist's way of expressing himself . . . In ancient sculpture and drama, the gigantic and colossal preceded the elegant and graceful. Read Shakespeare's early plays—you will find the same stresses and strains in them . . .

Having been reared in Moscow on Field's flowing, graceful playing, I could not at that time respond to the turbulent outbursts of a pianist who made his instrument shudder. I did not yet realize the rich potentialities that lay hidden in this kind of playing. I could not foresee the Liszt of today. I confess that at first I listened to him here with the prejudice that had been formed in Rome. But he soon vanquished me, and by the third piece I succumbed completely to the full might and power of his magic sounds . . .

No, it is no demon that moves this great artist's fingers, for a demon is lifeless and soulless, and Liszt's keyboard teems with life and passion! . . . Liszt's music is the cry of a vibrant soul in the desert of cold reason . . . He draws upon all the passionate themes that contemporary opera has borrowed from Shakespearian drama. And what a medium he has chosen for their portrayal! A limited, fashionable, drawing-room instrument, which the most ordinary people have at their disposal, and everyone given any kind of superficial education is taught to play. But the soul of this artist has wrought an astonishing transformation, and his effects are all the more telling because the language he has chosen seems familiar and understandable to every one . . .[1]

Shevyrev was entirely right. After his stay in Rome in 1839, Liszt was no longer the old Liszt—he was altogether different: matured and at the peak of his power. He himself understood this very well. On leaving Rome in November of that year, he wrote his Hungarian friend Count Leo Festetics:

I shall come to you [in Budapest] a little older, more matured and if I may say so, more "ausgearbeitet als Künstler" than I was last year, for since then I have worked enormously in Italy.*

A considerable part of the Petersburg public knew nothing about this —neither what Liszt had been before nor what he had recently become; they did not go in for making comparisons; they simply and naïvely felt, despite the Senkovskys and Bulgarins, that they were in the presence of a genius, the like of which they had never seen nor heard before. And they responded with all the enthusiasm of which they were capable.

On the basis of reports by contemporaries, Lina Ramann wrote:

Liszt's reception in Petersburg was as enthusiastic as it was glittering. Festivity followed festivity. After his concerts, fashionable ladies waited for him with wreaths of flowers on the steps of the Hotel Coulon, where he was staying. And when he left Petersburg, the aristocracy escorted him on a special steamer with a chorus of musicians all the way to Kronstadt, to the very entrance of the Finnish Gulf . . .'

During his stay in Petersburg, Liszt often played at receptions given by the Empress, the Grand Duchess Elena Pavlovna, Prince Peter of Oldenburg, at the homes of all the nobility—Count Vorontsov-Dashkov, Prince Yusupov, Prince Beloselsky, Count Sheremetyev and Count Benkendorf. But he spent most of his time at the homes of the two brothers, the Counts Vielgorsky, and Prince Odoyevsky, all of whom were very well-educated amateur musicians. Liszt also became very close to Henselt, who had come to Petersburg four years earlier (in 1838) and remained there for the rest of his life. There sprang up between them a sincere, warm friendship which was never darkened by the slightest cloud to the day of Liszt's death. They were always on intimate terms and dedicated a number of works to each other.

One of Liszt's ardent admirers, Lenz, a writer on music who, together with Vielgorsky, was present at Liszt's first visit to Henselt, tells the following anecdote. At Liszt's request, Henselt played Weber's Polacca

[1] *Moskvityanin* (1843), Pt. III, No. 5, p. 316.
* Letter of 24th November, 1839. [Trans.]

in E major. Liszt was taken aback by Henselt's playing but remarked: "I, too, could play with velvet paws if I wished."[1]

Liszt gave six concerts in Petersburg, including one for the benefit of the city of Hamburg, and another for a children's hospital. On 16th May, the practical Bulgarin offered him the following advice in *Severnaya Pchela*:

The great Liszt is leaving us, but they say that he plans to return to Russia next year, to visit Moscow and come to us toward the Spring. God willing, we'll meet again! They have fallen in love with Liszt here for his magnificent playing, his intellect and his rare geniality. However, we would advise him not to play at every concert, at the request of every musician. Our people quickly tire of everything, and we fear that Liszt might suffer the fate of the famous Field, whom everyone praised and then stopped listening to. Henselt has understood this and has flatly refused to give concerts, even though he is a brilliant virtuoso and a first-rate composer. People wait for him abroad, they invite him, but we are hardly aware that he is living in Petersburg. One has to be careful with our public; it is continually demanding something new, something different!

A year later Liszt returned to Russia and gave two concerts in Petersburg. On 16th April, 1843, *Invalide* wrote:

Liszt, who descended upon us like an unexpected snowfall, gave a concert immediately upon his arrival two days ago. The Engelhardt Hall could hardly accommodate the tremendous number of people who came to applaud this superb artist. Everyone was delighted, but their delight was mixed with sadness. They knew that this was to be the great musician's first and last concert here, as he has decided to leave for Moscow in three days.

Severnaya Pchela said that on this second visit, Liszt's "reception was no less glittering than it had been on the first"; that the artist chose the Engelhardt Hall more from modesty than from a fear that his concert might not attract a large enough audience to fill the Assembly Hall of the Nobility; that our public's taste is so highly developed that they would not, like many concertgoers in other countries, "turn their backs on an artist they had extolled the year before."[2]

In 1843 Senkovsky continued repeating what he had said about Liszt in 1842:

Only an extraordinary mind makes a man a great writer, a great artist, a great vurtuoso. This is the secret of the incredible impression that Liszt has made everywhere in Europe, in spite of intrigues, envy, rivalry, ill-will . . . Everyone

[1] In quoting this anecdote from Lenz's brochure, *Die grossen Pianofortevirtuosen unserer Zeit* (p. 104), Lina Ramann expresses doubt concerning the authenticity of this remark, maintaining that remarks of this kind were completely out of character for Liszt. But she did not know about the letter Liszt wrote to Lenz in 1872 (now in our Public Library), in which he thanks Lenz for this brochure and finds it truthful in every respect. Obviously, if Liszt had been misquoted, he would have objected.

[2] A reference to Berlin, where Liszt did not receive the acclaim in 1843 that he had in 1842 because of sneering attacks by a number of ignorant little satirical publications put out by the conservative music clique.

thinks that he is playing even better now than he did last year. But Liszt has not practised during the past year! Why, then, does his playing seem even better, even more wonderful? Only because he has thought through many passages again and given them a new, a different interpretation...

Then Senkovsky commented on Liszt's performance of Weber's *Konzertstück*, the variations on *I Puritani*, Hungarian "melodies", a Chopin étude, the overture to *Der Freischütz*, and the fantasy on *La Sonnambula*. Regarding the latter, he went so far as to say:

The transcription and performance of this piece were so carefully thought out that it actually sounded better than the opera on which it is based. The same may be said of the variations on the march from *I Puritani*, which Liszt played at the concert for the children's hospital. In these two pieces he again revealed his remarkable talent as a writer of music...[1]

Despite these reports of Liszt's brilliant success in 1843, this was actually not true. The guarded phrases in *Severnaya Pchela*, about his "modesty" having led him to hire the small Engelhardt Hall for his second concert instead of the large Assembly Hall of the Nobility, sound suspicious. Why had he not displayed this same "modesty" in Petersburg the year before? All of his concerts, except one devoted to chamber music (that is, for piano and stringed instruments), had been given in the Hall of the Nobility, and there had been no mention then of any "modesty". Now, the feuilletonists and critics who were kindly disposed toward Liszt had to resort to pretexts and excuses. No, it was not a question of "modesty"; it was simply that the public was less interested in Liszt than they had been before. Petersburg had a new fad, the Italians, and nothing could compare with this appetizing dish. It suited the capital's musical needs and tastes perfectly. People who knew nothing whatever about music did not need anything better than Italian opera and Italian singers. When Rubini and later other noted Italians came here, all other music faded into the background. The Italian furore blazed out of control. Even four years later, in 1847, Prince Odoyevsky, one of the few people capable of loving and understanding real music, wrote about Berlioz' concerts: "Berlioz is understood in Petersburg! He is understood despite his intricate counterpoint; he is understood, despite the deluge of Italian cabalettas that has diluted our stern Slavic feelings..."

In his *Memoirs*, Glinka, too, gives us an idea of our public's ridiculous and utterly incomprehensible enthusiasm for Italian music and singers. "When Rubini came to our country in 1843," wrote Glinka, "Count Mikhail Vielgorsky, dropping his chin in his huge cravat, said to me: 'Mon cher, c'est Jupiter Olympien!'"

Neither this great connoisseur nor anyone else said anything like this about Liszt.

[1] *Biblioteka dlya Chteniya* (1843), Vol. 58.

Glinka also tells us that when Mozart's *Don Giovanni* was performed here,

> The audience and even the newspapers were up in arms against the great master. It was to him and not to the mediocrity and musical ignorance of most of the singers that they attributed the failure of *Don Giovanni*. I wept from chagrin and then and there began to hate Italian warblers and fashionable Italian opera . . .

Apropros of the Petersburg public, Schumann wrote, in the spring of 1844: "Everyone here seems to have gone mad (*besessen*) over the Italians . . ."

Thus, the interest in Liszt was waning. In 1843 Petersburg was no longer in the mood for him, no longer cared about the wondrous poetry and artistry of his amazing concerts. The only thing the people wanted was the affected, stylized art of the Italians—meaningless, exaggerated passions or sweetness—*tastelessness*. There was no longer any talk about "lack of feeling", "too much intellect", "inability to move people to the depths of their soul". Now everybody was not only moved—they were shaken, overwhelmed, weeping tears of tender emotion. And so they turned indifferently away from Liszt. He had to be "modest", play in a small hall—and leave as quickly as possible.

In Moscow, on the other hand, Liszt was received brilliantly. The Italians had not yet settled there and destroyed the taste for good music. That is why one of the Moscow writers, who signed himself "A. B." (Glinka's friend Bulgakov, perhaps) could declare in *Moskvityanin* that

> Liszt surpasses all other pianists in the world in the secret of reaching the very soul of the true connoisseur, of delighting the ear. He has transformed the piano or, more correctly, has created a new kind of instrument with which, at will, he stirs, captivates or stuns the listener. He achieves effects that one would have thought only the human voice could.[1]

Thus, Moscow was still naïve, still unsullied. The excitement over Liszt still ran almost as high there as it had in Petersburg the year before. He gave six concerts in Moscow and every one of them was filled to overflowing. Among the large receptions in his honour was a gala dinner, which was described in detail in *Moskvityanin*.

> The sumptuous dinner was prepared by the masterful hand of the famous Vlas, who had once been the chef of our renowned Pushkin's uncle [the magazine reported] . . . Liszt listened indifferently to the famous overtures he himself plays better than any orchestra in the world. But when the Russian songs began, he became all ears and began beating time and making gestures in time with the music. "Not White Are the Snows" struck him as too sad, but when the dance song was sung, he could not sit still. His musical nature responded to each new sound. However, when several men carried in a sturgeon almost seven feet long and weighing a hundred pounds, Liszt forgot all about the

[1] *Moskvityanin* (1843), Pt. III, No. 5.

music. He had never seen anything like that. He began applauding the sturgeon, and everyone else followed suit. The applause grew so lively that the chef, who had walked out on the stage behind his enormous artistic creation, was obliged to take bows for the insensible fish . . .[1]

Moscow did not confine itself to sturgeon, however. At this dinner Liszt was also toasted, first by Pavlov and then by Shevyrev. The guest of honour replied in turn. After the second toast, he turned toward Shevyrev and said, among other things: "Your remarks on the social meaning of music have been very aptly put. In this the classics have served you very well. But permit me to observe that you have praised music a bit too highly, perhaps out of kindness to me. No, gentlemen, music is not more important than the word, for the word ordains, the word confirms, the word decides. I cannot possibly match your eloquence, wit and charm in words. You know, gentlemen, my eloquence is—at the piano."

Moskovskiye Vedomosti did not lag behind the general chorus. Through the lips of Fëdor Glinka, a well-known man of letters of the time, it exclaimed:

All you who have at last heard the great artist, tell me, did you ever imagine that art could ever attain such an incredible mastery of an ungrateful instrument that is so unyielding in its limitations that even the prime requisite of music—the duration of sounds—is beyond the control of the hand that produces them? Tell me, in your most ecstatic fantasies did you ever dream that such marvellous, fiery, exciting speed could be combined with such unfailing fidelity, distinctness and fullness of tone in every note, every phrase? No, this is a truly wonderful manifestation of that demonic quality which astounded Goethe in Paganini. It is utterly impossible to measure Liszt by any ordinary standard; he is beyond measuring . . .

(Later, this writer very gingerly suggested, however, that the andantino of the beautiful fantasy from *Lucia* might have been played a bit too fast, Schubert's "Ständchen" a bit carelessly, and that in the "Erlkönig," the epic element was given more emphasis than the dramatic. These criticisms were again followed by the most glowing tribute.)

They say of Thalberg, "See, he has a third hand!" If this is so, then each of Liszt's fingers is a hand! . . . Thalberg is a reputable, intelligent artist; his playing is clear, correct, highly proficient. But Liszt is above proficiency. Field's playing, which is dependable, sedate, pearl-like and often inspired, also makes the listener forget himself! . . . But what can one say about Liszt? Beneath his fingers, the piano is not a piano, and he is not a pianist; he is someone playing something! . . . He is the Paganini of the keyboard![2]

Besides the sturgeon and other culinary delights, Moscow regaled Liszt with still another of its wonders—gypsies. They made a deep impression on him. Fëdor Glinka, again in *Moskovskiye Vedomosti*, reported that:

[1] *Moskvityanin* (1843), Pt. III, No. 5.
[2] *Moskovskiye Vedomosti*, Nos. 51 and 54.

Liszt would listen to the gypsies and then generously play host to them. Once, after listening for a while very attentively, he suddenly sat down at the piano and the wild, semi-Asiatic gypsy themes were transformed on the European's keyboard into a brilliant fantasy filled with sparkling invention. One of Field's best pupils, V., later confessed that he had been utterly fascinated by this improvisation . . .[1]

Lina Ramann relates that Liszt arrived at one of his Moscow concerts unusually late, long after the scheduled time. The audience had become restive and terribly excited. Suddenly Liszt appeared, seated himself at the piano and, seemingly preoccupied, ignored the thunderous applause that had greeted him and began to play not the announced programme, but improvisations on gypsy songs. The whole audience was stunned, overwhelmed, captivated by the inspired quality of his playing; they listened breathless with excitement. Afterward, word got around that the reason for all this was that Liszt had stayed with the gypsies longer than he had realized and had left them deeply stirred. Later, however, Liszt spoke somewhat differently about the Moscow gypsies in his book *Des Bohémiens et de leur musique en Hongrie*. Naturally, their songs could not have held any particular interest for Liszt from a musical point of view. In our country they had long since lost their original, highly poetic, Asiatic character. The authentic, national songs had long since been replaced, in most cases, by cheap ballads and vulgar couplets of the latest make. There was very little left of the earlier, truly eastern flavour in either the songs or the singing that Liszt heard.

Here is some of what Liszt had to say about the Moscow gypsies in his book:

Being a thorough sceptic about the true worth of most of the art that becomes the fashion and rage among the highest aristocracy, I was not greatly charmed by the gypsies, though I did find the evenings spent listening to them less wasteful than those spent in elegant drawing rooms, listening to the cooing of a romance or some young talent's playing. For this reason, I often visited the famous gypsies and could easily imagine the ectsasy of those who were trying to attract the flamelets that flash from black gypsy eyes. Indeed, they could fill your sleep with visions of houris. On the whole, though, I found that in the strictly musical sense, the Moscow gypsies fall far short of their reputation: they are very inferior to the second-rate Hungarian virtuosos . . .

Then, after describing the gypsies' frenzied dances and the reckless, sumptuous life they led at the expense of their wealthy admirers, Liszt continues:

But the *gypsy sentiment*, which they cannot possibly shake off, is nowadays expressed very pallidly in their music; owing to continuous contact with European art, it has greatly degenerated among them. Still, this music has retained so much of the authentic rhythm, so many traces of its original wild energy and piquant modulations, that it delights tastes which are still little developed . . .

[1] *Moskovskiye Vedomosti*, No. 55.

In 1847, Liszt did not find in the gypsies of southern Russia, in the Kiev and Podolsk provinces, the vigour and charm that had captivated him in the Moscow gypsies. The songs and dances of these regions struck him as even more pallid and colourless.

We find some interesting comments concerning Liszt in Moscow in Herzen's *Diary*. There we read:

1843. 1st May. Last week I heard Liszt several times. When there is so much shouting, you expect Lord knows what, and often you are disappointed—because superhuman expectations are unrealizable. But true talents lose nothing from public acclaim. Such a one was Taglioni, whom I sometimes watched through tears, and such a one is Liszt, who also sometimes moves me to tears. An amazing talent.—Last night a wild gypsy concert. For Liszt this was new and fascinating. The music of the gypsies, their singing is not just singing but drama, in which the soloist lures on the chorus—unrestrainedly, furiously. It is easy to understand why gypsies create such an effect at bacchanals.

6th May. The reception given for Liszt by Pavlov somehow reflected the adolescence, the whole character of your society. Literati and spies, all giving themselves away. I was saddened. But Liszt is charming and intelligent.

Thus far I have not spoken of the impression Liszt made, in 1842 and 1843, on the greatest of the Russian musicians, Glinka, who was then in the prime of life and at the peak of his musical powers. Although Liszt's visits themselves made only a rather moderate impression on him, they had exceedingly important consequences for him later on. Here is Glinka's own account in his *Memoirs*:

Liszt's appearance in our country in 1842 caused a great flurry among all the dilettantes and even among the society ladies. I, who had been living a somewhat isolated life since the break with my wife, that is, since November, 1839, was forced to come out into society again. Thus, a Russian composer, forgotten by almost everyone, had to appear in the salons of our capital at the behest of a famous foreign artist. In spite of the general enthusiasm and, in some measure, my own, I can even now give a full account of the impression Liszt's playing made on me.[1] He played Chopin's mazurkas, nocturnes and études—that is, all the brilliant and fashionable music—charmingly but in a highly exaggerated manner (*à la française, c'est à dire, avec exagérations de tout genre*). However, I found his playing of Bach (whose *Clavecin bien tempéré* I knew practically by heart) and a transcription he had made of a Beethoven symphony less satisfactory.[2] His performance of Beethoven's sonatas and classical music in general was not what it should be; he struck the keys as though he were chopping meat. There was a suggestion of contempt in the way he played Hummel's Septet; and I thought that Hummel himself played it much better and more simply. Liszt played Beethoven's E-flat major concerto much better. On the whole, in terms of finish, I would not compare Liszt's playing with that of Field, Charles Mayer, or even Thalberg, especially in scale passages. I saw Liszt at soirées given by the Countesses Rostopchin and Palibina, as well as the Counts Vielgorsky and Count Odoyevsky. At Odoyevsky's Liszt played *à livre ouvert*

[1] This was written in 1854.

[2] Of the nine Beethoven symphonies Liszt transcribed for piano two hands in 1839, he played only the Scherzo and Finale from the Sixth Symphony in Petersburg.

several numbers from my autograph score of *Ruslan*, which no one knew at the time, and to the amazement of everyone, he did not miss a note.

Naturally, I found Liszt's behaviour and manners very strange, for I had not yet been in Paris and I knew *young France* only from hearsay.[1] Besides his very long hair, there was his manner, which was sometimes saccharine and at other times arrogantly self-assured. However, despite a certain patronizing air, especially with musicians and young people, Liszt was amiable; he readily participated in the general merriment and was not averse to joining us in our revels. Whenever we met in society, which happened fairly often, he would always ask me to sing him one or two of my songs. His favourite was "Fire of Longing in My Blood". He, in turn, would play some Chopin or fashionable Beethoven for me . . .

Liszt came to Petersburg for a second visit, and he often went on sprees with us . . . He heard my opera[2] and showed a true understanding of its key passages. Despite the many flaws in *Ruslan*, he reassured me as to its success. According to him, my opera, which was given thirty-two performances in Petersburg that winter alone, could be regarded as having been very well received and would have been considered so in Paris. After all, Rossini's *William Tell* was given only sixteen performances the first season.

I talked frankly with Liszt about my views on art and composers. I told him that I found Weber very unsatisfying (even in *Der Freischütz*) because of his excessive use of the dominant seventh in root position. To this Liszt replied, "Vous êtes avec Weber comme deux rivaux qui courtisez la même femme."

I remember the day of Liszt's departure very well. We had supper at Count Kutuzov's (I believe). The conversation turned to my opera, and Count Mikhail Vielgorsky said again, "Mon cher, c'est un opéra manqué." Tired of hearing the same old thing again, I asked for everyone's attention. "Gentlemen," I said, "I consider the Count one of the finest musicians I have ever met. Now, tell me honestly, Count, would you have signed your name to this opera if you had written it?"

"Of course, gladly," he replied.

"Then permit me, too, to be satisfied with my work! . . ."

Everything about this story is interesting, noteworthy, and significant. It gives a complete picture of our musical life at the beginning of the

[1] In her biography of Liszt, Lina Ramann relates that during Liszt's stay in Petersburg, the Emperor Nicholas expressed the desire that he play at the annual Lenten concert for the benefit of invalids (many of whom were veterans of the War of 1812), and that Liszt refused, saying, "I owe my education and my fame to France. Therefore I cannot join in the same chorus with her conquerors." According to Lina Ramann, the Emperor was deeply displeased by this reply and had word sent to Liszt that he liked neither his long hair nor his political opinions (meaning his sympathy with the Poles), to which Liszt replied, *smiling proudly*, "I let my hair grow in Paris and shall also cut it only in Paris; as for my political views, I have none and will have none so long as I have not got 300,000 bayonets to back them up."

This anecdote can be regarded as nothing more than a ridiculous fairy tale. Emperor Nicholas never had anything to do with arranging concerts and never entered into polemical discussions about hair styles and political opinions. All he did was issue orders that were immediately carried out. These unlikely tales probably originated from the fact that Nicholas did not care much for music and seldom attended concerts. He was so little interested in Liszt that, according to Lina Ramann, the Petersburg court was divided into two camps: the military, which, along with the Emperor, ignored Liszt, and the musical which, along with the Empress (and the Grand Duchess Elena Pavlovna) adored him and were eager to hear him.

[2] *Ruslan and Ludmila* had its première in Petersburg on 27th November, 1842.

forties: the musicians' revels; the highly cultured foreign artist placed in the position of having to rescue the wonderfully gifted Glinka from obscurity in his own country; the entire society consigning its great, un-understood, forgotten composer to the daily stupid gibes of some dilettante count, who understood hardly any music except banal Italian operas and the established classics; a society that did not dare to utter a word in Glinka's defence; Glinka, in self-defence and for his own peace of mind, having to compare his magnificent opera with this count's miserable scribblings—what a time, what people!

As for the "revels" of which Glinka speaks, we learn some details about them from an account by Yuri Arnold, one of those who participated in them. In her biography of Liszt, Lina Ramann quotes Arnold to the effect that many of the nobility in Petersburg entertained Liszt brilliantly, but

the composer Glinka gave the most original of all the fêtes in his honour. [Glinka was then living in Brunner's house on Gorokhovaya Street, near the Admiralty Square.] He invited a great many artists—musicians, poets, painters—and art lovers, more than forty persons in all. Among those attending were the musicians Dargomïzhsky, Arnold and Vollweiler; the singers Rubini and Petrov; the painter Bryullov, and the poet Kukolnik. The walls of the drawing-room were lined with fir trees, and flowered shawls were hung in such a way as to suggest a tent. In the centre stood a structure made of three poles, joined at the top, and from this was suspended an enormous copper cauldron on an iron chain. Carpets were strewn all about. In short, the gathering was meant to represent a gypsy camp.

After some music and supper, the guests, in the highest of spirits, sprawled about on the carpets, gypsy-style, their coats off and cravats loosened. With the help of his brother Platon, the poet Kukolnik began to prepare the famous crambambuli out of Jamaican rum, champagne and red Chablis. The flaming rum illuminated the jovial gathering and cast fantastic reflections on the arboreal walls of the tent. At this point they began singing Russian folk songs and then some by Glinka and Dargomïzhsky . . .

"Twenty-one years later, in 1864, during the music festival in Karlsruhe, I recalled all this to Liszt," Yuri Arnold wrote me. "'And do you remember the gypsy camp at Glinka's, docteur?' I asked. But apparently he did not want to go into details (there were strangers present, among them Brendel), for he only smiled and replied, 'Nous étions jeunes alors, cher ami, passons là-dessus.' " (By then Liszt was an abbé.)

Glinka could not but have thought highly of Liszt; he could not have failed to realize the uniqueness of Liszt's musical nature. Whom else might he have found who could have read at sight the complicated score of *Ruslan*, a work whose forms, musical material and style were so new, so unlike anything Liszt knew? What other musician from the West could have understood and appreciated the depth of this new opera, whose true significance virtually no one in our own country understood at that time? Amid this general lack of understanding, of whom else could Glinka have said, "He showed a true understanding of all the key passages in my opera"? And, on top of everything else, *this* man tried to elevate Glinka in the eyes of his musically uneducated compatriots! Yet, however close and deep the relationship between these two great musicians may have been, however richly endowed they both were, the Russian understood the Hungarian far less than the Hungarian did the Russian. The Russian saw the Hungarian only as an exceptional, highly gifted person and an excellent pianist, but even so, one who fell short of the mark because his playing did not fully fit in with the old classical ideal of pianism; he was not a pianist of the old school. Glinka found Liszt's playing "charming" but sometimes exaggerated. He preferred the old-fashioned, far from fully perfected technique of the Fields, Hummels, Charles Mayers and others. Among the younger pianists, he even preferred the cold, correct, passionless Thalberg to Liszt. And why? Because of his scale passages! All the fire, turbulence, tenderness, poetry, drama in Liszt's playing—everything that his playing expressed—was completely lost on Glinka. All he talked about was technique, accuracy, scales!

Serov tells us (in the magazine *Iskusstvo*, 1860, No. 3) that Glinka did not approve of Liszt's idea of playing orchestral works (overtures, symphonies, etc.) on the piano, maintaining that "compared with the effect produced by the orchestral masses, that of the piano is utterly insignificant!" Glinka simply did not understand the new, hitherto unheard-of rôle of the piano. Does this not seem strange for such a great man, a musician of such genius as Glinka? But such is the power of one's milieu. In this, the stupid musical training and pervading atmosphere in Russia made itself felt. As far as the piano and its performance are concerned, Glinka created nothing new, nothing of his own; he left everything exactly as it was, untouched by his own thinking. In this sphere, he adhered to the most routine and banal attitudes. That is why he never cared for Rubinstein's playing and found very little in it that pleased him when he heard this artist in 1849 and 1850. (Sometime I shall go into this in detail.)

When it came to instrumental and operatic music, however, it was quite another matter. In this sphere Glinka was a great artist, and every word he uttered regarding it was pertinent and meaningful. Here everything was tested and tempered by his own thinking, and therefore there is no trace of tradition, routine, custom. Here he dared to exercise his own judgement and did not hesitate to hold opinions directly opposite the generally accepted ones concerning Mozart, Weber, Italian music, Italian singers, the famous concerts of the Paris Conservatory, and so on. In all likelihood, he could also have appreciated the true significance of Liszt's great gift for composition, despite the views of the public and "critics" just as he did Berlioz' great talent during these years. In spite of the prevailing opinion, he called Berlioz "the foremost composer of our century".[1] It is very likely that had he known Liszt's works, he would have bracketed Berlioz and Liszt together. But unfortunately, Glinka heard Liszt only in Petersburg, and there he played nothing particularly important of his own, even though by then he had written such remarkable works as the *Sposalizio* and *Il Penseroso* (composed in 1838) and other pieces of the *Années de pèlerinage*. Consequently, Glinka knew none of this music, and since he did not consider the fantasies on operatic themes and the many superb transcriptions of special consequence, he looked upon Liszt only as a pianist—and wrongly, at that.

Thus, Liszt did not make the impression on Glinka that he should have, and he did not influence any of Glinka's subsequent creative work. Liszt's finest, his major compositions were still to be written and the important ones that did exist at the time were not played in Glinka's presence in Petersburg.

As for the rest of our musicians of that time and the public, neither Liszt's playing nor his music left any deep impression on them. Dargomïzhsky was already a man of thirty, but he had not yet produced anything out of the ordinary. He had written a fairly large number of songs, but they were quite mediocre. And although he himself was a very good pianist, he apparently was not much impressed by Liszt, for nowhere, in any of his letters, conversations or reminiscences, do we find the slightest reference to him.

In 1842–3 Serov was only in his early twenties and naturally, he was absolutely carried away by Liszt's playing. But neither then nor later did Liszt exert any influence on him either as a composer or music critic. All his life, Serov regarded Liszt as a phenomenal pianist, but he never shared Liszt's views and opinions about music (except in the case of Richard Wagner), and he never liked Liszt's works; in fact, in the last years of his life, he was openly hostile toward them. As for the Russian pianists, not one of them adopted anything from the Lisztian style (not even in the matter of technique), and after he left, they played exactly as they had before he came.

Thus, Serov was deeply mistaken when, in his youthful, pure enthusiasm over Liszt's concerts, he wrote me in one of his letters:

> Liszt has clearly made a tremendous impression on our public. His accomplishments are so staggering, so new to everyone, that I really believe now all the professional pianists are going to die of starvation and the amateurs of despair! Indeed, who will dare regale us with his playing after these supernatural sounds; who will have that leonine power, that lightning speed, that feminine tenderness? And who has that terrifying dramatic power, that all-embracing fidelity to nature, that angelic composure and furious, demonic fire? No one, because the world has never before known such a wonder, and it will probably be many centuries before anything like it appears again!

[1] In a letter to Kukolnik, 18th April, 1845.

Serov fretted and fussed needlessly. The momentary flame went out, the momentary gust of ecstasy and excitement suddenly abated, and every grain of dust returned quickly to its accustomed place. The public, as before, managed to get along on the most ordinary music, savoured it and extolled it; as before they were captivated by all sorts of worthless, mediocre stuff. But now, another new, precious banality was added—Italian opera and Italian singers, something heretofore almost completely unknown in our country.

While Liszt's visits to Russia left no deep imprint on the Russians, they left him with indelible memories. Foremost among them were those of Glinka, whose genius he had recognized and appreciated immediately. On his very first visit, in 1842, he came to know and admire both of Glinka's operas. In fact, he knew *A Life for the Tsar* so well that at his fifth concert he improvised extensively on some of its themes, throwing the entire audience into a state of indescribable rapture. His understanding of *Ruslan* was so sensitive and profound that Glinka himself said, "Liszt showed a true understanding of all the key passages." One can easily imagine, then, how puzzled Liszt must have been at the Russian public's strange attitude toward this great musician. ". . . forgotten by almost everyone," Glinka himself wrote. How do you like that! What scorn and pity Liszt must have felt for all of us—Liszt, that magnificent, cultured human being, that lofty, gentle, noble soul. Even forty years later, he still remembered a remark he had heard about Glinka in Petersburg. On 24th October, 1884 he wrote to the Countess Mercy-Argenteau:

> . . . I recall a striking remark Grand Duke Michael made to me in '43: "When I have to put my officers under arrest, I send them to performances of Glinka's operas."

How many times Liszt must have said to himself, as he looked at the audience, "Poor things! It's like casting pearls before swine!" And then he would play some fashionable rubbish for this senseless crowd that would dazzle them as shiny trinkets dazzle a savage. We know from Liszt's letters that he did not think very highly of European audiences. What, then, must he have thought of us Russians?! He stood *alone* in his appreciation of Glinka; indeed, for forty-three years, until the very end of his life, he never forgot this man and never ceased to esteem him highly. We shall see ample proof of this later on. We might add, in passing, that beginning with his first visit to our country, Liszt formed firm relationships with the Russian school of music which not only endured, but broadened, deepened and grew more cordial until his very last days.

Here, by the way, I should also like to mention that, in accordance with his usual custom of flattering local musicians and giving innocent pleasure to local dilettantes, Liszt made piano transcriptions (magnificent ones) of several of our amateurs' worthless "Russian" compositions. He transcribed Count Vielgorsky's songs "In Other Days" and "You Would Not Believe How Sweet You Are", Alyabiev's "The Nightingale" and a galop by Bulgakov. On the other hand, he also transcribed Chernomor's March, one of the greatest and most original musical creations of our time.

I shall conclude this review of Liszt's visits to Russia with a brief account of his concerts in Kiev, Odessa and Elizavetgrad.

Liszt came to Kiev at the beginning of 1847. His first concert, given in an exhibition hall at the end of January, attracted an enormous crowd and created an enormous stir. His second concert, in a hall at the University, also drew a large crowd. But the audience attending the third concert, on 2nd February, was not very large, and Liszt remarked, with a chuckle, that this time they were *en famille*. The most curious thing about these concerts, however, was the reaction of the Russian press. I doubt whether Liszt had ever encountered such hostility and such a lack of understanding of his genius anywhere before, except in certain conservative Berlin newspapers which, despite the public acclaim, abused him maliciously after his concerts in that city at the beginning of 1842.

One N.R., who reviewed Liszt's Kiev concerts in *Moskovsky Gorodskoi Listok* (No. 48, 1847), said that Liszt's playing offered nothing but "fireworks of sound, flickers of inspiration, bits and snatches of emotion, the caprices of a completely self-indulgent gentleman." According to this writer, Liszt played almost everything "in a slipshod, offhand manner, as the spirit moved him"; treated the audience too cavalierly, changed programmes, substituted one piece for another and even omitted many pages of them, "probably under the effect of the dinners that were given him." Only occasionally, asserted this critic, did his playing reveal his true talent. "On the whole, Liszt has no creative gifts," wrote N.R. "He can neither compose a melody of his own nor assimilate and elaborate an idea of someone else. As a result, his themes and the ornaments and embellishments he adds to them are poorly suited to each other . . ."

In conclusion, Mr. N. R. asserted that "Liszt's talent is sterile. He has wasted and ruined it amid the shallow, frivolous life of French society, which is susceptible to mere superficial effects . . . The impotence of present-day Western society is clearly reflected in the impotence of Liszt's talent . . ."

Such, then, were the views of this unknown Kiev critic. In fairness to our country, it must be said that this was the one and only instance here of such short-sightedness and lack of understanding of this great musician. Whether it represented the opinion of a single individual or was shared by the Kiev public, we cannot say. There were no reviews of Liszt's concerts in the Kiev press, for the simple reason that at that time Kiev did not have a single newspaper or periodical that carried art cirticism. To be sure, N. R. said that "After Liszt's first two concerts, most people felt that the artist does not fully deserve the adoration that surrounds him . . . In the end, most of the public decided that the rôle of a sheared lamb is an unenviable one, and that by attending two concerts, they had done their duty as cultured Europeans and could now sleep peacefully." But whether the majority of the people were of this opinion or not, we now have no way of knowing.

Half a year later, at the end of July, 1847, on his way from Constantinople to Germany and France, Liszt stopped in Odessa. He gave six concerts there, in the Hall of the Exchange, all with tremendous success. Of the first one, on 20th July, *Odessky Vestnik* (Nos. 58–59) wrote:

> Liszt's appearance in Odessa has excited and claimed the attention of everyone. His name is heard in every nook and corner, even in places where no music is ever heard except that of an organ-grinder or wandering gypsy violinist . . . And after the sounds of the *Galop chromatique* had died away and the great artist, looking slightly exhausted, had taken several curtain calls in response to the thunderous ovation and finally disappeared, the whole audience still stood there as if waiting for something . . . After the concert, a crowd gathered outside List's suite at the Richelieu Hotel to greet him with bravos and applause, and an Italian orchestra serenaded him . . .

Another critic, who signed himself "D", also expressed his own and the public's ecstasy. "All Liszt needed was one second," D's article began. "All he had to do was hurl one colossal bomb—the *William Tell* overture—and Odessa was taken by storm . . ." In conclusion the article stated:

> Liszt's *Galop chromatique* is descended, I think, from that Bucephalus, which only Alexander the Great was able to mount. This piece was given a stormy performance. Alexander was the son of Jupiter.

After Odessa, in August, Liszt gave some concerts in Elizavetgrad, but since at that time this city had no newspapers or magazines, we know nothing about them. It is an interesting fact, however, that these were the *last concerts* given by Liszt. With them he ended his career as a virtuoso and he never again played before the European public.

*

Schumann came to Petersburg a year after Liszt, during the Lenten season of 1844. He came to our country not on his own behalf but because of his wife, the noted pianist Clara Schumann, who decided to include Petersburg and Moscow in her concert tours. At that time Germany was astir with the glad tidings that Russian roubles were being handed out generously to musical celebrities, such as Liszt, Thalberg, Pasta, Rubini, Viardot, Tamberlik, Lipinsky, Leopold von Meyer and others. Schumann had no intention of appearing in public himself, despite the fact that he was then only thirty-four, was at the peak of his creativity and had already composed almost all of his major works: *Carnaval*, *Études symphoniques*, *Fantasiestücke*, *Novelletten*, the First Sonata, three string quartets, a piano quartet and quintet, the First Symphony, and *Das Paradies und die Peri* for solo, chorus and orchestra (the last he then considered his "best work").

In letters to friends, Schumann called his forthcoming trip to Russia the "Lapland journey", but his opinion of this Lapland soon changed.

On 1st April, he wrote from Petersburg to his father-in-law, Friedrich Wieck:

We have now been here for four weeks. Clara has given four concerts and has played before the Empress. We have made some delightful acquaintances and have seen many interesting things . . . But we made one great mistake: we came here too late. In such a large city as this, many preparations must be made. Everything here depends on the Court and the *haute volée*; the newspapers have little influence. Moreover, everyone here seems to have gone mad over the Italians. Garcia created an extraordinary *furore*. Because of this, the first two concerts were not fully attended, but the third was crowded, and the fourth (at the Mikhailovsky Theatre) was the most brilliant of all. Whereas in the case of other artists, even Liszt, the public interest has been waning, in Clara's case it has steadily increased, and she could probably have given four more concerts, had not Holy Week intervened and the time come for us to go to Moscow.

Our closest friends, of course, have been the Henselts, who received us most affectionately and, next to them, the Vielgorskys, two excellent men, especially Michael—a man of a truly artistic nature, and the most gifted amateur I have ever met. Both have a great deal of influence at Court and are received by the Emperor and Empress almost every day. I believe Clara is nursing a secret passion for Count Michael who, by the way, is already a grandfather—that is, he is past fifty, but is as fresh as a boy in body and soul. We have also found a most friendly patron in the Prince of Oldenburg (the Emperor's nephew), as well as in his wife, who is goodness and kindness itself. Yesterday they themselves showed us around their palace. The Vielgorskys, too, have been very kind; they gave a soirée for us with an orchestra, for which I prepared and conducted my symphony.[1] I will tell you about Henselt when I see you. He is the same as ever; but he is wearing himself out giving lessons. He cannot be persuaded to play in public, and is to be heard only at the home of the Prince of Oldenburg, where one evening he and Clara played my variations for two pianos.

The Emperor and Empress have been very kind to Clara. A week ago she played for two whole hours at the palace just for the royal family. Mendelssohn's "Frühlingslied" has become a favourite with everyone. Clara has had to repeat it several times at every concert; she even had to play it three times for the Empress. Clara will tell you herself about the splendours of the Winter Palace. Count von Ribeaupierre (who used to be ambassador at Constantinople) showed us over it a few days ago. It is like a tale from the *Arabian Nights* . . .

The musicians here have been very kind to us, especially Romberg.[2] They refused to accept any payment for their services at the last concert and permitted us only to send carriages for them . . .

[1] Schumann is referring to his symphony in B-flat major.
[2] The conductor.

For her part Clara Schumann wrote her father that at Count Vielgorsky's they had also played her husband's quartets, adding "These Vielgorskys are wonderful to artists; they live only for art and do not begrudge any expense, but they are the only ones here like this . . ."

We find an interesting detail in Schumann's letter of 14th May, 1844 to Friedrich Wieck. After extolling the Grand Duchess Elena Pavlovna, at whose home Clara played once, for her graciousness and wide culture, he adds: "We talked to her at length about the possibility of founding a conservatory in St. Petersburg and it seemed as though she would like very much to keep us here . . ." This shows how long ago the Grand Duchess Elena Pavlovna was nursing the idea of founding a conservatory in Russia (an idea which, incidentally, was not realized until 1862, some eighteen years later). Since only the previous year, Schumann himself had become a teacher of piano at the newly-founded Leipzig Conservatory,[1] he naturally was not at all opposed to the Grand Duchess's idea. He did not yet fully realize the effects, harmful or beneficial, that conservatories might have in our day; he did not disapprove of them as Glinka and Liszt did on the basis of some glaring examples. In any case, we now know that there was a moment when Schumann might have remained in Petersburg, and for a long time, and might very well have exerted a great influence on the course of Russian music and the direction taken by Russian musicians. However, this did not happen in 1844, and it was a long time before Schumann exerted even the slightest influence on our school of music.

Yuri Arnold, who saw Schumann and his wife in 1844 at a musicale at Alexis Lvov's, gave me the following interesting details about them:

That evening Clara Schumann played her husband's piano quartet, his *Kreisleriana* and some other pieces. We were deeply impressed by her, even though by that time we were becoming used to women virtuosi. During the thirties and forties, Countess Kalergi (*née* the Countess Nesselrode, later the wife of the Privy Councillor Mukhanov) often played at charity concerts, and a year or two before Clara Schumann came, the noted cellist Sophie Bohrer had performed in Petersburg. As always, Schumann was morose and taciturn the whole evening. He spoke very little. In reply to questions from the Vielgorskys and his host, Alexis Lvov, he only mumbled something. True, a kind of conversation developed between Schumann and the famous violinist Molique, who had come to Petersburg only a few days before, but this was carried on almost in a whisper and without any animation. Schumann spent most of the evening sitting in a corner near the piano (all the music stands for the performers of Mendelssohn's Octet were placed in the centre of the hall). He seemed lost in thought as he sat there, his head bowed, hair hanging down over his face, and his lips pursed as though he were about to whistle. The Schumann I saw that evening looked for all the world like a life-sized medallion by the sculptor Dondorf. Clara Schumann was somewhat more talkative than her husband, and she replied for him. In her playing she proved to be a very great artist with the energy of a man and sensitivity of a woman, even

[1] The Leipzig Conservatory was opened by Mendelssohn in April, 1843.

though she was only twenty-five or twenty-six. But hardly anyone found her a warm and gracious person. Both she and her husband spoke French with a Saxon accent and German like *ehrbare Leipziger*.

During the many weeks that Schumann spent in Petersburg and Moscow, he remained completely "incognito" as far as the Russian musical world was concerned. Neither Glinka nor Dargomïzhsky heard him; they were not even aware that he was here. Except for a small circle of aristocrats, no one had any idea that such a great musician was visiting Petersburg (I remember this vividly). No one talked about him, he gave no concerts, and he never appeared in public. Even most of the people interested in music knew only a few of his piano compositions, and then by no means the best and most important ones. With the possible exception of Anton Gerke, none of the music teachers here made their students play Schumann's pieces. Despite his friendship with Schumann, even Henselt never played his music nor gave it to any of his countless students to play. And no wonder: Schumann's piano compositions were so original, so new that they appealed to very few people at that time. Even Liszt did not dare play them at his concerts. He himself spoke of this in a letter to Wasielewski, Schumann's biographer:

> I was so often unsuccessful with Schumann's pieces both in public and in private circles [wrote Liszt],* that I became discouraged from including them in my programmes . . . Besides, I seldom, only in the rarest cases, planned my programmes myself . . .

If even Liszt could not force Schumann on his listeners in the thirties and forties, how much more difficult this would have been for others! As for our conductors, they never performed any of Schumann's orchestral or choral works. Neither our professional nor our amateur singers knew anything at all about his wonderful songs. In those days, the sole idol of the "cognoscenti and musicians" in the concert halls and drawing rooms was Mendelssohn, and in the theatre—the Italians, Italians, Italians. Therefore, our musical authorities, the Vielgorskys and Lvov, received Schumann and his wife graciously in their homes, showered them with kindness, presented them to the Court, had the composer's symphony and quartets played at their soirées (at considerable expense)—but that was the end of that. After Schumann left, they promptly forgot all about him. If those "highly gifted dilettantes", the Vielgorskys, had really liked Schumann, if they had understood him, of course, all they would have had to do was say the word, and Schumann's music would have been played at all the concerts, it would have been disseminated, and everything would have been done to arouse the public's interest in it. But alas! These "highly gifted dilettantes" were not the least bit interested.

* On 9th January, 1857. [Trans.]

They had ears and hearts only for Mendelssohn and the sweet, precious, charming, matchless Italians. Everyone else could wait.

And Schumann waited ten long years.

*

Berlioz first came to know and take an interest in the Russian musical world through Glinka. In an article on Glinka, in the *Journal des Débats* in 1845, he said:

I ran across him in 1831 in Rome,[1] and I had the pleasure of hearing several of his Russian songs sung superbly by the Russian tenor Ivanov, at a soirée at the home of Horace Vernet, the Director of the French Academy in Rome. I was deeply impressed by the charming turn of their melodies, which were completely different from anything I had ever heard before! . . .

Ten years later, in 1841, Berlioz was living in extreme poverty. Things were going very badly with him at that time. His relations with his wife, the former English actress, Henrietta Smithson, whom he had once loved passionately but now found utterly unbearable, were very painful. But even more painful were the repeated failures of his huge concerts, persecution by obtuse music critics and continual financial difficulties. He was subjected to endless suffering and worry, and only his indomitable spirit and tremendous will power sustained him. It was at such a moment that he suddenly received the news that in some far away place, barbaric Russia, at the end of the earth, his *Requiem* had been performed with brilliant success. This was an event of the utmost importance to Berlioz. He was overjoyed and on 3rd October, 1841 he wrote to his friend Humbert Ferrand:

You have no doubt heard of the "spaventoso" success of my *Requiem* in St. Petersburg. It was performed in its entirety at a concert given "ad hoc" by the combined forces of all the opera houses, the Tsar's Chapel and the choristers of two regiments of the Imperial guard.[2] According to the accounts of those who heard it, the performance, conducted by Henri Romberg, was incredibly majestic. Despite the financial risk involved, this worthy Romberg, thanks to the generosity of the Russian nobility, made a clear profit of 5,000 francs. When it comes to the arts, give me democratic governments! . . .* Here, in

[1] At that time Glinka was twenty-seven, and Berlioz twenty-nine.

[2] This concert was given on 1st March, 1841 in the Engelhardt Hall. *Severnaya Pchela* wrote of it: "Berlioz is the founder of a new school, as yet little known but rapidly spreading throughout all Europe . . . The *Requiem* reveals Mr. Berlioz to be an unusual and erudite composer . . . In an ordinary concert hall the three orchestras cannot achieve the composer's aims and are, for the most part, lost. The mass of horns and kettledrums only succeed in deafening the listener. For this reason Berlioz' *Requiem* pleases less, on the whole, than works in the same genre by Mozart, Cherubini and even Kreutzer. However, we cannot but commend our artists on their masterful performance of even the most difficult passages and contratulate Mr. Romberg, on behalf of all music lovers, for affording them such lofty musical enjoyment."

* This is clearly a mistranslation on Stasov's part. The original reads: "Parlez-moi des gouvernements despotiques pour les arts!" [Trans.]

Paris, I would have to be mad to think of giving this work in its entirety, unless I were resigned to losing as much as Romberg made . . .

The following year, convinced of Russia's musical solvency and, of course, encouraged by the recent enthusiastic reception given his friend Liszt, Berlioz wrote to the Petersburg music publisher Bernard, on 10th September, 1842:

In a few weeks I shall finish the *Treatise on Modern Instrumentation and Orchestration*. My articles on this subject, published in the *Gazette musicale de Paris* are nothing more than a brief enumeration. I believe this work will be useful to all amateurs and professionals engaged in composition. It will constitute a large octavo volume and will contain numerous examples, in full score and in parts, taken from great musical works as well as from several of my own unpublished compositions. It might be sold for fifteen or twenty francs. I would be very pleased if you would like to acquire the rights to this work for Russia. I should like to receive 2,000 francs for it . . .

Naturally, Bernard, who knew more about the state of music in our country than Berlioz did, rejected the offer. Thus ended Berlioz's first contact with Russia.

When Glinka went to Paris almost three years later, driven from Russia by the public's indifference toward him and his brilliant *Ruslan* and the ridiculous "madness" (as Schumann put it) over Italian opera and Italian singers, he soon got to know Berlioz. Prince Vasily Petrovich Golitsyn introduced them. "Berlioz was extremely friendly to me, unlike most of the Parisian musicians, who were unbearably arrogant", Glinka writes in his *Memoirs*. "I visited him several times a week and talked frankly with him about music, particularly his works, which I liked."

Glinka wrote to Kukolnik on 6th April, 1845:

The first rays of the spring sun have revitalized me, not only in body but also in soul. Chance has brought me into contact with several nice people, and in Paris, I have found not many, but sincere and gifted friends. Certainly, for me the most wonderful thing that has happened has been meeting Berlioz. One of my purposes in coming here was to study his works, which are so denounced by some and so extolled by others, and I have had the good fortune to do this. Not only have I heard Berlioz' music in concert and rehearsal, but I have also grown close to this man who, in my opinion, is the *foremost* composer of our century (in his own province, of course)—as close, that is, as one can to an extremely eccentric man. And this is what I think: in the realm of fantastic music, no one has ever approached his colossal and, at the same time, ever new conceptions. In sum, the development of details, logic, harmonic texture and finally, powerful and continually new orchestration—this is what constitutes the character of Berlioz' music. When it comes to drama, he is so carried away by the fantastic aspect of a situation, that he becomes unnatural and consequently untrue. Of the works I have heard, the Overture to *Les Francs-Juges*, the March of the Pilgrims from *Harold in Italy*, the Queen Mab scherzo, and the *Dies Irae* and *Tuba Mirum* from the *Requiem* have made an indescribable impression on me. At present, I have a number of Berlioz' unpublished manuscripts and I am studying them with inexpressible delight . . .

In his *Memoirs*, Glinka notes:

I often visited Berlioz. His conversation was very entertaining—he could be sharp and even caustic . . .

During this period Berlioz came to know many of Glinka's works, both through the *concert monstre*, which he gave in the Champs Elysées, and at a concert given by Glinka in the small Salle Herz. The following works by Glinka were performed at these two concerts: Chernomor's March and the Lezginka from *Ruslan and Ludmila* (the latter at Berlioz's request), Ludmila's cavatina from the same opera, Antonida's cavatina from *A Life for the Tsar*, the *Valse Fantaisie* and several songs. None of this music made the slightest impression on the French. Glinka's concert was completely wasted on them, and the considerable sum he spent on it went for naught. But with Berlioz, it was quite another matter. He had obtained an idea of what to expect of the Russian composer from Liszt, Glinka's first foreign admirer; now he came to appreciate Glinka on his own. In this these two great Western musicians were in full accord. Berlioz recognized Glinka's worth in Paris, despite the indifference of the Parisian public, just as Liszt had, three years before in Petersburg, despite the indifference of the Russian public.

Shortly after these two concerts, Berlioz wrote to Glinka.*

It is not enough, Sir, to perform your music and to "tell" many people that it is fresh, alive, charming in spirit and originality. I must give myself the pleasure of writing a few columns about it; what is more, this is my duty.

Must I not keep the public informed of all the most noteworthy events of this kind that take place in Paris? Will you therefore be good enough to give me a few notes about yourself, your early studies, the musical institutions in Russia, your works, and after going over your score with you so as to have a less imperfect knowledge of it, I may be able to write something tolerable and to give the readers of the "Débats" some idea of your excellence.

I am dreadfully bothered with these cursed concerts, the pretensions of the artists, etc.; but I will find the time to write an article on a subject of this nature. I do not often have such an interesting one.

Glinka did not provide Berlioz with the information himself. He was too modest; he did not like to talk about himself. His old friend Melgunov, who was living in Paris at the time, did it for him. On the basis of these biographical notes, Berlioz published an article in the *Journal des Débats* giving a brief account of Glinka's life, his works and his status in Russia. Then, for his own part, he said:

A Life for the Tsar is a truly national opera; it has scored a brilliant success. Quite apart from its patriotic slant, it has many fine qualities . . . But his second opera, *Ruslan and Ludmila*, differs so much from the first that one might imagine it had been written by an entirely different composer. Here the composer's talent manifests much greater power and maturity! *Ruslan* is unquestionably a step forward, a new phase in Glinka's musical development. In the first opera,

* In January, 1845. [Trans.]

in all the melodies marked by a fresh and truly national colour, one can sense a strong Italian influence; in the second, on the other hand, the important rôle given the orchestra, the beauty of the harmonic structure, and the masterful instrumentation reveal a predominantly German influence. Glinka's talent is unusually flexible and varied: he can change his style at will to fit the demands and character of his subject. He can be simple, even naive, but he never stoops to vulgarity. His melodies contain unexpected notes; his periods are strangely charming. He is a great harmonist. He is so painstaking with his scoring, he handles the instruments with such a deep understanding of their most secret resources, that his orchestra is one of the freshest, most alive orchestras of our time . . . Glinka's *Valse-Fantaisie* is charming, filled with piquant and coquettish rhythms; it is truly novel and superbly worked out. The most striking feature in his krakoviak and Chernomor's March is the originality of the melodic style. This is a rare quality, and when the composer combines his melodies with original, graceful harmony and superb orchestration—orchestration that is bold, transparent and colourful—he can rightfully take his place among the foremost composers of his epoch . . .

It goes without saying that Berlioz' article had no effect on the French whatsoever. They went right on worshipping their old idols. As for the consequences of Glinka's close acquaintance with Berlioz and his scores, this will be discussed later.

A year and a half later, Berlioz was even worse off than before. He had many debts and nothing in view. Both then and later he said many times that nothing ever wounded him so deeply as his compatriots' utter indifference to his *Faust*, which was given in December, 1846. It was then that he conceived the idea of improving his situation by going to Russia. Glinka writes in his *Memoirs* that at the time he met Berlioz, the composer "was thinking of going to Russia in hopes of a rich harvest, not only of applause, but also of money . . . I did everything I could to help make his trip to Russia a success . . ."

Since Berlioz had no money himself, he had to seek the help of various friends—editors, booksellers, instrument makers—in order to undertake the trip. Some lent him a thousand, some fifteen hundred, some five hundred francs. The French journals saw him off with their usual sneers and caricatures. For example, the magazine *Charivari* published a caricature, picturing Berlioz lying in bed with large chunks of ice being put on his head. The legend beneath said that "Berlioz' habit of shaking his head proves his Hyperborean origin"; that "in the summertime he has to have bucketfuls of ice continually poured on the back of his head every minute"; that "you can always hear a polar bear in his symphonies."

On 2nd March, 1847, the day before Berlioz' first concert in Petersburg, Prince Odoyevsky published an article in *S.-Peterburgskiye Vedomosti* titled "Berlioz in Petersburg", in which he tried to pave the way for a sympathetic reception of the great French musician. He even pointed out to Berlioz' credit, that he had understood Glinka and had done everything he could to make the French understand him too.

We might add—and this is rather remarkable [wrote Prince Odoyevsky], that Berlioz was one of the few in Western Europe to get to know about Glinka's music. He hastened to perform several numbers from *A Life for the Tsar* at his famous Paris "Festival". The reviews of the leading critics of Paris spoke with great respect about the original, distinctive melodies in Glinka's music, saying all the things that our journals were not half aware of and might very well learn. Berlioz' immediate response to Glinka, so unexpected, so strange for Paris, where we are still thought of as China, did not surprise us. One great talent always recognizes another . . .

In writing this article, Prince Odoyevsky was guided to some extent by a letter Berlioz sent him around that time, the original of which is now in the Imperial Public Library.

Here is some of the information you so kindly requested from me [wrote Berlioz].

Mr. Berlioz, who has just arrived in St. Petersburg, plans to give several concerts, at which large excerpts from his most important works will be performed, if there should be no possibility of giving them in their entirety. Included among the works with which he intends to acquaint us will be his latest composition, which was received with so much enthusiasm in Paris this winter, even though its author is a Frenchman. Artists and writers, under the chairmanship of Baron Taylor,[1] gave a banquet in his honour at which it was decided to raise funds (the entire sum was immediately collected) for the purpose of striking a medal to commemorate the first performance of this work.

In addition, we will hear the large choral symphony *Romeo and Juliet* and the famous *Symphonie Fantastique*, which was dedicated to Emperor Nicholas I. The *Romeo and Juliet* symphony was dedicated, as it well known, to the celebrated Paganini after this great virtuoso sent Berlioz 25,000 francs as his share of the subscription concert at which he heard the *Symphonie Fantastique* for the first time.

A curious feature of this letter is that here Berlioz speaks of the enthusiasm with which the Parisian public received his "descriptive symphony" (or "dramatic legend", as he also called it), the *Damnation of Faust*, in the winter of 1846–47. This assertion completely contradicts the facts previously known to us from Berlioz' autobiography and all his letters. According to these documents, *Faust* was received very coldly by the Parisian public, and this, added to the enormous debts incurred by the concerts, so distressed poor Berlioz that he almost perished. He simply did not know what to do next.

In his well-known biography of Berlioz, Jullien discusses this in detail and adds, in conclusion:

Berlioz said time and again that nothing in his entire artistic career ever wounded him so deeply as the public's unexpected indifference to his *Faust*. And his disappointment was particularly keen because this followed immediately the tremendous ovations he had received in Germany. What is more, he was ruined, burdened by huge debts from which he saw no way of escaping.

[1] Baron Taylor, one of the leading art patrons in France, was then that country's Inspector of Fine Arts and had enormous influence among artists and the public.

And suddenly, just at this moment, he was presented with a totally unexpected opportunity to extricate himself from his difficulties; he had only to undertake a journey to Russia . . . He did just that. He went and he brought back from Petersburg and Moscow enormous new fame and several thousand roubles, enough to cover all his disappointments and all the debts incurred by *Faust*.

Thus, Berlioz' letter to Prince Odoyevsky did not state the full truth when it claimed that *Faust*, whose best pages were about to be performed in Petersburg, had scored a tremendous success in Paris. This was not so. On the other hand, it cannot be said that what Berlioz wrote was sheer fiction, that he told an out-and-out lie. At that time, as always, he was surrounded by a group of people who were truly devoted to him, sincerely loved his music and, what is more, were capable of understanding true genius. These connoisseurs were few in number, of course, but their quality and importance made up for this. Included among them were all the most important musicians of the Paris of that day, with Liszt and Meyerbeer at the head, and all the best, most important and most gifted artists, poets and music lovers, among them such people as Heine, George Sand, Baron Taylor and many others. It was these people who comforted Berlioz and cheered him with their warm friendship; it was they who contributed the money and had the medal struck in his honour. Thus, Berlioz had reason to be proud in his letter to Russia. Incidentally, in due course, the stupid, ignorant crowd also came to adore Berlioz, but this was not until considerably later, some forty years later, long after Berlioz had gone to his grave.

On 5th April,* two days after Berlioz' first concert, Odoyevsky published an extended piece in *S.-Peterburgskiye Vedomosti* in the form of a letter to Glinka, which reads:

Where are you, dear friend? Why are you not with us? Why are you not sharing the pleasure with all of *us*, whose hearts beat as one? Berlioz is understood in Petersburg! He is understood despite his intricate counterpoint; he is understood, despite the deluge of Italian cabalettas which have diluted our stern Slavic feelings; he is understood despite the barrenness of our musical criticism, which, far from enlightening our public, has only confused them . . . With pure, genuine delight the public has succumbed to Berlioz' spell . . . Berlioz has advanced music dozens of steps—a pity, perhaps!—but fortunately by now the public has lost its faith in the drivel of the knights of the guitar and balalaika! It is beginning to put more trust in its own musical instinct and rightly so; now and then there are even signs of conscious conviction. Nowhere was this so noticeable as at Berlioz' concert . . . The enormous Assembly Hall of the Nobility was filled to overflowing. Of course, the *Rákóczy March* and *The Dance of the Sylphs* had to be repeated. This did not surprise me. But would you believe it, the audience listened attentively to and fully enjoyed the marvellous chorus "Christus resurrexit" in the first part of *Faust*, in spite of its strict, sharply-etched forms. I was very apprehensive about how they might respond to the Soldiers' Chorus, which is combined so felicitously with the

* This date is clearly an error. Two days after Berlioz' first concert was 5th March, not April. [Trans.]

Students' Chorus . . . This chorus, which is rather difficult to follow, was received with unanimous applause. The scene from *Romeo and Juliet*, in which Romeo's melancholy theme is combined with the glittering playful phrases of the music of the Capulet's ball was also greeted with a shower of applause . . . Berlioz was called out at least a dozen times in the course of the concert . . . What a delight it is to hear this marvellous music a second time: how unconscious feeling and conscious conviction become one! I must confess I fully realized the charm of many passages in *Faust* and *Romeo* only on the second hearing. I was even more delighted with the enthusiastic response of our public, to most of whom Berlioz' music was utterly new. There must be a special affinity between his music and our innate musical sense: only this could account for such a response. How long has it been said that there is nothing new in music, that everything is stale, trite, hackneyed! Everything in Berlioz is new, and there is not a chord in his brilliant imagination that does not strike a responsive chord in the soul of the listener, a new chord whose existence we did not even suspect! How many untapped treasures lie hidden in the depth of human feelings!

In contrast to this review by a true connoisseur and estimable amateur musician, the same publication printed a review a few days later, by its amateur feuilletonist who said:

It seems to us, and we say this humbly and with trepidation, that Berlioz' music is designedly original, even somewhat contrived in its effects . . . On the whole, we think that it speaks more to the mind than it does to the heart, that it awakens more puzzled surprise than pure delight. This is music of the nineteenth century; it is a vigorous, powerful embodiment in sound of our anxious age, with its suffering without belief, striving without purpose, sorrow without submission, gaiety without joy. In this sense, there is something profoundly meaningful in Berlioz' music, something titanic, something that automatically strikes one with terror and bewilderment. In it there is ceaseless struggle but neither the plaintive moan of the captive nor the ecstatic cry of the free. In it there is neither victor nor vanquished. Above all, it lacks that touching, comforting element of reconciliation which emanates from the creations of the great musical poets . . . It grieves us to say this, but we must confess that, while the art of our day has attained the most perfect finish, it lacks the divine spark . . .[1] (Incidentally, in two other articles, this same writer, who signed himself "S", praised many many parts of Berlioz' works, such as the *Rákóczy March*, *The Dance of the Sylphs* and excerpts from *Romeo*.)

Berlioz himself was highly pleased with the audience, concerts and substantial box-office receipts.

When the concert was over, the embraces concluded, and a bottle of beer consumed [he writes in his *Memoirs*], I decided to inquire about the financial result of the experiment. Receipt, *eighteen thousand francs*; expenses, six thousand; clear profit, twelve thousand francs. I was saved!

Then, I automatically turned toward the southwest, towards Paris, and could not refrain from murmuring:

"You dear Parisians!"

A week and a half later I gave a second concert with similar results. I was a rich man. Then I went to Moscow, where material difficulties of a strange

[1] *S.-Peterburgskiye Vedomosti*, 9th March, No. 55.

nature awaited me:[1] third-rate musicians, fabulous choristers, but a public quite as sensitive and enthusiastic as that in St. Petersburg, and the result—a clear profit of eight thousand francs. Again I thought of my indifferent and blasé fellow countrymen, and again turned towards the southwest and exclaimed: "Oh, dear Parisians!"

Moskovskiye Vedomosti (No. 40) called Berlioz the "Victor Hugo" of the latest French music.

> . . . an original mind [wrote the author, one "L"], a free and independent talent who knows how to combine strict theory with an unrestrained revolutionary passion for innovation. And that is why he has always been unhappy about the pedantic academicism of the conservatory and the frivolous tastes of the public, the blind devotion of those who frequent Italian and comic opera . . .
>
> A combination of the lofty and the strange, an imagination riotous and wilful yet held within the bounds of the established system; odd forms and strict basic ideas, exaggerated effects, a love for masses of sound, a profound loathing for everything trite and hackneyed, a spirit of rebellion against the old—all this we find in the wonderful works of the French master, and we cannot help being attracted by their unprecedented boldness, their destructive, yet seemingly prophetic character. Listening to Berlioz' music, one has the feeling that everything has been turned upside down, everything questioned . . . But there is no doubt that the revolution which Berlioz has brought about in music, especially instrumental music, will have a mighty and fruitful impact on the art of the future. As an orchestrator Berlioz probably has no equal: no one else seems to have attained such a profound knowledge of the orchestra and its effects, such an ability to combine instruments, to draw from the orchestra sounds never heard before and to transform them into an arcane language for the expression of all the nuances of human feeling . . .[2]

Of all the journals, *Biblioteka dlya Chteniya* was the least friendly to Berlioz. The information it published differed greatly from that which Berlioz himself had provided and its opinions ran counter to those of the rest of the press. It said that Berlioz had given two concerts in the Assembly Hall of the Nobility, the first, before an enormous audience, the second, before a much smaller one; that his music is "deficient in melody. His works stem not from deep feeling but from reflection, from a rich mind and an extraordinarily lively and vivid imagination"; that "the striving for the new, the unprecedented sometimes lures Berlioz beyond the bounds of the truly beautiful", that he is forever painting "musical pictures" and often "depicts subjects that are completely outside the province of music—for example, the aerial journey in *Faust*, the Capulets' ball in *Romeo and Juliet*, the scene in the country and the execution in the *Symphonie Fantastique*, music, that is, which should be perceived through feeling and not require explanation. These pieces convey the expected

[1] This refers to a curious experience Berlioz had with the Marshal of the Nobility, who refused to let him have the Assembly Hall of the Nobility because he could not and would not play an instrument at a concert for the nobles.

[2] *Moskovskiye Vedomosti*, No. 40.

impression only when the listener knows the programme. Consequently, works of this nature cannot truly be called music . . ."

For all this, *Biblioteka* praised the composer for certain parts of his works. But it observed that in general, "Berlioz does particularly well with marches . . ."

However, when Berlioz returned from Moscow and gave two big concerts at the theatre, which included many excerpts from *Harold, Romeo and Juliet* and *Faust*, the critic of this magazine spoke more favourably of him:

> Although in many respects we do not agree with Berlioz' trend, we must confess that the more we listen to his works, the more we like him. We find much in his music that is new—new ideas, new forms, new rhythms, new orchestral effects. When he tries to achieve the impossible (that is, to produce all the impressions created by poetry and painting by means of instrumental music alone), he should not be ridiculed but respected for his unswerving resolution. After all, who knows what lofty results he may achieve?

After giving a detailed account of *Harold* and *Romeo*, the author concluded as follows:

> Even though we are not in accord with the trend embodied in Berlioz' *Romeo*, we cannot disregard the truly beautiful music it contains . . . When Berlioz is not inhibited by self-imposed restraints, he attains heights accessible only to the greatest geniuses . . .

I, for my part, reporting on Berlioz' concerts in *Otechestvenniye Zapiski*, could not help revealing the confusion and anxiety of the contradictory impressions Berlioz' music had produced on me. On the one hand, I found that "Berlioz' works are utterly devoid of music; he has no gift for musical composition whatsoever"; that "Berlioz and Liszt are strikingly alike in every respect—in taste, ways of thinking, and in their entire manner of performance, down to the smallest details", but that "neither of them has composed anything that could be considered music." At the same time I expressed my deep conviction that "they are both the most brilliant heralds of the future".

"Although we fail to see a Byron in Berlioz, as some of his well-wishers have called him," I said at this point, "we leave each of his concerts in a most extraordinary mood, a mood entirely different from that produced by the usual concerts . . ." After describing several excerpts from *Queen Mab*, the *Dance of the Sylphs* and the *Pilgrims' March*, which had impressed me deeply, I said in conclusion: "One has the feeling that this man will go on developing forever; there is no way of knowing what new wonders can be expected of him . . ."[1]

During all this period, the Petersburg aristocracy treated Berlioz exactly as they had Liszt five years before—they were friendly, sympathetic, and respectful. They may not have grasped the essence of his

[1] *Otechestvennïe Zapiski* (1847), Vol. 51, "Smes," pp. 222–7. (For Stasov's full report on Berlioz' concerts, see Chapter I of this book.)

music, they may have found little in it that suited their taste, especially now that the Italians were the rage, but they gave heed to their aristocratic arbiters in matters musical—two counts (Vielgorsky), one prince (Odoyevsky) and one general (Lvov). The arbiters gave the pitch and the rest, in chorus, sustained the note. And so, the fashionable world made a fuss over Berlioz. Lvov, of course, arranged for him to hear our famous Imperial Chapel. Berlioz thought very highly of it.

Four years later, on 1st February, 1851, he wrote to Lvov from Paris:

> Please give my kind regards to the artists of the Imperial Chapel and tell them that I remember them with the greatest affection and sincerest admiration. I have at last succeeded in making them known in Paris and valued almost as much as they deserve. The Parisians no longer believe that the miserable castrati of the Sistine Chapel in Rome are the best and only church singers worthy of the name . . .

He wrote to Lvov again on 21st January, 1852:

> Remember me to your wonderful Chapel and tell the artists belonging to it that I long to hear them so that I might weep . . .*

Berlioz was also highly pleased with the Petersburg theatre orchestra and chorus when he heard them in 1847. But he felt differently about a performance of *A Life for the Tsar* which he attended in Moscow.

> The immense theatre was almost empty [he wrote in his *Memoirs*], and the stage almost constantly represented pine forests covered with snow, steppes covered with snow, people white with snow. I still shiver whenever I think of it. The opera contains many graceful and highly original melodies, but the performance was so poor that I could hardly make them out . . .

Berlioz left Petersburg filled with the most pleasant impressions and memories. We might mention that Empress Alexandra Fedorovna was as kind and gracious to him during his stay there as she had been to Liszt in 1842 and 1843, and she attended his concerts just as she had those of Liszt.

On his return trip from Russia, Berlioz gave a concert in Riga and even in this provincial city, he found ardent admirers. On 22nd May, 1847 he wrote Count Vielgorsky from Riga:

> The audience was as enthusiastic as it was small. There are eleven hundred ships in Riga at present, and all the men are busy buying and selling grain from eight in the morning until eleven at night. As a result the audience was composed almost entirely of women. Nevertheless, I regret neither the fatigue I felt after the concert nor the time devoted to it, after the enthusiastic demonstration of the orchestra, whom I had not known but I now count as my friends . . .

* Here Berlioz' letter reads: ". . . pour me faire verser toutes les larmes que je sens brûler en moi et qui me retombent sur le coeur." This is an example of the way in which Stasov sometimes compressed the original style. [Trans.]

Then, after extolling Shakespeare (whom he always adored) and a performance of *Hamlet* in German that he had seen in Riga, he told Count Vielgorsky:

Oh, if I were very rich, what performances I would give for myself and my friends! And I would not even let the others in the door, the outsiders whom God has placed on earth to order artists about and clip their ambitious wings! Fortunately, he has also placed on earth some beings with great minds, and warm and wonderful hearts, to lift the spirits of these artists when they fall, crushed by the crowd of cretins . . .

Then followed compliments on Vielgorsky's unfinished opera *Gypsies*, which Berlioz urged the author to complete as soon as possible.

What a difference there is between a great musician and an insignificant amateur! The musician praises the amateur's opera, which will forever remain unknown, while the amateur bluntly and unashamedly tells the musician that he "does not understand" one of his works and has him remove it from the programme. (Berlioz related this in his *Memoirs*. The work in question was the *Roman Carnival* Overture.) Count Vielgorsky was only remaining true to his old rôle. Was it not he who, five years before, had gone mad about the Italian warbler Rubini and had told Glinka that his *Ruslan* was a worthless opera? For all this Berlioz liked the Russians, even the dilettante Counts; he found respite among them from the scorn and indifference of his own countrymen, and he was grateful to Russia. He had such need of rest, warmth and a chance to heal his wounds!

In a letter to Lvov on 29th January, 1848, Berlioz wrote:

Oh, Russia! And its warm hospitality, its literary and artistic ways, the organization of its theatres and chapel, that precise, clearly defined, inflexible organization without which, in music, as in many other things, nothing good, nothing beautiful can be accomplished—who will give them back to me? Why are you so far away? . . .

It was so good of you to speak about me to His Majesty and to allow me still to hope that I may one day settle near you. I am not counting too much on this idea: it all depends upon the Emperor. If he wanted it, in six years we would make Petersburg the centre of the musical world . . .

On 28th November, 1848, Berlioz wrote to Count Vielgorsky:

I still have not written my "Letters about Russia"; I still have not been able to make any arrangements about them with the *Journal des Débats* . . . I have so much to say about St. Petersburg that I would like to have a fitting tribune. Mr. Bertin thinks, of course, that I am too infatuated with the Russians. I'll make him see the light.*

* "Je n'ai pas encore écrit mes *Lettres sur la Russie*; M. Bertin ne m'avait pas paru disposé à les imprimer dans les *Débats*, et je ne puis me décider à les donner ailleurs. Je ferai une nouvelle démarche auprès de M. Bertin; peut-être a-t-il changé d'avis maintenant. Je ne sais quelles pouvaient être ses raisons. J'ai tant de choses à dire sur Pétersbourg que je veux une tribune convenable. M. Bertin me trouvait trop *engoué* d'eux sans doute. Je le convertirai." [Original text]

Then, rejecting even the most basic concepts of the new French nationalism, Berlioz, in the spirit of an out-and-out conservative, complained bitterly about the regime that had displaced the House of Orleans.

> The new invasion of cholera in Russia makes me long for your letters [he told Vielgorsky] . . . How many changes have occurred in our unhappy Europe since I left you! What shouting, what crimes, what madness, what stupidities, what atrocious deceptions! Be grateful to God that your cholera is only physical; moral cholera is a hundred times more deadly. Paris always has a fever and frequent attacks of "delirium tremens". When one thinks, under such conditions, of the peaceful labours of the intellect, of the quest for beauty in literature and art, it is like starting a game of billiards on a ship during a storm in the middle of the Antarctic, just at the moment when the hold has sprung a leak and the sailors have mutinied below deck . . .

A month later, on 22nd December, 1848, Berlioz wrote to Lenz:

> And you are still thinking about music! What barbarians you are! What a pity! Instead of working for the great cause, the radical destruction of the family, property, intelligence, civilization, life, humanity, you busy yourself with the works of Beethoven!! . . . You dream of sonatas! You write a book on music!
>
> Joking aside, I am very grateful to you. There are still some worshippers of beauty alive . . .

And again, on 21st January, 1852, Berlioz wrote to Lvov:

> The opinions of our press and public are more stupid and frivolous than any you will find in any other nation. In our country the beautiful is not the ugly, it's the commonplace: they do not prefer the bad to the good, they prefer the mediocre. The sense of truth is as dead in art as the sense of justice in morality . . .
>
> . . . It will always be a pleasure for me to keep the few serious readers we have in France informed about the great and serious things being done in Russia. Besides, this is a debt I should like very much to pay. Believe me, I shall never forget the way the Russian people, in general, and you, in particular, received me, and the kindness shown me by the Empress and every member of your great Emperor's family. What a pity he doesn't like music!

Did Berlioz visit have any effect on Russian music, Russian musicians, the Russian musical public? In my opinion, none whatever. Neither the trend of Russian music, the form and content of our musical works, our orchestration nor, finally, even the style of conducting changed in the slightest after Berlioz left. Everything remained exactly as before; it was as though Berlioz had never been here at all. Our musicians attended his concerts, listened and left, and the next day they went right on doing exactly what they had done before. It was the same with the public. They enjoyed listening to, reading and talking about Berlioz' "innovations" in this, that and the other thing. They willingly called him a genius, a giant, and so on, who had introduced "new elements", but their musical tastes did not change a hair's breadth, and they remained quite happy with the "old elements". They paid a kind of lip service to the "new elements", but in reality they preferred the "old" and went on revelling in them. It is very doubtful that Berlioz would have influenced and educated these people very quickly even if he had settled in Petersburg, as there was talk of his doing in 1848. It would not have been so easy to make our capital the "centre of the musical world".

There was only *one person* in the entire Russian empire on whom Berlioz had a profound and powerful effect and that was Glinka. But this had happened before Berlioz came here. As early as 1845, Glinka had written his friend Kukolnik from Paris:

> The study of Berlioz' music and the tastes of the Parisian public has had extremely important consequences for me. I have decided to enrich my repertoire with a few and, my strength permitting, many concert pieces for orchestra to be called *Fantaisies pittoresques*. It seems to me that it ought to be possible to reconcile the demands of art with those of our time and, by taking advantage of the improvements in instruments and performance, to write pieces equally accessible to connoisseurs and the general public . . .

The results of this idea were: the *Jota Aragonesa*, *Night in Madrid*, and *Kamarinskaya*. These are brilliant and entirely original works; there is nothing of Berlioz in them—neither in composition, execution, musical ideas, forms nor, finally, orchestration. The person who gave the world *Ruslan* had nothing to learn from Berlioz, nor from anyone else, for that matter. Even if we consider only the orchestration of his second opera, we find that Glinka created effects as novel, beautiful and original as any that Berlioz or any other of the most gifted composers of that day had. Berlioz and Glinka made tremendous innovations in orchestration during the thirties and forties, simultaneously and entirely independently of each other, when they did not know each other at all. Berlioz' *Requiem* was performed in Petersburg in 1841, but Glinka seems not to have heard it. At that time, he was living the life of a hermit and seldom went anywhere—he was, in his own words, "forgotten by almost everyone". At any rate, in his *Memoirs* he speaks of hearing the *Requiem* in Paris in 1845 as though for the first time. Before writing *Ruslan*, he might possibly have heard the new European orchestration in Meyerbeer's *Robert* and *Huguenots* and in some of Mendelssohn's overtures. But there is not a single trace of either of these composers in Glinka's second opera; it is entirely his own. Equally so are the *Jota, Night in Madrid* and *Kamarinskaya*, which were written after Glinka's stay in Paris. What is more, the latter proved to be the first example of a completely original truly *Russian national scherzo*. On the other hand, Glinka himself tells us that it was his acquaintance with Berlioz and his careful study of Berlioz' music that first prompted him to write these purely instrumental "programme" pieces. Therefore, we must believe this and be grateful that they met. The meeting of these two great musicians in Paris did not count for nothing as did Glinka's meeting with Liszt in Petersburg. This time Russia benefited enormously.

*

About twenty years after their visits here, Liszt, Schumann and Berlioz began to exert an enormous influence on the Russian school of music. The composers of this school were Glinka's heirs and successors, and their enthusiasm and esteem for this musician of genius equalled that they had for Beethoven and certain other composers of earlier days. But at the same time, they had a high regard for the three great Western composers of our day, Schumann, Berlioz and Liszt because they were well aware not only of their enormous gifts, but also of their independence of thought and innovatory daring. In his excellent article on Schumann, Liszt says that his two principal contributions were first, that he advanced music further along the path opened by Beethoven and second, that he firmly fixed the direction of this path, which the musicians before him had too seldom followed. Schumann clearly understood the need to bring music (including instrumental music), poetry and literature closer together and this he did. Here is what Liszt said in 1855 about the trend which today is called "programme music":

> Beethoven was groping toward this, but he did not fully realize it in his music; it still remained somewhat obscure (this striving is quite evident in *Egmont* and certain other instrumental works with specific titles).

And then Liszt added:

> The programme is the means by which music will be made more accessible and comprehensible to the active, thinking part of the population, which is at present far removed from it and regard it with a certain scorn. And this does not surprise us when we remember how little music till now has concerned itself with the interests of these people. For hundreds of years music afforded only a kind of sensuous pleasure, which was of scant interest to those who had little time to get used to it. Besides, it was drenched with sentiments that these people could not understand because they could not respond to them . . .

What Liszt ascribes here only to Schumann was equally true of Berlioz and himself. All three of them belong to that group of musicians who not only need a "programme", but to whom music without a programme seems utterly unacceptable, an idle plaything. Having been reared on the vitalizing principles of our forties and fifties, the young composers of the new school of Russian music, which made its appearance at the end of the fifties, felt the same need. They responded immediately to Schumann, Berlioz and Liszt when their magnificent works, embodying this idea, began to be performed at our concerts. By 1855, Schumann was no longer on the scene, but a considerable number of his finest creations had not yet been published, and consequently were not known at the time of his death. Many of them did not appear until the end of the fifties and during the sixties. Similarly, a considerable number of Berlioz' works had not been published, were unknown and began appearing only about this time. Some of them were not even written until the mid-fifties and beginning of the sixties. This is true, for example, of all of the most important ones—*L'Enfance du Christ*, which was composed in 1854; *Te Deum*—in 1855; *Les Troyens*—in 1855.* As for Liszt, all of his major works were either written or given their final form during the fifties and sixties.

All this proved of great value and interest to the new Russian musicians. They plunged avidly into studying these new compositions which, though strange to the general public, to them were works of genius. The new school had been reared mainly on Glinka and Beethoven; now they sought to learn from Schumann, Berlioz and Liszt. They did not make a fetish of these great musicians, however. With their characteristic independence and honesty, they understood very well that the music of Schumann, Berlioz and Liszt contained many flaws. They studied them, analysed them, and regarded them as unfortunate blemishes. For example, the young Russian musicians were fully aware that the symmetry and adherence to strict form, which at times marred some of Schumann's works was a consequence of excessive classical training. They knew also of Schumann's complete ineptitude for orchestration. They were very well aware, too, of the incoherence, vagueness and pomposity of some of Berlioz' writing, the pretentiousness, affectedness and ornateness of some of Liszt's. But the great, the predominant qualities in the music of these composers—imagination, fire, depth of feeling, matchless poetry and descriptiveness—made our young musicians overlook these shortcomings. It is doubtful whether even the most ardent compatriots of Berlioz, Schumann and Liszt valued them as highly as this little group of young Russian musicians did. It should be noted, however, that in this they stood almost alone. Most people here were just as indifferent or hostile toward these three foreigners as their fellow-countrymen in France and Germany. Their true significance came to be recognized very gradually, very slowly and then only long after they had entered into the flesh and blood of the new Russian school. Our school had to endure a great deal because of this.

During the ten years that remained to Schumann after his visit to Russia, he had no contact whatsoever with any Russians. Indeed, this would have been impossible in view of his mental condition—his ever increasing moroseness, melancholy and withdrawal. He died without ever knowing the impression his music made on the northern barbarians, and the profound, fruitful interest he awakened here. We began to know his symphonies at the end of the fifties, first at the performances of the

* According to *Grove's Dictionary of Music and Musicians*, *L'Enfance du Christ* was composed 1850–4, *Te Deum* in 1849, and *Les Troyens* 1856–9. [Trans.]

Concert Symphonic Society given by Lvov in the Imperial Chapel and later, from 1859 on, at the concerts of the Russian Musical Society conducted by Rubinstein. The major credit for including Schumann's works in the programmes of these concerts is due to Dmitri Vasilyevich Stasov[1], who managed them. Meanwhile, thanks to the excellent Belgian pianist Mortier de Fontaine, who lived in Petersburg and Moscow during much of the fifties, Schumann's keyboard compositions also became increasingly known and soon even loved here. The leading exponent of these piano compositions, however, was Anton Rubinstein, who was beginning to win great renown in the fifties. He was always at his best in the music of Chopin and Schumann. But the Free School of Music contributed even more to the dissemination of Schumann's music in Russia. Balakirev, the School's director and conductor of its concerts, and all his colleagues of the new Russian school loved this music passionately and made a profound study of it. Thanks to Balakirev who was on the alert for everything new and highly talented that appeared in European music during the fifties and sixties and brought it to the attention of his colleagues, our school was the first in Russia to get to know Schumann and immerse itself in his wonderful creations.

*

Throughout the last twenty-two years of his life, from his first visit here in 1847 right up to his death in 1868, Berlioz was in continuous contact with Russia. I have already referred to some of the letters he wrote to Count Vielgorsky and Lvov during the forties. Now I shall deal with other letters written to the Russians.

Delighted with some of the magnificent works which had been performed at Berlioz' Petersburg concerts but had not yet been published I wrote the composer in 1847 asking for permission to copy the orchestral scores. Those I inquired about were *Queen Mab*, the *Dance of the Sylphs*, the *Marche Triomphale*, and parts of *Romeo and Juliet*. I hoped to arrange to have them played at our concerts after Berlioz' departure. At the same time, I asked him what he thought of the possibility of using the organ in orchestral works, not combining it with the orchestra and making it repeat what is already in the score, but giving it a separate, independent part. I addressed this question to him because I found no answer to it in his excellent and precise *Treatise on Instrumentation*. Berlioz replied to me on 10th May:

I have barely the time to write you a few lines; I am on the point of leaving. I cannot possibly do without my scores, as I am going to Germany and I will need them for my concerts. As for the organ, it can be used successfully in certain cases, in religious music where it might alternate with the orchestra. But I

[1] The writer's brother.

do not think that a good effect is achieved when it is used simultaneously with it.

Not long afterward Berlioz put this into practice. On 23rd February, 1849 he wrote to Lvov:

At the moment I am working on a large *Te Deum* for double chorus with orchestra and organ obligato. It is beginning to take shape . . .

The *Te Deum* is probably Berlioz' greatest, most masterly work. In line with the ideas set forth in the letter to me, he used the organ throughout independently, apart from the orchestra. As Fouque so correctly put it in *Les révolutionnaires de la musique*, "The giant instrument is almost always separate from the other instruments, and answers them like a voice from heaven answering voices on earth."

When this monumental work was published and became known to our young musicians, they were very enthusiastic about it and eagerly began studying it, mainly under Balakirev's guidance. When I was in Paris, in 1862, I saw Berlioz. I told him how much our new school enjoyed his magnificent works, especially the *Te Deum*, and asked him to give us Russians an original autograph of it. He promised to try to find one and the following day, 10th September, he wrote to me:

By good luck I have found one of my manuscripts in sufficiently good condition, and I am happy to present it to the Public Library of St. Petersburg. It is precisely the manuscript of the *Te Deum* about which you had asked . . .

When I wrote the work I still had faith and hope. Today I have no other virtue left but resignation. But I am nonetheless capable of feeling lively gratitude for the interest which is shown me by true friends of art, such as yourself . . .*

Berlioz' autograph, which has been in our Imperial Library since 1862, is especially valuable because it contains a superb number, *Prelude* for orchestra (designated "No. 3"), which Berlioz did not include in the published score and, therefore, is not known to the rest of Europe. Balakirev included this number in a performance of the *Te Deum* at the Free School.

In 1867 Cui also saw Berlioz in Paris. At the time the composer was ill and deeply depressed over the recent death of his only son. Cui wrote to ask if he might see him to discuss the performance of *Les Troyens* at our Free School concerts, either in part or in its entirety, and also if he might copy the score. Berlioz, who was confined to bed when he received Cui, was delighted to learn that his guest was so familiar with his music that he could even sing many themes from it. Immediately the ice was broken and Berlioz lent Cui the proofs of his *Memoirs*, which had already been printed but were not to be published until after his death. As a memento,

* *New Letters of Berlioz*, 1830–68. With introduction, notes and English translation by Jacques Barzun, 1954. Columbia University Press, p. 221. [Trans.]

he gave Cui a photograph of himself, which he autographed with the main theme of the love scene from *Romeo and Juliet*, a theme he particularly liked and considered his most profound inspiration. Upon returning to Petersburg, Cui published a biographical sketch of Berlioz in *S.-Peterburgskiye Vedomosti*, based on the then unknown *Memoirs* and his conversations with the composer. He described Berlioz as follows:

> He is now sixty-three. He is extremely nervous and sensitive; his imagination is vivid to the point of morbidity. He speaks a most elegant French. He is handsome and impressive in appearance—lean face, high forehead and thick, curly, snow-white hair; eyes that are deep-set, piercing and wise; a prominent, slender, aquiline nose; thin lips; a few sharp lines on his forehead and at the corners of his mouth. There is an elegance about his figure and in all his movements . . .

Here are some excerpts from their conversations:

> Naturally we talked mostly about musical matters. "Mozart's operas are all alike. His imperturbable composure (*beau sang-froid*) irritates and exasperates," said Berlioz. He remarked that Meyerbeer had not only the good luck to have talent but a great talent to have luck. In Rossini's music, Berlioz finds melodic cynicism, a perpetual, puerile crescendo, a coarse bass drum. . . . Of all the conductors he has come across his favourite is Nicolai (composer of *The Merry Wives of Windsor*). In this connection he also thinks highly of Meyerbeer, Wagner and Litolff. But he dislikes Wagner's affected retards, when the orchestra reaches a climax and there is no change in either the tempo or expression. "Liszt conducts and plays on the inspiration of the moment," said Berlioz. "He doesn't convey the composer's thought, but his own feeling at the time. He takes liberties with other people's works, and each time they sound different . . .[1]
>
> Berlioz was very pleased to learn that parts of his *Lélio*, *Faust*, *Romeo* and other works are often performed in Russia, but he regretted that they are not played in their entirety . . .

Cui did not achieve the main purpose of his visit to Berlioz, however. After having agreed to permit him to copy certain numbers from the score of *Les Troyens* for Petersburg, the composer later changed his mind and in a letter, dated 7th August, he asked Cui to give up the whole idea.

> I have thought over our plan . . . [he wrote], and I see great difficulties in it. My publisher may think badly of it and may interpret it in a light very prejudicial to me . . .

Thus, the Petersburg performance of *Les Troyens* was put off for a while. It was not until January, 1868 (while Berlioz himself was here) that a copy of the score was made for Petersburg and sold to the Russian Musical Society.

Berlioz came to Petersburg for the second time in November, 1867. He had been invited by the Grand Duchess Elena Pavlovna, the patroness

[1] In this connection, I would remind the reader that during the last years of his life, Berlioz' opinion of Liszt changed considerably; he was by no means as enthusiastic about Liszt as he had been in his youth.

of the Russian Musical Society, to conduct six of its concerts in Rubinstein's absence. The financial terms were very favourable, especially in view of Berlioz' perpetually straitened circumstances.

On 24th September he wrote to his friend Mme. Damcke:

The Princess is paying my travelling expenses there and back, is placing one of her carriages at my disposal, providing me with living quarters in the Mikhailovsky Palace, and paying me 15,000 francs. If I should die, at least I will know it was worth it . . .

As originally planned, five of the six concerts were to be devoted entirely to classical music (the Grand Duchess was a great lover of the classics) and the sixth to works by Berlioz. But Balakirev, a great admirer of Berlioz and at that time conductor of the Russian Musical Society's concerts (at the insistence of Kologrivov, one of the Society's bigwigs) succeeded in changing this. He arranged to have some of the exceedingly old-fashioned things by Mozart and Haydn replaced by Berlioz' more interesting modern ones. Presented at the first concert were: the Overture to *Benvenuto Cellini* and the song "L'Absence"; at the second—the *Symphonie Fantastique;* at the third—the *Roman Carnival* overture and *Rêverie et Caprice* for violin; at the fourth—the Offertory from the *Requiem* and the overture to *Les Francs-Juges*; at the sixth—excerpts from *Romeo and Juliet* and *The Damnation of Faust* and all of *Harold in Italy*.

Concerning these concerts Berlioz wrote to his friend Edouard Alexandre on 15th December:

. . . The public and press are extremely cordial. At the second concert I was called out six times after the *Symphonie Fantastique*, which was given a stunning performance. The fourth movement had to be repeated.

What an orchestra! What precision! What ensemble! I do not know whether Beethoven ever heard himself performed in such a way. I must also say that in spite of my sufferings, when I reach the conductor's stand and see all these sympathetic people around me, I feel revived and I conduct, perhaps, as I have never conducted before.

Yesterday we played the second act of Gluck's *Orpheus*, the symphony in C minor [Beethoven's Fifth Symphony] and my *Roman Carnival* overture. Everything was played sublimely. The young lady [Lavrovskaya] who sang Orpheus (in Russian) has a matchless voice and performed her part very well. There was a chorus of 130. All these pieces had a marvellous success. And these are Russians who know Gluck only from horrible mutilations made by incompetent people!!!! Oh, what an immense joy it is for me to acquaint them with the masterpieces of that great man! Yesterday there was no end to the applause . . . The Grand Duchess has ordered that I am to be obeyed in everything; I am not abusing her order, but I am taking advantage of it . . .

. . . Here they love what is beautiful; here they live a musical and literary life; here they have a fire within them that makes one forget the snow and frost. Why am I so old, so worn-out? . . .

A week later, on 22nd December, he wrote other friends, the Massarts:

I am as ill as eighteen horses; I cough like six donkeys with the glanders, and yet I want to write you before going to bed again.

Our concerts are going wonderfully. This orchestra is superb and does exactly what I want. If you heard them play Beethoven's symphonies, you would, I believe, say many things you never dream of at the Paris Conservatory. The other day they played the *Fantastique*, which was included in the programme of the second concert by special request, with the same perfection. It was electrifying . . . The "March to the Scaffold" occasioned loud shouts of "Encore"; and the adagio (the Scene in the Country) made many people weep unashamedly . . .

I have been invited to Moscow. These gentlemen of the semi-Asiatic capital have irresistible arguments, whatever Wieniawski may say; he believes that I should not have accepted their offer immediately. But I do not know how to haggle, and I would be ashamed to . . .

From Moscow Berlioz wrote to Damcke (on 31st December):

Twelve thousand five hundred people attended my concert at the Manège.

I will not attempt to describe to you the applause that greeted the Fête from *Romeo and Juliet* and the Offertory from the *Requiem* . . . As I listened to the chorus of three hundred voices repeating the same two notes, I suddenly pictured to myself the increasing boredom of the crowd, and I was afraid that they would not let me finish. But the audience understood my thoughts, their attention redoubled, and this expression of resigned humility held them in its grip.

After the final bar, there was a tremendous burst of applause. I was called out four times; then the orchestra and chorus also applauded; I did not know where to stand. This was the greatest impression I have ever produced in my life . . .

In speaking of the warm response of the press, Berlioz, of course, had in mind particularly Cui's articles in *S.-Peterburgskie Vedomosti*, which expressed the views of the whole group of new Russian musicians. In one of these articles Cui wrote of the *Symphonie Fantastique*:

Berlioz wrote this in 1828, when he was only twenty-five and still a student at the Conservatory. It is a work brimming with lush fantasy, powerful imagination, vigour, poetry, and originality (although *Der Freischütz* had already been written, Berlioz was not yet acquainted with it). In view of all this, in view of the abundance of Berlioz' young creative powers, and the new musical world into which he is leading us, who can reproach him for the undeniable eccentricities and exaggerations found in the symphony's programme, orchestration and music! This is the brilliant beginning of a giant, destined to lead music into yet unknown realms. The *Symphonie Fantastique* was written before *Robert*; Meyerbeer heard it at Berlioz' concerts, and the critics have yet to call sufficient attention to the *enormous* influence it had upon Meyerbeer's works. All of the qualities that distinguish Meyerbeer's style and constitute his major contribution to opera—colour, vivid effects, brilliant orchestration—all these are to be found in the *Symphonie Fantastique*. Meyerbeer borrowed from it very freely, at times specifically. The famous "Resurrection from the Graves" in *Robert* is identical, in character, to the "March to the Scaffold", and the orchestral effect of the bassoons in the low registers is simply a copy of the same effect in Berlioz. The dialogue between the winds at the beginning of *The Prophet* is identical in mood (though inferior musically) to the opening of the "Scene in the Country", etc. Liszt's *Danse Macabre* is undoubtedly one of his finest works, but he, too, borrowed a great deal from the finale of Berlioz' symphony: the "Dies irae" theme, many of the variations, the opening bells, the glissandos—all this was in Berlioz' music thirty-five years earlier! . . . There is not another conductor whose performances are truer to the composer's intentions, who has a greater understanding of the spirit of a work, who preserves so completely all of its nuances . . . What a grasp he has of Beethoven; how meticulous, how thoughtful his performances are; how effective yet free of the slightest concession to false, tawdry brilliance. As an interpreter of Beethoven, I prefer Berlioz to Wagner who, despite excellent qualities, is sometimes affected and here and there inclined toward sentimentality. For us Gluck became utterly new, alive, unrecognizable. Even though he is now outmoded, it cannot be denied that he was a brilliant innovator, a genius. As for Berlioz' own works, the magnificent performances under his direction have revealed many wonders that we had not suspected were there, even after the most careful study of his enormous, complex scores. And how simple, how restrained Berlioz is on the podium; yet how amazingly *precise* his gestures are! And how modest he is! When the audience called for him after the first piece, he came out, and with a charming wave of the hand, indicated that it was the orchestra, not he, who deserved the honours. Of all the conductors we have heard in Petersburg, Berlioz is certainly the greatest; as an artist wholly dedicated to music, he deserves our admiration, respect and unbounded affection . . .

During his stay in Petersburg, Berlioz was in frequent contact with all the musicians of the new Russian school. The one he saw most often was Balakirev, who was assigned to rehearse the choruses and soloists for him and assist him at concerts. Berlioz thought very highly of Balakirev. He saw all of our other young composers frequently, too; they called on him when he was well, when he was ill, whenever he was not at rehearsals or visiting the Grand Duchess Elena Pavlovna, to whom he read his beloved *Aeneid*, Byron and Shakespeare in French. His young admirers would speak to him about the great new works they expected of him, but he would only sigh and answer sadly that this was no longer possible, he was too old, sick, and broken. Once he attended a performance of *A Life for the Tsar* in Kologrivov's box with Balakirev and me. But we heard none of the fresh, profound remarks we expected from one who had been so enthusiastic about this opera twenty-two years before. By now it was too much of a strain for Berlioz to sit in a theatre an entire evening (he was accustomed to retiring at nine o'clock). He praised Glinka's opera as a whole but made only one specific comment, concerning the orchestration: "How pleasant it is to come upon such restrained, beautiful, sensible orchestration after all the excesses of today's orchestras!" Of course, at this moment Berlioz was thinking of Wagner, whose music and orchestration he strongly disapproved of and whose failure in Paris not so long before this (in 1860), he had all but rejoiced at. By now he did not even like Liszt. He no longer cared for the brilliant innovations in Liszt's latest works, his orchestration, piano transcriptions (which had so captivated and delighted him before) or even his conducting. He now found Liszt's conducting too arbitrary, subjective, capricious and arrogant. Berlioz was getting old and, like Glinka in his last years, he was beginning to love only the great composers of earlier days, particularly Gluck and Beethoven, the main idols of his youth. This is why what pleased him most in Glinka's music was the "restrained" orchestration in *A Life for the Tsar*.

On the whole, this visit to Russia proved very exhausting for Berlioz, and he was anxious to get back home, to France, as soon as possible. On 1st February, 1868 he wrote his friend Holmes:

> The trip to Moscow has finished me . . . The concert which was to be given "for me" in March would keep me here for more than a month. I prefer to sacrifice the eight thousand francs and return immediately.
>
> The kindness everyone has shown me—artists and public alike; the dinners, the gifts mean nothing to me. I long for the sun; I want to go to Nice, to Monaco . . .
>
> Six days ago we had 32 degrees of frost. Birds are dying; coachmen are falling off their boxes. What a country! And in my symphonies I sing of Italy, sylphs and bowers of roses on the banks of the Elbe!!!

Berlioz' birthday, 11th December, was celebrated by his Petersburg admirers, foremost among whom were the young composers affiliated with the Free Music School, and members and associates of the Russian Musical Society (whose conductor was Balakirev and Dargomïzhsky, the vice-president). He was given a supper which was attended by many people. On this occasion he was presented with a certificate of honorary membership in the Society which read: "The Russian Musical Society, in recognition of your enormous rôle in the history of art and regarding you as one of the most important creators of the new school, considers it a special privilege to count you among its honorary members and asks you to accept this title in the hope that the ties which will unite one of the prime movers of contemporary art with our music centre will exert a most felicitous influence on the development of music in our society."

In his reply to the many speeches and toasts given him, Berlioz stressed the hope that Russian musicians would always be artists and never artisans (*toujours artistes and jamais artisans*).[1]

[1] This supper gave rise to the following curious incident. Although Berlioz was aware of how hostilely Serov had spoken and written about him, he included him among the guests invited to a dinner he gave at the suggestion of the Grand Duchess Elena Pavlovna, for his musical acquaintances at the Mikhailovsky Palace. Serov, who was hostile and unpleasant to all the colleagues of our new school of music, sat through the entire dinner silent and ignored. When the invitations were issued to the supper in honour of Berlioz' birthday, Serov was not invited. He was incensed and, in a strongly worded letter, demanded to know why he had received no invitation. Dargomïzhsky, the Vice-President of the Russian Musical Society, replied in an

Berlioz left Petersburg on 1st February, 1868, leaving his baton as a memento to Balakirev, and to the Russian Musical Society the little cymbals (*cymbales antiques*) he had had made in Paris for the performance of his wonderful *Queen Mab* scherzo.

After his departure, Cui wrote in *S.-Peterburgskie Vedomosti*:

> The Russian Musical Society is at present copying the score of *Les Troyens*, so for the time being this unusual work is to be found only in Paris and here. The Theatre Directorate would render a great service to art if next season they would produce *Les Troyens* at the Maryinsky Theatre. In this case Berlioz might not be averse to coming to keep an eye on the rehearsals and might even conduct once or twice. We would gain immense honour in the eyes of the whole music world if we were to produce properly this important work, of which Carvalho could give only a very shabby performance at his Théâtre Lyrique in Paris.

However, these fond hopes were never realized: neither the "great service" on the part of the Theatre Directorate nor the "immense honour" in the eyes of the musical world. Twenty years have passed and no one in our country has yet thought of producing *Les Troyens*.

Meanwhile, Berlioz was suffering a steady decline in health; he was growing weaker and wearier. On 1st March 1868, he wrote to me:

> I don't know why I do not die . . .
>
> Don't be too strict with me, write to me despite my brevity; remember that I am ill, that a letter from you will do me good, and don't talk to me about composing, don't tell me any nonsense . . . Please remember me to all your family . . .*
>
> Music . . . Ah! I was going to say something about music, but I shall refrain.
>
> Farewell, write me soon, your letter will revive me and so will the sun . . . Poor unfortunate! You live amid the snow! . . .

In another letter Berlioz told me that he had had a fall at Monaco and hurt himself severely on some rocks.

Finally, on 21st August of the same year, he wrote to me about the great ovations he had received in Grenoble, adding in conclusion:

---

official letter on behalf of all those who attended the Berlioz celebration that "only people who knew and respected each other had been at the supper".

The following humorous verses by P. M. Kovalevsky refer to this comic incident:

"I am not invited to dinners
—The creator of Judith and Rogneda!!
Only malicious gossip could fail
To see a luminary in me.
Me, on whom Moscow has chosen
To bestow her honors!!!

(*S.-Peterburgskie Vedomosti*, 1867, No. 358)

Also Mussorgsky's lines in *The Peepshow:*

Invite him to the dinner,
The genius dearly loves homage!

* Original here reads: "Assurez-moi que vous m'avez rappelé au souvenir de votre charmante belle-soeur, de votre gracieuse fille et de votre frère." [Trans.]

I returned to Paris exhausted and suddenly received letters from Russia and Löwenberg asking impossible things of me. They want me to speak highly of a German artist, of whom I do, indeed, think well, but on condition that I speak ill of a Russian artist, whom they wish to replace by the German and who, on the contrary, deserves the highest praise. This I will not do. What kind of devilish world is this?[1]

I feel that I am going to die; I no longer believe in anything. I wish I could see you; perhaps you would cheer me up; Cui and you might put fresh life into me.

What's to be done?

I'm terribly bored. There is not a soul in Paris. All my friends are away, some in the country, some hunting. Some have invited me to visit them, but I haven't the strength . . .

Oh, I beg you, write me as briefly as you wish. I still feel the effects of my fall in Monaco; Nice, too, has given me cause to remember her.

Perhaps my letter will not reach you. I am prepared for anything.

If you are in Petersburg, write me *six lines*. I will be eternally grateful to you.

A thousand greetings to Balakirev.

Farewell. It is very difficult for me to write.

You are kind; prove it to me once more.

I press your hand.

Your devoted Berlioz!

This was Berlioz' *last* letter as far as is known. He died six months later, after a long and agonizing illness.

Thus, Berlioz' closest, most intimate relationships, on his second visit to Russia, were almost exclusively with the composers of the new Russian school. These young people appreciated his genius and understood his importance more than any of their countrymen. That is why his influence on them was so powerful and profound.

*

During the fifties and sixties, Liszt underwent a complete transformation. Until then he had had only one desire—to be the world's foremost pianist—and this he had become. He had astounded the world. For him it had not been simply a matter of satisfying his own vanity and thirst for fame: he had had to raise the piano to an unheard of height, to give it the importance of the orchestra. He had had to play on this new instrument in his own way, as his genius inspired him, all the greatest and loftiest works that had been created for the orchestral instruments and the human voice.

[1] This refers to the following incident. After Berlioz left Russia, a certain group of leaders in the Russian Musical Society wanted to remove Balakirev as conductor of its concerts and replace him by Seifriz, the Löwenberg conductor. With this aim a letter was sent in August, 1868 to Berlioz, Liszt and Wagner, asking them to give their opinion of Seifriz. The letter to Berlioz contained the further request that he speak unfavourably of Balakirev. Liszt and Wagner replied that Seifriz was an experienced conductor—diligent, intelligent and amiable (*Golos*, No. 124, 1869, article by Famintsyn). Berlioz did not reply to the Russian Musical Society but wrote me the above.

In those days, when friends would tell him that it was time he gave up his constant preoccupation with the piano and turn to something weightier, more important, he would reply (as he did in a letter to Pictet in the autumn of 1837):

> And you too! You do not realize that you are touching a very sensitive spot. You do not know that in suggesting that I give up the piano you are foreshadowing my day of mourning, you are taking from me the light that has illuminated the entire first half of my life and has become a part of me. For can't you see, to me the piano is what a ship is to a sailor, a horse to an Arab—even more. Till now it has been my *I*, my language, my life . . . How can you possibly want me to forsake it for the pursuit of more glittering, more resounding successes, theatrical and orchestral? Oh no! Even assuming that I am ready for these harmonies, I am resolved to give up studying and developing the piano only after I have done everything that is possible, everything that is now within my reach... If I am not mistaken, with my piano transcription of Berlioz' *Symphonie Fantastique* I have begun something quite the opposite of former piano transcriptions. I have worked on this as conscientiously as if it were a matter of transcribing the Holy Scriptures. I have sought to transfer to the piano not just the general structure of the music, but all its separate parts, as well as all its varied harmonic and rhythmic combinations . . . After my efforts, I hope that it will no longer be permissible to *arrange* the works of the masters as they have been before . . .

Only two years later, in 1839, Liszt was ready to state in the preface to his transcription of Beethoven's Fifth Symphony: ". . . the piano in recent years has acquired the importance of the orchestra . . ."

This is how Liszt thought and spoke then: he was not averse to composing, he was simply putting it off for the time being, for an indefinite period. But none of his friends who were kindred in talent and direction had any doubt that he would be not only a composer but a great, an extraordinary one. Even before he had reached thirty, Berlioz said, after hearing his fantasy on Halévy's *Juive*: "Well, now we can expect *anything* of Liszt as a composer." And, indeed, Liszt's fantasies on *La Juive* (1836) and *Don Giovanni* (1841) are not just simple transcriptions, adaptations or arrangements of the themes of others—they are major compositions in their own right, works in which the composer's creative ability reveals itself in its full power and brilliance. As early as the thirties another great musician and admirer, Schumann, wrote: ". . . Had Liszt . . . devoted the same time to composition and to himself that he has given to his instrument and to the works of others, he would have become a very remarkable composer . . ." But Liszt seems not to have been sufficiently aware of this. He still did not consider himself ready for composition. He did not think that he had completed his work as a creator of pianism, a piano orchestrator, and piano composer. One of the most striking proofs of this is the fact that even though he had written two such piano masterpieces as *Sposalizio* and *Il Penseroso* as early as 1838, he neither played them at any of the countless concerts he gave throughout all of

Europe nor had them published until twenty years later. These two great works did not appear in print until 1858.

The change in Liszt occurred during his "Weimar period", that is, during the years when, having given up his career as a pianist, he settled in Weimar, became conductor of the theatre there and devoted himself entirely to composition. During this period and later (after he stopped conducting), Liszt exerted a tremendous influence on the new Russian school.

The first contact Liszt had with the Russians after his visits here in 1842 and 1843 was an exchange of letters with Serov. In 1847, Serov was serving in the Simferopol Criminal Department and, on hearing that Liszt was nearby in the south of Russia, he sent Liszt his arrangement of Beethoven's *Coriolanus* overture for piano (two hands), asking his opinion of it. In this arrangement, Serov had tried to imitate Liszt's style.

Liszt replied from Elizavetgrad on 14th September:

> I am deeply grateful to you for the kind remembrance you have kept of me since our meeting in Petersburg and I ask a thousand pardons for not having replied sooner to your most charming and interesting letter. Since the musical opinions you have set forth coincide exactly with those I have held for many years, I shall not enlarge upon them. There is only one point on which we differ, but since it concerns me personally, you will understand that this subject is very embarrassing to me, and therefore I shall handle it in the most ordinary way by thanking you sincerely for your too flattering opinion of me.
>
> The Overture to *Coriolanus* is one of those masterpieces *sui generis*, unlike any works of this kind that preceded or followed it. Do you recall the beginning of Shakespeare's tragedy of the same name (Act I, Scene I)? It is the only pendant to it that I know of created by man's genius. Read it again and compare it, thoughtfully. You are worthy of these lofty emotions of art for the fervour with which you serve art. Your piano arrangement of the *Coriolanus* overture does great honour to your artistic conscience and bears witness to a rare and patient intelligence which is indispensable to realizing this task well. If I should publish my version of this Overture (it should be among my papers in Germany), I shall ask your leave to send you, through Prince Dolgoruky,[1] whom I cannot commend to you highly enough, an inscribed copy, which I will beg you to add to the insignificant autograph which you value far beyond its worth!

We might note that Liszt's transcription of *Coriolanus* was never published.

Another of Liszt's letters, addressed to the half-German, half-Russian, Lenz, the author of very well-known works on Beethoven, bears the date Weimar, 2nd December, 1852. Lenz, a very well-educated musician and fairly competent pianist, had spent much of the late twenties in Paris in order to study with Chopin and Liszt. At that time he had introduced Liszt, who though still very young was already famous, to the piano music of Weber.

[1] A landowner in the Crimea, a music lover, and friend of both Serov and Liszt.

In 1852 Lenz sent Liszt his book, *Beethoven et ses trois styles*. Liszt replied with a long letter full of praise for the author, declaring, among other things, that in his study of the subject he combined "the diligence of a mole and the soaring of an eagle." Further Liszt wrote that the latest Russian writers on music justified anew Voltaire's remark: "C'est du Nord que nous vient la lumière." Here he had in mind Ulybyshev's book on Mozart and Lenz's on Beethoven. After praising both authors, he added that there was no need for Ulybyshev to have made a kind of Dalai Lama of Mozart, after whom no one else counted.

As for Beethoven, Liszt wrote:

> For us musicians the work of Beethoven is like the pillar of cloud and fire which guided the Israelites through the desert . . . Had I to classify the different periods of this great musician's thought, as expressed in his sonatas, symphonies and quartets, I would not stop at dividing them into three styles, a procedure adopted by almost everyone nowadays, including yourself, but, bearing in mind the questions raised thus far, I would weigh candidly the great question around which all musical criticism and aesthetics revolves at this point to which Beethoven has led us: namely, to what extent does traditional or conventional form determine the thought process.
>
> The answer to this question, implicit in Beethoven's works themselves, would lead me to divide them not into three styles or periods (these terms are only vague and confusing) but into two categories: the first, that in which traditional and conventional form constricts and governs the composer's thought; and the second, that in which the thought expands, breaks, recreates and forges the form and style to fit its needs and inspirations. To be sure, we thus come face to face with the eternal problems of authority and freedom. But why should they frighten us? In the realm of the liberal arts, they, fortunately, entail none of the dangers or disasters which occur as a consequence of changes in the social and political world . . .

This letter is one of the most important and most interesting of all Liszt's letters. It dates from that period when the matured great musician, having given up his career as a virtuoso, had begun once and for all to compose and was charting new, independent paths, free of "tradition". He wanted to follow the path opened up by Beethoven, but he was resolved to present to the world new material, new content and new form, all, from first to last, his own. During the fifties and sixties he did this in brilliant forms and with the persistence of genius.

In 1857, when Serov and I were still very close, I wrote to Liszt about four- and eight-hand piano transcriptions my friend had made of a vast number of important works, particularly those of Beethoven's last years, and asked his help in getting them published in Germany. Liszt replied to me from Weimar on 17th March, 1857:

> . . . Several people, among them M. de Lenz and Prince Eugene Wittgenstein, have spoken of him to me in the highest terms as an artist in whom genuine talent is combined with a most conscientious intelligence. It will be of great interest to me to evaluate the work to which he has devoted himself with

such praiseworthy perserverance and thus avail myself of the opportunity of hearing again these sublime creations of Beethoven's last period (I purposely avoid the inappropriate term "manner" or even the word "style")—works which, whatever Ulybyshev and other learned men . . . may say,[1] will forever remain the crowning point of Beethoven's creative career . . .

Then Liszt promised to try to get Serov's transcriptions published, though he admitted frankly that he had almost no influence in Germany and the German publishers paid little attention to him. ("I have as little influence on them," he said, "as on the above-mentioned experts, who do their utmost to keep all kinds of nonsense in vogue and prevent the publishers from taking foolish risks.") Encouraged by the help Liszt promised, Serov sent him his transcriptions of the late Beethoven quartets (Ops. 127, 131, 132). But nothing came of this.

In "Letters from Abroad" (published in *Muzykalny i Teatralny Vestnik*), Serov tells of a visit he paid Liszt in 1858:

My friendship with this idol of the musical world came about very simply. He had noticed my article taking issue with Ulybyshev, which appeared in German musical publications in Berlin and Leipzig, and in turn, he had written a brief but important one for the Leipzig *Neue Zeitschrift für Musik* regarding my views on the subject . . .[2] Finding myself in Dresden that summer, I wrote to Liszt that I was planning to visit him. He was pleased with the idea, so I went to Weimar. He receive me like an old friend, *à bras ouverts*, and I stayed with him a whole month. He played a great deal in my presence and sometimes for me alone . . . I heard many, many wonderful things. He is still the same Liszt, a giant compared with whom all other pianists are pygmies. What is the strength of a ladybird compared with that of a lion, or the height of a blade of grass with that of a cedar of Lebanon? I am not exaggerating. You have to know Liszt! Why, he seems to have improved, even in his playing. For us unworthy sinners (Dräseke and me) he played either sketches for his orchestral works (more about this in its proper place), Bach, or Beethoven. What can one say—it was utterly incredible!

At one of the "matinées," after playing my two-piano transcription of Beethoven's C-sharp minor Quartet with Markull, a musician from Danzig, he played, especially for me, Beethoven's big B-flat major Sonata, Op. 106 . . . The performance was a veritable act of creation, which reduced to naught all other sonatas that had come before. What words could possibly describe the vastness of its conception and expression? In this work Liszt's playing was particularly inspired. In the adagio he sang on the keyboard, as though divinely inspired, as though witnessing some other worldly mysteries. He himself was deeply moved, and he reduced all of us to tears. For such moments it would be worth journeying from Petersburg to Weimar on foot! . . .

How strange! Since his youth, Serov had been so used to thinking of

[1] Here Liszt's text contains an untranslatable play on words: "M. Oulibicheff et d'autres docteurs qui réussissent plus aisément à *verser* en ces matières qu'à y *être versés* . . ."

". . . whatever M. Ulybyshev and other learned men who succeed more easily when it comes to conversing about these matters than they do in becoming conversant with them . . . may say . . ." [Trans.]

[2] Article titled "Ulybyshev and Serov," 1858, No. 1.

Liszt only as a phenomenal pianist and nothing more, that now he did not even notice Liszt the composer. Liszt played "sketches for his orchestral works" for him. But which ones—*Dante, Hunnenschlacht, Die Ideale, Hamlet*, or *St. Elizabeth*? All these were in the process of composition or had just been composed but had not yet been published. And what do we find? Despite the fact that Liszt's genius was revealed in all its power, Serov heard nothing, observed nothing, was impressed by nothing and only promised casually to discuss these things "in their proper place"—a promise that was never carried out! The point is that by then Serov was no longer the progressive he had been in his youth; he was becoming more and more conservative, more and more set. He recognized no one but Beethoven (he added Wagner in 1858–59) and was beginning to turn against everyone else. Not long after this Liszt became one of the composers he disliked most—and this is understandable. The musical reactionaries, the musically backward people, the musicians who took their ideas from the conservatories always disliked Liszt, as they did Berlioz. When Berlioz and Liszt were young, all sorts of blockheads—the Scudos, Fétises and their ilk—refused to recognize them, treated them like dirt. Later, in their maturity, the Hanslicks and their clique treated them the same way. It was the same in our country. The Serovs, Laroches and their henchmen from the conservatories viewed them contemptuously from the heights of academic pedantry and despised them. As recently as this year, in fact,[1] Liszt's works were declared a "caricature of music" at public lectures at our conservatory, and young musicians were told to stay as far away from them as possible.[2] The short-sightedness of conservatives, musical and otherwise, it seems to me, surpasses all other kinds of short-sightedness. It goes without saying that once he had taken his stand with the reactionaries, Serov had to begin to hate Glinka. It was for this reason that he was the first to attack him. This has to be borne in mind when discussing Liszt.

A few months after Glinka's death, his sister, Ludmila Ivanovna Shestakova, had four of her brother's orchestral works—the overtures to *A Life for the Tsar* and *Ruslan and Ludmila*, the *Jota Aragonesa*, and *Night in Madrid*—published in Leipzig. She wanted to dedicate the *Jota* to Liszt and asked for his consent.

On 7th October, 1857 he replied:

I wish I were able to tell you how deeply your letter moved me! Thank you for having remembered me as one of the most sincere and ardent admirers of the great genius of your brother who was so worthy of a noble glory for the

[1] This article was written in 1889.

[2] "It is strange that Liszt has nowhere taken hold as he has here in Russia. The youth speak only of his works and this is very harmful for them. I think very highly of his poetic quality, artistry and virtuosity, but I find that sometimes it is all a caricature." (Cavos-Dekhtereva, *Anton Rubinstein*, pp. 262–3.)

very reason that he was above popular success. I thank you, too, for your kindness in wishing to dedicate to me one of his orchestral works which enjoys the highest esteem and favour among people of taste.

I accept with true gratitude the dedication with which you honour me, and it will be both a pleasure and a duty for me to do my utmost to promote the performance of Glinka's works, for which I have always entertained the most sincere sympathy and admiration . . .

Three months later, on 8th January, 1858, Liszt wrote to V. P. Engelhardt from Weimar:

Thank you for sending me Glinka's four scores, published through your efforts. I am very pleased to inform you at the same time that the *Jota* has just been performed (on New Year's Day) at a grand Court concert with the utmost success.* Even at the rehearsal, the intelligent musicians whom I am fortunate to count among the members of our orchestra were both struck and charmed by the lively and piquant originality of this delightful piece, formed of such delicate lines, proportioned and finished with such taste and artistry! What exquisite episodes, ingeniously linked with the principal theme! What subtle nuances and colouring distributed among the various timbres of the orchestra! What spirited rhythmic movement from beginning to end! How lavishly the most felicitous surprises flow from the logical development! And how everything is in its proper place, keeping the mind continually on the alert, by turn caressing and tickling the ear, without a single moment's drowsiness or fatigue! This is what we all felt at the rehearsal, and the day after the performance we firmly resolved to hear it again soon and to become acquainted, as soon as possible, with Glinka's other works . . .

Liszt retained the deep admiration for Glinka expressed here until the very end of his life. He never missed an opportunity to praise his works. In view of this, the derogatory remarks about Glinka which Serov ascribes to Liszt are utterly inexplicable. According to Serov, Liszt once told him that he found the overture to *Ruslan and Ludmila* contrived, forced, and in many respects inferior to the overture to *A Life for the Tsar*. Liszt was supposed to have said, "Ça sent l'exercice, c'est une oeuvre mediocre.'[1] He was also supposed to have found fault with the introduction to *Ruslan and Ludmila* because of the excessive use of the B-flat major tonality, and so on. All this sounds questionable, unbelievable. It was Serov who changed, who attacked *Ruslan* and tried to find unfavourable criticism of it wherever he could. Liszt could not have changed, he could not have ceased to understand what was great in Glinka, what made him the genius that he was.

* Here the original reads: "En vous faisant mes très sincères remercîments pour votre obligeant envoi des Partitions de Glinka publiées par vos amis, il m'est très agréable de vous informer en même temps que le Capriccio sur le thême de la *Jota Aragonese* vient d'être exécuté (le jour de l'an) à un grand Concert de la Cour avec le plus complet succès." Stasov obviously wanted his Russian readers to know that Liszt was sent four scores. For some reason he attributes their publication to Engelhardt's "efforts" not to his "friends" as Liszt does. [Trans.]

[1] *Muzyka i Teatr* (1858), p. 114.

When Ludmila Shestakova sent him the published score of *Ruslan* in 1879, he was very grateful. On 14th June he wrote her:

> Your illustrious brother Glinka occupies an important place among the very carefully chosen idols of my youth. His genius has been known to me since 1842, and at my last concert in Petersburg in '43, I played Chernomor's March from *Ruslan and Ludmila* and a brilliant transcription by Vollweiler of several themes from the same opera.
>
> Glinka remains the patriarch-prophet of music in Russia . . .

All in all, Liszt had the highest regard for Glinka. During the fifties and sixties his own position in Germany was very precarious. Most of the German public ignored him; they refused to acknowledge him as worthy of any attention as a composer. In his letters of 1858 he speaks repeatedly of the widespread attacks on him, the lack of recognition, the constant hostility shown him on all sides. (*Anfeindungen, die ich allerorts zu erleiden habe.*)[1] And yet? Instead of thinking only of himself and his own selfish interests, he consistently propagated the works of his contemporaries, among them one who was totally unknown in Germany, a foreigner, a musician from far away Russia—Glinka. This was the very opposite of Serov's attitude. But, then, what a difference there was in their characters, natures, talents. This is why, as time went on, Liszt grew less and less disposed towards Serov and his trend and more and more sympathetic to the trend, works and fortunes of the new Russian school which Serov did not at all understand and tried in every way to denigrate. Liszt saw with the unerring eye of a true artist that this school was Glinka's rightful heir, that it was following an original, truly national path and that it was for this reason that it was not recognized and was persecuted.

It may seem strange that Liszt twice declined invitations to come to Russia: first in 1863 and then in 1885, that is, twenty years and forty years* after his first visit here. He still loved our country; he still felt well-disposed to the Russians and remembered with warmth the way he had been received here—yet he refused to come. Both times he had good reasons for this.

The first time, he wrote about this to his friend Brendel, the editor of the *Neue Zeitschrift für Musik*, on 11th November, 1863:

> In spite of my retirement and seclusion, I am still very much disturbed by visitors, social obligations, music students, an extensive, mostly unnecessary correspondence and duties. Among other things, the St. Petersburg Philharmonic Society has invited me to conduct two concerts of my works during the next Lenten season. Their letter is, of course, somewhat more intelligent than the one from the Chairman of the Committee for Building the Cologne Cathedral (of which I told you); but nevertheless these good people cannot refrain from prattling about my "former triumphal tours, unrivalled mastery

[1] La Mara, *Musikerbriefe*, Vol. II, p. 215. Letter to Dräseke dated 10th February, 1858. [Stasov is in error. The correct date of this letter is 10th January, 1858].

* Liszt actually visited Russia first in 1842, then in 1843. [Trans.]

of the piano, etc." and this has become as sickening to me as flat, lukewarm champagne! Committee gentlemen and others should really feel ashamed of their inane platitudes and should leave off rehashing this antiquated business . . .[1]

The fact is that after Liszt had given up performing in the Autumn of 1847, he had turned to conducting in Weimar and other places and had also begun to compose on a very large scale. But by 1859 he had grown tired of being attacked and hounded by the most backward elements in Germany, not only as a composer but as a conductor as well. He wearied, finally, of the ceaseless hostility of his detractors and gave up conducting. The German blockheads had worn him down. How could he go to Russia to conduct when this business had long since become so distasteful to him!

The Berlin *Allgemeine Musik Zeitung* of 26th June, 1896 (No. 24) published Liszt's reply to the St. Petersburg Philharmonic Society. Dated Rome, 10th November, 1863, this letter reads:

Gentlemen:

The letter which you did me the honour of addressing to me on 26th September did not reach me until 4th November. I must therefore beg you to pardon me for my belated reply and also for its content, which is necessitated by a variety of circumstances.

Assuredly the great renown enjoyed by the St. Petersburg Philharmonic Society cannot but make every artist long to appear with you, either as a performer or as a composer. This rule naturally applies first of all to the members of your society, among whom I am honoured to count myself. However, if you would be good enough to take into consideration the fact that I long ago absolutely refused to din my ten fingers into the public's ears and for fifteen years have persistently declined to participate in any concert whatsoever as a pianist, a rôle I can no longer recapture save, perhaps, by reminiscence; also that I do not suffer in the least from a craving to personally advance my own works and am content to write with care, reflection and conscientiousness without concerning myself further—then you will not be surprised, gentlemen, that I am not thinking of undertaking any journeys. The fatigue I should have to experience would in no way compensate me for the interruption of my work which, if it continues, promises to add considerable honour to my name;[2] in my, perhaps, unique situation I must think of how best to utilize my time.

After having played the piano for a long time, I did, in fact, conduct many orchestras in Germany (in Weimar, Berlin, Prague, Vienna, Leipzig, etc.) for a dozen years, from '48 until '60, to be exact. During this period of my career I, of my own accord, filled the post of Kapellmeister to his Royal Highness the

[1] La Mara, *Musikerbriefe*, Vol. II, p. 133.

[2] Liszt wrote the following works in 1863; a piano transcription and an organ transcription of Arcadelt's *Ave Maria*; organ transcriptions of two Preludes by Chopin (Op. 28, Nos. 4 and 9); a piano transcription of Schumann's song "To the Sun"; his own *Ave Maria*; two concert études for piano, *Waldesrauschen* and *Gnomenreigen*; a revision of his *Berceuse* for piano, composed in 1855; two "legends" for piano—*St. François d'Assise, La prédication aux oiseaux* and *St. François de Paule marchant sur les flots*; L'*Hymne du Pape* for organ ("Tu es Petrus"); a revision of his piano transcriptions of Beethoven's first eight symphonies and a new transcription of the ninth symphony; finally, organ variations on Bach's theme *Weinen, Klagen, Sorgen, Zagen*.

Grand Duke of Weimar, in honour of which one of the members of your Philharmonic Society, Mr. Ulybyshev, in his regrettable book on Beethoven, paid me compliments which are almost as erroneous as most of the opinions and arguments in this volume.[1] But for some time before I left Weimar, I decided not to wield the baton or play the piano in public any more, so much so that—to cite but one example—I did not even conduct the choir, of which I was still nominally the leader, at the concerts of the Tonkünstler-Versammlung in Weimar in August, 1861, even though I was very much interested in them. Baron Hans von Bülow was kind enough to replace me in conducting many of my works, at my request. How could I now, in Rome, be tempted by the idea of again assuming a responsibility which, I believe, I gave up as honourably as I had once fulfilled it? Batons and pianos will continue to flourish without any difficulty everywhere, quite well without me!

Therefore, excuse me, gentlemen, if I find it impossible to satisfy either of the requests of your kind letter, and my reply offers you nothing but regrets, and accept, I beg you, my esteem and respect. F. Liszt.

The second time Liszt was invited here, in 1885, he felt too weak and therefore, despite the favourable financial terms (which at that time would have been most welcome—what a bitter lot for a great man!) he again refused. We shall go into this later on.

In 1864 we find Liszt once more commenting on Glinka. In August of that year, Yuri Arnold spent some time with him in Karlsruhe during the Allgemeiner Deutscher Tonkünstler-Verein festival. Liszt was one of the founders of this Society and its honorary Vice-President, and Arnold served as its Secretary. In a *Note* which Arnold wrote at my request, he tells us that on the way to the hotel where they were all to dine together, Liszt said (apropos of his ballad for alto to Mey's poem, "Somehow Among All People"):

Evidently you are following the path toward the creation of a genuine national Russian school charted so well by Glinka. Your folk songs are richer melodically, harmonically and rhythmically than those of any other people in Europe. And you are quite right in loving and adoring your great-little Glinka. His genius has not yet received sufficient recognition in the West, or even in Russia for that matter. Follow him, follow him, don't ever leave him—he is the best model you Russian musicians have . . .

Another time, upon hearing that Brendel and Riedel knew almost none of Glinka's music, Liszt suggested that Arnold acquaint them with it and then added:

[1] On page 324 of his work *Beethoven et ses trois styles,* Ulybyshev says of Liszt: "I have presented, as accurately as I could, Richard Wagner's views on Beethoven. Why should it surprise anyone, then, that Mr. Franz Liszt, friend, patron and student of Wagner, has sung the praises of the 'great Beethoven', in poetic fantasies, in prose, as inexpressibly wonderful as any of his piano fantasies [There follows a quotation from Liszt expressing boundless adoration for the genius of Beethoven]. While Mr. Liszt does not indicate the exact chronology of these visions of the future, Mr. Wagner clearly does. 'Poetry,' he says, 'will not flourish until we have a new life, and this will not happen until politics vanish, that is, until *the state ceases to exist.*' Oh, then the public will have a long wait for the dramas of the future."

Indeed, *Kamarinskaya* is excellently wrought and truly Russian. But the music to *Kholmsky* is also a splendid work (*ein Prachtwerk*), deeply thought through and subtly orchestrated.

In the summer of 1869, I myself spent some time with Liszt. This was during the International Art Exhibition in Munich. Wagner's *Nibelung's Ring* was scheduled to be given and Liszt had come there especially to hear it. Owing to a variety of unforeseen circumstances, the operas were not given, but I saw Liszt, for the second and last time in my life. Later I wrote in *S.-Peterburgskiye Vedomosti*:[1]

> ... I wanted to see once again this extraordinary man who, even though he has embarked upon a strange, incomprehensible life (he was now an abbé) is still one of the most influential teachers and leaders of contemporary art ... I wondered: ... once he becomes caught up in conversation, his clerical posture vanishes. His movements lose their restraint and pious humility; he raises his head and, shedding, as it were, his monkish pose, once again becomes forceful, dynamic. You see before you the old Liszt, the genius, the eagle ...

I then told how he had played excerpts from his new mass but had flatly refused to play even a part of his *Totentanz* or any of the other magnificent creations of the fifties and sixties.

"All these are works of *that* period! No, I don't play them any more," he said.

He played a short excerpt from *Ce qu'on entend sur la montagne*, but then, as if he had suddenly remembered something, he stopped. He refused to tell us the programme of the *Totentanz*, saying he felt that this was one of those works "whose content must not be made public". Thus, it remains an enigma to everyone. Even Richard Pohl, an intimate friend of the composer, gives only an approximate idea of its meaning in his book.[2]

Beginning with the late sixties, Liszt came to know and appreciate the works of the new Russian school. Reports began to reach him that the composers of this school had a high regard for him, that they studied all his works as soon as they were published and sought to have his finest orchestral and choral compositions performed at the concerts of the Free School. Liszt's increasing interest in the new trends in Russian music had two very important consequences for us. First, in his personal meetings with many Russian musicians throughout the seventies and eighties, he never missed an opportunity to speak of his great regard for our new composers, a sentiment he also expressed in numerous letters. Secondly, during this period he made a great effort to promote the performance of the new Russian music in Europe.

In order to support the conclusions I shall present at the end of this

[1] *S.-Peterburgskie Vedomosti* (1869), No. 263. The full translation of this account is given in Chapter I of this book, pp. 47 ff.

[2] Richard Pohl, *Franz Liszt* (Leipzig 1853), p. 40. *Danse Macabre*.

article, I shall now cite all of Liszt's most important statements on our new school.

On 20th September, 1872 Liszt sent a letter to Lenz thanking him for his enthusiastic essay on him (Liszt) in his book *Die grossen Pianoforte-virtuosen unserer Zeit.* At the same time, he vigorously defended Chopin against certain groundless criticisms (which had to do particularly with the harmful influence the aristocratic Paris salons were supposed to have exerted on him).[1] Then Liszt concluded his letter with this unexpected postscript:

> Are you in touch with *young musical Russia* and its very notable leaders: Messrs. Balakirev, Cui, Rimsky-Korsakov? I have recently looked through many of their works; they are deserving of attention, praise and propagation.[2]

Not long after this, in May, 1873, Liszt wrote to Cui from Weimar concerning the latter's opera *William Ratcliff*:

> It is the work of a master, worthy of attention, fame and success, as much for the wealth and originality of the ideas as for the skilful handling of the form. As I am persuaded that all intelligent and honest musicians will be of the same opinion, I wish I were in a position to add to this some assurance that your *Ratcliff* will be performed in Germany soon. It would be performed in Weimar immediately if, as in former years . . . I still held an active post in the theatre; but since I left, I am no longer in a position to make decisions and must confine myself to recommendations, which are more often rejected than accepted . . .

Again, in May of that year, Liszt wrote to the music publisher V. V. Bessel thanking him for sending him a number of works by Dargo-mïzhsky (*The Stone Guest*, *Finnish Fantasy*, *Baba Yaga*), Rimsky-Korsakov (*Sadko*), Tchaikovsky, and Mussorgsky (*The Nursery*). He told Bessel that he was "greatly interested in them" and would try "to arrange to have the instrumental ones performed in the near future." Accordingly, he asked the publisher to send him the scores and orchestral parts (at his expense) as soon as possible. Liszt was so taken with *The Nursery* that he wanted to transcribe it for the piano and dedicate one of his own pieces to the author.

In a letter to me, Mussorgsky wrote:

> Liszt amazes me. I may or may not be a fool in music, but in *The Nursery* I don't think I'm a fool, because an understanding of children, seeing them as people in their own little world, and not as amusing dolls, should preclude anyone from considering the composer a fool. I never would have thought that Liszt, who deals with colossal themes, could seriously understand and appreciate *The Nursery* and, especially, be ecstatic about it. Why, all the children in it are Russians, with a strong local smell . . .

[1] "His soul was not in the least affected by them," Liszt wrote, "and his work as an artist remains transparent, marvellous, ethereal, and of incomparable genius, outside the erring ways of a school and the foolish trifling of a salon."

[2] Virtually the first of the new Russian works Liszt came to know was Balakirev's *Islamey*. He liked it so much that he always kept it on his piano and made all of his pupils play it.

In November 1873, Liszt's fiftieth anniversary was celebrated in Budapest. Among the countless telegrams he received that day from every corner of the globe was one from the members of the new Russian School which read: "A group of Russians, devoted to art, believing in its continuous progress and striving to further it, greet you warmly on the day of your anniversary as a composer of genius and a performer who has expanded the boundaries of art, a great leader in the struggle for vitality and progress in music, a tireless artist, whose great and ceaseless work we salute." This telegram was signed by M. Balakirev, A. Borodin, C. Cui, A. Lyadov, M. Mussorgsky, N. Rimsky-Korsakov, M. Shcherbachev, and several music lovers closely associated with the new Russian School.[1]

Liszt replied in a letter in which he said that he "highly admired and respected" our musicians; that insofar as he could, he would "promote their works"; and that he considered it "an honour to reciprocate in this way the warm feelings expressed by these valiant colleagues."

On 20th June, 1876, Liszt wrote to V. V. Bessel:

> Once again I wish to assure you of the lively interest which I take in the works of the new Russian composers—Rimsky-Korsakov, Cui, Tchaikovsky, Balakirev, Borodin . . . You know that the ballad *Sadko* was recently given a fine performance at the Tonkünstler-Versammlung at Altenburg and was well received. Next year I shall suggest that other works by these composers be performed. They deserve serious attention in musical Europe.

During the summer of 1876, Cui met Liszt for the first time, in Weimar. Later, in an article in *S.-Peterburgskie Vedomosti*,[2] he gave a detailed account of their conversations and also told us much that is interesting about Liszt's classes. Our compatriot, Vera Timanova, was one of his most brilliant and favourite pupils at the time. Liszt himself no longer refused to play, as he had in 1869. By then his "priestliness" had assumed an altogether different character. Indeed, it had all but disappeared.

> I had the feeling that Liszt would have liked to play a great deal for me and talk with me at great length [wrote Cui]. But unfortunately the constant stream of visitors prevented this. Nevertheless, he did play two pieces for me—Chopin's C-minor *Polonaise* and his own latest work, music to Count Alexis Tolstoy's ballad "The Blind Singer". This is a charming little piece—graceful, delicate, unusually beautiful and poetic. In it Liszt has said nothing he had not already said in his earlier compositions, but it is amazingly good and fresh for a sixty-four year old composer. I was struck by the extraordinary simplicity and depth of feeling expressed in Liszt's playing. His touch is unusually light and gentle; the transparency, poetry, delicacy of his playing—unparalleled. Yet, I repeat, the qualities that impressed me most were its simplicity, sincerity and expressiveness. Indeed, his playing is unique; it is his alone.

[1] The text of this telegram was written in Russian by Cui. At my colleagues' request, I translated it into French, and it was in that form that it was sent.

[2] *S.-Peterburgskie Vedomosti* (1876), No. 205.

As for Liszt's views on music, he feels that at the present time there are no outstanding composers in Germany. Brahms, Raff, and the others are all good musicians, they have written good works, but they have said nothing new, they have not advanced art. We, in Russia, have outstanding composers, who have said *something new* and have advanced art. Liszt spoke with special warmth about Balakirev's *Islamey* and his transcription of Glinka's *Jota*. At his request, Mme. Timanova played this transcription and also Borodin's Symphony for me at one of the classes.[1] He was amazed at the original rhythmic effects, masterful crossing of themes, and completely new harmonic progressions in Borodin's Symphony (he played the progressions of the basses in the scherzo for me from memory). I was especially pleased by Liszt's high opinion of Borodin, since he is studiously ignored by the musical powers-that-be in Petersburg (which, we must admit, is partly his own fault because he composes too little). Liszt does not like the works of Rubinstein and Serov.[2] Quantities of newly published music are sent him from all over Germany and also from Russia. He often throws away what he receives from Germany without even glancing at it, but he always looks through what comes from here. I found all of our latest published works on his piano. I told him that he is very popular in our country, that there is scarcely a concert that does not include his works. He was particularly pleased and surprised to learn of the frequent performances and success of the *Totentanze*[3] and the fact that I prefer the first episode from Lenau's *Faust* ("Nocturnal Procession") to the second ("Mephisto Waltz"). He beamed with delight, for these two magnificent works are completely ignored and unappreciated in Germany. Liszt is now sixty-four . . . His expression is always one of imperturbable geniality. Once in a while, very seldom, his eyes twinkle mockingly and an ironic smile appears on his lips; except for this his good humour knows no bounds . . .

Drawing on his recollections, Cui recently amplified the foregoing in a special "Note":

My first evening with Liszt was spent at the home of his devoted friend, Baroness Meyendorf. I played a great deal of the music from *Angelo* for them. Liszt and I played the introduction four-hands. At one point he made a mistake

[1] This refers to Borodin's First Symphony. Liszt did not come to know the Second until 1877.

[2] This was corroborated in conversations Borodin had with Liszt in 1877. Liszt had nothing good to say about the works of Serov and Rubinstein. In a letter to his wife from Jena on 3rd July, 1877 (during the time of his visits to Liszt), Borodin wrote: "Liszt apparently does not think very much of Serov's operas. He told me that Serov wanted at all cost to produce *Judith* abroad and that he had told Serov frankly that it would certainly be a failure there. 'Serov was very annoyed with me, of course,' said Liszt, 'but I told him the truth; in my opinion, it is not very original.' (*Borodin. His Life, Correspondence and Articles*, p. 129.) Liszt's letters to Anton Rubinstein, which have now been published, deal only with the publication of the latter's works and their performance in concert or in the theatre. Apparently, except for the *Persische Lieder*, Liszt did not like Rubinstein's works at all (La Mara, *Liszt's Briefe*, Vol. 1, p. 200). In one letter, dated 19th November, 1854, he told Rubinstein bluntly that his "excessive productivity prevents him from turning out anything original." (*Ibid.*, pp. 177–8.) Yuri Arnold tells me that in conversation with him, Liszt had this to say about the *Ocean Symphony*: "Its realism is astonishing. Listening to it, you feel everything you would during a sea voyage, even sea-sickness."

[3] Only the new school of Russian music and its adherents liked Liszt's *Totentanze* and other works of genius. The Conservatory ridiculed them, and the public did not like them at all.

and was very annoyed with himself. Later, over tea, I told him what I thought of Wagner,[1] the falseness of his system, the insignificant rôle he assigns to the voice, the melodic poverty that results from his repeated use of the same themes, and so on. The Baroness listened with horror, Liszt—with a slight smile. Then he said, "Il y a du vrai dans ce que vous dites là, mais je vous en supplie, n'allez pas le répéter à Bayreuth!" Wagner was always afraid of Liszt and felt rather inhibited in his presence, like a youngster in the presence of a strict tutor. And this is not surprising in view of the difference in their natures—Liszt's gentleness and leniency, Wagner's brusqueness, curtness and fanatical egotism. I saw Liszt for a second time that year in Bayreuth, at Wagner's house, where he occupied a small room . . .

In articles on *The Nibelung's Ring*, published in *S.-Peterburgskie Vedomosti* in 1876. Cui described this visit as follows:

There I heard Liszt again. He still possesses considerable technique and power, but again the most striking quality in his playing was its remarkable simplicity, expressiveness and matchless delicacy, the lightness of his passage work, the inconceivable *piano*. Beneath his magic fingers, the piano sounded like an aeolian harp . . .

During the summer of 1877, Borodin spent a great deal of time with Liszt. He describes his visits in a series of unusually well-written, colourful, vivid and original letters. There are no better, more faithful portraits of Liszt and his everyday life in all European literature. It would be impossible to present excerpts from these letters here: there would be too many of them. They are filled with warm, sympathetic remarks Liszt made about the new Russian school, particularly about Borodin. But here is one of his most characteristic comments: "You know Germany, of course," he once said to Borodin. "They're writing a lot here. I'm simply swamped with the music they keep sending me. But good Lord! How flat it all is! There's not a single fresh idea! You Russians on the other hand, have a steady stream of them. Sooner or later (more likely later) it will find its way to us!"

Once, when Borodin, on being asked whether he had studied at a conservatory, replied that he had not, Liszt burst out laughing and said: "You're lucky. You have an enormous, original talent. Don't listen to anyone. Just work in your own way . . ."

Thus, Liszt's views concerning conservatories and conservatory training coincided exactly with those of Berlioz and Glinka. The new Russian composers shared these views, too, and therefore, they were highly pleased with what Liszt had said.

The following year, on 11th March, 1878, Liszt wrote Bessel:

. . . You have sent me some of the other publications of your firm: six piano pieces by Lyadov; they have an appealing gentility; and a collection of Russian folk songs by Rimsky-Korsakov, whom I highly esteem and admire. Frankly speaking, no one could feel Russian folk music more deeply nor understand it

[1] Cui was then on his way to the Bayreuth Festival.

better than Rimsky-Korsakov. His notation of the folk songs is most intelligent and musically appropriate; and his harmonies and accompaniments seem to me admirably fitting . . .

In 1879 Borodin, Cui, Lyadov and Rimsky-Korsakov sent Liszt their *Paraphrases* on a children's tune.[1] Liszt replied from Weimar on 15th June:

Dear Sirs:
In the form of a jest you have created a work of serious value. I am delighted with your *Paraphrases*: nothing could be more ingenious than these 24 variations and 14 little pieces on a favourite obbligato theme . . . Here, at last, is an admirable compendium of the science of harmony, counterpoint, rhythm, fugal style, and what is called in German *Formenlehre*! I shall gladly suggest to the teachers of composition at all the conservatories in Europe and America that they adopt your *Paraphrases* as a practical guide in their teaching. From the very first page, Variations II and III are true gems, as are all the subsequent numbers, including the Fugue grotesque and the Cortège,[2] which gloriously crowns this work. Thank you, Gentlemen, for this feast, and when any of you publishes a new composition I beg you to bring it to my attention. You have had my warmest, highest esteem and sympathy for many years; please accept, also, the expression of my sincere devotion.

In her book on Liszt, the Hungarian writer Janka Wohl, a sincere friend and admirer of the great musician, says that Liszt often played these *Paraphrases* at large gatherings in Budapest and made the guests take turns tapping out the theme on the piano.

He was delighted with this work [she writes]. "It is as ingenious as a Chinese puzzle" he exclaimed—a plaything, if you will—but a very precious one." He played Borodin's little polka and Lyadov's waltz very often and endowed Rimsky-Korsakov's *Bells* with unforgettable colour.

In accordance with the wish expressed in the above letter, at the end of the year, Lyadov sent Liszt his newly published *Arabesques*. On 25th December, 1879, Liszt replied from Villa d'Este (near Rome):

All your compositions bear the stamp of distinction and good taste. It is a delight to find this also in your *Arabesques* . . .

Shortly after receiving the *Paraphrases*, Liszt transcribed Dargomïzhsky's *Tarantelle Slave* for solo piano. Most likely one of the Russians had told him that we have another composition, like the *Paraphrases*, based on a single, continually repeated theme. Here the bass part consists of one note, repeated at the octave like an unbroken pedal point. Liszt was enchanted with this graceful work. He made an unusually fine piano arrangement of it for two hands and sent it to the Moscow publisher Jurgenson, its original owner. In the accompanying letter, on 15th December, 1879, he called the *Tarantelle* a "charming" thing ("reizende

[1] Two editions of these talented compositions were bought up in a short time.
[2] The Cortège was composed by Lyadov.

Tarantella").[1] At that time, on commission from Jurgenson, he also arranged the Polonaise from Tchaikovsky's *Eugene Onegin* for two-hand piano. When sending it, he wrote:

> Please convey my heartfelt thanks to Nicholas Rubinstein for the interest he has shown in my works for many years.[2] With his magnificent, dazzling virtuosity he adds special brilliance and effectiveness to everything he plays. I would be happy if he would undertake to play my transcription of Tchaikovsky's *Polonaise*.

Cui wrote to me:

> I saw Liszt for the third time in 1880 when I was passing through Weimar with my family. We all dined at his home. There was another guest besides us. When the dessert was served, Liszt thought that there were not enough strawberries, even though there really were, and turning displeased to his servant, the Montenegrin Spiridon, he said several times: 'Sind das Erdbeeren für sechs Personen'.[3] After dinner I stayed on for Liszt's regular class. During this class he played our *Paraphrases* in their entirety. I do not think I shall ever again hear them played so elegantly, so transparently. He had all his students play the theme in turn. He called this a "grand pique-nique musical". In the evening he joined us for supper at our hotel, the Russischer Hof. The next morning, before our departure, Spiridon appeared with a bouquet from Liszt for my wife and a card for me, attached to which was a variation he had composed for the second edition of the *Paraphrases*.

On this variation was written: "To be placed between pages 9 and 10 of the published edition, after Cui's Finale and as a prelude to Borodin's Polka. A variation *for the second edition* of the *marvellous* work by Borodin, Cui, Lyadov and Rimsky-Korsakov. Their devoted F. Liszt. Weimar, 28th July, 1880." This variation was printed in a facsimile of the autograph in the second edition of the *Paraphrases*.

During their conversations in 1877, Liszt had spoken to Borodin very warmly about the latter's First Symphony, which he heard performed.

On 3rd September, 1880, he wrote to Borodin from Rome:

> The orchestration of your very remarkable [E-flat major] symphony is done by the hand of a master and is excellently suited to the work. For me it was a genuine pleasure to hear it at rehearsals and at the concert of the Baden-Baden Tonkünstler-Versammlung. The finest connoisseurs and a large audience applauded you . . .

In the summer of the following year, Borodin again met Liszt, at the festival in Magdeburg, and again he wrote much that is interesting and

[1] In another letter Liszt calls this tarantella "tick-tock". Long before this, the group of young composers had called the *Paraphrases* "Tati-Tati" because of the rhythm of the theme.

[2] Nicholas Rubinstein was one of the most ardent exponents of Liszt's works in our country. He was the first to play his *Totentanz*, concertos, and other compositions, at important concerts in Moscow. This cannot be said of any other of our leading pianists except Balakirev.

[3] Borodin's letters contain many references to this servant whom Liszt called "Spiridon", obviously in honour of George Sand's famous novel of the same name.

highly important about the great musician. All of this is to be found in Borodin's recently published letters. Of particular importance and interest is something he related to Cui in a letter dated 12th July, 1881: "Look at this," said Liszt, showing Borodin one of the many scores that had been sent to him. "This is how they write here! Just look at this stuff! . . . Just wait, you'll hear it all at the concert today! You'll see for yourself what kind of music it is. No, we need you, Russians! I need you. I cannot do without you—*sans vous autres Russes*!" Liszt chuckled. "In your country, there is a living vital stream. You have a future—but here, we are mostly surrounded by carrion . . ."

In August of the same year, V. V. Bessel also saw Liszt in Weimar.

When I gave him the proofs of Lyadov's A-flat major Étude [Bessel related among other things], Liszt immediately opened them and glanced quickly through a few pages with obvious delight. Then he sat down at the piano and played it, exciting the interest of all the musicians present. He spoke very warmly about the new composition and immediately suggested that Mme. Timanova play it at the next class . . .

Among the many other things played that day were the music Liszt had written as accompaniment to Count Alexei Tolstoy's ballad, *The Blind Singer*, Rubinstein's ballad *Leonora*, and Liszt's transcription of one of the latter's most popular songs.[1]

On the day of my departure [continues Bessel], while bidding me farewell, Liszt said many nice things about our composers—Borodin (of whom he has grown very fond), Cui and Rimsky-Korsakov, and he asked me to send him, if possible, the libretto of the latter's *Snow Maiden* in German. He liked Cui's *Miniatures* very much; he attaches great significance to Borodin's and Rimsky-Korsakov's symphonies.[2]

In 1883 Henselt's anniversary was celebrated. He and Liszt had been close friends since the latter's first visit to Petersburg in 1842. Even though, according to Lenz, Liszt had told Henselt at that time, "I, too, could play with velvet paws, if I wished," he would not permit anyone to speak ill of his friend in his presence. When, on his second visit to us in 1843, Lenz had tried to court Liszt's favour by telling him, "Henselt has made great progress since last year"; Liszt had immediately replied irately, "You know, Sir, artists like Henselt do not make progress." (This Lenz himself related in his brochure *Die grossen Pianofortevirtuosen unserer Zeit.*) Indeed, Liszt was in continuous correspondence with Henselt and always addressed him by the familiar *du* (these letters contain nothing of musical interest, however). When a presentation album of autographs was being prepared for Henselt's anniversary, Liszt, at the request of mutual acquaintances, copied out and sent two lines from

[1] Among the works of Anton Rubinstein which Liszt transcribed were two of his songs from *Persische Lieder,* namely *Der Asra* and *O! Wenn es doch immer so bliebe*. It was the former that Bessel heard played that day.

[2] *Novoye Vremya,* 12th September, No. 1990.

Henselt's Concerto. Above them he wrote: "Motive of the wonderful Larghetto in A. Henselt's Concerto," and at the end, "etc. (ever more and more beautiful) . . . For 40 years the composer's devoted and highly respectful F. Liszt."*

Liszt wrote to Cui on 30th December of the same year:

Very honoured friend,

The high esteem in which I hold your works is known in many countries. As I am convinced that the "Suite"† of which you speak will prove worthy of your earlier compositions, I consider it an honour that you have dedicated it to me and am very grateful to you. Your musical style rises far above phraseology; you do not cultivate the convenient, barren field of the commonplace . . . Of course, the expression of ideas and feelings requires artistic form: it must be appropriate, flexible, free; sometimes vigorous, sometimes graceful, delicate, sometimes even subtle and complex, but always free of vestiges of decrepit formalism.

Recently, at Meiningen, where Bülow's admirable conducting is achieving wonders of rhythm and nuances with the orchestra, I had the honour of speaking with the Grand Duke Constantine Constantinovich about the present development of music in Russia and the well-known ability of its courageous exponents. His Highness justly appreciates their true worth, noble character and profound originality: consequently, dear Mr. Cui, the Grand Duke accords full praise to your gifts and merits . . .

A young Russian pianist, Mr. Siloti, who has attained remarkable virtuosity through the tutelage and example of Nicholas Rubinstein, is presently enjoying substantial success in Germany. When he comes to Petersburg, I commend him to your favour.

In the spring of 1884, Glazunov met Liszt in Weimar, on the occasion of the performance of his First Symphony. Here is part of a letter Glazunov sent to Balakirev at the time:

As we (Belyaev and I) entered the anteroom, Liszt appeared on the threshold of his study and, on hearing my name, graciously extended his hand, said he had played my quartet and immediately began to talk with feeling about our group, mentioning you, Rimsky-Korsakov, Borodin and Cui. Myself as well. I had the good sense not to stay long, as he was getting ready to go to a performance of his *Elizabeth* from six until ten. Besides, he had spent the morning at a rehearsal (from ten until one, if not longer); after that he had had music at home (beginning at 4 o'clock) and there was to be more later in the evening. I do not understand how he is able to stand all this. I had only one such day—the day my symphony was played—and I was in a complete stupor. And he is an old man of 73! . . . The following day I saw Liszt in the restaurant where everyone gathers after the concerts . . .

In the course of the conversation that evening Glazunov told Liszt that his *Du Berceau à la Tombe* had been played in Russia.

He was very pleased but felt badly that it had not been successful in Germany . . .

* Letter to Wrangel, 20th May, 1883. [Trans.]
† For piano, Op. 21.—G.A.

On the day of the concert there was a dress rehearsal. I sat down near Liszt and watched him closely. My symphony went very badly at the rehearsal. But Liszt applauded after each movement. He remarked that the repeat should not be taken in the first movement. He was very pleased with the chords in the scherzo, and the double-pedal in the flutes and strings* at the very beginning of the finale. The symphony went much better in the evening . . . At about four o'clock that day I went to Liszt's and took him the score of my D-flat major Andantino and the *Serenade*. After listening to the latter, he suggested that I use a guitar in it. He liked the descending scale in thirds and sixths very much. I noticed that on the whole Liszt is very partial to piquant harmonization. Later he made his pupil Friedheim, a Russian, play my piano suite, but he played the *Prelude* so badly that Liszt chased him away from the piano and made me continue. He particularly liked the agitato in the *Prelude*. After a few words about my suite, he began to talk about the *Paraphrases*. He called them his "conservatory" and insisted that I play something from them. Meanwhile more and more people arrived. Various composers came, among them Saint-Saëns. They played their works. Apropos of something, Liszt said that if a work contains something Russian, it is certain to be good. He is very witty. When I seated myself at the piano and apologized for playing badly, he remarked that that is as it should be. If a composer plays well or a pianist composes well, he said, there is good reason to suspect that each is passing off someone else's works as his own. Liszt is full of witticisms like this. Another amazing quality is his memory. He remembers Stasov, Shcherbachev, and, of course, Borodin and Cui. One thing, however, I find a little overdone—he never criticizes anyone to his face, probably out of tactfulness; except for some remarks, like *trop de mineur*, he praises everything. I saw Liszt for the last time at a soirée at the Duke's. He asked me to give you and the others his regards. I told him about *Tamara* . . .[1]

In August, 1884, Liszt wrote to the music publisher Rahter to thank him for sending him the *Fantasia on Russian Themes* by the Petersburg conductor Napravnik and Rimsky-Korsakov's *Lullaby*. He called the *Fantasia* "a brilliantly successful concert piece" and expressed confidence that many of his young pianists would be delighted to play it at musicales and in concerts. Speaking of Rimsky-Korsakov's *Lullaby* he added: "I have a high regard for Rimsky-Korsakov. His works are among the rare, uncommon, the exquisite."†

When a few months later, Balakirev asked Liszt to accept the dedication of his symphonic poem *Tamara*, Liszt replied to him in a letter on 21st October, 1884:

Highly esteemed colleague,

My admiration for your works is well known. When my young pupils want to please me, they play for me compositions by you and your valiant friends. In this intrepid Russian musical phalanx I hail, with all my heart, great masters endowed with a rare vitality. They by no means suffer from poverty of ideas—a malady that is very widespread in many countries. Their merits will become more and more recognized and their names renowned. I gratefully accept the

* In the published score the flutes are replaced by clarinets.—G.A.

† Letter of 28th August, 1884. [Trans.]

[1] This refers to Balakirev's intention to dedicate *Tamara* to Liszt.

honour of the dedication of your symphonic poem *Tamara*, which I hope to hear played by a large orchestra next summer. When the four-hand transcription is published, please send me a copy . . .

Please accept, dear colleague, my profound respect and heartfelt devotion.

Meanwhile, in 1884, the Countess Mercy-Argenteau, who had come to know the works of our new school, began to champion them ardently in Belgium and France. On her initiative several concerts, devoted either entirely or largely to the new Russian music, were given in Liége, Antwerp and other Belgian cities. This new enthusiast even exerted some influence on the Lamoureux Concerts in Paris.

On 24th October, 1884 Liszt wrote to her:

You are most assuredly right, my very dear, kind friend, to value and take delight in present-day musical Russia! Rimsky-Korsakov, Cui, Borodin, Balakirev are masters of striking originality and worth. Their works make up for the ennui caused me by others which are more widely played and more talked of, works of which I would find it difficult to say what Léonard once wrote you from Amsterdam after a performance of one of Schumann's songs: "What soul, and also, what success!" Rarely is success in a hurry to accompany *soul*. In Russia, despite their remarkable talent and knowledge, the new composers have thus far had but a limited success.—The fashionable world of the court is waiting for them to win recognition elsewhere before applauding them in Petersburg . . .

For several years, at my suggestion, some work of the Russian composers has been performed at the annual concerts of the Allgemeiner Deutscher Musik-Verein. Little by little a public will be formed . . .

The following year, on 20th January, 1885, Liszt wrote to the Countess Mercy-Argenteau from Rome:

What a miracle you have just achieved with your "Russian concert" at Liége, dear admirable one! From the material standpoint, the Institutes for the Deaf, Dumb and Blind have benefited from it; artistically, deaf and dumb of another sort heard and spoke; the blind saw and, beholding you, were entranced.

I will most certainly not cease my propaganda for the remarkable compositions of the new Russian school, which I warmly esteem and value. For the past six or seven years, the orchestral works of Rimsky-Korsakov and Borodin have appeared on the programmes at the grand annual concerts of the Allgemeiner Deutscher Musik-Verein over which I have the honour to preside. Their success is growing despite the malicious prejudice there is against Russian music. It is not out of eccentricity that I persist in disseminating it, but out of a simple sense of fairness based on a belief in the true worth of these highly artistic works . . .

My best pupils, brilliant virtuosi, play the most difficult piano compositions of Balakirev and the others superbly. I shall bring Cui's Suite for piano and violin to their attention.

Since few singers are endowed at once with a voice, intelligence and a taste for unhackneyed things, there is some delay with regard to the vocal compositions of Borodin, Cui, etc. Nevertheless, we will manage to give them suitable performances and make them appreciated and successful. Your translations of the Russian texts will be of great help in France. The same sort of translation must be made available in Germany . . .

The Hamburg music publisher Rahter, correspondent of Jurgenson in Moscow, will send you three of my Russian transcriptions—Tchaikovsky's *Polonaise*, Dargomizhsky's *Tarantelle* . . . and a song by Count Michael Vielgorsky. Let us also add Chernomor's March by Glinka and especially the prodigious "kaleidoscope" of variations and paraphrases on an ostinato theme . . .

. . . I know of no worthwhile piece more entertaining than this. It affords us a practical manual, par excellence, of all musical knowledge. The treatises on harmony and composition have been summarized and synthesized here in some thirty pages, from which one can learn a great deal more than from the usual instruction . . .

At the Countess's request, Liszt made a piano transcription of Cui's orchestral *Tarantelle*. On 18th October, 1885 he wrote to the composer:

. . . I hope you will not disapprove of the few liberties I have taken and the additions I have made to your brilliant *Tarantelle* in order to adapt it to the requirements of virtuoso pianists . . .

On 24th October Liszt wrote to the Countess Mercy-Argenteau regarding this transcription:

. . . If you will deign to illuminate it with your fingers, it will appear in all its splendour.

. . . I hope that Cui will not be angry about the changes and additions I have made in order to bring the pianist more to the fore. In transcriptions of this kind, one must be able to take liberties . . .*

On 21st November, 1885 he wrote to the Countess again from Rome:

Dear admirable propagandist,

Herewith is a variant of the trill with the indication in the left hand of the motive which then appears in full. This new trill is a trifle awkward but not too difficult. Be so kind as to send it to Cui and ask him to serve as my intermediary with the publisher of the original brilliant *Tarantelle*. Unfortunately, my modest income obliges me to do everything I can to make money out of my transcriptions, for which I am now paid at the rate of 1200 to 1500 marks in Germany, Russia and France, for the copyright in all countries.

Note that I choose the works to be transcribed and refuse other proposals. This year, for example I have confined myself to the opuscule which you deign to accept and will, I hope, bring to light with the diamonds and pearls of your fingers . . .

This arrangement of Cui's *Tarantelle* was Liszt's last work. His strength was failing. By the end of the year, his eyesight had become so impaired that he wrote to the Countess on 23rd December:

My eyes have grown so weak that it tires me to write three brief lines. If this continues, I shall be unable to use a pen.

Yet Liszt had to work. Such was the financial situation of this man through whose hands hundreds of thousands, even millions of francs had

* "Dans ce genre de transcriptions, il faut de la marque . . ." [Original text]

passed, this man who had always given so generously right and left, for a monument to Beethoven, a monument to Bach, or simply to various needy people, musicians and non-musicians. On the other hand, how many mediocre and ungifted musicians live their entire lives in wealth and comfort! This was not so with Berlioz and Liszt. They had to work when they were old, weak, sick; to work beyond their strength, to be grateful for invitations anywhere, no matter how far, just to earn a bit of money; they had to concern themselves about a few roubles "for living quarters and a carriage!" What a wretched tragedy! What a sad end, what an ugly spectacle!

In December, 1885, Liszt's former pupil, the noted pianist Sophie Menter succeeded in having Liszt invited to Petersburg to conduct several concerts to be given by the Russian Musical Society in April, 1886. Liszt wanted to accept this invitation, but he could not, and he wrote her from Rome on 30th December, 1885:

> Kind diplomatist and dear friend,
>
> I am sending my most humble thanks to the Grand Duke Constantine for his gracious invitation, and also telling him of my apprehensions about my age and failing eyesight—especially about my *unfitness* to play the piano and conduct. All this deters me from making any claims to a fee. But, you know, dear friend, that my small income is not sufficient to pay for living quarters and a carriage in St. Petersburg . . .
>
> In the next letter of the Grand Duke Constantine I hope to find a decision as to whether or not my journey to Petersburg in April has been approved.

Finally on 18th April, 1886,* Liszt again wrote to Sophie Menter from the Countess Mercy-Argenteau's estate:

> Highly esteemed, dear diplomatist,
>
> A week before 19th April (Russian style) I will be in Petersburg. I beg you to trouble yourself as little as possible about my humble self. The programmes of both concerts seem excellent to me, but I will not tell you what my small part in them will be until I get to Petersburg. On 19th April, then, *Elizabeth*; on the 23rd—a concert . . . Tell me, what is going to be done about my lodgings in Petersburg, for which my meagre means are insufficient? . . .
>
> I enclose a letter and the photographs requested for our friend Zet. I consider it quite superfluous to autograph these for the newspapers. I do not like overdoing things.

None of these plans materialized. Liszt did not come to Russia. His health continued to fail and four months later, on 31st July, 1886, he died in Bayreuth. Among the many wreaths placed on his grave was a magnificent one made of silver overlaid with gold and enamel from the musicians of the new Russian school and their colleagues with the following inscription (in Russian): "To Franz Liszt from admirers of his genius." This wreath was placed in the chapel later erected over Liszt's grave.

* According to La Mara this letter was dated 18th March, 1886. [Trans.]

In this article I have quoted from a great many of Liszt's letters. This I had to do for a number of reasons. First of all, most of these letters were hitherto completely unknown and it is important that people interested in the new music and the great musicians of the nineteenth century know much of what this man thought and said about our new school of music and our new musicians. Everything in these letters is so deeply felt and thought through, so fresh, so original that they should, I believe, prove of enormous benefit to our new school and all those who sympathize with it. They should no longer remain unknown.

Secondly, I had to present all these forceful statements from such a quantity of letters in order to counteract the falsehoods of the many enemies of our new school who would have the Russian reader believe that Liszt's remarks about it were nothing but the usual gentlemanly courtesies and compliments. "It's all conventional and put on," these people say. "This is the way people in fashionable society always talk when they have to tell an author to his face what they think of him." I cannot agree with this—it is malicious slander and libel.

Are Liszt's letters to the Russian composers, his statements about them really like the countless other letters he wrote and statements he made during his lifetime? Do we not sense here an altogether different tone, a different mood, feeling, thought? Indeed, here we find something quite different—profound, sincere, totally unlike the platitudes, the usual "courtesies" and compliments Liszt paid to all sorts of Russians like General Lvov and Count Vielgorsky. No, this was a matter of infinite importance, something that meant a great deal to Liszt himself. Moreover, it had to do with an *entire school*, which Liszt recognized as a highly significant event and one that held enormous promise for the future, the very antithesis to the other, ordinary happenings in contemporary music. Liszt's statements about the Russian composers can be compared only with those he made about Berlioz and Wagner at the beginning of their vast creative work, which he saw as the dawn of a new era in music. No, this was not a matter of politeness. Liszt wrote no other letters like these. Let the enemies of the new Russian school try to find such letters among Liszt's correspondence!

My third reason for quoting from these letters at such length is that they clearly refute certain views which some of Liszt's closest friends ascribe to him. I have in mind particularly the Hungarian writer Janka Wohl, who was on intimate terms with Liszt from her childhood almost until his death.

In Chapter 13 of her interesting but over-anecdotal and superficial book about the great musician, she discusses his attitude toward the new school of Russian music. Despite all the praise Liszt heaped on it, she quotes him as having said, apropos of some composition by one of his Russian pupils:

Although a genuine, fully developed school of Russian music has not yet appeared, the Russians already have excellent composers who constitute an epoch. The Russian spirit which, on the one hand, is in a state of perpetual ferment and on the other, is lulled by its environment, still has much to do before it can find its true direction. This is a consequence of the climate and the Slavic character in general. Just as the long, dead months of the Russian winter are followed by a brief, lush spring, so in Russian music there is a kind of continuous monotony, coloured only here and there by clearly stated melodies. But, instead of this, these melodies, which are so sparsely strewn, ought to express the mighty power that characterizes the Russian summer Besides, there is too much in this music that is nebulous, undefined, too much of the incorporeal dream. Nevertheless, I believe it has a great future. At the present time one has the feeling that the Russian composers approach their work in a more or less sentimental frame of mind, that they are not impelled by a vast, all-embracing universal idea. If Russian music possessed the resolute force and originality of the sculptor Antokolsky, it could by now have laid the foundation for a new era. This it will do, in all probability, in time . . . The Russians have not yet found the key to their own highly complex nature; they are not yet able to plumb the depths of their own character, their own national music. They do not know how to utilize the originality which is rooted in their national soil, springs only from this soil and is inseparable from its snowy wastes and steppes and from the way its sons feel about and understand life and death. All this will one day give their music that individual character without which Russian music, however superb it may be, will remain only a variant of European music. Given their drive, their faith in their own strength and talent, the Russians will surely find one day what they have so far missed. The art of the Russians is still young, and in art youth is rarely an advantage. They have already done a great deal worthy of admiration and will advance further and further along the path toward perfection and renown!

It is unbelievable that Liszt could ever have indulged in such a tirade. Under no circumstances can we or should we give it credence. In the final analysis, the statement which Janka Wohl ascribes here to Liszt amounts to a charge that the music of the new Russian composers is not sufficiently *national* in character and is too *European*. Even if we disregard everything we find in his letters over a period of many decades, it is inconceivable that Liszt ever made such an assertion. It is utterly inconceivable that a man of such genius, particularly a musician of such genius, could have failed to see, as if from nyctalopia, the principal distinguishing feature of the new Russian music—its profound, genuine, clear and unmistakable *national character*!

What, since the time of its great founder Glinka, has always been the most important element in our music? The national element. All the greatest music that has been created in our country thus far, all the music that holds the most promise for the future is permeated with the national spirit. Over the past decades the motivating force of all the striving of true Russian musicians has been to penetrate to the roots of Russian national music, to deepen their knowledge of the Russian folk-song, Russian liturgical chants and their original modes. Yet some would have us believe that Liszt did not see this, did not understand it! They would have us believe that Liszt thought quite the opposite—Liszt who heard and knew not only Glinka's *Life for the Tsar*, *Ruslan and Ludmila*, and *Kamarinskaya*; Dargomïzhsky's *Rusalka*, *Baba Yaga*, *Kazachok*, and *Finnish Fantasy*; but also Borodin's *Prince Igor* and *In the Steppes of Central Asia*; Rimsky-Korsakov's *Maid of Pskov, May Night, Sadko* and *Snow Maiden*; Glazunov's *Stenka Razin*; the Russian overtures of Balakirev and Rimsky-Korsakov, Mussorgsky's *Nursery* and a great many of his other songs, as well as those of Borodin, Balakirev and Rimsky-Korsakov.[1] And Liszt was supposed not to have noticed the *national* element in all this music, to have counselled the Russians not to overlook it, to make full use of it! What nonsense! Liszt would have had to have been an utterly insignificant musician, one totally wanting in perception and understanding, not to have seen, not to have sensed the pulsating national element in all these works, but instead to have uttered platitudes about Russian "steppes and snow".

When we turn, however, from second-hand reports to facts, that is, to Liszt's letters and conversations, we come across a thousand instances which prove that Liszt always thought and spoke about the new school of Russian music entirely differently from the way Janka Wohl claims he did. It was precisely its *distinctiveness*, its original national character and innovatory daring—to say nothing of the talent of its composers—that Liszt valued most in this school and it is because of these qualities that he contraposed it to all the other schools of music in contemporary Europe. There he found anaemia, here—a vibrant, fresh life, a bubbling spring, and he exclaimed: "I need you, Russians! I cannot do without you!" It is as if Liszt, contemplating the new Russian musicians, were fervently echoing Pushkin's magnificent lines:

> "I hail you, race of youthful newcomers!
> I shall not witness your maturity,
> When you shall have outgrown my ancient friends,
> And with your shoulders hide their very heads
> From passers-by . . ."

1896

[1] Liszt seems not to have known Mussorgsky's *Boris Godunov* and *Khovanshchina*.

VII. A Friendly Commemoration

This was Stasov's last published article: an amusing demonstration that his power of invective was as effective at 82 as it had been in his fiery youth.

G.A.

NOT LONG ago Germany commemorated the fiftieth anniversary of the death of one of the great musicians of the nineteenth century. This anniversary was not marked only in Germany, however. In our country, too, there were some solicitous people who felt the need to declare publicly their boundless devotion and burning love for the deceased great man, and at the same time display their own virtues, their profound learning and incorruptible love of truth. With this in view, they began by berating the rest of their countrymen, that is, we Russians, for our indifference, our lack of esteem for great talents, our backwardness as compared with the rest of Europe. All this would have been fine had their efforts succeeded. But, unfortunately, there is a vast difference between making a great show of wanting to do a thing and actually doing it. Our zealots only acted out the scene from Krylov's fable: "Though help in need is precious, indeed, not everyone knows how to give it."[1] "Walked into one room, found himself in another," it says in *Woe from Wit*.[2]

Now, sometimes it is very bad to find oneself in the wrong room. This is exactly what recently happened here.

The "hermit" of the fable was the great and famous composer Schumann, and the solicitous bears—not one but two in this case—were his Russian friends, Mr. Ivanov and Mr. Koptyaev.[3] Both of them are music critics by profession; both, alas, as yet scarcely known. To help their adored friend both of them armed themselves not with one rock, as in the fable, but with a dozen ("For a friend that is dear, I'll give the ring from my ear"). And they pelted him so heartily in columns of *Novoye Vremya* and other periodicals that "the bear's friend was left lying there for good".

[1] This is a reference to the fable *The Hermit and the Bear* by the great Russian fabulist, Ivan Andreyevich Krylov. It tells the story of a hermit who fell asleep in the desert. Observing that a fly was disturbing him, his friend, a bear, seized a rock and killed the fly. But in killing the fly, he also killed the hermit. [Trans.]

[2] A play by the early nineteenth-century Russian playwright Alexander Sergeyevich Griboyedov.

[3] Mikhail Mikhailovich Ivanov (1849–1927) and Alexander Petrovich Koptyaev (1868–1941)

One of the friends, not, by the way, the leader, Mr. Ivanov, but his perpetual apprentice, Mr. Koptyaev, starts out by declaring that "certainly Schumann was not endowed by nature with great musical gifts..." "Schumann," says he, "had an innate sense of the beautiful, but this manifested itself first in the field of literature. Did he not write plays about the life of highwaymen? And when his interest in music first emerged, Schumann turned not to composition but to playing the piano..."

Mr. Koptyaev's patron, Mr. Ivanov observes that "it was not until he was twenty that Schumann began to devote any special attention to music..." But this is completely untrue. Poor zealous friends! They have never heard that Schumann began to show signs of great musical ability when he was only seven years old, and that a few years later, his teacher, the organist Kuntzsch, told his parents that the boy was already capable of working by himself.

In a letter he wrote later on, Schumann expressed his profound gratitude to Kuntzsch for having been the *first* to recognize his musical ability when he was a small boy. The "plays about highwaymen" came much later than the music. Schumann started to compose at a very early age on his own, without the help of anyone. He passionately loved to improvise at the piano, even though he knew nothing about the basic principles of music. He was writing little melodies at the age of seven or eight. Even in those days he tried to portray in music the characters, personalities, gestures and physiognomies of his little schoolmates.

At the age of nine Schumann was carried away by the works of the noted pianist Moscheles. By the time he was twelve, he knew a great deal of classical music and was himself diligently writing compositions for chorus and orchestra, evoking amazement and interest in his friends as much by his youthful compositions as by his excellent piano playing. That is how much his "Russian friends" know about it.

But the more intense their zeal grows, the further they wander from the truth.

Schumann was struck by Clara Wieck's talent and extraordinary musicality when she was still a young girl. The "friends" maintain that from an artistic point of view this famous German pianist, who later became Schumann's wife, was absolutely insignificant, that she played the piano "like any well-bred young lady". Mr. Ivanov heard this, he says, thirty years ago from an old piano-teacher in Moscow by the name of Dubuque,[1] and later on from Liszt himself. What the Moscow piano

[1] Far from being a nonentity, as Stasov implies, Alexander Ivanovich Dubuque (1812–97) was the leading Moscow piano-teacher of his day. He was a pupil of Field; among his own pupils were Balakirev, the critics Laroche and Kashkin, and the pedagogue N. S. Zverev who in turn taught Skryabin, Rakhmaninov and Siloti.—G.A.

teacher (who, according to Mr. Ivanov, had "pretty much given up the piano") might or might not have told him, we do not know, but as far as Liszt is concerned, we are quite at a loss whom to believe—Mr. Ivanov or Liszt himself. Of course, we would prefer to believe no one but Mr. Ivanov, but after all, there *was* such a person as Liszt.

In his writings, Liszt spoke again and again of his high regard for Clara Schumann's talent. In 1855 he devoted an entire article to an expression of his enthusiasm and admiration for her. He called her a "great artist" and said that she and her husband had created so many things in collaboration and for their mutual benefit that the annals of history would always speak of them as one; that one star and one star only should shine above the heads of this "immortal pair".

Schumann played a prominent rôle in his wife's artistic development and, according to the music historian Naumann, her performances of his works, like those of the works of Beethoven, Bach, Chopin, and others were "beyond compare". Mendelssohn, who was himself a celebrated pianist, often played four hands duets with her in concerts. As for her technical ability, this may be judged from the fact that Liszt dedicated his stupendous *Paganini Études*, which at that time perhaps only four or five pianists in all of Europe could play, to her. All the German newspapers of the 40's are filled with endless praise for the talent of Clara Schumann. When she and her husband came to Petersburg in 1844, the Russians flocked to her concerts, and at that time she enjoyed an even greater success here than Liszt himself had on his second visit. Yuri Arnold, one of Petersburg's music critics of that day, tells of the "enormous" impression she made in Petersburg. He himself was astounded by her great artistry, vigour, and fine feminine sensitivity. Serov, too, recalls with delight her concerts in our capital. But as far as the "Russian friends" and their friends "who had given up the piano" were concerned, Clara Schumann played "like any well-bred young lady".

Pressing his interesting campaign against this gifted woman precisely because she was so highly gifted, Mr. Ivanov's apprentice tries to convince his readers that "from a spiritual point of view, Clara Schumann had a deleterious effect on her husband." She made a Philistine of him! "After 1840 when he married her, Schumann somehow quietened down, and you never would have recognized the stormy Florestan (Schumann's pseudonym) in this burgher in the dressing-grown with a pipe in his hand . . ."

What foolish and ridiculous slander! Anyone who has even a slight acquaintance with Schumann's music knows how fiery, passionate, deeply poetic, magnificent and youthful he was until the very end of his life (save, of course, during the period of his final illness, his terrible mental breakdown). Page after page of his letters reflect his kindness and goodness, his concern and boundless love for art, his indignation at the bourgeois character of the little towns and the petty interests of most of the public and music scribblers.

But the "Petersburg friends" know nothing about this, and Mr. Koptyaev assures us that "Clara Schumann was a narrow-minded and sentimental musical bluestocking . . ."

"What a pity Schumann did not run away from Clara Wieck," says he. What appalling stupidity! This about Schumann, who repeatedly told everyone who would listen that he owed the best moments of his life to his dear, his matchless Clara. She was the one who inspired his finest, most poetic creations! And Mr. Ivanov's assitant charmingly and inanely bemoans the fact that Schumann "did not run away from" the creature he adored, the being whom no one in the world could have replaced!

Only a few months before his awful final illness, Schumann wrote about the wonderful performances of his works that his wife was then giving in Germany and Holland. In letters to friends at that time he also spoke of the continual growth of his dear Clara's art.

Finally, the "friends" are so utterly lacking in an understanding of Schumann that the only works of his which they regard as important are those he composed before his marriage, that is, prior to 1840. "By 1840 he had achieved immortality. Had he died then he would have left us with the impression of something complete and perfect!" states Mr. Koptyaev. Thus, Schumann had the misfortune to compose many great and truly talented works after 1840, but we must not regard them as great! His symphonies which even today, many decades after his death, are considered great creations by Tchaikovsky (himself a highly gifted symphonist) just as they have been by all of musical Europe from Liszt on; his marvellous overtures (particularly *Manfred*); the incomparable "Mystic Chorus" and astonishing scenes from *Faust* (especially the one in the cathedral in which the evil spirit addresses his tragic, sombre speeches to Gretchen's tormented soul); and finally, his portrayal of Cologne Cathedral in the fourth movement of the "Rhenish" Symphony which, in grandeur and power, surpasses all the greatest and mightiest works of Schumann's entire career—all these are things unworthy of the earlier, the young Schumann, things which prevent him from being "complete and perfect"!

Out of some insatiable desire to disparage Schumann (while, at the same time, showering him with meaningless praise), his "Russian friends" resort not only to absurdities of various kinds but also to outright aspersions. As proof of this wonderful composer's mysticism and eccentricity, the apprentice, Mr. Koptyaev, cites as something quite out of the ordinary Schumann's use of the letters of family and first names as musical themes (A.S.C.H., A.B.E.G.G., etc.). But what is really so surprising about this? Everyone who knows anything at all about the history of music will recall that, back in the eighteenth century, the great Bach used the letters of his name as a theme (B-A-C-H); that many of his contemporaries did the same; that in the nineteenth century, both Liszt and Schumann wrote works based on Bach's name; that Glazunov wrote a charming suite on the letters S-A-S-C-H-A (Sascha), and Cui wrote one scherzo on the letters B-A-B-E-G, from his wife's maiden name (Bamberg) and another on his own initials C-C. Are we expected to regard all these as indications of "mysticism", eccentricity, as strange aberrations?

In the writings of the principal "friend", Mr. Ivanov, we find things that are even more ludicrous. He has the effrontery to assert that the great figures, the luminaries of the 40's thought no more highly of Schumann than the ordinary public did.

> They turned to him only when they needed his support as a critic. All of them—Chopin, Mendelssohn, Berlioz, Hiller—did this. They looked upon him as a critic, whose opinions might, on occasion, prove helpful to them . . . They thought little of him as a composer . . .

Some people, reading this, might say, "How brazen!" But I say, "How abominable!" How dare this Mr. Critic of *Novoye Vremya* cast such base aspersions on all the most outstanding people and talents of Europe! . . . And especially on Liszt, who adored Schumann, Mr. Ivanov's vile fabrications notwithstanding! How dare he accuse Schumann of being corruptible, and Liszt, Berlioz, Mendelssohn—in fact, everyone—of being corruptors! Where are the facts, where is the evidence? What kind of putrid swamp does Mr. Ivanov live in? Where did he acquire these deplorable practices which he so readily ascribes to other lands, other times, other people, people great not only in talent but also in soul! And why did Schumann have to be the object of the ignorance, stupidity and malice of these musical pariahs and spiritual paupers?

What a wonderful commemoration! Had there been none at all, there would be a less shameful stench in the air.

If the need should arise, I am prepared to present the readers with many other charming excerpts from the articles of Messrs. Ivanov and Koptyaev.

1906

Index